And introducing

DEXTER GAINES

A NOVEL
OF OLD HOLLYWOOD

Mark B. Perry

AMBLE
PRESS
ANN ARBOR

2025

PRAISE FOR MARK B. PERRY

And introducing
DEXTER GAINES:
A NOVEL OF OLD HOLLYWOOD

"Mark B. Perry is a wonderful writer and I'm sure we will all enjoy his novel *And Introducing Dexter Gaines: A Novel of Old Hollywood* as well as anything else he puts his mind and talent to. I was very proud of the 'Two Doors Down' episode he wrote for my *Heartstrings* series on Netflix."

—Dolly Parton

"Take me to Mark B. Perry's Hollywood party! The one that opens his sensational new novel *And Introducing Dexter Gaines*. In fact, I insist. Do you like a page-turner? You got it, sweetheart. Tell Zanuck I said so."

— Sam Staggs, author of *All About All About Eve,*
Close-Up on Sunset Boulevard,
When Blanche Met Brando, and *Born to be Hurt*

"Forget the studio backlot tour at MGM. Mark B. Perry's deft and deliciously immersive *And Introducing Dexter Gaines* is the only guide you'll need when it comes to getting inside those fabled walls (plus a few bedrooms, poolside cabanas, and ocean liners) from the Golden Age of 1950s Hollywood. You'll feel for his main character, stud-to-star wannabe Dexter Gaines, who dares to be himself; you'll even feel for the studio bigwig who shapes Dexter's career, who can't be himself. In Perry's hands, the research comes alive; he feels what the period must have been like, and his characters come alive too, with hilarity and heartbreak. *And Introducing Dexter Gaines* is like a wonderful weekend binge on TCM: you don't want Monday to ever come."

— Kim Powers, author of *The History of Swimming*
and *Rules for Being Dead*

"If you hate being submerged in a time when movie stars were still idols, when movie palaces were still shrines, and Hollywood still seemed like magic, when supper clubs and transatlantic crossings made the pages of Hedda Hopper and Walter Winchell, then *And Introducing Dexter Gaines* is not for you. Mark Perry recreates all of that with the loving specificity of someone you might assume believes he was born at the wrong time. But in *Dexter Gaines*, he is up to something much deeper and more complex, much more emotionally wrenching. Set in the waning years of a golden age, this is a novel about the cruelty of the rules by which we live and the lies the movies tell us, about the desire to be somebody and the unbearable need for love. Like the last flickering frames of a movie that has broken your heart, *Dexter Gaines* will not easily leave you."

—Christopher Keyser, *Party of Five* (co-creator), *The Society, Max's Julia,* and past president of the Writers Guild of America West

"Mark Perry's poetic way with words and his beautifully drawn characters bring to life the opulent bygone era of 1950s Hollywood in delicious fashion. His main character's narration through two different eras brings to mind the way Billy Wilder used William Holden's voice throughout Sunset Boulevard. The back and forth between periods heightens the drama which has as many twists and turns as a fast car careening down Mulholland Drive. Fasten your seatbelts, darlings!"

— Laurie Jacobson, Hollywood historian and author of *Hollywood Haunted, Dishing Hollywood,* and *Hollywood Heartbreak*

"Fascinating and entirely captivating . . . a page-turner replete with authentic period details, excellent and witty dialogue, and a layered plot worthy of the finest of Hollywood's golden age."

—Anthony Caplan, author of *Savior*

"Deftly mixing fictional characters with well-known personalities of Hollywood's golden age, this subtly powerful novel is . . . finely drawn with foibles of the flesh in a Truman Capote–like piece . . . deeply affecting and tinged with pathos."

—*Kirkus Reviews*

"Displays an excellent sense of plot and pacing as the storyline alternates between the young Dan of 1952 and the aging Dexter of 1994. The historical settings sparkle. . . ."

—*Foreword Reviews*

Amble Press

Copyright © 2025 Mark B. Perry
Previous edition copyright © 2014 Mark B. Perry

Print ISBN: 978-1-61294-313-8

Amble Press First Edition: May 2025

Printed in the United States of America on acid-free paper.

Cover designer:
TreeHouse Studio

Amble Press
PO Box 3671
Ann Arbor MI 48106-3671

www.amblepressbooks.com

This is a work of fiction. All characters and situations
depicted herein are entirely fictitious, other than
actual historical persons and firms that are portrayed
or referenced in entirely fictional scenes and dialogue.

For Mark and Cayce,
who both inspire in their
own inimitable ways

"My mother thought Hollywood was a den of iniquity, and people came to terrible bad ends there."

—Kitty Carlisle Hart

ONE

Entertainment Tonight barely gave a passing nod to the news Milford Langen had died of a heart attack outside a liquor store on Melrose Avenue. Mary Hart, her eyes scanning the words on her teleprompter, delivered the announcement of his passing with the somber tone she reserved for such obituaries, listing a handful of titles Langen had produced at 20th Century Fox in the '40s and '50s before she filled the remaining few seconds with a litany of the innocuous television series he had either created and/or produced up until the late '70s. The only mention of Lillian Sinclair, his actress wife of some forty-one years, was the same tired line about her suicide in 1982. No reference was made to Langen's brief association with a once-promising young actor named Dexter Gaines.

Milly, as his inner circle called him, had always hated to be upstaged, so he had chosen the worst possible time to drop dead, the bulk of the telecast being devoted to the low-speed O.J. Simpson police chase. For a moment, as I listened to Mary's recitation, which ended with "Academy Award-winner Milford Langen, dead at seventy-five," a long pent-up rage tightened my stomach, threatening to linger and consume me. I muted the television and sat in the ensuing silence of stuttering blue light in my shabby apartment, trying to breathe into the knot, calling on the relaxation techniques I'd learned after years of therapy. But these feelings were deep-seated and stubborn, an unhealed wound in my soul now salted by the news he was dead. Recent events hadn't helped, as I

1

was still struggling with my newfound status as widower at the reality-altering age of sixty-three.

Impossible after forty-some years that just the mention of Milly's name could still trigger emotions that should have been long dead. Impossible how the sight of his smiling face from a studio photograph taken sometime in the mid-1960s, inset over Mary's left shoulder, could still cause my hands to tremble even more than usual—so much I had to set down the fork I had been using to eat my Lean Cuisine and fold them in my lap.

Breathe out.

Breathe in.

God. Damn. It.

The anger was still there, nearly as raw and horrible as it had been my last day in Hollywood when I'd smashed most of Milly's Steuben glassware and then tried to strangle him on the imported marble floor of his Hancock Park mansion.

Breathe out.

I was losing to the now familiar dark shroud of one of my "spells" as it crept over me, blocking out the dwindling light in my apartment and the surreal tableau of the never-ending aerial shot of the infamous white Ford Bronco. They were less frequent now, these episodes, but had never really left me. My life since that autumn in 1953 had been a frantic escape, running from place to place, seeking anonymity while contemplating suicide—until, that is, I had met Carol some twenty-one years ago and discovered the bliss of healing. Death had landed me here, scars and baggage intact, in a one-bedroom at the Briarwood Arms in San Jose. Not as far from Hollywood as I would have liked, but enough that I'm no longer recognized by self-styled film buffs who've actually heard of Dexter Gaines or perhaps even seen one of the three films I did while being mentored by a powerful young producer at 20th Century Fox named Milford Langen.

I had neither seen nor spoken to Milly since the day I'd tried to kill him, and the pain had gone unresolved in all the gaping, empty years that followed. I looked down at my quivering hands, searching for the faint scars from Lillian Sinclair's claw-like fingernails, almost as if for reassurance my current life had not begun with some disturbed dream. Weeping and hysterical, she had tried to pull me off of her husband, gouging three parallel slashes of blood in the back of my right hand before I at last succeeded in hurling her across the floor where she cowered, her legendary face contorted into a mask of despair made all the more convincing by the rivulets of black mascara washing down her perfect cheeks as she sobbed over and over again, "I don't understand, I don't understand." It was her eyes, desperate and childlike, that snapped me to my senses. In them, I saw the enormous horror of what I had become—of what we all had become. I stared at her in disgrace as Milly gagged, choking on the words, "Get out." Lillian then met my gaze and nodded, hugging herself, still splayed against the wall where I'd thrown her like a discarded doll.

It was to be the last time I would see him, his wife crawling over to her coughing husband as I wailed, "Oh no oh no," before turning to run out the front door and headlong into all the silent years that lay ahead. Until Milly's smirk popped up over Mary Hart's shoulder, taunting me with the knowledge he had died on his own, of natural causes no less, in his ultimate declaration of victory over me.

Just one more reason to hate him.

And so it went, my obsessive thoughts of Milly pulling me in a downward whorl. I was too tired to resist, and Carol was no longer around to nurse me through, so instead I gave in to my weary ritual of closing the yellowed shades, unplugging the phone, and burrowing into the relative calm of darkness and the smell of unwashed sheets.

I would remain that way for two days.

In the nightmare fervor of my spells come the visions. Milly's face from the *ET* segment, his smile incapable of masking the haunted madness in his eyes. The vivid memories of moonlight glinting off the prisms of a crystal ice bucket set neatly on the drink cart next to the lawn chair where I sat wearing my sailing clothes, utterly alone and wallowing in my childish yearning for an unattainable love, watching three toy steamships cut their tiny wake across the surface of a still pool glowing blue in the night as the laughter and swing of some ancient Hollywood party lilted from the open doors of the exquisite mansion behind me. The indelible vision of Barbara Stanwyck's pitying look as I stood over her, now in a uniform, holding a silver tray neatly set with china cups of steaming broth, my hands shaking—goddamned hands always shaking—now the squeaking of my mother's wheelchair as she rolled into my bedroom and caught me masturbating. Her gin-ravaged voice a cruel rasp as she commanded, "Put your hands flat on the floor, you dirty boy." The indescribable agony as she ran her wheels over my fingers to ensure I wouldn't touch myself again for almost a year. The stench of the holding cell where I spent my first night in Los Angeles, New Year's Eve, 1951. The bald humiliation of that evening that had been my welcome to the promise of Hollywood. Now Lillian Sinclair's sad, dead eyes as the weight of her soaked sable coat pulled her spiraling down toward the bottom of the sea, the last tiny spray of bubbles bursting from her red, full lips. Did she think of me in those final moments as death clouded over her? Now Carol gasping for that last breath, too, both without me there to comfort them as they gave up and moved on. A kaleidoscopic pastiche of faces and words and feelings, like something out of a B horror movie when the protagonist slips into madness and his life is superimposed in spinning vignettes around his horrified features, looking for all the world like that painting *The Scream.*

I still have a lifetime of lurid visions, and in the darkness, alone, they are as vivid as yesterday.

TWO

The Buck sputtered his displeasure as we drove west on Wilshire Boulevard, the radio playing a static-filled live broadcast of the New Year's Eve ceremonies in New York, as if the Big Apple had final say over when the rest of the world would be allowed to follow them into 1952. He was still exhausted from the cross-country drive that had ended late that afternoon when we stopped alongside a road in Griffith Park so I could snooze in the back seat—until a policeman tapped on the window and told us to move on. We had arrived in Los Angeles with eight bucks and change and no place to live. The brief shut-eye hadn't helped either of us much, and he didn't like being rousted from his slumber any more than I did, but my survival hinged on this mission, and The Buck was, after all, just a 1937 Buick with rusted-out running boards, three bald tires, and an "i" that had corroded off its grill emblem.

Trying to steer while reading the scribbled directions by the quavering flame of my Zippo, I made a right onto Wilton Place, then a left on Sixth Street, and at last another right onto South Windsor Boulevard where we found ourselves dwarfed by an umbrella of towering palm trees and awed by the celestial opulence of Hancock Park in the early 1950s. The woman at the catering company had told me to look for "a monstrous building surrounded by expensive cars," then had added, almost as an afterthought, "Oh yes. And stay off the grass and don't forget to use the kitchen door." I had to wonder if anybody at a jam-packed Hollywood shindig would even notice if one of the waiters

5

slipped in through the front—or if they'd spot it right away as a bald attempt to be "discovered." Whatever the case, I planned to play by the rules because all I knew about the inner workings of Tinseltown came from reading the fan rags and watching the newsreels we screened at the Arcadia Theater back in Tyler. So I'd do as I was told, daring to offset the indignity by daydreaming how this was a temporary situation, and that someday maybe entire armies of servers would be lined up at my kitchen door, competing to see who'd get to work one of my parties. I liked that shimmering future in my head, so while I was there, why stop at the servers clamoring for an invitation? Why not throw in a who's who of the picture business like all the Lana Turners and William Holdens and Bette Davises? "Yes, well, sorry darling. Can't make it. Dan Root's having a soiree at his pad in Malibu and . . ."

Dan Root?

Not exactly marquee, I admit. Dan being too dull, and Root too embarrassing. I needed something catchy and classy, sophisticated and alliterative like Cary Grant, Gary Cooper, or Clark Gable. All big stars, all guys who used *C*s and *G*s in their names. With their formula for success, I'd devised a moniker for myself I hoped would impress even the most stalwart of studio press agents: I was going to become *Clifton Garrow* and leave poor Dan Root behind forever. But for now, I needed to pull my head out of the clouds because rising above me was the house I'd been looking for.

It was, in fact, monstrous. A gleaming white moderne mansion of geometric corners and sweeping curves with a two-story half-rounded wall of glass brick towering over the semicircular driveway, severe and out of place among the more traditional Tudors, Cape Cods, and Mediterraneans. *Cripes.* The neighbors must've raised Holy Ned when this thing went up. It was more like a post office than somebody's home, with an oversized front door painted glossy black to accent the round, chrome rims of its three vertical portholes, their frosted glass glowing multicolored from the lights of a huge Christmas tree inside. I slowed as I passed, considering my parking options on this now crowded street, but my eyes kept returning to that house on the corner, its symmetrical metal-trimmed windows blaring like searchlights, casting clever silhouettes of the partygoers inside as they drifted like horny ghosts from room to room. Even with my windows up, I could hear the boppity-bop of a live orchestra and the shrill screaming laughter of a woman having much too good a time.

I started to slide The Buck into the first spot I came to, right behind a sparkling new roadster like nothing I'd seen before, then changed my mind, opting to move him well away from all the Cadillacs and Packards that overflowed from the driveway and seemed to be looking down their hood ornaments at him. The Buck deserved better. Having been the only car I could afford after years of popping corn and ushering at the Arcadia, he had aided my escape from a dead-end life in Texas, so I spared him the judgment from all those snooty automobiles, drove him around the corner, and parked in the middle of the block on Fifth Street. The Buck was the only jalopy within a ten-mile radius, meaning he'd be safe in this swanky neighborhood, so I hopped out and didn't even bother to lock him up. Just put the bricks behind the rear tires and prayed he'd start again in another few hours when this job was done and I could go in search of the local YMCA—if they even had such a thing in this crackerjack town—ten clams richer and maybe a step closer to stardom.

I stared at the house for a long time, wondering what kind of fancy people might call this municipal building home. Then, remembering myself, I yanked the car's side mirror up to check my appearance. Now bear in mind I had shot up to six-feet-one and a hundred and-seventy-five pounds before my fifteenth birthday, and ever since then I'd been told I had a face ready-made for the silver screen. God knows I'd been hit on by enough women that I almost believed it, but the reflection now looking back at me didn't live up to the hoopla. The ebony mop on my head was in need of a cut and comb, so I spit on my fingers and tried to tame it as best I could. There wasn't much I could do about my nose and mouth, which were too small for my face, or my pale brown eyes which were too big and made me look startled to see myself. They were also bloodshot after hours of driving on precious little sleep. I could only hope this being a Hollywood party, the lighting would be optimized for all the dolled-out dames wanting to hide their real age in shadow, and I might also benefit from their vanity. Of course, this bash would have to take place in a cave to hide the damned birthmark on my upper lip, so I reached through the passenger window and unhooked the bent paper clip that held the glove box closed, fished out a small tube of theatrical pancake, then dabbed the offending blot until it disappeared. Satisfied, I retucked my shirt, tightening the belt on the too-big waist of my second-hand tuxedo trousers, looking down at my feet and praying the low lighting would also work its magic on my shoes.

As I approached the house, I scanned for anything resembling a kitchen door, then spotted a discreet paper sign with the scrawled word "HELP" attached to a wooden gate in a stucco wall, just above eye level running the full periphery of the colossal backyard. I did my best to ignore the sting of this derogatory word—ten bucks was ten bucks, after all—and let myself in. Around the side of the house, I noted a single cement walkway winding down a slight embankment and toward a distant glittering pool with adjacent cabana, where it then wrapped around and returned toward the house a good fifty feet away. I considered my options. It seemed silly that these wealthy people—whoever they were—expected a guy to snake all the way down to the lower yard then back up and through the trees just to avoid leaving footprints on their pristine grass. The first glimmerings of resentment tightened my stomach, and I knew I had best nip it. My temper could be my worst enemy, so I smothered it with the commitment that my someday lawn in Malibu would be free for all to tread upon, and I would never force my guests—or the "help"—to feel the blush of intimidation now shaming me.

Nervous, I ran my palm over my hair again then tried to smooth the lapels of my frayed white short-waisted jacket, drawing my attention to my quaking fingers—fingers that would be, at any minute now, handling dainty and oh-so-expensive china. Not the brightest idea. Through the fabric of my shirtfront, I could feel the cool metallic cylinder of my grandmother's match safe hanging on a ball chain around my neck, always there for such emergencies. I fished it out, unscrewed the top, and tapped its contents onto my waiting palm.

My Zippo clanked and sputtered to life as I sucked the familiar sting of Mary Jane into my lungs, held it there until tiny stars swam the periphery of my vision, then exhaled before following up with another long, deep drag. After extinguishing the reefer and returning it to the safety of its hiding place, I blew the final streams in sharp bursts hoping to dispel the odor. That's when the memory of my grandmother brought a wistful smile to my lips. She'd given me the little safe shortly before her death the previous year, and as I stood over her casket, hell-bent on holding back my tears, I'd promised her I'd do whatever it took to someday get to Hollywood and chase her dream of seeing me become a star. It was when she'd given me the little safe she'd told me—one last time—how much she believed in that possible future for me. I'd go a long way in life on just my looks alone, she'd always said, and she sounded so sure of it, she'd at last convinced me, too. Of course, neither one of us knew at the time I was one of those guys who were just too good-looking to be taken seriously. Yet here I was hoping to cash in on my face, just as soon as the marijuana's friendly sensation soothed my ever-shaking hands—the bitter legacy of my mother's drunken cruelty.

With the high came an intense awareness of the party on the other side of the wall. The music, which had at first struck me as old-fashioned and sentimental, seemed to take on a new life, the rhythm kicking in and feeding my pulse. Not too bad for a small group playing standards interspersed with holiday tunes. In fact, the number so arresting me at that moment turned out to be a thumping version of "Here Comes Santa Claus." And, with my senses now good and properly altered, the guy on clarinet sounded a lot like Benny Goodman—an observation that could only mean I was ready to put up with just about anything.

I cut across the dark grass and gave a sharp knock under the porthole in the kitchen door tucked beneath a flagstone verandah spanning the house's rear and forming a terraced row of stairs down to the impeccable grounds. On the second knock, the door was yanked open by a plump sausage of a man who must have put up quite a battle to stuff himself into his chef's garb.

"What you want?"

9

"I'm . . . Clifton Garrow."

The fat man squinted at me. A total blank.

"I'm here to work second shift. Are you Tony?"

His thick eyebrows shot up. "Late, late, late!" he spat the words in my face even as he opened the door wider and pulled me into the warmth of a modern kitchen swarming with "help" and sizzling with garlic and basil.

"And it's An-*ton*-ia." He stopped a passing waiter to sniff the delicate display of shrimp canapés on the silver tray, fanning their aroma toward his hairy nostrils with his fingers. "No no no. More garlic. This smells like my wife." The waiter spun on his heels and headed back to yell at one of the cooks. The little man turned to me, inspecting me top to bottom with a sharp snap of his head. I shifted my weight and gave him an uncomfortable smile before the first blink of approval flashed across his pudgy face.

"Okay, you serve drinks."

Before I could protest this unwise choice, An-*ton*-ia had already handed me a tray of delicate stemware fizzing with the laughter of pale champagne. "And don't talk. Tonight, you're a waiter. A servant. A—how you say—*eunuch*. You talk, you tell anybody you sing and dance and act like Gene-goddamned-Kelly, I not only fire you, I *kill you*."

As much as I wanted to see him try, I nodded. "Yes, sir," I said, then took the tray and hurried toward the pantry door, the glasses already tinkling above my trembling hand.

"No no *no*. This way, *stupid!*" He held another door open for me, shaking his head and staring at me with disdain. My head rocked back, my temper flaring as I considered slamming the tray of champagne into his swollen pustule of a face.

*Ten bucks, Danny. Ten whole bucks. One day soon you'll hire this bloated slug just so you can fire him and blackball An-*ton*-ia from all of Hollywood.*

The satisfaction of this vengeful fantasy allowed me to grin and brush past him, stepping through the butler's pantry and into a burst of laughter, chatter, music, and the sound of someone doing a pretty good Louis Armstrong. As I dodged and weaved through the smartly dressed partygoers, ever vigilant of the tinkling tray of bubbling amber, I found myself in the ballroom-sized, two-story entry foyer with its curved wall of glass brick behind a sweeping staircase outfitted with an elegant, brushed nickel railing that looked as if it were suspended in midair. I had to maneuver around the kickin' quintet, and that's when I realized the guy on clarinet *was* Benny Goodman and the singer *was* Louis Armstrong. I couldn't help but grin.

Pushing on, I had to maneuver past Bing Crosby who had a pipe stem clamped in his teeth as he chatted with a rather faded beauty. I didn't recognize her until she spoke in the cancerous rasp of Tallulah Bankhead.

"Excuse me, *dah*-ling," she croaked, swinging Bing's pipe away with her finger, "but my *nose* is toasting."

Criminy. I had seen Mr. Crosby hundreds of times on the silver screen at the Arcadia and was surprised to realize I was a good four inches taller than one of the most beloved stars in Hollywood's galaxy. Go figure. As for Miss Bankhead, I recalled seeing her in that Hitchcock movie *Lifeboat*, but mostly knew her from *The Big Show* radio program on NBC. She never failed to make me laugh, and now was no exception.

When Mr. Crosby caught me grinning at them, I covered by offering the tray of tinkling glasses. Miss Bankhead plucked one as she sailed past, her eyes locking with mine for a brief lecherous moment. "Well now," she said, the corners of her blood red lips twisting upwards, "Thank god *you* got here." I returned her smile, but she was already slinking off through the foyer to seek grand adventure elsewhere, pausing with dramatic impatience to disentangle her chinchilla from a branch of the towering Christmas tree before moving on.

"*Dear Christ*, will it *ever* be midnight?" she asked of no one in particular, the smoke from her cigarette trailing like a gray, silk ribbon.

I stood rooted in place, taking in the bobbing sea of dancers on the inlaid marble floor, the room so alive with people—famous people—that it brought a singe of shame to my cheeks.

You don't belong here.

My mother's voice. Only tonight, I refused to listen as I pushed on into the party with my tray of bubbly. I stepped down into the chic living room, noting with awe the fireplace mantel was also brushed steel, with recessed lights glowing soft through its milk glass top. I'd seen houses like this only in the movies, usually the ones starring Fred Astaire and Ginger Rogers. The room was packed, and the noise from the overlapping conversations competed with Goodman's band playing in the foyer, punctuated by trumpet bursts and explosive gales of laughter. A second Christmas tree adorned a corner near the fireplace, and just beneath it Katharine Hepburn sat cross-legged on the floor having an amiable chat with Judy Holliday. *Adam's Rib* being one of my favorites, I approached them and leaned down to offer my tray, trying not to look like a starstruck maroon. The two women didn't even pause in their intimate and animated conversation as they exchanged their empty coupes for full ones. Hepburn sloshed hers a bit over the rim so I handed her a cocktail napkin.

"—oh, no, my dear. Lilly can barely tolerate Bette, and she knows damn well not to invite her whenever Tallu's in town," Hepburn said without so much as glancing my way. "And of course Bette's fully aware and considers it a professional courtesy. Same for Tallu!"

Though I wasn't in on the joke, I laughed right along with Miss Holliday until both women gave me a perplexed and somewhat annoyed look. "Sorry," I muttered, realizing my *faux pas*. Just as I straightened to continue circling the room, another waiter dashed by, barking at me as he passed, "Mr. Langen's asking for more champagne. Now."

"Who's Mr. Langen?"

The other waiter huffed. "You're in his house, Einstein. They're in the study. Hurry."

"Where's that? I just got here—"

He jabbed a thumb in the direction of a hallway off the foyer where the musicians were just heating up with "Winter Weather." I closed my eyes for a second, tapping back into the easy buzz of the weed, and headed in that direction.

"Oh for god's sake, Darryl, keep your shirt on," a man's voice said with a laugh as I neared the door. It was followed by the distinctive crack and rumble of someone breaking a fresh rack of billiard balls.

"Frank here says I'm old. But I'm still built like a man in his twenties!" It was an enormous voice. A voice of such power and authority I almost jumped as I stepped into the exquisite room paneled in bird's-eye maple with more metallic accents, looking for all the world like a movie set. It was an oversized space, with a Streamline leather sofa and matching chairs clustered into a conversation pit around the sputtering fireplace. A gigantic desk sat in the very middle of the room, centered within a huge, curved bay window of symmetrical steel. To the left, a dozen or so tuxedoed men were standing around a pool table, pausing for a moment from their game, their heads encircled in a low-hanging cloud of smoke like the tops of buildings rising out of a thick fog. They were all looking at a powerful bulldog of a man with an enormous forehead who was in the process of loosening his tie and ripping the studs from his shirtfront, a smoldering cigar clenched in his gap-toothed mouth.

"We know. We've seen it. You want some coffee?" This from a younger man in his early thirties, polished and elegant in a stylish tux. He tapped a Chesterfield on his gold cigarette case as he stood surveying "Darryl." I wondered if he was some debonair leading man I had yet to see on the screen—he was certainly handsome enough. I hoped I'd never have to go up against him for a role. The guy made me look like Jimmy Durante.

"No, I don't want any goddamned coffee. *That's* what I want," Darryl said, noticing my arrival and pointing at me with his fat cigar. The other men in the room followed his gaze to where I now stood frozen and self-conscious.

"Changing horses on us, Darryl?" someone asked in a low, lascivious voice, bringing a titter of sleazy laughter from the other men.

"Not *him*, you idiot, *champagne*," Darryl yapped, and I made sure he got some. As he knocked it back, he grumbled, "Sure, I was already in this business when most of you were still sucking your mama's teat, but I'm not out of touch. You see this box office slump we're in? I'm telling you these goddamned plywood boxes are *killing* us."

"The studio's called Twentieth Century Fox, Darryl; too bad you're still living in the nineteenth. Television's going to change the way we do business." It was the matinee idol again, a twinkle of mischief in his eyes.

"Everybody said talkies would kill the movies, too."

Darryl slammed back another glass of champagne. "This is different. It'll ruin us. We need bigger pictures."

"Bigger? Jesus. We've already got *Nearer My God to Thee* in development. The latest draft is terrific," added another voice.

"And I'm getting a rewrite on *The Trojan War* any day now if that goddamned writer will sober up long enough to put paper in his Underwood," again from the elegant guy.

"I got news for you, Milly," said another man in round tortoise-shell spectacles, "Stutz got himself on the wrong end of McCarthy's boot."

The classy guy named Milly exhaled.

"Just as well," Darryl grumbled, "Nobody'll pay a penny to see your precious *Trojan War*."

"Trust me, Darryl, just you wait. You say we need bigger pictures? *Trojan*'s gonna be huge."

"I mean bigger literally. In widescreen. Technicolor. With that new stereo-optican sound."

"Stereophonic," someone corrected.

"We're trying to get our mitts on that French Anamorpho-Scope process. The name stinks, but we've *got* to give people a goddamned reason to pry their eyeballs away from *I Love Lucy*. That traitorous redhead is gonna kill the whole goddamned industry!" Darryl turned his attention to a stout gentleman perched on the arm of a club chair and caught him mid-sip. "You're a layman, Frank. You wanna stay home and watch a test pattern or you wanna take the old lady to a *movie*?"

"All depends," the stout one considered, "on what's playing."

"You see, Darr? Both are gonna thrive. Movies *and* television," said Milly, the undiscovered movie star.

"You're crazy. We gotta kill this damn toy before it gets too popular."

Milly stepped closer, about to speak, when he seemed to notice me for the first time. His eyes flickered across my face, ever so briefly, then snapped away as he tried not to miss a beat. I continued to pass drinks around, swapping out overflowing ashtrays for clean ones as I took in the details of this fashionable and masculine room. The walls were lined with books and pieces of art. Framed photos hung everywhere, mostly of the guy named Milly posing with a cavalcade of movie stars. There was also a built-in phonograph like nothing I'd seen before, and shelves upon shelves of records. Man, this pad was the *gas*, and everybody in it was *cookin'*.

"Kill it? Why the hell would you want to do that? It's just like an animal. The bigger it gets, the hungrier it gets," Milly said.

"All the more reason to kill it. Like an animal. And what the hell are you talking about, hungry?"

"Darryl, nobody's gonna stay home and watch television unless there's something worth watching. Even Frank said so. And where do you think those shows are gonna come from?"

"Oh, that's genius, Milly. We might as well drive over tonight and burn the goddamned studio down."

Wait a minute. Darryl? And Milly?

Holy mackerel.

This mustached bulldog must be Darryl F. Zanuck, the emperor of 20th Century Fox Studios, and if that were true, then Milly—Mr. Langen—the dashing fellow I mistook for a heartthrob, had to be Milford B. Langen, *the* Milford B. Langen, Zanuck's second in command and lord of this post-modern Xanadu, host of this incredible shindig, and the man who had single-handedly discovered Lillian Sinclair and made her number one at the box office toward the end of the war. When that nickel dropped, I remembered seeing his picture in *Modern Screen* with the caption, "Milford Langen, Hollywood's Heartthrob Behind the Cameras."

Captivated by these men and their important conversation, I circled the room with my tray, offering glasses to a few more takers, wanting to linger there as long as possible without being obvious. I noticed how, even as he spoke, Milly managed to steal a few curious glances my way. Could this be it? Was I being "discovered"?

He walked over to a built-in cabinet surrounded by bookcases, and yanking open its doors revealed the stark, blind eye of a television receiver. But all I could see was the incongruous object sitting on top of

15

it: an honest-to-god Oscar.

"You *bought* one of the damned things? That's aiding and abetting."

"They're gonna show movies on this 'damned thing,' Darryl, and—"

"Not *my* movies!"

Milford Langen switched the set on and the men stared at the black screen, waiting for it to warm up.

"Listen to me," Milly continued. "What about all that nitrate just sitting there, rotting in the vaults? You can't rerelease them. Once a picture's played, it's worthless. Nobody'll pay to see a five- or ten-year-old film. Unless they can turn on the television set and watch it for free."

"*Free?!*" Zanuck nearly did a spit take.

"To them, but not the broadcasters. They have to rent the pictures from us, and then make their money with advertisements."

"Oh, right. What cement head's gonna stay home and watch some old movie on a screen the size of a goldfish bowl?"

"I might." Frank shrugged, scoring no points with Zanuck.

"What do you know? You're a cop for chrissakes, and I'm telling you—"

"I went to the pictures a lot when I was younger. Saw some good ones, too. Some I wouldn't mind seeing again. Long as they're free."

Milly chimed in. "KTLA's been showing the Hopalong Cassidy serials for the past five years. It's free money for the studios. And think about original programming. American Broadcasting is already blazing that trail with *The Lone Ranger.*"

The image on the television screen at last appeared: a test pattern with the profile of an Indian chief in full headdress. Darryl rolled his eyes.

"Kid stuff, Mill. Now remind me to fire you after the holidays. Maybe you can get a job in your precious television."

"I don't want a job in television. You know I love the picture business. All I'm saying is this could be a gold mine for us, Darr. A deep one. Before you know it, all the studios will be in the television program business. Cheapie half-hour westerns. Comedies. Mysteries. Like the old serials. We shoot 'em on standing sets with B directors, and writers are a nickel-a-dozen in this town. Plus, if we hire unknown actors we can get them for next-to-nothing, and before you know it—"

He shot a quick glance my way and stopped dead, his vivid emerald eyes locking into mine as he cut himself off. This was it. Any minute now, he'd be offering me a screen test.

"Do I smell dog shit?"

At first I wasn't sure I'd heard him right.

"Excuse me?" I stammered.

He looked down at my feet, pointing with his eyes.

I lowered my head, getting the first rancid whiff, saw the slick brown clump clinging to the side of my battered patent leather. Panicked, I looked back toward the door, seeing with horror the rhythmic brown impressions of my shoeprint on the expensive carpet, then felt the hairs on the back of my neck upend themselves as humiliation crawled over and immobilized me.

Stay off the grass.

"Do you mind?" Milly said, the hint clear. Then, to my hesitation he added a condescending, "*Please.*"

Flustered, I turned to make my way toward the door.

"Excuse me. You might want to take off the shoe first. That way I'll only have one room to recarpet."

I fumbled with the tray of glasses, looking for a place to set it down so I could do as he'd said. Wanting nothing more than to get the hell out of there. And fast.

"Give it to me." He was losing his patience as I handed it to him and started to remove the offending shoe, hopping in the process which caused the clump to dislodge and plop onto the carpet where my jumping smashed it flat into the rug before I could regain my balance. By now, the other men in the room were laughing. But Milly just stood there, his face both menacing and inscrutable. I took the bar towel from my arm and started to clean up the mess.

"Just go," Milly snapped, the other men still laughing. "Get out."

It wouldn't be the last time he'd say those words to me.

I nodded and backed out of the room, hobbling as I went, trying to walk and take off my other shoe. I almost collided with Tallulah Bankhead in the narrow corridor. She took wry note of me over the rim of her highball, "Want some help with the *pants*, *dah*-ling?" I was trapped. It was a crowded party and everyone was stopping to look at me, this ridiculous figure with a hole in his sock, carrying a shit-covered shoe. I turned and bolted back down the hallway, brushing past Langen and Zanuck as they emerged from the study.

"Are you still here?" I heard Milford ask as I pressed on, not looking back. I hurried through the foyer and toward the kitchen when a man stepped into my path, blocking my way.

"Whoa, what's your hurry?"

"I'm just, I—" I stammered, falling silent when I realized I was face-to-face with an up-and-coming actor I recognized from a handful of pictures I'd seen at the Arcadia. His name was Rock Hudson, and I recalled my grandmother whispering, "You're a far sight better lookin' than he is" as we'd shared a bag of popcorn. Standing right next to him in the flesh, wearing my threadbare Eton jacket and reeking of dog shit, I wasn't so sure.

In a small act of kindness, Hudson pretended he hadn't noticed. "You look like you could use a drink."

"I . . . have to go," was all I could manage before finding the French doorway that took me out onto the wide verandah overlooking the backyard. I hobbled toward the stairs with one shoe on and when I jumped a low flagstone wall, found myself ankle-deep in a koi pond.

"God damn it!"

But I kept going, humiliation fueling my pace. To my right, the kitchen door opened and sausage man poked his swollen head out. How could he have heard about this so fast? I pressed myself against a tree and waited, breathing hard while he hocked a wad of snot from his throat and spat it onto Milford Langen's prized lawn.

Once he had vanished, I stood in the ensuing calm, leaning against the tree, then ripped off my other shoe and my now soaked socks. That's when I realized my hands were sticky with a thick sap from the trunk of the tree. And now, the back of my white uniform was ruined as well.

"Shit."

By the time I reached the poolside cabana, tears were clouding my vision. I wasn't even good enough to serve drinks to these people, let alone become part of their rarified world. I was sure my mother would have laughed herself hoarse if she could've seen me, and my father would have smacked me around until I bled. Standing there, I considered tying one of the deck chairs to my ankle and jumping into the pool. Hell, at least I'd make the headlines and maybe even get a mention in *Daily Variety*: "Z-List Actor Drowns at A-List Party."

The double doors to the cabana were open, so I stepped into its darkness and dropped, defeated, onto a lounger. I just wanted to hide. To let everyone in that house forget about the demeaning disruption I'd caused, to go on about their business and give me a chance to skulk back to anonymity.

The band ended their break, and a plaintive version of "Moon Glow" drifted across the lawn and into the safe haven of the cabana as I became aware of the faint scent of gardenia. I studied my hands in front of my face, trying to will them to stop shaking, then remembered the reefers encased in cool metal next to my heart. I was well into my second substantial hit when a woman's voice scared the living bejesus out of me.

"Is that marijuana?"

I leapt up and spun around, searching the darkness, at length spotting, in the far corner, the amber beacon of a cigarette.

"It is, isn't it?" It was a calm voice, lilting and controlled, with a dash of a Southern accent and not a hint of judgment. "I've always wanted to try some. May I?"

I squinted, hoping to see the woman who went with this remarkable, silken voice.

"Sure. Sure. Please." I offered it in her general direction, wondering if I should go over and serve it to her.

She stubbed out her cigarette and rose from the chair. Her long evening gown rustled as she drew nearer, the sweet smell of gardenia growing stronger until she materialized in a patch of moonlight filtering through the open shutters, revealing her exquisite features. Diamonds sparkled from her earrings and the necklace encircling her flawless throat. Her skin was pale, almost alabaster, and her eyes, perhaps a bit too close together, were narrow and bright. She looked at first what we called "delicate" in those days, yet there was nothing about this woman that suggested frailty. Instead, there was a playful yet haunted sparkle in those too-small eyes.

"It's a little chilly to be running around barefoot," she said, glancing down at my feet.

I couldn't answer, because in that moment, I realized I was in the company of a no-buts-about-it movie star. I'd seen every Lillian Sinclair picture back home in Tyler, and now this icon was taking a step toward me and extending a slender hand with long, dark nails, to take the smoldering remains of the joint I held.

"You're trembling," she said, drawing near, using two of her manicured talons to carefully pinch the Mary Jane from my fingers.

"Yeah, I know. It's sort of a . . . nervous condition. My mom, she—I mean, I had an—*accident* when I was kid. The weed . . . helps a little."

She took a long drag, exhaling through her nose. "I see," she said, a slight smile curling her lips, "so it's for medicinal purposes?"

My own laugh surprised me. "Something like that. And you have to hold it in. Don't exhale so fast."

"Oh." She took another drag, following my instructions while trying not to cough as she carefully asked, "Have you been crying?"

"Well no. I was just, you know, supposed to work the party—as a waiter—and I sort of stepped in dog sh—stuff before I went in. Then I sort of tracked it all over your husband's study."

This beautiful creature threw her head back and laughed a deep throaty laugh, the sound of which coupled with the knowledge I'd inadvertently caused it, gave me a tiny thrill, bolstering my confidence.

"Or maybe that's not such a bad thing."

"Maybe. I'm Lilly."

She extended a hand. I took it, noting how cool and dainty her flesh felt when pressed into mine. "I know," I said. "I'm Clifton. Clifton Garrow."

"What's your real name?"

I deflated. "Dan Root."

"Ouch." She gave me a sad, indulgent smile, and as she stood closer I could see she was probably ten years my senior. Spotting the match safe around my neck, she idly toyed with it as if fascinated, already under the weed's creeping witchery.

"This gives you a rather interesting sensation, doesn't it?" she said, eyeing the glowing ember between her fingernails as she handed it back to me.

"Yeah. It does."

"I like it. Perhaps I'll get some." Lillian slipped her arm through mine. "Now come on. Let's go brave the party together."

"That's . . . probably not such a good idea."

"As a guest. You'll be *my* guest."

I looked at her, dumbfounded. I had done nothing to earn this woman's kindness.

"Like hell he will."

It was Milford Langen, standing in the open doors of the cabana with Frank, the stout policeman. Lillian let out an exasperated groan and returned to her chair in the corner, leaving me standing there with the remains of the reefer, the air now pungent with its bittersweet smoke.

Milford's eyes lingered on her for a moment, but she was already resting her chin on the tops of her fingers and staring off, face set and impenetrable. He turned back to me. "I thought I told you to leave."

"I was—I mean, I did . . ."

"No. I watched you jump off the verandah—and into my koi pond I might add—and come in here where you have no business. You're trespassing."

"Oh leave him alone, Milly," Lillian said, her voice rising.

"Forgive me, darling. I didn't realize this was some prearranged tryst. What'd you do, slip him a note during the party?"

This was getting out of hand. "I didn't even know she was in here."

"So you came in to see what you could steal. Is that it?"

"No. I just—I don't know—I wanted to sit down," I said through a

21

crack in my voice.

It was Frank the cop who spoke next. "And smoke a marijuana cigarette?"

I had forgotten about the now dying roach in my hand, despite the monstrous high clouding my senses. "Well, no," I said, "I was just . . ." and trailed off, realizing the futility of my situation.

Milly put a hand on Frank's arm. "Uh, Frank, a word?"

He led the policeman out onto the patio where they stood, backs to me, framed by the wavering blue light of the swimming pool. Milly spoke to Frank in hushed tones, only fragments of which reached me. ". . . can't have this sort of thing under my roof . . ." then something garbled, ". . . if this gets out, that you were here and this was going on . . ." My heart was sinking, and I looked to Lillian. She shrugged her sympathy and shook her head, as powerless as I. At length, Frank and Milly came back into the cabana, both looking grim.

Frank looked at me. "I'm afraid I'm going to have to place you under arrest."

"*What*?" Lillian stood again, knocking her champagne glass to the floor where it shattered. "For god's sake, Milly!"

"This young man here is using a controlled substance and if people find out I was in attendance at a party where this was going on, well, let me just tell you there'd be hell to pay. Excuse my language, Lil."

"God damn it, Frank. It's New Year's Eve," Lillian replied. "Have a heart. No one has to know."

Frank shook his head. "In this town?"

She sized him up, standing firm. "Fine, then. I had some myself. So I guess you'll have to arrest me, too."

"Lilly—"

"It's a possession charge. And at the moment I became aware of the situation, this young man was the one holding the controlled substance. Not you."

"Arrest me."

"No one's arresting you," Milly said, exasperated. "Are you insane? You want this to be in the morning papers?"

"I don't give a good goddamn what's in the morning papers," she snapped.

There was a brief silence. As the four of us stood there, I could feel the dread rising like vomit. The music from the house broke off mid-song, replaced by a sudden and portentous drum roll, followed by the united voices of the revelers counting down. "Ten ... Nine ... Eight ..."

"Perfect," Milly said, looking panicked, "I'm going back in. I have no intention of ringing in the New Year with some deadbeat drug addict."

Lillian eyed him. "Then why'd you invite so many?"

He started to respond, then stopped himself. "Handle this, Frank. Just get him off my property."

"Four ... Three ... Two ..."

Lillian didn't move. Milly shook his head and took off toward the house just as a roar of whistles and cheers gave way to the exuberant but melancholy strains of "Auld Lang Syne."

Frank shrugged. "Happy New Year, Lillian."

"Go to hell, Frank."

The policeman looked away, almost as if to take a breath to control himself, then: "Law's the law. Put your shoes on, son. You're coming downtown with me."

As soon as I stood up from tying the wet laces, Lillian rose on tiptoe and kissed me square on the lips. Frank averted his eyes, giving her a chance to discreetly clip the cold joint from my fingers. "Happy 1952 ... Clifton, wasn't it?" she asked with a wink.

"Uh ... that's right."

Frank shook his head and put his hand on my arm. "Let's go. Good night, Lil."

Only Lillian didn't answer as she relit the poached reefer and stood there sucking the smoke with the slightest trace of a defiant smile, watching Frank the cop lead me out of the cabana, my wet shoes squish-squishing. He was careful to keep us on the twisting sidewalk as we rounded the pool like two idiots, one leading the other off to jail.

1952 was off to one hell of a start.

THREE

I was already questioning my decision to attend Milly's funeral, even as the pilot announced our imminent landing at LAX, though I couldn't help savoring the irony that the deceased had paid for my trip. The pawnbroker had barely glanced at me as he examined the solid gold cigarette case then pressed the catch and popped it open, scanning the inscription inside before grunting, "Are you Dex?"

"No," I lied, "it belonged to my father."

He looked at me. "Milly was your mom?"

"What're you, writing a book? Can you give me anything for it or not?"

With a shrug, he'd opened his cash drawer and counted out three hundred and fifty bucks.

I was relieved to be off the plane, now free from the incessant chatter about O.J. all around me. The terminal at LAX was bright and noisy as I headed for the nearest payphone. Armed with what sparse news clippings I could find about Milly's death, I double-checked the name of the funeral home in his three-inch *Variety* obituary. My shaky hands flipped through the Yellow Pages until I spotted a display ad for "Culver Mortuary, All Undertaking Needs Our Specialty," and jotted down the address on Washington Boulevard. The service was scheduled to start in half an hour. If I hurried, I could just make it.

LA had changed a lot in forty years. Everything except the weather, and I was already starting to sweat in the dry, smog-flavored heat. It wasn't until the cab driver exited the car-choked 405 and crawled his way over to Washington Boulevard that things started to look remotely familiar. He was prattling on about O.J. being innocent, but I wasn't listening as I took in the brown, dying palm trees interspersed with flowering shrubs. Flat Spanish-style houses next to gas stations and video stores. Whatever charm this city had possessed so long ago was gone. Everything looked as forced and faded as an aging beauty queen's desperate attempts to appear young. I noted with sorrow the MGM back lot was gone, the remnants of the once thriving studio now cramped and piled on top of itself, dolled up like an amusement park. Columbia Tri-Star.

Jesus.

Across the street was the Culver Mortuary with maybe eight cars total in the lot. Hardly the turnout Milly would have expected for his little bon voyage soiree. It was already five after two, so I quickly paid the cabbie, grabbed my overnight bag, and got out to stand on the sidewalk as the taxi farted exhaust and drove away. The traffic on Washington swished by with indifference as my gnawing anxiety deepened. What did I really hope to accomplish by attending Milly's funeral? But I'd come this far, and the muted organ music wheezing from behind the closed red doors seemed to draw me in. Still, I just stood there, feeling stupid, hating myself for wasting over a hundred dollars on airfare to pay my last respects to the man who had nearly destroyed my life.

My next move was not by choice. The automatic sprinklers that kept the tiny lawn an unnatural green sputtered to life, soaking my trouser legs.

"God damn it," I said, and hurried beneath the cross and into the tiny chapel.

The air conditioning blasted in my face, chilly with the sickening odor of molded flowers and disinfectant. I felt clammy and a little ill as I lugged my suitcase into the small sanctuary where a handful of people were seated facing the open casket. *Milly would have hated this.* It would have offended his impeccable sense of taste and decorum. Like a fool, I scanned the room for signs of Lilly before remembering she had offed herself in 1982. I felt both sad and relieved I wouldn't have to face her.

Those in attendance seemed to be aging and now-powerless studio executives, relics from the old regime that had been trampled by the industrial revolution of the business and its ensuing influx of baby-faced MBAs in Italian loafers, toting beepers and cellular phones. But this flew through my mind in an instant, for all I could really see at the room's other end was Milly Langen's haggard and waxen face, neatly packed as if for shipping in tufted white satin.

The ceremony had not yet begun, so I put my suitcase down behind one of the pews and took a few hesitant steps down the center aisle, drawn toward the open casket to get a closer look, unable to turn away. As I approached, a rush came over me, the frustration of impotent silence that masked two tumultuous years of Milly's life. And Lillian's. And mine. Those two years in the early 1950s had left so many scars. A time only the three of us and a few disinterested third parties knew about. Or suspected. Fortunately, they were all now long dead. Besides, it was just another myth of Hollywood decadence and desperation. It didn't even make the gossip rags at the time, some things in that era not meeting the criteria of what's fit to print or being just cheap enough to bury with a few thousand dollars of hush money.

The eyes of the mourners seemed to bore into the back of my head as I walked down the aisle, moving ever closer to Milly's corpse, noting a head-turned whisper as I passed. I overheard the distinctive sibilant hiss of the "x" in Dexter and knew I had been made. People were talking after all, but none of them with the facts about what had really transpired.

I neared the casket and paused to take in Milford Langen for the first time in forty years and the last for all eternity. Jesus, he looked like hell, as if all the flesh of his once chiseled face had been sucked by a vacuum into every crevice and opening of his skull. His still handsome features were no more lined than my own, but his cheeks were so sunken as to create a near pucker to his lips, leaving his mouth rigid and set, void of any hint, any glimmer of emotion. He seemed neither peaceful nor satisfied. Merely tan, dead, and perturbed about it. His hair, once thick and dark auburn and a great source of pride to him, was now thin and gray, combed perfectly over the ridges of his near translucent scalp. Had his eyes been hazel or green? I couldn't remember. Maybe because they used to change shades depending on the light.

For reasons that eluded me, the undertaker had opted to perch Milly's reading glasses on his nose. What was he going to do? Skim *The Hollywood Reporter* every morning in the hereafter? It seemed freakish and perverse and somehow all wrong for Mill. If he had been anything, Milly Langen had been meticulous about his appearance and only wore his spectacles when he absolutely had to. Then again, maybe old age had eroded such vanity. I wouldn't have known. Throughout the ensuing time that was to become My Life, Milly had always been out there somewhere, lurking like some menacing ghost just beyond the reach of memory. Our paths had crossed exactly twice, and this, as I stood over his shriveled corpse in a shabby earth-toned mortuary, was the second time.

Damn it. I brushed away a surprising tear. I had come here with insane thoughts of throttling his corpse, of exploding with all the years of imagined conversations and pent-up rage, shouting to the world what this man had done to me. How he had destroyed my career, ruined any hope I had of stardom, left my self-worth in shambles, and driven me to contemplate suicide. Only now, confronted with the reality of him, this withered old man laid out with a paltry handful of people to mourn him, I felt only a consuming sadness for all of us who have lived beyond our usefulness. Maybe it was self-pity, or maybe it was the final acceptance of everything I had lost, back then and recently, but as I stood there looking down at him, I knew there was only one thing to do.

I leaned over and gently kissed his forehead.

FOUR

I greeted the first morning of 1952 with my face pressed flat against a cold metal bench, blinking as I tried to get my bearings. I sat up, clutching my head as if to keep the pain in my skull from migrating down my spine, then looked around the crowded and rank cell, squinting in the harsh light, squeezing my eyes shut as I rubbed my face and tried to block out the memories of my miserable debut at my first and probably last Hollywood party. So here I was, waking to my new life in a new year behind bars, my tongue as rough as a cat's. The clatter of keys and the booming sound of the heavy door sliding on its track forced me to open my eyes.

"Okay, Sunshine, you're free to go."

The other bums, drunks, and hooligans in the cell merely glanced at the middle-aged cop now standing there, one hand holding the bars, the other resting on the butt of his billystick. This was the same huddle of men with whom I'd spent most of the previous night trying to avoid eye contact, knowing full well a broken nose, black eye, or gash across my face could ruin my chances of auditioning in the near future for anything other than a boxing picture.

"I said you're free to go," the cop repeated, but nobody moved.

"Are you deaf? C'mon!"

It was then I realized he was glaring my way.

"Me?"

"Yes, you. Unless you'd rather stay here with your girlfriends. No skin

29

off my dick."

Even though I was sure there had been some mistake, I grabbed my filthy waiter's jacket, which I'd been using as a blanket, and stood up, at first uncertain of my balance, but managed to make my way toward him without saying a word. Whatever came out of my mouth was bound to cause him to toss me right back in, so I kept it shut and followed him down the corridor, past the row of holding cells filled with the stink of so many New Year's Eves gone wrong.

"I don't . . . understand," was all I could manage.

"Your bail's been posted."

"It has? By who—?"

And that's when I saw her, sitting on a wooden chair just beyond the front desk. She was wearing a long fur coat and sunglasses, her long chestnut hair bundled in a scarf, no trace of last night's makeup, utterly unrecognizable as she tapped cigarette ash onto the linoleum with her black gloved hand. She looked for all the world like some beautiful vampire daring to venture into the daylight.

"Mrs. Sinclair . . .?" I stammered, confused.

"Shhhh, just gather your things. I can't bear this place another instant."

I blinked, wondering if perhaps I was still in that cell, asleep and dreaming. Another cop processed my release quickly enough, handing me a manila envelope with my wallet, keys, Zippo, and some change. My belt, bow tie, and shoelaces were also there.

"Where's my match safe?"

The cop glanced impatiently at the paperwork. "Confiscated. Evidence."

"But my grandmother gave it to me."

"Really? Sweet ol' Grandma the dope fiend?"

My fists tightened. I had only one connection to my family worth fighting for, but I knew better than to tangle with a cop. Still, the smirk on the guy's face was testing me. That's when I felt a gentle hand on my arm and turned to see Lillian Sinclair, my savior, now at my side. I flinched, pulling away from her touch with a quick reflex, and took a half step back, self-aware of how my breath and clothes must reek after a night in that cage. Her response was to apologize and reassure.

"Everything's fine now. The car's waiting for us."

"Put your John Hancock right here," the cop said, then added under his breath, "Lucky bastard."

I signed for my pathetic possessions and followed Lillian through the busy precinct and out into the brightest daylight I'd ever seen. But the sun was as deceptive and untrustworthy as everything else in Hollywood, because despite its brilliance, the air was cold. Idling at the curb was a brand-new Cadillac limo, and no sooner had we appeared than a disapproving and impossibly skinny Chinese fellow jumped out, his uniform as black and shiny as the car itself. Without a word, he yanked open the rear door.

"Thank you, Deming," Lillian said, "Just take us home and you can have the rest of the day. So sorry to make you work on the holiday."

He wore a tight-lipped smile that barely masked his contempt for me. As Lillian got into the car, she glanced over her shoulder. "I'm afraid I don't drive."

"Looks to me like you don't have to," I replied. Her smile was genuine. I slid in to join her, catching the smell of the soft, mauve-colored leather as I noticed the retractable armrest already pulled out. There were two fold-down seats in front of us, but the passenger space was so cavernous we still would have had plenty of legroom even fully loaded. A cat like me could get used to this.

As Deming started the engine and pulled into the deserted street, Lillian tapped another cigarette on the back of a slim silver case. She put it to her lips, still between her slender, gloved fingers, and looked at me. It took me a second to remember my manners. I fished out my Zippo and lit it for her, but the flame wobbled because my hands were shaking again. Gently, she cupped hers around mine to steady them, and I detected a faint whiff of gardenia before she exhaled thick smoke through her nose.

"Poor thing," she said as I extinguished the flame and tried to hide my hands in my pockets. "Would you like one?"

"No, thanks. I don't smoke."

"*Cigarettes*," she smiled, dropping her chin a bit and revealing just the faintest slits of her incredible hazel eyes over the rims of her dark glasses. A knowing smile curled her perfect lips.

We were silent for a moment, then I steeled myself.

"Why did you . . . I mean, I'm grateful, but . . ." I felt like such a jackass. I was tongue-tied around this legendary creature, desperate for my grandmother's match safe with its calming marijuana.

"I don't know. Maybe because I was like you, once."

"I find that hard to believe."

"It's true. I came to Los Angeles with nothing. Endured my share of degradation."

"When did things turn around for you?"

"When I met Milly, of course," she said, staring at nothing outside the window. "I'm sorry for the way he humiliated you last night. Sometimes he . . . can't help himself." Then, changing the subject, "I assume that Buick parked up the street from our house is yours."

"How could you tell?"

She laughed now, smiling at me as she put her cigarette out in the little ashtray in the door panel before snapping it closed, then watched the idle wisps of smoke that still managed to escape and laze upward. "You're going to do just fine, Clifton."

I smiled in return, grateful for her kindness, and for the implicit respect she had shown by calling me by my new name.

"Anyway, shall we drop you at your car or where you're staying?"

"Well, my car *is* where I'm staying." I said without thinking, not realizing how pathetic it made me seem until it was too late. "Temporarily, I mean. I got into town yesterday."

"And we've already made such a bad first impression," she said with all sincerity. Was she actually apologizing? To me?

Lillian Sinclair scrutinized my face. "You've got something on your lip."

She reached toward me to dab it with her gloved finger, but I turned my head away from her, feeling the embarrassment blush my cheeks. Of course last night's hasty makeup job had worn off.

"Whatever is the matter?"

"It's a birthmark. I usually cover it up with a little pancake. When I'm auditioning or anything."

"I didn't mean to make you self-conscious."

"Trust me, you had nothing to do with *that*."

She frowned, and I could tell her remorse was genuine.

"It's okay," I said, surprised to find myself reassuring one of the most famous women in the world.

We drove in silence for a while, and the next thing I knew Lillian Sinclair was gently shaking my shoulder. I had nodded off in the safety and comfort of that luxuriously expensive cocoon.

"Cliff? We're here."

Again, I blinked awake. We were stopped just up from their house, a blinding white beacon in the California sunshine. The streets were wide and empty, and despite the glorious sun, our breath was now steaming. I shivered.

"You should put your jacket on."

I did, and as I reached for the door handle, it was yanked open from the other side by the dour Deming. I got out, aware for the first time of my urgent need to pee. I had refused to use the filthy toilet in the holding cell the night before, there being no privacy. So this was it. I'd thank Lillian Sinclair, hurry over to The Buck, beg him to start, then vanish forever, praying I could find an open service station somewhere along the way where I could relieve myself.

"I can't thank you enough, Mrs. Sinclair."

"It's Lilly. And it was my pleasure," then, with some authority, "Deming, would you get back in the car?"

With a frown the servant followed orders, and I could have sworn he slammed the door a little too hard.

"Cliff . . . before you go . . . I feel so awkward asking you this . . ."

"Under the circumstances, I'd say you can ask me anything." Of course, I couldn't imagine what this exquisite creature might want from the likes of me.

"Did the police take *all* of your marijuana?"

I hesitated, unsure I'd heard correctly.

"I'm sorry. I shouldn't have asked."

"No, no. It's okay. I have a stash in the car."

"Would you mind terribly if . . .?"

"Are you kidding? Lady, after what you've done for me, be my guest."

Happy I could repay her unsolicited kindness, I turned toward The Buck. My heart sank. The trunk lid was raised an inch or two.

"Oh no."

I hurried over and flung it open, panic setting in when I saw that my suitcase—packed with everything I owned—was gone. Of all the neighborhoods in all the world . . .

"God damn it!"

"What is it? What's the matter?" Lillian hurried over toward me.

"Some bastard stole my stuff . . ."

"Your marijuana, too?" she asked with genuine concern. The ridiculousness of it caught me off guard, and rather than venting my frustration on The Buck, I laughed.

"Let's hope not."

I yanked the flat spare tire aside, revealing a small, battered tin with a picture of two Scottie dogs on it. Prying it open, I showed her it was packed full.

"I'm sorry, I didn't mean to seem unconcerned about your belongings . . . it's just. I get these migraines. Crippling, really. I had one coming on last night, from the party, which is why I was in the cabana when you . . ." She trailed off before at last finishing her thought. "The marijuana helped."

"Take all you want. It's the least I can do."

"I could pay you," she said, already digging for her wallet when I stopped her.

"God, no. It's on me."

"Then let me feed you some breakfast at the very least. I make dazzling eggs Benedict. And Milly has some clothes we were going to give to charity."

"I'm not charity," I snapped, then regretted it.

"Sorry. I didn't mean to imply . . ."

"No. *I'm* sorry. I don't know what's wrong with me sometimes."

"Will you come into the house? It's cold out."

I hesitated. All I really wanted to do was find a dark place to pee and let one of my spells come over me. But here was this kind woman, who seemed almost haunted by some unspoken sadness.

"Can I use your bathroom? Maybe take a shower?"

"Of course. There's eight to choose from."

FIVE

So that's how a nobody from Tyler, Texas with the unfortunate name of Daniel Root came to be sitting in the modern yet cozy kitchen of a famous movie star and her producer husband, wrapped in said husband's luxurious smoking jacket, fresh from a hot shower and eating the last of the best eggs Benedict I'd ever tasted. Never mind they could've been horrible for all I knew, but in my marijuana haze, with Lillian Sinclair watching me through a veil of cigarette smoke, I was sopping them up as if they were the greatest delicacy on earth, only a tad distracted by the Tournament of Roses Parade on the television receiver concealed in a cabinet in the breakfast nook. There was no sign of Milford Langen, and the house staff had the day off, though they must have worked late the night before as there was not a trace of the party to be seen anywhere. The mansion was spotless, almost sterile, with everything precise and in its place. Even the two Christmas trees were already gone, disposed of due to Lillian's deep-seated superstition about leaving holiday decorations up past the new year—one of the many strange beliefs she later told me she'd acquired from her Southern mother.

I was laughing so hard it was difficult to eat while she recounted growing up in Valdosta, Georgia, a tiny town with Spanish moss-draped trees that was so far south it was practically in Florida. After being crowned The Azalea Festival Queen, she'd come to Hollywood where she worked diligently to lose what she called a very "cornpone accent." It was difficult to believe this fetching and sophisticated woman could have come from such humble roots, but the more she told me about herself—things that never once made it into the fan magazines—the more I felt a kinship with her. I, too, had come from a difficult childhood in a poor family. I, too, was determined to rid myself of any traces of my upbringing. As Lilly put it, her family was "country-er'n slop." In fact, her poor widowed mother was terrified of any mode of transportation, so the only time Lillian ever saw her was when she herself could make the trek to South Georgia—seldom if ever. As she chattered on, her blow-by-blow description of watching her obese father drop dead in front of her elicited the most inappropriate of responses: I laughed so hard I thought I'd faint, and to my surprise Lillian joined me.

"I'm sorry . . . I don't . . . mean to be disrespectful," I managed through gulps of air.

"No, no. It's fine. In fact, this 'weed' makes everything funny! What a marvelous tonic!" She stubbed another cigarette out into her plate. "I smoke too much," she added, almost to herself. "Anyway, I was an unknown when I auditioned for Scarlett O'Hara. That role should have been mine."

"I'm sure you'd have been brilliant."

"And now we'll never know," she said with matter-of-fact simplicity, then fell silent before she went on. "Milly set it up. He was one of David Selznick's army of assistants at the time—still only a teenager—and yet he somehow managed to get me a screen test. I didn't get the part, but I did get a husband out of the deal."

"How long have you been married?" I asked, making conversation.

"Oh, ten years or so. He had just enlisted in the Navy and was about to ship out . . ." She trailed off, staring at me.

"What?"

"When's the last time you had a haircut?" she asked.

Not what I'd expected, but direct enough to warrant an answer. "Oh . . . maybe a month ago. I've been a little short on cash."

"You should let me cut it for you."

I laughed. "In your condition, I don't know about that."

"I'm quite good. I was a beautician when I came to Hollywood way

37

back when. You're a very handsome young man. Dare I say even gorgeous. The raw material is there. What you need to survive in this town is an image all your own."

"*You* used to cut hair?" I asked, dodging the discomfort I always felt around the subject of my looks.

"Oh, and dye and perm . . ."

"Is that how you met Mr. Langen?"

"Please, everybody calls him Milly, so you might as well, too."

"Yeah, we'll see about that."

"C'mon. I'm dying to make you over," she said, pushing away from the table and standing, avoiding my question. I thought better than to press. She took my plate and put it on the floor, whereupon two dogs appeared from nowhere, lapping up what little was left. One, maybe fifteen pounds, looked to be some kind of terrier, jet black with a huge white spot on its side. The other, a scrawny thing with tufts of wispy gray fur poking from its otherwise mottled skin, looked as if it had been through an atomic blast. The latter was the more skittish of the two, eyeing me warily as it licked the rim of the plate farthest from the terrier.

"I didn't know you had dogs," I said, unable to mask the delight in my voice as I knelt down and petted them. When they realized the snack was gone, they turned to me for more. Soon, the scruffy little one was licking my face.

"Milly makes me lock them in the laundry room when we have parties, poor things."

"What're their names?"

"The big one is Trouble, and the little one is Puck. He doesn't usually take to people, other than me. He likes you."

"Puck? That's funny, I played that part in high school."

"You must've been wonderful."

"I was okay," I said, not wanting to go into details of the beating my father had given me after opening night, drunk and screaming at me for running around the stage in nothing but leaves. Then, to the scruffy dog, "Hey there, Puck. You're a special little fella, aren't you? Awww, Trouble, you're special, too. Look at you two. Puck and Trouble."

"Or 'Fuckin' Trouble' as Milly likes to call them. He isn't much for dogs."

The mention of her husband brought me back for a moment, but the pooches remained content to have me scratch behind their ears as they fought to see who could lick my hands the most.

"Looks like you're making new friends."

"Hope so," I said, glancing her way.

A few minutes later, I was sitting on a stool in the middle of the kitchen with a sheet draped over me as Lillian Sinclair scrutinized my face, clipping away with comb and scissors, both of us still giggling as Puck and Trouble tried to get in on the action by jumping up on me. All of the previous night seemed like a bad dream now, and I had a little glimmer of happiness twittering in my stomach. She was genuine and likable. A real person who just happened to be a movie star. Even if she shaved my head, I wouldn't have cared.

Finally, she bundled up the sheet to keep the shorn hair from getting all over the linoleum and handed me a small mirror.

"Go on. Worship me afterwards," she grinned.

The man staring back at me was a surprise. I had always worn my hair longish in front, so as to get just the right double wave when combed back. Lillian had taken that away, cutting the sides close to the scalp and leaving just enough in front to flip back once. The way she'd tamed my once unruly mane now gave me a cool and crisp look, and by taking attention away from my hair, drew focus to my eyes and nose, which by some miracle now seemed to be in proportion to the rest of my face. Lillian's reimagining of me had given my appearance a smoldering sensuality and made it possible for me to see for myself what others had so often remarked about. The eyes, nose, mouth . . . though I was still tormented by the sight of the penny-sized chocolate-stain birthmark marring my upper lip. I sat there, looking at my reflection, contemplating what now seemed like a less uncertain future, when I realized Lillian was tickling the back of my neck with a kiss. I jumped up from the stool.

"Oh god," she said, embarrassed. "I'm sorry. I simply cannot resist the nape of a man's neck after a haircut."

"Good thing you changed careers," I quipped to defuse the awkwardness, for the first time questioning her motives.

"Please don't look at me that way. It's the dope."

"Yeah, it does weird things to a person."

"I'm still hungry; are you?"

I didn't answer, just watched as she yanked open the door of the Frigidaire and gazed inside.

"I'm going to make a traditional southern New Year's dinner later. You must stay."

"I don't know . . ."

"I won't take no for an answer. Fried ham. Collard greens. Black-eyed peas. Cornbread . . ."

I had to admit it sounded good.

"The collards are lucky," she continued. "They represent greenbacks. The peas are coins and the ham just tastes good. I've been eating it every New Year's Day since I can remember."

"Then obviously it's paid off for you."

She closed the Frigidaire's door, losing interest, and moved over to the kitchen table where she plopped down and lit another cigarette.

"Come on," she said, "tell me all about yourself."

"That won't take long," I replied.

"Modesty doesn't suit you, Clifford."

"Clifton. And I'm serious. I think I've already told you everything."

I joined her at the table as she sat there, drawing on her cigarette and staring idly at the television screen. A float filled with roses and beautiful young women was drifting by the camera.

"What sort of girls do you like?"

I was surprised by the question; in fact, had to think for a minute. "I don't know."

"Oh c'mon. Every man has a type."

"I guess maybe I don't."

"Do you have a girlfriend now?"

"I wouldn't've driven myself to Hollywood if I did."

"You must've left right after Christmas."

40

"That's right. Wasn't much keeping me there."

"Your family surely was devastated."

I thought of my mother in her wheelchair, drunk and soaked in her own urine as I'd walked past her with the suitcase containing everything I cared about, which wasn't much. The same one some very disappointed thief was now going through, looking for anything of value to hock. I grinned. The joke was on them.

"You'll be back," my mother had said without even looking at me.

"They're managing in their own way," was my only reply to Lillian.

"You're smiling. What aren't you telling me?"

"I was just thinking about the stupidest guy in the world."

"Who's that?"

"Whoever broke into my car and stole my stuff. On *your* street."

She laughed now, throaty and real. It was a sound I found addictive, and I was determined to make her laugh as much and as often as possible. Fueled by the marijuana, a drug that makes brilliance from the mundane, I couldn't help but join her. The two of us giggled, me in her husband's robe that had fallen open to expose the cleft in my chest, and her in a simple blouse and pants, smoking a cigarette and laughing so hard she was coughing. It was exhilarating and like nothing I'd felt before in all of my twenty-one years. We were being deliciously silly, and soon we were watching the televised parade and ridiculing its participants, which brought renewed gales of laughter. So much so we hadn't heard the front door.

"What the hell . . .?"

We snapped out of our gaiety, realizing Milford Langen was now standing in the archway to the kitchen, wearing riding clothes along with the most astonished expression I'd ever seen on another human's face.

"Milly. You're home."

"That's obvious. What's *he* doing here?"

"Oh, talking, getting a haircut, watching the television . . ."

Milly's entire face twisted downward into a disapproving frown. It was a look I'd get used to over the next few months, but in that moment it was unsettling.

"You know what I meant."

"It's simple," Lilly said, standing and clearing the table. "I went downtown and bailed him out—"

"You *what*?"

"It was the least we could do after the horrible night he had. Most of it thanks to us. Well, mostly *you*. How was your ride?"

Milly leveled a displeased look at me. "Is that my smoking jacket?"

"I—" but before I could finish, Lilly intervened.

"Well, he couldn't very well be sitting around the kitchen naked, now could he?"

"Lillian, we need to talk."

I stood up so fast, it startled the dogs. "It's fine. I need to be going, anyway. I'll just . . . get dressed and . . . thanks for the breakfast."

As I hurried out of there, trying to find my way back up to the guest room where I'd showered and shaved, I could hear their hushed argument echoing through the cavernous mansion.

". . . a murderer for all you know . . ."

" . . . oh Milly, he's perfectly charming . . ."

". . . I'm calling Dr. Sturner . . ."

". . . stop it, I felt sorry for the poor thing . . ."

". . . you've taken leave of your senses . . ."

I closed the guest room door to shut them out, and as I took off the robe and gathered my clothes, I heard a faint scratching. It was Puck, who'd followed me, looking a little scared.

"Hey little fella. It's okay," I said, kneeling down and rubbing his scrawny ears.

Puck watched with cocked head while I slid into my pants, shoes and socks, and just as I was reaching for my shirt, the door burst open. It was Milly, impossible to read, but there was something unnerving about the way he looked at me as I stood there half-naked, my tuxedo trousers still unbuttoned. Puck darted under the bed and I hurried to put on my shirt and stuff it into my pants.

"I'm really sorry, Mr. Langen. Your wife was being very kind, and I just got into town yesterday, and . . . anyway, you don't want to hear about me, so I'll just . . . be going." I grabbed my shoes, figuring I could put them on once I got outside.

"My wife . . ." Milly said, stopping me as he chose his words with precision, "her judgment isn't all it should be. But she's explained your situation to me and . . ." This last part seemed hard for him to say: "She'd like it very much if you'd stay for New Year's dinner."

I should have bolted then and there, but in my shock, the only reply I could manage was, "I've caused enough trouble . . ."

Milly eyed me, and a glimmer of some weariness shown through with a hint of melancholy, which, for a fleeting moment, made him seem kind. "There's some clothing I'm getting rid of. Lilly told me about your suitcase. That's a hell of a way to start a new year. Anyway, they're in boxes in the laundry room. Take whatever you'd like. Out with the old, right?"

He left me then. I stood in the ensuing silence, wondering what could possibly have been said between the two of them in the kitchen that would have led to this abrupt about-face. I was determined to get out of there, but as I finished buttoning my shirt, my eyes fell on its tattered cuffs, and I turned toward the opposite mirrored wall that made the room look twice as big. My shirt was sweat-stained and still smelled of the city jail. It was wrinkled and my pants had dusty scuffs all over them. My waiter's jacket was in ruins, and I realized what a fool I'd look driving around Hollywood in the bright sunshine. I surveyed this well-appointed home, sensing a sadness that permeated these two famous people, and considered my situation.

Maybe it wouldn't hurt to accept a little charity for a change.

The laundry room seemed bigger than the tiny house I'd shared with my mother and father in Tyler. There were three large pasteboard boxes stacked near the washing machine, and as I sorted through them, I couldn't imagine why anyone—even people with money to burn—would be disposing of their contents. There were elegant gabardine slacks, silk shirts monogrammed *MBL*, a blue serge suit, a silvery gray sports jacket, even two pairs of custom-made oxfords by some so-called "shoemaker to the stars." Quality stuff. The labels were all well-known tailors in Beverly Hills and Miracle Mile, and the clothes were immaculate and neatly folded. Hell, no sense letting these threads go to some hobo.

I could hear Lillian puttering around the kitchen, accompanied by the occasional clang of a pot. Her voice was almost sing-song as she talked to Trouble who stayed constantly by her side, his claws clicking on the floor as he followed her, then a burst of running water and the sizzling hiss of something being thrown into hot oil in a skillet. The aroma made my stomach growl so loudly that Puck cocked his head and looked at me with alarm. I chose a white brushed cotton shirt and teal trousers, and, rummaging further, I found a bunch of neckties. Soon I was knotting a steel-colored silk one in the tiny mirror over the maid's sink.

I looked so good it startled me. The haircut, the fitted clothes, all transformed me into a man I knew I wasn't, but I didn't mind projecting the image, nonetheless. Isn't that what Lilly had said really mattered anyway? Besides, these were powerful people, and since the situation had presented itself and my luck seemed to be turning on a dime, why not exploit it for all it was worth? Hell, I knew I was a damn good actor, and not only on the stage.

"C'mon, Puck," I said with a wink. "It's showtime."

SIX

I emerged from the mortuary and blinked in the brilliant afternoon sunshine, relieved that the insincere ordeal of Milly's memorial service was over. The dour-faced undertakers were already handing out "Funeral" banners for those who wanted to drive to the cemetery and make sure Milford Langen was dead and buried for good, but I waved them off, standing there like a fool with my suitcase and no means of transportation. LA isn't exactly the kind of place where you can hail a cab, so I considered my options. The few mourners straggled out of the little chapel, making their way toward their cars in the heat, some tugging at their ties and slipping off their jackets, others already on their mobile phones the size of shoes. That's when I heard a voice behind me.

"Excuse me. You're Dexter Gaines, aren't you?"

I was surprised to see a pretty blonde woman I guessed to be in her thirties, squinting at me as she dug her arm deep into her mammoth purse, rooting around for something. She was what we used to call voluptuous, meaning there was meat on her bones, only well distributed. Her dress was black with tiny white polka dots and big plastic earrings to match. The whole outfit had a dated feel to it. Still, no one under fifty should have even had a clue who I had been all those years ago, let alone this girl.

"I was once. My name's Dan."

"Tally," she said, then waited for a response from me. I gave her a blank stare, even while sensing something familiar about her.

"Milford Langen's my father. Was, I mean."

"Then, I'm so sorry." As soon as the words came out of my mouth, I realized their double meaning. Tally nodded absently. If she had picked up on it, she didn't comment.

She found her sunglasses. "Jesus, I need a smaller bag," she muttered to herself as she slipped them on.

"How did you recognize me?"

"From your movies, of course. And Mom told me you had a bit of bittersweet chocolate on your lip."

Even after so many years, I reached to touch the birthmark that had so bedeviled my self-esteem throughout my life, stunned to hear my name would have ever been mentioned by Lillian after the way things had ended.

"You seem surprised," she added.

"Yeah, sorry. I remember reading about them having a kid, but once I left town, I . . . never really looked back."

"She spoke very fondly of you," Tally said.

"She did?" I asked, perplexed.

"Well, usually when she was drunk. Which means she spoke of you often." This last she added with a wry raise of her eyebrow, almost as if she herself could see the humor in being the spawn of Milford Langen and Lillian Sinclair. I pondered the impossibility of her words as she eyed my tattered suitcase, "You came into town for Dad's funeral? I'm sure it would have meant the world to him." I could tell she was just being polite. Later she told me she'd been bewildered to learn her father had *any* friends at all.

"It would've meant *something*," was all I managed, figuring Tally didn't know of my tawdry and violent past with her parents.

"Did you rent a car?"

"No, I, uh . . . took a cab from the airport. Barely made it, as it turns out."

"Well, I'm glad you're here. You can ride with me," she said even as she spotted my hesitation. "Please. Otherwise, I'll be all alone. Looks like you will be, too."

She tugged her sunglasses down her nose and stared at me over the rims. Our eyes met, and I was startled and moved to see in them Lillian Sinclair staring back at me, filled with the same winsome mischief and melancholy. The moment vanished when she pushed her shades back into place.

Unnerved, I said, "All right."

And so I found myself in another chauffeured limo in Los Angeles, some forty-three years later, following the hearse with Milly's remains as it snaked through the snarl of afternoon traffic, unable to shake the *déjà vu* of the situation. Tally sat beside me, absently plucking at a loose thread on the lap of her skirt.

"So . . . I'm guessing the lawyers called you about Dad's death?"

"Nope," I said, shaking my head. "Saw it on *Entertainment Tonight*."

"Funny. That's more or less how I learned about my mother's little midnight swim. Except it was *The Today Show*." The tone in her voice betrayed someone trying to make light of a lifetime's pain. A tone I knew all too well.

"Your father and you . . . were close?" I asked after a long, uncomfortable silence.

She gave a rueful laugh. "Not really. I always thought someday I'd break through, but it never happened. I spoke to him last Christmas. Then I got a call from the coroner's office three days ago. Unfinished business, I guess." She grew a little agitated by whatever was going on in her mind. "Look, would you freak out if I smoke?"

"I didn't know people still did."

"Well . . ." She trailed off, pushing the button to raise the privacy divider and shut out the funeral home's driver. "I don't mean cigarettes." Whereupon she snapped open her purse, found a dented and scratched Altoids tin, then produced a half-smoked joint. "Scandalous, I know."

"It's fine. There was a time in my life I would've joined you."

For the first time since I'd met her, she smiled. "Mom told me you were all right," she said, torching the spliff with a vintage Zippo lighter. She then cracked her window and exhaled a thick plume before licking the tips of her finger and thumb to extinguish the joint with a faint sizzle.

After putting it back into its hiding place and snapping the lid closed, she sighed, fanning her hands to dispel the sweet, musky aroma.

"There now," she said. "All better. You'll help me get through this, won't you, Dex?"

"We'll help each other," I replied, "but only if you call me Dan."

"Something tells me your memories aren't as fond as my mother's."

"You could say that." I nodded, still marveling at how Lillian Sinclair would have told such lies to her own daughter. "I didn't exactly have what you'd call a storybook Hollywood experience."

"Mom always said you were quite talented. She really hated that you gave it up and left."

"That's very generous of her," I said, my voice a surprised whisper.

"Why *did* you leave?" she asked, her face a mask of innocence.

It seemed pretty clear her mother had omitted the more salacious truth, and I wasn't about to scandalize this young woman at her father's funeral. So I decided to pass the awkward time in the limo by telling her a story that would shed only the feeblest light on my brief flirtation with stardom.

I shifted in my seat and shook my head slightly as I began, "It's hard to make it as an actor when you can't handle props."

She glanced at my jittering fingers. "Oh right, she told me . . ."

"But that was a long time ago."

The first time I walked onto a real movie set as a working actor was on Stage 14 of the 20th Century Fox lot. A small army of grips and gaffers and production assistants was swarming over an enormous set four stories high: the middle section of a massive ocean liner, complete with a funnel that reached nearly to the catwalks above. I was already in makeup and wardrobe, in my case the tailored uniform of a deck steward. As I stood there, taking in the lights, the camera, and a cluster of costumed extras smoking cigarettes and eating doughnuts at the craft service table, I felt a hand on my shoulder.

"Well, you certainly look the part," Milly said, giving my arm a squeeze.

"Yeah, I'm drawing on my vast life experience as a waiter." I tried to smile, but the truth was I was nervous, and more than a little bitter.

"You know your lines?"

"Line," I corrected, then, in my best British accent, "Would you like some bouillon, Madame?"

"Hey, kiddo," Milly said, grinning, "you gotta start somewhere."

"I'm not complaining" was all I could muster, lying through my teeth.

The assistant director, Henry Weinberger, called for first team to take their places.

"That's you," Milly said with a gentle nudge. "I'll tag along and introduce you to everyone."

We headed over to the set and a production assistant named Pook showed us around back where the clever illusion abruptly ended. The ship was just a façade, of course, its back a mishmash of wooden beams and a narrow staircase.

"Welcome aboard," Pook said, then gestured toward the steps. "Bon voyage."

I emerged onto the partial deck of the steamship where the extras were already in place, bundled up in steamer rugs and gloves despite the excruciating heat of the lights overhead. Behind us, a huge rear projection screen flickered to life with a black-and-white film loop of the ocean rolling by, and a giant wind machine began to spin, ruffling our hair. If you squinted, you'd almost believe you were in the middle of the Atlantic—on an impossibly hot day. Milly approached a poised and regal woman, already seated in a deck chair with a blanket over her legs.

"Milly," she exclaimed, delighted to see him, "what on earth are you doing here? Don't tell me you've taken over the picture?"

"Just visiting, Missy," he said, leaning down to kiss her elegant cheek. "I'm grooming a young actor." He turned to me now, very formal. "Allow me to introduce you to Dexter Gaines. Dexter? I'd like you to meet Miss Barbara Stanwyck."

I'll admit it, the kid from Tyler in me was awed and starstruck.

When she extended her hand, I took it in mine.

"I'm thrilled to meet you, Miss Stanwyck," I croaked. "*The Lady Eve* is one of my favorite pictures."

"You're very kind," she smiled, putting me at ease. She was genuine, unlike so many other people I'd met in the months since I'd been living in Milly and Lilly's cabana. "And here I am on the set of another luxury liner. Too bad this one has to sink in the end."

She was referring, of course, to the *Titanic*, on whose faux decks we now stood, awaiting our cue to shoot the one scene Milly had managed to secure for me. It was early November 1952, and Milly had been successful in his campaign to ditch the working title *Nearer My God to Thee* and go with the more recognizable name of the actual doomed liner—an idea I had suggested to him poolside one Saturday afternoon, by the way. I had been in Hollywood for almost a year before he'd pulled enough strings to get me in front of the cameras. If you've seen the movie, you'll remember Robert Wagner out on deck when he spots Barbara Stanwyck, who plays the mother of Wagner's love interest. He chats with her, and she reads a poem to him. What you won't remember is the very beginning of the scene where Stanwyck is seated alone with her book, and a handsome young deck steward approaches and offers her morning bouillon.

"Well look what the cat dragged in," said Robert Wagner, approaching and chucking Milly affably on the shoulder. Milly beamed when he saw the young actor.

"R.J., a little respect."

"For you? Please," Wagner said, all in fun. Milly stared at him for a moment before remembering his manners.

"R.J., this is Dexter Gaines," Milly said, pivoting to include me in the conversation.

"How are you, Dex?" Wagner said, shaking my hand so firmly I almost flinched. "Nice to meet you."

"You, too" was all I managed in return.

"Places everyone!" called an authoritative voice with the slightest trace of an Eastern European accent. "And will someone please help this poor lost producer off my set?" It was the director, Jean Negulesco, a kind man in his early fifties, his eyes twinkling as he came rising over the deck railing, riding alongside the cameraman on a huge crane. He gestured toward Milly. Everyone snapped to attention.

"Johnny, you shouldn't work so hard," Milly said to the director. "You need to rest up for croquet at Darryl's this weekend."

"Pfffft" was his only response. "Good morning, Barbara. Lovely day to hit an iceberg," he quipped.

Miss Stanwyck frowned. "I don't think we should joke, considering the true story."

"I meant no disrespect," the director replied.

"I was just leaving," Milly chimed in. Then, as he passed me, "Okay, kiddo, break a leg." Which was more or less exactly what I was afraid of.

"Any questions, anyone?"

"Let's shoot," Wagner said, hopping over a railing with the ease of an acrobat and trotting down the ship's stairs to assume his place on the deck just below. I admired his self-assured athleticism, but the fact that he had the role that should have been mine filled me with resentment from the moment he shook my trembling hand.

My first screen test at Fox had been the very scene Wagner was about to play with Miss Stanwyck. After months of gentle badgering from Lillian, Milly had finally acquiesced. I tested opposite a woman I didn't recognize playing Barbara Stanwyck's part, and while the bulk of the experience has been blocked from memory, I do remember Milly telling me how well I'd done afterward over drinks at Ciro's, one of his favorite haunts. I didn't bother to tell him I'd been so high I could barely remember the dialogue. In the end, Wagner got the part, and I got a walk-on as a consolation prize, so here I was.

As we were getting ready to roll camera, the prop master, a diminutive man in his forties, brought over the silver tray of china cups and saucers, steaming with hot bouillon. "Here you go," he said, thrusting the tray with its dangerous contents into my hands. I heard the delicate and foreboding rattle, but the prop master had already moved off, checking to make sure Miss Stanwyck had her small book of poetry for the scene.

"On a bell!" the first A.D. boomed, startling me and bringing another wave of clattering from the tray as a loud buzzer sounded. I stared at the roiling sea of broth, as agitated as the fake ocean projected behind me.

"Rolling!" "Camera!" "Speed!"

"*Titanic*! Scene thirty-five! Take one!" the camera loader barked, then snapped the clapperboard, startling me and triggering a renewed round of tinkling bone china.

There was a long pause as I stood out of frame, clinging to the tray, kicking myself for not having the sense to toke up prior to leaving my tiny dressing trailer outside.

"Aaaaaand . . . action!" Negulesco shouted.

I turned toward Miss Stanwyck, who sat serenely reading her little book, the fake breeze ruffling her scarf. I approached.

"Good morning, Madame, lovely day." I said, so far so good. "Would you like some bouillon?"

"Cut!"

I turned, annoyed. I wasn't done yet.

"Something technical?" Miss Stanwyck asked.

"No, Missy. Uh . . ." Negulesco looked at me. "I'm sorry, what's your name again?"

I bristled, tried to hide it. "Da-Dexter."

"Well, Da-Dexter, please stick to the script," he said, good-naturedly enough. "You will not want to meet the angry writers."

"I just thought it would be more courteous if I—"

"Just stick to the script," he said firm but not unkind, then nodded to the first A.D.

"Back to one! Two is up!" the A.D. shouted. "We're on a bell!"

In retrospect, I probably shouldn't have taken it all so personally, but that was always my knee-jerk reaction. My cheeks were warm with humiliation as I caught a sympathetic look from Miss Stanwyck. "You're doing fine," she said, and I mustered a smile as I balanced my tray back to my starting mark.

"Rolling!" "Camera!" "Speed!" "Thirty-five, take two!" "Aaaaaand . . . action!" The ritual was repeated. I turned again and approached Miss Stanwyck exactly as I had done before. She looked up, marking her page with her finger, and smiled.

"Would you like some—?" was all that came out of my mouth before my shivering hands spasmed and the entire tray of delicate china and steaming bouillon landed all over Barbara Stanwyck's lap in a horrible cascade of clattering metal and shattering crockery.

With a yelp, she threw off the blanket which had fortunately spared her from being scalded. "Oh my god!"

"Cut! Cut it! Barbara, are you okay?"

"I'm fine. But I'm afraid my coat isn't . . ."

In the ensuing pandemonium of wardrobe, makeup, and hair people swarming their star, I remained frozen in abject horror, ignored. At length, Miss Stanwyck caught my eye. "Dexter? Are you all right?"

The only words of kindness spoken to me.

"I'm so . . . sorry, Miss Stanwyck . . . I don't know what happened . . ."

"It's all right, really."

"Everybody take ten!" the assistant director shouted, and I spun around and made my way down the hidden stairs, blowing past a frowning Milford Langen standing near the director.

"Dex!" he shouted after me, but I kept going. I couldn't face the man I knew I had so bitterly disappointed.

Outside the soundstage, I hurried into the empty trailer I shared with the other bit part actors—stinking bit part actor, that's what I was. I found my stash and was well into my third significant hit when the door swung open and Milly came in. I braced myself for the worst.

"Are you okay?" he asked, surprising me with the genuine concern in his voice.

"I'm sorry, Mill. I know you stuck your neck out to get me this part, but . . . it's my *goddamned hands*."

He came in and closed the door, sat down opposite me.

"Let me see," he said, and I held them up. They were still trembling even though the marijuana was slowly working its magic. I saw his expression as I put away the now cold joint.

"It's the only thing that makes it better," I said.

Milly nodded. "I spoke to Johnny. You'll get through it. Just relax."

"I'm so sorry, Mill."

"Dex," Milly said with reassurance in his voice, "stop saying you're sorry. You can do this. I know you can. *I believe in you.*"

No one had ever said those words to me in my entire life. I nodded and looked away, grateful for his kindness, but still not wanting to let him see me cry.

Of course, everyone was bending over backwards to be nice to me when I returned to the set. No harm done, they all said. The prop master wisely changed the contents of my tray, but even my amended line of dialog, "Would you like a fresh scone, Madame?," was cut from the final picture.

"You poor thing." Tally patted my knee as I finished my story.

"Yeah, well . . . like I said, a long time ago. I mean, it's funny now, but when your father screened the rough cut for us one night, I just sat through the whole movie with a knot in my stomach. There was R.J. dancing with the girl, swinging from the lifeboat ropes, playing a scene with Barbara Stanwyck, just being, you know, a hero. But 'what if' is a waste of time."

Neither of us had noticed the limo was now gliding amid a sea of elaborate tombstones, some of them cracked or toppled, all surrounded by a brown, dying lawn. The backs of a few soundstages and the Paramount Studios water tower loomed incongruously in the distance, framed by wilted palm trees. We were in Hollywood Memorial Park, an overgrown and neglected depository for the dead located on an unattractive stretch of Santa Monica Boulevard. As our driver parked, I noticed some of the crypts showed signs of damage, no doubt from the Northridge earthquake just six months before.

Once we stood at the gravesite, I noted the look of regret on Tally's face as she stared at the adjacent granite marker engraved in simple block letters, "Lillian Sinclair, 1921–1982." Tally and I then watched in silence as Milford Langen began the rest of all eternity in the shadow of the studio where he had long ago destroyed his once precious career.

SEVEN

The first time I fooled around with Lillian Sinclair, she rolled off of me after we'd both been satisfied and started to cry. Being a young man, this caught me off guard.

"Did I hurt you?"

"No, no. Quite the opposite," she said, wiping her tears, exhilarated. "I just realized why people scream out 'Oh god oh god' when they're having marvelous sex."

This, too, caught me off guard. "Why?"

"It's giving thanks. A prayer of gratitude."

True. In the ecstasy of the moment, I thought she'd alarm the whole neighborhood. Not to mention the servants, who had been looking at me with the same quiet disdain since that first morning when I had plodded out of the cabana and into the lives of Lillian Sinclair and Milford Langen. It had been—what?—maybe a month since then, and even though Lilly talked of preparing for her role in Milly's upcoming *The Trojan War*, I'd seen little evidence of it. Mostly, we'd spent our time smoking dope, watching the television, and just that afternoon, before she pulled me to her and kissed me like a starved person with a bowl of rice, she'd enlisted my help in a bizarre arts and crafts project involving wax fruit and gold leaf. Even more unsettling was Milly's apparent lack of concern over this handsome young man who'd moved into his cabana. Milly and I were still maneuvering around each other like two fencers, foils parried and waiting, sizing up their opponent and waiting to lunge for the kill. Little did I know at the time.

In the weeks since we'd shared collard greens and black-eyed peas with Tallulah Bankhead on New Year's Day, Lilly and I had become what I can only describe as very deep friends. Although she'd never tell me her age, and I never dared to ask, I guessed she was probably nine or ten years older than me, but when we talked to each other, laughed, even argued, there was no divide evident to either of us. We saw eye-to-eye on most things, not at all like the other thirty-or-so-year-olds I'd known back in Tyler.

Truth is, Lilly was decidedly *unlike* any other person I'd ever met before. She took her fame in stride, as "part of the job" she'd put it, and "a goddamned nuisance." Still, she loved her work, the films she'd done, and was very fond of running them for me, both of us as high as the Hindenburg, sitting in their plush screening room while Deming operated the projector from its concealed booth in what felt like a scene from *Sunset Boulevard*—only without Norma Desmond. Her favorite was *Ready! Set! Go!*, a very funny comedy she'd done with Cary Grant, and sometimes, she'd ask the dour Deming to run the last reel where she felt she looked her best and her performance was perfect. The film had been released a decade ago, but I always made a point of laughing at all of Lillian's best lines.

Another favorite was *The Widows Wore Blue and Gray*, where she'd played alongside Katharine Hepburn and Bette Davis as three sisters on different sides of what Lillian jokingly referred to as the "War of Northern Aggression." She wasn't what you'd call fond of either costar, but felt her work in the film, a Civil War melodrama Milly produced early in his career to capitalize on the success of *Gone with the Wind*, *Jezebel*, and *The Little Foxes*, had been Oscar-worthy. I didn't have the heart to tell her, but there's a reason nobody remembers *The Widows Wore Blue and Gray*. For me, the most fascinating thing about the film was how real Lillian was in her performance. She'd let her natural Southern accent through, and even when she delivered the ridiculous line, "Yankees are like dogs: give them a bone and they'll worship you forever," she'd been riveting. Lillian shared with me that the line she'd wanted to say was

"Yankees are like dogs: let them sniff your butt and they'll worship you forever," but the Hays Office had a thing or two to say about that.

Her warm flesh pressed against mine under the cool sheets. "We should probably get up," I said, now aware of the time. Milly was at the studio, but he might be home soon if he didn't call as was his habit. Neither of us had heard the phone ring, but then a bomb could have destroyed the house and we wouldn't have noticed, not over Lilly's enthusiastic cries of ecstasy.

"Yes . . ." she replied, trailing off. I could sense her trouble.

"I'm sorry. This shouldn't have happened."

"Don't be silly. It *had* to happen. You have no idea, my dear sweet Clifton Garrow."

She rolled back to me now, nuzzling into my chest as I stroked her sweet shoulder with light caresses. She kissed my nipple and I caught sight of our reflection in the mirrored wall, liked what I saw. "I'm glad it happened," she whispered. "And I want it to happen again and again and again."

"Right now?"

She laughed. "Of course not. Now we'll both shower and get dressed and see what Blanche has come up with for dinner and then tell wondrous lies to my darling Milly." She kissed me, lingering, then cupped my face. "Thank you," was all she said.

I watched as she got out of bed, her naked figure backlit by the afternoon sunlight filtering through the blinds. She was as gorgeous then as she'd been some ten years earlier in *The Widows Wore Blue and Gray*, but Lillian Sinclair, like most perfect women, never saw herself that way. She was scrutinizing her features in the glass wall as she pulled on a robe.

"How old do I look to you?" she asked with an innocent expression.

"Twenty-four, twenty-three?" I may have been young, but I wasn't stupid.

Lillian laughed. "Someone trained you well."

"Yeah," I said, "the movies."

She stared at herself a moment more, patting the back of her hand under her jaw line as she frowned and fretted, then turned away.

"I hate mirrors," she said, draining a glass of wine on the nightstand before heading for the door. "Now you'd better hurry, or the servants will go mad with gossip," Lillian giggled, then left me. I rubbed my face, remembering her touch, her sounds, her enthusiastic gratitude, then lazed in the tangle of gardenia-scented sheets. It was almost five o'clock and the ritual of cocktail hour loomed. I rolled over to get out of bed, spotted the half-smoked reefer in the ashtray, then bolstered my already monstrous high.

Our journey had begun together on New Year's Day, 1952, with Milly's baffling one-eighty turn, and my staying not only for a traditional Southern dinner, but for the night and into the surreal months that dragged into the two years still ahead. Too drunk to drive, and with no place to go and only eight bucks to my name, I accepted when Lilly insisted they make up the bed in the cabana for me. With the servants having the day off, she changed the sheets herself—with deft precision I might add—as Milly leaned in the open French doors, puffing on a cigarette and chatting away, the chilly night seeping in behind him.

"I don't know about your choice of friends, Lillian," he said, smoke expelling from his nose.

"We can't just toss him out into the streets, Milly."

"I was referring to Tallu. You do realize she wasn't wearing any underpants again, don't you?"

"For Pete's sake, Milly, just say 'panties' like everybody else. And how do you know, anyway?"

Milly grimaced, stubbing out his cigarette in an ashtray. "She made certain I didn't miss her little floor show. She loves to needle me, that one."

As for me, next to Lillian, Tallulah Bankhead was my second-favorite new friend. When she had talked to me, no doubt wondering why I was there in the first place, her interest had seemed genuine. She was further enchanted to learn my father hailed from her home state of Alabama and pronounced us "practically next of kin." Struggling to make conversation, I'd asked her, "So . . . Miss Bankhead . . . what advice would you give to a new actor coming to Hollywood?"

She'd rattled the ice cubes in her nearly empty bourbon glass and raised an eyebrow, saying, "Take Fountain."

Milly and Lilly found this uproarious, but I looked at her, having no clue what she meant. Then, Milly baited her: "Isn't that Bette Davis's line?"

"*Fuck* Bette Davis, not that I'd want to. She's *forever* robbing from *me*, you know. *Little Foxes, Dark Victory,* and don't even get me *started* on *All About Eve*! She stole my entire *persona* lock, stock, and hairdo! Even went so far as to *claim* she had laryngitis as an excuse to mimic my very *voice*!" she roared, then patted my hand by way of explanation. "Fountain's an east-west street, honey child. And if you *ever* call me Miss Bankhead again, I'll make *certain* you're the end of your lineage. Now who cares? My glass is empty."

"So's your bottle," Milly said in an undertone, unfazed by her histrionics.

"There's more in the pantry." Lillian yawned.

"I'll get it," I said, rising, anxious for some air.

"Would you mind grabbing the champagne from the icebox?" Lilly asked.

"And bring more collards, darling! I feel just like I'm down home again!" Tallulah added.

"Happy to," I said, then moved through the butler's pantry and into the kitchen. Even before I was out of the room, I could already hear Tallulah trying to be discreet. But lowering that voice was a near impossibility.

"Who exactly *is* this *divine* creature?" was all I heard before the door swung closed behind me. Puck and Trouble perked up from their cushy little bed in the breakfast nook, and Puck stood, stretched, and shook himself before trotting alongside me as I fetched the champagne and then rummaged in the pantry until I found an unopened bottle of Old

Grand-Dad. I gave the scruffy mutt a scrap of ham from the platter on the counter. He gobbled it up, then just sat there, watching my every move with a dog's vigilant look of adoration tinged with worry.

By the time I returned to the dining room with the improbable combination of champagne, bourbon, and collard greens, there was an explosive sound like an air raid siren after too many Lucky Strikes, and I realized it was Tallulah laughing. The three of them sat up as I entered with the bottles, their brief conspiracy interrupted.

"Please, darling," Tallulah said, lighting yet another cigarette, "I simply *must* have sustenance before I fly back to New York tomorrow."

"So soon?" Lilly asked, genuine disappointment in her voice.

"Oh, you know, it's this *goddamned* trial. I didn't even want to press charges, I mean, *honestly* darling, the publicity is simply *ruinous*," she said between puffs, referring to some legal trouble she was having with a former housekeeper. "And I'm still doing *The Big Show* on Sundays, and then, of course, there's my *goddamned* book. My cup over-*turneth*!"

They spoke now of her impending memoir, which was to become a bestseller later that year. But I only knew Tallulah Bankhead as a comedienne and radio personality, aside from her memorable turn in *Lifeboat*. It wasn't until Lilly explained to me a few days later that I realized just how important a figure Tallulah was in the international theater. Still, it was a little unsettling how this delightful and outrageous woman always seemed to be staring at my crotch.

My hands were once again shaking as I managed to get the foil off the top of the champagne bottle. I had just started on the cork when Milly leapt to his feet. "Good Lord, man, where were you raised?"

I stopped, feeling shamed and embarrassed but trying not to let it show. "We . . . didn't drink a lot of champagne in Tyler."

Milly softened, as if he could tell he'd been too cruel. "I'm sorry. Here. Let me teach you the proper method. It's not supposed to pop, you know, and you never let the cork fly out. Instead . . ." He picked up his crisp dinner napkin and draped it over the bottle, then began to nudge back and forth until there was a faint hiss. His movements had an elegance and precision to them, and my hurt gave way to admiration when he whisked the cloth away with a flourish, revealing the sparkling steam of the now open bubbly. "It's supposed to make the sound of a satisfied woman."

"In which case you obviously haven't a *clue* what you're doing," Tallulah rasped; then she and Lillian giggled.

Milly balanced the bottle with his thumb pinched in its recessed bottom, and reached to refill my glass. "You first, young man," he said, "with apologies for my brusque behavior."

"Hey," I laughed, tossing it off, "at least I learned something."

He nodded as I toasted him, the situation defused. Heck, a Joe could pick up a thing or two from these powerful, sophisticated people.

After a dessert of old-fashioned strawberry shortcake, Tallulah downed the dregs of her bourbon, stubbed out the last cigarette from the pack she had opened when we first sat down for dinner, and announced, "Well, darlings, I *must* be off. Or so my detractors say."

"But it's still early," Lilly protested. "Can't you stay the night?"

"Not this time, darling. There's this *gorgeous* bartender at the Beverly Hills expecting me."

"Picking up another strange man, Tallulah?" Milly asked, always teasing her.

"Who said anything about a *man*?" she growled as she knelt to let the two dogs lick her face, wobbling when she stood up again. She glanced at me, then pulled Lillian into a tight hug. Being as there was no such thing as speaking under her breath for Tallu, I heard her whisper to Lilly, "Take good care of your little pets, darling. All *three* of them."

While we waited for her taxi, Milly went into his study and emerged with an expensive Argus still camera, insisting on pictures to record the occasion. Lilly and Tallu posed together, comfortable and dear old friends; then, at Lilly's insistence, Milly snapped a few of me flanked by those two captivating women. Outside, we watched as her cab pulled away into the night, with Tallulah shouting at the driver, "Good god, I *hate* fucking Los Angeles!"

To which the hack simply shrugged and replied, "Then don't." Tallu roared a braying, guttural laugh as they drove off, and Milly and I joined her. We didn't realize Lillian was already crying. She would miss her dearest friend terribly in the months ahead, unaware of her impending betrayal.

"The good news is, I think I got studio publicity to convince Frank to make the charges go away," Milly said, sipping his second champagne cocktail. The three of us were sitting by the fire in the living room, waiting to be summoned for dinner. Lilly and I were both freshly showered, which she'd insisted on doing together after we'd had sex. I was having trouble looking Milly in the eye, for fear of discovery.

"Milly, that's wonderful!" Lillian said, throwing her arms around him and adding a little kiss.

"It took some doing, seeing as how he isn't even a day player."

"I don't know what to say." My head was cloudy from the dope and the martini Lilly had made for me. Of course, what I really wanted to say, what was really on my mind, was why have you so openly embraced me? Given me a place to stay? Clothes to wear? Idle weeks of getting high and screwing your wife?

"Then say nothing. New Year's Eve was a horrible misunderstanding. What shall we do tonight?"

"Let's go dancing," Lilly said with uncharacteristic enthusiasm.

"Really?" Milly asked, surprised.

"Why not? We'll have dinner here, then head over to the Cocoanut Grove. I think Les is playing tonight."

Milly considered. "All right."

Lilly beamed, gave her husband another kiss, then, as she hurried out of the room, "I have to change."

And just like that, I found myself alone with Milford Langen.

"How is it?" he asked.

"Strong," I replied, referring to my martini.

"I meant things with you and Lillian. You seem to be getting along."

I hesitated, unable to tell if it was an accusation or a blessing. But

Milly seemed so nonchalant about the whole thing, I decided to proceed with caution.

"You've both been more than kind." Even if he suspected the truth, he didn't seem to be bothered by it. Still, the whole situation, being there alone with him in the firelight, his now jade green eyes boring a hole through me, was more than a little awkward.

"Clifford," Milly said, "You know . . ." He trailed off, then seemed to change the subject. "You know, I don't think Clifford suits you."

"It's *Clifton*. And really?" I stammered. "Because if you look at Clark Gable, Cary Grant, and Gary—"

"I know, I know. C's and G's blah blah blah. It's passé. We have to give it some thought."

"We?"

"You want to be an actor, don't you?"

"I want to be a movie star."

Milly seemed pleased by my response. "Good boy. But take it from me, you won't get there with the name *Clifford Garrow* or even *Clifton Garrow*. I'll see what the boys and girls in publicity think. A face like yours needs a *name*. Now excuse me, won't you? I think I'll change, too."

And he was gone.

I was spinning, or the room was reeling, or maybe Lilly mixed especially potent martinis, but whatever the reason, I had to sit down. The situation had started as a lark, but now Milford Langen was talking about helping me break into the picture business, seemingly unfazed by whatever might be going on between his wife and me. They had taken me in, and I couldn't help wondering if this was the normal way of things in Hollywood. Hell, I was just a hick kid from Texas—nowhere near as worldly as these rarefied people—and even though I liked them both, the whole thing was unsettling.

As I drained the last of my martini, Puck tried to leap into my lap, but fell short. I scooped him up, hugging him, and scratched the belly of the only new friend I completely trusted.

EIGHT

We had christened the pool and cabana at Milly and Lilly's house the "Urban Idyll" late one night in the spring of 1952 when the three of us were stoned and soaking our feet in the warm water. Earlier, we had listened to Tallulah's radio program, *The Big Show*, laughing at her quips and routines, and now Milly's hi-fi was playing Chet Baker through the concealed outdoor speakers. The air tickled with a whiff of orange blossom as Lillian demonstrated the proper way to suck the nectar out of a honeysuckle flower. The sheer sensuousness was unnerving, but Milly seemed amused as he imitated his wife's every succulent move. "First, you pinch off the little button, then carefully pull the stamen through the flower to coat it in nectar, then *voila*, put it on your tongue."

Milly chuckled. "Yum," he said, "you're very clever, my darling Southern belle. Clifford-ton? Wanna try?" he asked, taking a not-so-subtle dig at my chosen stage name as he held out a handful of freshly plucked flowers.

"I'm going for a swim," I said, and slid into the pool in hopes of hiding my uninvited erection. Earlier, Lillian had had those same red lips wrapped around something else entirely just before Milford came home from the studio, and her latest display was yet another of her dangerous games to toy with her husband. It had been four months since I'd first moved in, and the three of us had become a kind of ersatz family. Embracing the spirit of "if you can't beat 'em," Milly had even taken to smoking dope with us in the evenings, sometimes forgoing his usual three or four cocktails and heading straight for the rolling papers. Personally, I was relieved, because Milford Langen on pot was a sweet, congenial man who could be gregarious and generous with his wife and her lover. Restaurants, premieres, nightclubs . . . you name it.

He was also under the common delusion that the dope was making his work with the writers on *The Trojan War* all the more brilliant even while Zanuck continued to resist the project. Still, Milly never lost faith in his sprawling epic, battling Darryl and his sycophants who were dead set against Lillian playing Helen of Troy. None of this dissuaded Milly, and he vowed the film would be made even if he had to bankroll it himself.

"Darryl's not the only one who knows how to produce a picture, you know. I'm having two budgets worked up. One for shooting on the lot, and another for location," Milly said, dipping his toes in the pool.

Lillian perked up. "You mean in Greece?"

"Of course. *And* I'm thinking we could go over this summer, scout the locations, and make it a holiday. Our anniversary's coming up, and I see no reason we can't combine business and pleasure. Would you like that, darling?"

"Oh, Puppy. Can we go back to Venice?" Lillian asked, growing excited.

"And Paris and Barcelona and Rome. We could easily stay for six weeks . . ."

Lilly threw her arms around her husband. "When do we leave?"

"How does June or July sound? Right after you wrap *They Came to Die*?"

"Perfect!" She kissed his cheek, then turned to me as I stood waist-deep in the water, running my fingers through my wet hair. "Cliff? Have you ever been to Europe?"

I almost laughed at the absurdity of the question. "Unless that's the name of a blink-and-you-miss-it town between here and Tyler, can't say as I have."

"Then you simply *must* come with—"

"Lillian," Milly said, cutting her off with a disapproving chuckle in his voice.

65

"But wouldn't it be—"

"That's very kind of you, Lilly," I said, meeting Milly's eye. "But I can't take off for six weeks. Not when I just got here."

Milly smiled and nodded. "He's right, of course."

"Of course," Lilly said, but I could tell she was disappointed.

The truth is, so was I. But I was still hungry to break into the film business, which meant I needed to stay in town. When the day came for me to see the world, I was going to do it as a movie star.

At Milly's insistence (and on his dime), I was taking acting classes with a handful of other students at a small studio in West Hollywood. Our teacher was a New York snob who called himself only "Dante" and let you know he was a protégé of Lee Strasberg every time he opened his mouth. Personally, I thought the so-called Method was kind of silly. Just pretending to be your character was a whole lot easier. Especially for a guy like me who'd rather forget his past than wallow in it. Still, it was a pretty good place to meet people, so I sucked it up and did my scene work. I later learned Milly called Dante the morning after every class to discuss my progress, and I was thrilled he took such lively interest in my career. At Lillian's urging, he was committed to helping me break in. But despite our constant badgering to get me a screen test, Milly held firm: "Not until I say he's ready."

As part of his mentoring, he shared his physical fitness trainer with me, insisting I be in the best shape to maximize my sex appeal at the box office. One day, he joined me for a workout at the Easton gym on Beverly Boulevard, and as his trainer put us through the paces in front of the floor-to-ceiling mirrors, both of us sweating as we flexed, I was struck again by his matinee idol looks and swashbuckling torso.

"You ever think about acting?" I asked just to make conversation as I huffed through a set of bicep curls.

Milly laughed. "You have no idea how many times I've been asked that question."

"Well, have you?"

"Honestly? Yes. When I first came to Hollywood. Though I quickly learned it wasn't for me."

"Why?"

"Simple, kiddo. Because I'm lousy at it. Godawful, really. And besides, I do my best acting *behind* the cameras."

As it turns out, that may have been one of the most honest things he ever said to me.

I don't know how to explain the dynamic of our treacherous trio. It was a situation that had seduced all of us into an off-kilter everyday life. Evenings were spent smoking dope and drinking by the pool, our heads dancing to whatever new jazz records Milly had discovered. Deming had the thankless task of sitting in the study, waiting for the music to end before flipping the stack on the changer for us. Our needs attended to, we chatted at length about the latest scandals in town and the weekend's box office grosses. Though Lillian was bored by the topic, Milly and I discussed the movies enthusiastically.

I had explained to him how my alcoholic mother would give me two bits and send me off to the Arcadia so she could drink in peace. As a result, I spent most of my childhood afternoons staring in speechless wonder at whatever new fantasy was unspooling on the screen while dear old Mom got so loaded she'd be passed out by the time I came home. Sometimes, my grandmother Mawmaw would go with me, and the two of us would often be shushed by the other theater patrons. I was so enamored of the movies I got a job ushering at the Arcadia in high school, watching the latest Hollywood offerings over and over, sometimes until I could play all the parts along with the film.

Milly seemed impressed by my encyclopedic knowledge of his and Lillian's careers—from his beginnings as a wunderkind producer in his early twenties, his discovery of the now world-renowned Lillian Sinclair, and their catalog of successes since then. He was curious to know what I'd thought of his latest masterpiece, *Too Many Dreams*, which had just opened to lackluster reviews but colossal grosses. I replied there's a reason the picture was a hit: Milford had a touch unlike any other producer in Hollywood. This seemed to make him happy, and I smiled at having pleased him.

As for my presence in their lives, if anyone bothered to ask, Milly and Lilly would explain they were renting me the cabana, and they both believed I was destined for stardom. While Milly was at the studio, Lillian and I were left to our own devices which usually meant more weed, the occasional shopping spree, several unsuccessful attempts to teach her how to drive, destroying the kitchen in our quest for the perfect brownie, and an overdose of sex the likes of which I won't describe here. She was a voracious and eager lover who seemed to find me irresistible. I went along with it all. We read every script she was offered during that period, and despite my urging her to take the part, she turned down the starring role in *All My Yesterdays* because the character was required to age forty years over the course of two hours. "I can't face myself in age makeup," she'd insisted. "Nor I'll warrant could my fans."

"Hey," I'd said, "when's your birthday?"

Lillian had bristled at the question, replying in a way to end the conversation: "I don't have one."

Although she wouldn't admit it outright, Lillian had been vexed the night she and Milly had come home from the recent Academy Awards ceremony. Her rival Vivien Leigh had won her second Oscar for playing another Southerner, this time in *A Streetcar Named Desire*. I'd tried to console her by pointing out she was a good ten or fifteen years too *young* to play the deranged Blanche DuBois, but Lillian shot back, "She isn't even Southern. And her accent is laughable." I'd been mesmerized by the film, but bit my tongue and agreed.

I emerged from an underwater lap to the surprising sound of Milford and Lillian laughing. It was almost conspiratorial, confirmed when they fell silent upon realizing I was within earshot.

"What's so funny?" I asked, trying to disarm them both with a smile. In answer, the pop of a flashbulb blinded me. It was Milly snapping a shot as I rose out of the water. He then picked up his 16mm Bell & Howell movie camera and started to wind it.

"Oh, dear boy," Milly said, "I think I've finally convinced my wife you'll never be a star."

I was stunned by the abrupt cruelty until Lilly chimed in. "Stop it, Puppy," she said, swatting her husband before turning to me. "He means as long as you insist upon going by Clifton Garrow."

"I'm leaning toward just Cliff," I said in my own defense.

"Cliff, Clifford, Clifton. It's a bad name. Monty Clift already owns any version of it. And as for Clifton, well, there's Clifton Webb. You don't want to be thought of as an erudite mamma's boy, do you? Publicity did some research for me and I think they've hit it."

I took the bait. "What is it?" I asked, planning to look up *erudite* later.

Milly took a long drag on his cigarette and made us wait while he extinguished it in the pool and then flicked it into the shrubs.

"Dexter Gaines," he announced with emphasis amid a plume of exhaled smoke, like some fire-breathing dragon.

Both Lilly and I were silent for a moment.

"Dexter? You're joking, right?" I said, sloshing up the steps. My calf brushed Milly's bare thigh as I got out of the pool and grabbed a towel. "Sorry."

"I'm dead serious. It's good."

For the record, I despised the name from the instant it came out of Milly's mouth. Unfortunately, I was in the minority.

"Dexter Gaines . . ." Lillian tried it out. "I rather like it."

"Maybe because you're toasted."

"No, it's good. Dex has the x, rhymes with sex. And Gaines gives you the 'G' you wanted . . ."

"I hate it," I said, toweling off, my trunks clinging to my loins as I grabbed one of the many terry cloth robes and covered myself. I sat down at the little patio table and, spotting Milly's slim gold cigarette case, popped it open and lit one.

"Since when did you take up smoking?"

"It's hard to be around you two and not pick up a few bad habits," was my reply. "Come on, we have to do better than Dexter Gaines."

Lillian dabbled her toes in the water. "You should listen to Milly when it comes to names. You won't believe who I was when I arrived in town."

"A hairdresser, I know," I said.

"A hairdresser named Edna Mae Loudermilk."

Milly rose from the flagstone coping around the edge of the pool and joined me at the table, not bothering to put on a robe. The US Navy dog tags that he still wore on a chain around his neck glistened in the moonlight, clinging to his wet skin. "She's right, you know." He lit a cigarette, tipping the last of the scotch into his glass, then sipped, eyeing me over the rim as he swirled the ice cubes.

"And at any rate, it's too late to change it."

"Too late? It's not like it's already on the marquee," I protested.

Now Lilly joined us at the table after snuggling into a robe. She pulled her wet feet up in the chair, and she, too, lit a cigarette. The three of us sat there in all of our collective ridiculousness, until Lilly finally broke the silence, shaking her husband's arm playfully.

"Puppy, tell him. This is agony."

Milly looked at me and flashed his most devilish grin, exhaling jets of smoke from his nostrils as he lifted his movie camera and snapped on the blinding spotlight attached to it. I squinted and shielded my eyes as he started the camera rolling to film my reaction. After a pause, he announced, "You're testing for the role of Gifford."

I blinked. Had I heard him right?

"A screen test?"

"You two have been nagging me nonstop about how you're ready, and Dante says you're showing some promise in your classes. Besides, the role is tailor-made for you—good-intentioned, a bit rough around the edges, often maddeningly naïve. And you *are* the perfect age to play Gifford, so . . ."

"Who's Gifford?" Now I was excited, having forgotten all about Dexter Gaines as I ignored Milly's playful jibes.

"He's the young love interest in *Nearer My God to Thee*—dreadful title, sounds like a sand and sandals thing—anyway, I have the script in my study. You should read it. It doesn't shoot until late October, so there's plenty of time to get you ready. Oh, and I didn't even tell Lillian this last bit . . ." He poised his 16mm again.

"What? *What?*" I asked, unable to contain my enthusiasm.

"If you do well, there might be a studio contract in it for you."

I was speechless. Milly's camera hummed, capturing my open-mouthed expression.

"Milly, that's wonderful!" Lillian said, throwing her arms around her husband and kissing his ear. His camera whirred the whole time, glued to his eye, even as his wife nestled into his neck.

"Trouble is, they're expecting Dexter Gaines. I've been campaigning for you, you know. Telling a few select people I've discovered the next Bob Wagner."

"Dexter Gaines," I said again, mulling it over and trying not to hate it. "Dexter. Dex."

"Rhymes with sex," Lilly reminded.

"All right, then," I said, putting out the cigarette. "Dexter Gaines it is. Can I read the script?"

"Right now?"

"Hell, yes," I said, grinning.

Milly seemed charmed. "On my desk in the study."

As I trotted across the cool grass toward the house, I heard a very stoned Lillian say, out of the clear blue, "Puppy? You know what would be perfect back here?"

"What's that, my love?"

"A swing."

NINE

"But I thought *you* went to Europe with my father in '52," Tally said as she lifted the bun off of her turkey burger and coated it in mustard before piling on the extra pickles she'd ordered on the side, along with a mountain of French fries. The funeral over, she had insisted we grab something to eat at the Denny's in Gower Gulch. I found her likeable if neurotic and largely withholding about herself. Resourceful, too. She'd managed to sweet-talk the funeral home chauffeur into waiting for us outside.

"I did," I said, signaling the waitress for more coffee. "Two weeks before their trip, your mom was loaned to Warner Brothers for *Bring Them Back*."

She squeezed the last of the ketchup out of the plastic bottle with a loud splat. "And we both know how well that turned out."

In fact, it hadn't. Although she'd been set to costar with Joan Crawford, in the third week of shooting Lillian had "blown her top" at director Mervyn LeRoy before locking herself in her dressing room. Jack Warner canned her and recast the role with Gloria Grahame who ended up with a nod for a Golden Globe. Joan and Gloria had already worked together in *Sudden Fear*, which was to open later that long ago summer, and while their real-life lack of chemistry had been infamous among the town gossips, they nevertheless clicked on screen. It was to prove one of many setbacks from which Lillian never recovered. And I was probably the only person still alive who knew her notorious breakdown had been triggered by a disturbing transatlantic call from Paris.

"So what about you?" I asked, trying to nudge the conversation away from the whitewashed tales of my failed career. Of course, I'd been careful to omit any hint of sexual indiscretion.

"What about me?" she replied with indifference, then bit into her burger and wiped mustard from her lip.

"What part of town do you live in?" I asked, making strained small talk.

"I don't," she said, swallowing. "I flew in from San Francisco. For the funeral. I was the only contact listed for my father. Sorry for talking with my mouth full."

"That's . . . sad."

"Are you surprised?" she asked, snatching another bite. "You knew my dad."

"Only for a couple of years."

"People don't change," she said. And I could tell she was politely trying to mask her anger.

"Some do," I said, knowing it to be true. "You can be honest with me, Tally. I promise. What was your gripe with your dad?"

She dabbed the corners of her lips before turning into another person. "My father—dear old Daddy—was a sonofabitch. No, wait, that's an insult to Grandma. He was a bastard. No, that's disrespecting Grandma again." She threw her burger down onto her plate and shoved it away. I won't say I didn't recognize her barely contained fury. "Asshole? That's pretty safe. Sometimes he could be the most wonderful, magical man in the world—calling me 'Daddy's little gift' and showering me with affection. And then, without warning, he'd get in one of his moods, and be so . . . *cruel*. I never could figure out what was wrong with him. So I went into therapy and gave up trying."

I put my coffee cup down now, feeling a connection with this damaged young woman as I stared into the brown liquid, watching the tiniest pieces of curdled Half and Half swim around as if alive. "He was a very tormented man," was all I said.

"But *why*?" she nearly shrieked in frustration. I didn't answer, so she

73

went on as I shrugged. "He was trying the past few years. But I didn't want to let him in."

I shifted in my seat. "You want some dessert?" I asked, seeing she was now gulping down the pile of French fries.

"No. I'll probably just throw this all up later, anyway. You must think I'm nuts."

"Not at all," I said, then managed to catch the eye of our server and pantomimed the universal gesture to ask for our check.

"So . . . your dad had a heart attack?"

"Yeah, guess he overexerted himself carrying all that liquor."

"Milly always did like his booze."

"Yup, and it finally killed him, though maybe not in the way you'd think."

She took a deep breath. I swirled my coffee some more. Something seemed to be bothering Tally as she asked, "So when was the last time you saw him? My dad, I mean."

"That's easy. It was my birthday back in November of 1953. Not a great day."

"Scorpio or Sagittarius?" she asked, changing trains, now holding her hand over her mouth to hide her chewing.

"Scorpio, why?"

"A survivor who wants to triumph."

"I don't put much faith in the stars."

"Me, neither. But it doesn't stop me from reading my horoscope every day hoping, just once, it might be useful. I'm Aquarius for what it's worth. And I'm prone to chatter, in case you hadn't noticed."

She went back to her unfinished burger, and I began to sense she was avoiding some bigger, unknown conversation. I tried to steer us back on course.

"What about you? When's the last time you saw him?"

"When he came up for Christmas two years ago. But we talked on the phone, maybe once or so every, I don't know, six months. And we'd talk about the weather, and my store—I'm a vintage clothing dealer— and he'd go on and on about his AA meetings and working the twelve steps and, this will blow your mind, he said he'd taken up gardening."

"Milly?"

"I know, right? Said he was taking care of the yard, and planting, and I was like—who the hell am I talking to? Where's my dad? But we never talked about anything real. Or that actually mattered. And all of it smothered in distrust."

"I had a few of those conversations with him, myself."

"Then you get it. And, of course, the whole time he was lying to me. About getting sober, I mean."

I nodded and sipped my now cold coffee, the server nowhere in sight with our check. I started to get up. "I'm gonna go find our waitress."

But Tally stopped me, her guard down, now a raw and vulnerable person grabbing my arm. "Why'd he do it?"

"Do what?"

She clutched at me. "Why'd he leave you everything?"

"I honestly don't—*what?*"

There was no way I had heard her correctly.

"When he changed his will just after Mother's suicide. You're the *only* beneficiary."

The desperation in her voice made it clear she was serious, and I now understood why she'd asked if the lawyers had called to tell me of Milly's passing. I just stared at her stupidly, managing only a feeble: "I had . . . I didn't know."

"And I believe you. I can actually tell. You're a sweet guy, so god only knows what my dad did to you to make you hate him so much that the only way he could make it up to you is . . . he cut me out of everything. And you . . . you haven't seen or spoken to him in, what, forty years?"

I sat back, stunned. "Forty-one."

"He left everything to you. Five and a half million dollars."

In response, I broke wind, having lost control of every muscle in my body. Tally pretended she didn't notice.

"Five and a half . . . million?" Then, because my brain had clouded over, "Dollars?"

"*And* the house in Hancock Park."

The waitress waddled over and plunked our check down on the table. Tally looked at it, then at me.

"You mind gettin' that?"

TEN

No matter how many times I turned the little convertible down Windsor, I never tired of delighting in the symmetrical rows of giant palm trees gliding past overhead on either side of the street. I preferred to drive North from Wilshire so I could take in their lofty magnificence, aligned so as to form a towering corridor that converged into a perfect frame for the recently refurbished sign on the distant ridge: HOLLYWOOD. The sight served as a mental pinch for myself, telling me I really was living this surprising life—especially with the radio blasting the latest Dean Martin and the sun tanning my bare torso. It was kind of titillating, the looks I'd get from people at the streetcar stops when I'd slow to turn and they realized wide-eyed that I was tootling around town shirtless in a $4,000 sports car. Milly had long ago insisted I sell The Buck and drive the "champagne ivory" '51 Nash-Healey two-seater that mostly sat unused in the garage. I got thirty-five bucks for the old Buick from a junkyard, which I'd blown through by taking Milly and Lilly to dinner at Musso and Frank's. The Nash was a head-turner wherever I went and gave me a confidence I wasn't really entitled to. Sure, I missed The Buck and all he had come to represent to me, but this was Fat City! The new wheels were like a ton-and-a-half mask of steel to hide my insecurities. Driving around Hollywood half naked was changing that; it was easy to justify my outrageous behavior by saying I didn't want to get a farmer's tan from riding with the top down.

It had been a good day in early June of '52. I'd been to lift weights with Milly's fitness trainer, both of us pleased to see how my physique was shaping up, followed by acting class with Dante, then drinks at the Cock 'n Bull on Sunset with some of my fellow thespians. Afterward, I hit the men's stores along Miracle Mile, inspired by a chance meeting at the bar and now determined to get some nice threads of my own. No more of Milly's hand-me-downs—never mind he was paying for it all. I was driving up Wilshire, knowing Lillian would be waiting for me, and most likely she'd want to fool around before Milly got home. I knew she sometimes spied on me from the upper guest room window when I'd pull into the driveway, hoping to watch me get out of the car and then put my shirt on, taking my sweet time to button it, feeling her hidden eyes licking me. Once I even caught sight of the curtain snapping shut. Right now, I was feeling swell, coming home with some news of my own to be celebrated in bed with one of the most beautiful women in the world.

Only as I cruised up South Windsor, I saw Milly's car already parked in the circular drive in front of the house below the curved glass brick wall. I glanced at the gold Bulova wristwatch Lilly had given me. It was only three-thirty, so something must be going on. I drove around the corner to the garage entrance, hopped out with the engine still purring, and raised the door. After I'd put the Nash away, I exited through the back while wiggling into my shirt and headed past the cabana and straight for the huge open French doors on the verandah. Puck came jingling toward me, having been awakened from his pool-side nap by the sound of the car. The poor dog was slowly losing his eyesight and his hearing, but he never failed to recognize my scent and welcome me with all the enthusiasm he could muster. I bundled him up in my arms, not even minding the stench of his breath while he kissed my face hello.

As I neared the house, I saw Deming leaning against the side wall, stealing a smoke. He gave me a warning look that I ignored, just then hearing the sounds of a ferocious argument going on in Milly's study.

"It wasn't my decision!" Milly was shouting.

"Then make it your decision. Tell Darryl I won't do it."

"At least read the script."

"I don't give a good god damn about the script. I want to go to Europe."

Perfect. For once, I had some good news to share, but as usual, it would have to take a back seat to the latest Douglas Sirk playing out in the house. "C'mon, Puck," I said, turning around, resigned, "let's go for a float."

Fifteen minutes later I was getting the last of the afternoon's direct sunlight on an inflatable raft in the pool, letting Puck guzzle the final drops of a cold beer, when Lillian came striding across the lawn, wearing a summer frock and obviously upset, her devoted Trouble trotting at her heels, panting.

"What's going on?" I asked.

"Darryl Zanuck's driving me mad, that's what. He's loaned me to Warners for some movie with that hussy Joan Crawford. It shoots in July in the Mojave Desert."

"But what about your trip?" I feigned innocence.

"Milly says I can't go. He claims he nearly lost his job when he stood up to Darryl. God. Where's the Mary Jane?"

"Where it always is," I answered, not bothering to move. "I'm sorry, Lil."

"Yeah, well . . ." was all she said as she went into the open cabana and retrieved the little tin, angrily prying it open to get at the reefer inside. She was well into her second toke when Milly came out of the house, a glass of scotch in one hand and a screenplay in the other.

"Lillian, can we please talk about this?"

"What's left to say?" She put out the joint and dove into the pool, fully clothed. Without hesitation, Trouble leapt in next to her. Once in the water, she tore the dress off over her head, threw it at Milly, and started swimming back and forth in her bra and panties, causing the pool to surge and ripple, Trouble paddling along behind. Puck was clinging to me for dear life on the bobbing raft as they passed us, splashing.

"Oh for god's sake," Milly shouted, tracking alongside her on the patio. "I have an idea. Let's have dinner out here, get loaded, and have our own read-through of the script. Then you'll see—" He stopped, noticing me in nothing but my trunks, sunglasses, and tan, the drenched little dog shivering next to me. "Hello, Dex."

"Milly." I nodded in return, feeling as naked and awkward as the situation. I carefully put Puck on dry land where he shook himself, splattering me as I got out of the pool and wrapped a towel around my waist. That's when we both noticed Lillian had been underwater a few seconds too long, Trouble anxious and circling above. I started to dive in, but Milly waved me back with his scotch and shook his head. We waited for what felt like an eternity until Lillian at last spluttered to the surface, gasping for air as the relieved Trouble licked her face. She took him into her arms and sloshed toward the stairs.

"Tell Darryl I quit."

"He'll sue you," Milly said, again walking alongside her on the patio. "There's good news, too, Lil. Darryl said if you do this picture for Warners, he'll green-light *Trojan War*."

Lilly stopped, waist-deep in the pool. "Fuck *Trojan War!*"

As soon as the words were out, Lillian realized she'd gone too far.

"I didn't mean that, Puppy."

"I know," he said with a sigh.

Lilly considered. "With me as Helen of Troy?"

"*The most beautiful woman in the history of the world.* That's the deal. I told him I want it in writing, so he's having the lawyers draft it up."

Lillian chewed on her lower lip, a habit she had whenever she was vexed. It's a wonder she wasn't bleeding all the time. "What's it called?"

"*Bring Them Back*," Milly answered. "Mervyn LeRoy's set to direct, and the schmuck who wrote it has two Oscars." He peeled open the script to show her the title page. "They want you for the role of Nora."

"And Joan gets the better part, I'm sure."

"Actually, she plays your sister. Your much *older* sister. C'mon, let's read it together. It'll be fun."

"Fine," she said, surrendering as she came up the pool stairs, looking gorgeous in her wet bra and panties. Trouble shook himself as Milly helped his wife into a robe. I thought about death to kill the tingling nerves in my groin, watching these two stunning people as Lilly absently reached into her husband's jacket for his cigarette case, tamped a Chesterfield on its gold surface, and waited while he lit it for her. Regardless of what was really going on, their casual interaction suggested a couple who had grown comfortable with one another. I looked away, forcing down the rising voices in my head that kept telling me I had no right to be there.

"I'm just . . . disappointed. About the trip. Can't you reschedule?"

"I'm afraid not. Darryl said we can start production as early as the fall, which means we have to lock up the locations before August." Milly went into the cabana. I didn't know until sometime later that he was leaving out one important fact: Milford Langen had agreed to finance half of *Trojan War* out of his own pocket. It was the only way he could get Zanuck to bite and have Lillian Sinclair as the star.

Milly brought the phone out, snaking the long cord around the patio furniture and over to the table where we spent so much of our time. Dialing a single number, he waited, then, "Blanche. If anyone other than Darryl or Jack calls, we're not to be disturbed, understood?" He hung up, tossed the screenplay onto the table, and plopped down, exhausted.

A few minutes later I was dressed and seated with him. Lillian had gone inside to shower off and change.

"What are you smiling about?" Milly asked.

"Nothing," I replied. "I just had some good news to share with you two. But I guess it's not the best time."

"Oh please. What is it? Some breakthrough in your class?"

"Nope," I said, feeling smug, then fished into my shirt pocket and produced the business card I'd been given earlier that afternoon. I waved it, grinning. "I got an agent."

"You . . . what?" Milly asked, his eyebrows arching upward.

"I went out for drinks with some of the class and this guy's staring at me, right? Then he comes over and introduces himself, hands me his card, and tells me to call him. You'll never guess what his card says."

I knew I was being goofy, but for the first time since I'd known him, I wasn't scared of Milly. It felt good to be toying with *him* for a change.

Milly looked at me, and after an eternity he laughed. "Where'd you say you had a drink?" he asked, surprising me.

"The Cock 'n Bull, why?"

"In which case I can tell you what the card says: 'If you're interested in getting into the movies, I can help you.'"

Sure, it pissed me off, still: "How'd you know that?"

He snatched the card from me, stared at it with a cigarette burning between his fingers. "Henry Willson. Jesus. Absolutely not, Dex." Then he looked me in the eye as he tore the business card to shreds.

"What are you doing? You have no right to—"

"Do you have any idea who Henry Willson is? Or more importantly *what* he is? Besides being a goddamned parasite like every other agent in town?"

"I know he represents Bob Wagner and Natalie Wood and Rock Hudson and he did okay by Lana Turner and Joan Fontaine. He invited me to a barbeque at his house on Saturday—"

"He's a *homosexual*," Milly snapped, cutting me off with a whispered hiss of disgust. "As are more than a few of his clients. Notoriously so, I might add."

He brushed the last of the card from his palm and sat back, agitated as he lit a cigarette. I didn't bother to point out he already had one going in the ashtray. I was angry and confused.

"So what?"

"I'm protecting you, Dex. If you throw in with his lot, you'll be guilty by association. There are so-called reporters for *Hollywood Confidential* who loiter around his neighborhood, waiting to bust one of his 'barbeques.' And if Joe McCarthy gets so much as a whiff of it, your career will be over before it even starts."

"Rock Hudson's a queer?" I asked, surprised.

Milly paused before he answered carefully, "There are rumors. Persistent ones. You don't want to know the stories I've heard about the things Willson does with some of his clients."

"Wow," was all I could say. I picked up Milly's other burning cigarette and finished it off. This was a subject no one had ever discussed openly with me before. In fact, I'm pretty sure it was the first time in my life I'd ever heard anyone say the word "homosexual" out loud.

"You're anxious, Dex, understandably. But you have to trust me. I know what I'm doing."

"I got this on my own, Milly. The one thing that hasn't just been handed to me since I came to this crazy town. And he *is* legit, with some real stars as clients to prove it. Besides, in case you hadn't noticed, I've got taking care of Number One down pat."

"Fine." Milly put his hands up and shrugged. "Don't say you weren't warned. Where's the scotch?"

We were interrupted by the return of Lillian and her ubiquitous Trouble. She'd thrown on a pair of oversized linen pants and a crisp white shirt with upturned collar and was headed toward us, barefoot, in a headscarf. She was carrying a large platter of her favorite summer delicacy, crisp rind-less triangles of ice-cold watermelon. The sun was dipping below the trees now, so I took off my dark glasses. Milly was pouring himself a drink from the circular bar cart.

"All right," Lilly said, "let's read the goddamned script."

The new wooden swing screeched as she plopped down and devoured a slice of melon. Milly had resisted its installation, but Lillian said it reminded her of her nana's house on Saint Simon's Island. How was Milly supposed to argue with that?

"Great." Milly seemed relieved, moving over to sit next to her and motioning for me to join him on his other side. I squeezed onto the swing as Lillian offered us the melon, then laughed and challenged me to a seed-spitting contest. Milly soon grew impatient with our antics. "The script," he reminded us, then opened the screenplay and folded back the first page. "Okay, let's see. You're Nora. Dex, you read all the other characters except for Irene. That's the Joan Crawford part."

"*You're* gonna be Joan Crawford?" I asked, amused.

"Trust me," Milly said, downing his scotch. "Even I'm a better actor than *he* is."

Lillian patted her husband's arm. "Oh, Puppy, just read the lines in a monotone, no inflection, and you'll sound just like her." Milly laughed and slipped on his reading glasses.

"I want some more pot before we start," Lillian said, reaching for the little tin with the Scottie dogs on it.

"Me, too," Milly sighed.

"I'm in."

Within minutes, we were once again soaring, and I checked my watch. It was just now cocktail hour. In truth, we seemed to be smoking a lot of Mary Jane earlier and earlier with each passing day, long before the sun dipped below the row of pine trees like it was doing now, throwing us into mottled shadows. Milly used his Zippo to light a couple of candles on the arms of the creaking swing, and I was pretty sure I caught a glimpse of Deming watching from the open French doors, wearing his usual mask of disapproval.

"*Bring Them Back*," Lillian mused. "Bring who back?"

"Your husbands in the picture. They've gone off to the Spanish-American War," Milly said as he polished his tortoiseshell reading glasses with his handkerchief before slipping them on.

"Another costume piece?"

"A good one. You'll see."

Lillian scanned the first page of the script, and Milly began.

"Fade in. Exterior, the desert. Angle on Nora Dawson as she walks through the rippling heat towards camera. She's gorgeous." Here he paused to give a good-natured poke to his still pouting wife. "That's you."

"'I guess we'll never know,'" Lillian read the last line of the script, and I could have sworn I saw a tear glistening in the candlelight. Puck shifted in his sleep in my lap, as if dreaming of chasing squirrels. A lazy fly buzzed in the watermelon juice. Milly waited in silence, filling the time by folding his spectacles, slipping them into his pocket and lighting another Chesterfield. One thing was for certain: we all knew the script was pretty damn good.

Lillian sat there, immobile, just staring at the last line of dialogue typed simply on the page. Then, without taking her eyes from it, "Well, as long as I have to be in the Mojave Desert for six weeks, you might as well take Dex with you to Europe."

I was as surprised as Milly seemed to be. Obviously, she wanted the part, but this was something else. The only traveling I'd ever done was driving from Tyler to Hollywood.

"I'd feel better knowing you had someone with you."

To keep an eye on him, more likely. I wasn't keen on the idea of being Milly's chaperone, but as Lillian explained to me later after Milly had gone to bed and we'd fooled around in the pool, she knew her husband strayed sometimes.

"Kinda ironic to say that considering the circumstances," I said, holding her naked body close to me in the warm, dark water.

"He doesn't do well when he's alone," she said with genuine concern. "Promise me you'll go with him."

"All right," I said, unaware I was choosing a fork in the road that would change my life forever.

The next Saturday, I got out of bed in time for lunch in the kitchen. Milly had gone riding as usual, and Lillian was nowhere to be seen. Most likely she'd be upstairs in her bedroom, the thick drapes closed, an eye mask further blocking the light, sleeping off her latest champagne and marijuana hangover, or perhaps fighting another of her migraines. Blanche had made sandwiches, which she'd wrapped in waxed paper and put in the Frigidaire on the off chance anyone actually got out of bed and wanted something to eat. She'd left a note on the counter, in her immaculate penmanship with its implied priggish disapproval: "Gone to market. Back by 3." I glanced at the clock over the sink. It was twelve forty-five. I had heard Deming out washing the cars in the side driveway as I'd left the cabana with Puck stumbling alongside me. He was all too eager to finish the last of my second ham on rye and the only sound in the massive house was the voracious little mutt licking his lips after gobbling it down.

I got up from the table and looked around. The place was, as always, in perfect order. I made my way through the hallway toward the vast two-story entry foyer, noting the mail hadn't yet arrived. It had been a month since I'd sent my parents a postcard with Lilly and Milly's address, just in case either of them wanted to drop me a line with the good news the other had died. I glanced up the staircase with its polished nickel railing, then moved toward the hallway that led to Milford Langen's study. "You stand guard," I whispered to Puck as he curled up in the open doorway and promptly went to sleep. "Good dog."

Milly's inner sanctum was, to me, the most pleasing room in the house with its maple paneling and cabinetry, and the exquisite artworks mixed with various framed photographs of Milly, Lilly, and their circle of famous friends. Some of the pictures were signed, hanging near the numerous awards and citations Milly had accumulated over the years. The desktop extended on both sides, looking like the wings of a small aeroplane, and its surface was neatly stacked with scripts, clippings from *Daily Variety*, and various ideas for movies jotted down on monogrammed notepaper. The pool table was covered, and I noted a few headshots of actors under contract to the studio laid out in precise columns, as if Milly were casting his next picture. I walked over and sat down in his leather desk chair, sensing the pure power all around me, then paused to listen for sounds other than Puck's snoring before carefully pulling open the top drawer. It was filled with pens and pencils, postage stamps, a bottle of paste, and a few stray paper clips. The next drawer revealed a .22 snub-nosed revolver and a box of bullets. The larger drawer beneath wouldn't open, and I realized it was locked. Intrigued, I slid the drawer above it all the way out to see if it would provide an opening to the one below, but soon discovered the whole desk was partitioned with wood. I'd have to remember to find Milly's keys when he wasn't around.

Next to the metal lamp was a cigarette box engraved MBL. I wondered what the "B" stood for as I helped myself to one of Milly's Chesterfields and lit it with a chrome lighter also shaped like a plane. I turned to the drawers on the other side of the kneehole. Nothing but a few household bills and three check ledgers among other odds and ends. Squinting from the smoke clamped in my mouth, I opened the first ledger and flipped through the check stubs. I wasn't looking for anything in particular, but this had become my secret whenever I had a few moments alone in the house on Windsor: going through Milly and Lilly's things, trying to figure out as much about them as I could. I knew it was wrong, but my curiosity always got the best of me. I'm sure had Blanche or Deming or even Lillian walked in, they'd have thought me a thief. But I never stole anything from Milly and Lilly. Nothing tangible, anyway.

The checks chronicled an innocuous history of mundane transactions, and it wasn't until I got to the second book, whose records dated from about a year ago, that I saw several made out to someone named Michael Spencer. Fifty dollars once a week, then a hundred, and the last one for a whopping twenty-five C notes. It had been written on June 16, 1951, and the notation read "good riddance" in Milly's elegant, masculine handwriting. I put out my cigarette and flipped back through them. Fifty dollars a week. Exactly the same amount he'd been giving me as a "loan against impending stardom." The deal was I'd pay it all back. But *twenty-five hundred*? And *good riddance*?

After carefully replacing everything, I looked around the room, gingerly fingering through a new stack of long-play records Milly had purchased earlier that week. Thelonius Monk, Dave Brubeck, Billie Holiday, June Christy, Miles Davis, Jeri Southern, Charlie Parker and some others I'd never heard of. All smoky and moody artists whose music set the tone each night in the Urban Idyll. Finally, I spotted Milly's Oscar. He knew it drove Darryl Zanuck crazy, but it amused him to no end to display it not on the mantel, but on top of the custom-made cabinet of his Philco television receiver. I got up and went over, wrapped my trembling fingers around the base, and picked it up, feeling its surprising weight in my hand. God, how I wanted one of these. I was enjoying its heft when I was startled by the front door closing and Milly's voice booming in the cavernous mansion, "Lillian? Are you up?" Panicked, I put the statuette back, nearly dropping it in the process, and made a hasty exit into the hallway to the foyer, stepping over the slumbering Puck, undisturbed by Milly's return home. Luckily, Milly didn't notice me as I heard him trotting up the stairs, calling for his wife. I was back in the kitchen, pouring myself a glass of Blanche's lemonade when Milly came in.

"I swear my wife could sleep through the Blitzkrieg," he said, yanking open the Frigidaire and helping himself to a sandwich. "Where the hell is everybody?"

"Deming's washing the cars and Blanche went to the market."

"Good. I need a dip in the pool. I smell like horse sweat. Join me?"

"Sure," I said.

The air was hot as I emerged from the cabana in my trunks and dove straight in, then surfaced and bobbed lazily in the cooling wet. Milly was folding his riding clothes over the back of the swing, having grabbed a swimsuit from among the towels and bathrobes. As he sat on the coping to dangle his feet in the pool, I swam over, lazily treading to keep my head above the water. That's when I noticed three things which interested me immediately: One, I'd never realized the dog tags weren't the only things dangling against the dusting of hair in the center of his chest. Nestled between them at the end of the silver chain was a key—just the right size to fit the locked drawer in his study. Two, his trim and muscular torso was marred by a small but rather nasty-looking scar in his right side, just below the rib cage. And finally, most intriguing of all, he had what looked like tiny clumps of dried semen clinging to the trail of fine hair leading down from his naval. So that explained his Saturday morning rides. I was more curious than ever now about the contents of the drawer in his desk. *What was he hiding?*

"So, did you read the whole script and not just your part?" he asked, lowering himself into the pool up to his neck. *Your part.* I liked the sound of that. I started to answer, but he had ducked under.

Once he surfaced, slicking his thick hair away from his eyes, I said, "It's a good role. The dialogue's a little corny at times, but it's pretty solid."

I was referring to the role of Giff in *Nearer My God to Thee*, the young Purdue student who romances the snooty daughter of the wealthy couple ultimately played by Barbara Stanwyck and Clifton Webb. My screen test was scheduled for that coming Tuesday, and Milly had volunteered to spend Sunday helping me prepare.

"I think you should call the picture *Titanic*," I said, pulling the inflatable raft into the pool and climbing aboard to catch some sun. Puck found his way to the water's edge and waited for me to bring him aboard.

"I like it," Milly said, swimming over and putting his forearms on the foot of the float, resting his chin on his wrists, drifting along with me. "Dex, you're a genius. I'll make Darryl think it was his idea."

I grinned. *What a thrill*. Milly fell silent for a moment, then changed the subject, "You'll need some proper clothes for Europe, you know."

"I guess so."

"Black tie for the boat, a dinner jacket. I'll have Lillian take you shopping. She has impeccable taste."

"I know." Then, self-conscious, I added, "Thanks."

"Did you get your passport?"

"I can pick it up on Wednesday."

"Then we're all set."

Milly looked at me for a brief moment, oddly thoughtful, then half-smiled and pushed himself away from the raft. I lay there with Puck again asleep at my side, rocking gently from the water's motion as Milly swam a few slow laps of the pool. It was one of the rare times we'd been alone together and feeling comfortable with one another. Did he know what was going on between me and Lillian? He'd have to be an idiot not to. But perhaps his Saturday morning rides (rather his weekly visits to his mistress) actually made him grateful so that he sanctioned his wife's indiscretions without judgment. The more I was around Milly, the more I understood and liked him, though in the years following my departure, I would never admit it. Not even to myself.

I must have dozed off, because the next thing I was aware of was catching a glimpse of Blanche's back as she lugged her groceries into the French doors and disappeared. I blinked. Milly was lying in a lounge chair, a *Daily Variety* over his face, its pages rustling in rhythm to his steady breath as he slept. Could it be three o'clock already?

I gently lifted Puck back onto the patio. He growled in harmless protest as was his habit, then climbed off the float and I made my way into the cabana. Later, as I emerged freshly showered, shaved, and changed, the keys to the Nash in my hand, Milly was still there. Only he wasn't sleeping. He spoke without removing the *Variety* that covered his features.

"Ah, the telltale aroma of aftershave," he said. "Where are you off to?"

I stopped, clutching the keys in my hand. "Out for a bit. To see some friends."

Milly sat up and folded the newspaper. "Dex. We already had this conversation. You're *not* going."

"Excuse me?" It was his tone that set me off.

He tossed the *Variety* aside and looked at me, taking in my pressed short-sleeved shirt and shorts, and the new leather sandals I'd purchased just for that day.

"Oh, Henry Willson's gonna *love* you."

"I told you he represented Lana Turner and—"

"More than his fair share of *pansies*," Milly nearly spat out the words.

"So *you* say. Look, you and Lillian have been very generous with me, and I appreciate it, but I can't go on having everything just given to me. I gotta earn something for myself."

"Oh, that's priceless. Who bought your little ensemble there? And when's the last time you even offered to pay some rent for god's sake?"

"Okay, fine, you want to tell me what this is about? You want to put your damn cards on the table?"

"Lower your voice."

"Fuck you." I turned to head for the garage when I saw Lilly, still groggy, standing on the verandah watching.

"What now?" she asked.

"I'm going to a party."

"Oh, it'll be a party, all right," Milly said, grabbing his clothes from the swing and starting toward the house. He stopped beside me, leaning in close. I could feel the spittle from his lips as he hissed at me, "Have a good time 'cause you'll be celebrating the end of your career."

"Or the beginning for all you know."

"Fine. But I'm through helping you. You go to Willson's party, I'm done. After your screen test, you're on your own."

I couldn't believe this was happening, and all over a backyard barbeque. I knew I should stay and patch this up, but Milly had given an ultimatum, and that was something that always pushed me right over the edge. He might as well have been my father bossing me around. I was still hot-headed and stubborn, after all, and regardless of whatever trepidation I felt about attending this particular party, nobody was going to tell me what I could or couldn't do. Stupidly, I turned and left him there. Lillian called after me, but I didn't stop. In fact, I made a point of slamming the garage door so hard I shattered one of its windows.

If Hancock Park was Ginger Rogers, then Bel Air was Hedy Lamarr. Some of the mansions, set off from the twisting street by their well-tended rolling lawns, were easily twice the size of Milford and Lillian's and situated on much bigger sprawls of land. Maybe Milly was just jealous of the guy because he had more money. Schmuck. It had taken me an hour to get there in cross-town traffic on Sunset Boulevard, even on a Saturday, most of the other cars looking like they were either going to or coming from the beach. I had taken my shirt off, lying to myself that I'd done so to keep it from getting too wrinkled in the heat, but a few extra rays wouldn't hurt. Stone Canyon Road rolled into view so I turned right, heading up into the hills, where the houses were mostly hidden behind walls, trees, and shrubs. The homes were smaller than the sprawling mansions further below, but much more private. I spotted a row of cars clustered around a gate and, checking the number, parked the Nash and wriggled into my shirt, grabbed the keys, and headed up the slope. Halfway there, I remembered I was chewing gum, so I looked around before spitting it into some bushes. As I neared the address, I could hear laughter and splashing.

The front lawn of the house was carpeted in purple jacaranda blossoms that I knew to be pretty sticky from my afternoon walks with Lilly and the dogs. I tried to avoid stepping on any of them as I approached the front door, which was slightly ajar. Some bouncy if outdated big band bubbled from a radio in the living room. I tapped on the door.

"Hello? Mr. Willson?" I got a whiff of hamburgers cooking and my stomach growled, reminding me I hadn't eaten anything since the two small sandwiches. The laughter and splashing was much louder now. I knocked again, then after waiting for what felt like an eternity, wiped my feet on the mat and took a hesitant step inside.

"Hey there! You made it," Henry Willson boomed, coming in from the patio and spotting me. He was dressed in an open collar shirt with long sleeves, cuff links, and double-pleated trousers pulled up over his naval, perhaps in a futile attempt to hide his largish belly. With his long, oval face, nonexistent chin, and somewhat vacant expression, he reminded me of the director Vincent Minnelli whose picture I'd seen in *Photoplay* back home.

"I did," I said. "Traffic was murder on Sunset."

"Right." He gave my arm a squeeze. "I should have warned you about that. C'mon out back. I'll introduce you around."

As we stepped out into a backyard secluded by high stucco walls, shade trees, and exotic native California plants, I was greeted by the sight of a dozen or so young guys, all no doubt actors and wannabes, lounging around the kidney-shaped pool chatting and sunning themselves in the still-warm afternoon glow. Two fat older men sat on lawn chairs in the middle of the yard, smoking cigars and fanning the heat away with their hats. The only woman in sight was flipping burgers on the grill, her lined mouth puckered as if she'd just eaten a lemon.

"New client, Henry?" a voice asked from behind.

It was Rock Hudson, in swim trunks and flip-flops, coming out of a double doorway that led to the back of the house.

"I hope so. Rock, allow me to introduce . . ." He turned to me, almost blushing, "I'm sorry, I forgot your name."

"Clifton Garrow," I said, defying Milly's rechristening.

"Huh," Hudson said, shaking my hand, "that'll have to change. Henry's the king of names."

"It's, uh, nice to meet you," was all I could manage, wanting to keep my mouth shut about having collided with him in the hallway at Milly's house what seemed like decades ago.

"We'll fix you up," Henry said. "I've already got some ideas."

"Nice haircut," Hudson said, scrutinizing me as if sizing up potential competition for movie roles.

I smiled. Lilly had just cut it again for me the day before. "Thanks." The warmth in my cheeks made me realize I was blushing. Nerves, I guessed.

"Well, welcome to the fold."

I smiled again as he leaned in and whispered something to Henry Willson before striding over toward the bevy of boys by the pool, walking for all the world as if he owned the place.

"Let's get a drink, and then I want to hear all about you," Willson said, leading me toward the outdoor bar.

I'd never had a Manhattan in my life, and after two of them on an empty stomach, I realized I'd been chattering away nonstop. Willson, to his credit, seemed riveted. I wished I'd visited with Mary Jane before coming in, but it was too late for that. I spotted a Bakelite cigarette box on the bar. "You mind?"

"Go right ahead," Willson said as I took one. He lit it for me, noticing my shaking hands. "You chilly?"

"Nah, it's just, um, yeah, a little," I replied, not wanting to go into further detail. My hands could be my worst liability, so better to keep that to myself for now. Willson was just staring at me.

"Your face was *made* for a close up. What's that on your lip?"

"Oh." I touched it, self-conscious. "Just a birthmark. It covers up pretty easily."

"I've got it," Willson said, not taking his eyes off me.

"What?" I asked, no clue what he was talking about.

"Dirk Hardin."

"Excuse me?"

"Your new name . . . if you let me represent you, I mean."

It might have been the buzz from the bourbon and vermouth, but it sounded brilliant to me.

"Oh no you don't." It was Rock again, joining us at the bar, his torso glistening after just emerging from the pool. "You might as well name him Dick Hard-on."

"Rock," Willson admonished, "will you behave?"

"We're out of ice," Hudson said, staring at Henry.

After a moment, Henry stood up. "I'll get some." And he left us sitting there. It was pretty clear who was the real king of this clambake. Rock and I chatted for a while, and he struck me as a really solid guy. I don't know if I was naïve or just plain stupid, but I was still convinced there was no way what Milly had said was true—despite the all-male pool party going on behind me. Rock Hudson was a budding movie legend, well on his way to an iconic career, but as he talked to me that day, he seemed downright bashful about the modest success he'd had thus far.

"Don't kid yourself," I said, gaining confidence. "You were terrific in *Iron Man*."

"You saw that?" he asked.

"Only about a million times."

He laughed, intrigued and puzzled. "You liked it that much?"

"Well, no," I said, the booze getting to me before I realized. "I mean, yeah, I liked it, but see, I used to be an usher. At the Arcadia back home. So I saw every picture over and over again and wow . . . I'm babbling. Henry makes a strong drink, huh?"

"You bet he does. You gotta watch out for him."

Before I could ask him to explain what he meant, Henry returned and took me around making introductions. I didn't like the way the two fat men eyed me from beneath the brims of their hats, but the rest of the guys there seemed nice enough. Hudson joined us with two drinks in his hands. "Manhattan, right?" he asked, holding out a fresh one before giving me a wink. "Not quite as strong as your last one."

"Thanks." I grinned and took a sip. *Holy Toledo.* Rock Hudson was making drinks for *me*. Could this be the first step toward realizing my long-ago fantasy of hosting the best parties in the world? Two of the boys were arguing about something and called Henry over to mediate.

He excused himself, and Rock leaned in a little closer to me. "Just watch yourself around him."

"Sorry?"

"Henry and his heavy pour. You don't have to do anything you don't want to."

My stomach flipped. This was strange advice. I downed the last of my third Manhattan.

"You should see his house. Want a tour?" Hudson asked, grinning.

"Sure," I said, hoping I could walk without staggering. As we crossed the lawn and headed through the open door into the back of the house, I went to put my drink down on a low table but missed it, the tumbler landing unbroken on the grass. The sour-faced housekeeper snatched it up as I apologized.

"C'mon," Hudson said.

Rock led me through what appeared to be Henry's office. My cheeks again felt warm, and there was a pounding in my temples. My heart was pumping adrenaline, as if some part of me sensed danger. Hudson was oblivious, pointing out pictures on the walls, all of various handsome young men posed with Henry Willson. Then I followed him into a hallway where he showed me the den, Henry's master suite, and the built-in intercom system, before stopping at a closed door.

"This," he said, "is the most fun room in the house."

He grinned again and opened it. The room was dark except for what light filtered through the thick bougainvillea outside the half-closed Venetian blinds. I was puzzled by the strong stench of dank perspiration that seemed out of place in this fussy home, but when my eyes adjusted to the gloom, it made a stark and alarming sense to me. There were three or four naked guys on the huge bed, doing god-knows-what with each other, their voices low and dirty as they moaned and egged their buddies on.

"Rock? Where the hell'd you go?" came a husky growl from the darkness.

"Your friend's welcome, whoever he is," said another.

I was frozen in place. Terrified and humiliated with the realization

Milly had been right. So immobilized I wasn't aware that Hudson had slipped out of his swim trunks and was now reaching to unbutton my still crisp shirt.

"Let's get you out of this," he said, winking at me, "so you can join the club."

I fought through my panic and snapped back to my senses.

"What the *hell?*" I clenched his wrists hard and yanked him off me.

"Whoa, whoa, sorry," Hudson said, stepping back and raising his palms. "Guess I read the wrong—"

I cut him off with a sucker punch to his face that was so hard he snapped backwards and slammed into the wall. I didn't see the impact, just heard the thud because I was already halfway down the hall, running blindly for the front door. Once outside, I sprinted back to the car, horrified and unable to catch my breath, inflamed by the knowledge I had most likely just broken Rock Hudson's nose. Hands jittering, I dropped the keys twice before managing to get into the Nash and starting the engine. It wasn't until I hit Sunset that I realized the soles of my bare feet were gummy with the purple jacaranda blossoms from Henry Willson's courtyard. I'd left my new leather sandals by the pool where I'd taken them off shortly after I'd arrived at his party.

Too bad. They were really nice shoes.

Lillian was waiting up for me, immobile in her swing, smoking and staring into the glimmering darkness of the pool when I got home at one in the morning. I had found a dive bar in Malibu, gotten good and properly smashed, and then somehow managed to drive home on those twisting roads without killing anybody or being arrested. She was silent as I approached her, but looked at me with such heartfelt sympathy and understanding. Drunk and disgraced, I dropped to my knees in front of her and curled up, my head resting in her lap. She stroked my hair. So gentle.

"There there," was all she said, before taking my hand and leading me into the cabana to comfort me.

I screwed her with abandon that night, though Lillian didn't seem to mind. And the entire time, all I could think about was how I'd have to find a way to repair things with Milly in the morning.

ELEVEN

Hancock Park hadn't changed much in forty years, and I easily recognized the streets as Tally drove us east on Third in her subcompact rental car. It was late enough that the sun was already waning, but she had insisted I come along with her to see the house I hadn't set foot in since 1953. A house I would soon inexplicably own. Tally hadn't been home in over ten years and was afraid to face it alone. I was still reeling from the news of my inheritance, and I'm embarrassed to admit I was filled with a nagging distrust of her motives. Was she befriending me because of her father's will? Did Milly really have five and a half million dollars squirreled away when he died? We chatted about him in the car, and the subject at last turned to Lillian, still a painful memory for Tally as she told me again how she had learned of her mother's suicide on *The Today Show* before her truly shaken father had called her to relay the bad news. Milly and Lilly had had one of their endless fights the week before Christmas, and Lilly had taken off. Her car was found parked at the marina with the keys still in the ignition. She'd taken their yacht out, headed toward Catalina Island. The *Jubilee* was spotted by the harbormaster, bobbing in the heavy swells the next morning, adrift and empty. Ever courteous, Lillian's handwritten note read simply, "I'm done."

"Your dad bought that boat in the fall of '52," I said, trying to imagine the desperation that had led to Lillian's actions.

"And sold it right after Mother died," Tally added.

As we turned onto South Windsor and made our way through those same mammoth palm trees I'd been so fond of in my youth, Tally slowed when we neared the enormous old house on the corner. Neither of us could believe what we saw. The whole structure was barely visible now, the yard so overgrown, the shrubs so tall, that the rundown mansion was unrecognizable as the sleek streamline moderne manor of my memory. Giant birds of paradise had taken over and obscured the simple lines of the house; only patches of curled paint hanging off the stucco exterior could be glimpsed through their massive leaves. The southern side was covered in ivy, which was now making its way around front, gradually devouring the half-round wall of glass brick that had once sparkled in the evenings. As she parked in the cracked, weed-sprouted circular drive, we both saw the front door had been boarded over with a water-damaged sheet of plywood where some infuriated neighbor had scrawled in angry orange spray paint: "TEAR IT DOWN!"

"What the hell . . .?" was all I could manage.

"I guess his gardening went about as well as his sobriety."

"No kidding."

I got out of the passenger seat and stared up at the decrepit old house. It didn't make sense. A man with that kind of money, with that kind of pride, had allowed his castle to decay. What could have possibly happened to Milly?

"C'mon," Tally said, joining me. "The lawyer said the entrance is around back. Dad was getting pretty paranoid in his old age."

"Among other things."

It was almost dark as we made our way through the old wooden gate where a simple paper sign reading "HELP" had once so insulted me. Stepping into the backyard, we saw the elegant, curved footpaths were now covered with the voracious ivy.

"Watch your step," I said, as we moved past the drained pool where Milly and Lilly and I had shared so many evenings. A jagged, nasty crack marred its far wall, and I wondered if it had resulted from the recent earthquake. The Urban Idyll was definitely a thing of the past. The cabana, too, was boarded over. I considered the ruins, noting the overturned and rusting shopping cart at the bottom of the leaf-filled pool, Lillian's cherished swing now covered in ivy and hanging from only one chain. A tangle of discarded patio furniture was piled nearby, the cushions long gone. Had Milford Langen really lived here all those years? With his palace in apocalyptic ruins?

A flagstone on the verandah steps dislodged under my foot as we went up to the double French doors that once overlooked the gorgeous landscaping, but Tally steadied me as I stumbled.

"You okay?" she asked.

"Honestly, I don't know," I said, taking in the dark windows, some broken, and one missing a pane on the second floor that had been replaced with a soiled scrap of cardboard and duct tape. The same French doors that had stood wide open all those long-ago summer evenings now had a black iron accordion burglar bar padlocked across them. I could almost hear the faded music from Milly's hi-fi drifting out to us as we drank and swam until all hours. Straining to see in the encroaching darkness, Tally finally got the combination lock open after three failed attempts. It took both of us to slide the rusting bars aside before she produced a key and unlocked the doors. They creaked in resistance as she pushed them, then fumbled for a light switch. Lucky for us, the power was on, and a single working bulb in one of the six art deco sconces in the rear foyer popped to life.

"Holy god," I said, my voice hushed in the gloom.

We stood there for several seconds, taking in the unimaginable sight before us. The house, once kept immaculate by Blanche and Deming, was in total chaos. Cardboard boxes were piled to the ceiling in places, their contents bulging with old screenplays, reels of 35mm film, and newspapers. Everywhere. Near the archway leading to the kitchen, a hodgepodge of old pots and buckets still held brackish traces of the last rain that had seeped through an ugly brown water stain in the ceiling, a chunk of its plaster dangling precariously overhead.

"I guess he must've fired the housekeeper," Tally said, trying to keep herself from crying.

"Yeah, in 1962."

She gave a halfhearted smile and moved farther inside, turning on a bare light bulb in the hallway where I'd once encountered Rock Hudson coming out of the bathroom. The walls were cracked and flaking, and the remaining artwork hung at ridiculous angles. Tally started toward the front of the house, and, with no choice, I followed. The living room was the only place that bore any resemblance to its former magnificence. The furniture was different than I remembered, looking as if Milly and Lilly had redecorated sometime in the '70s when deco made a brief and gaudy disco-era return. The fireplace was plugged with an irregularly cut piece of drywall, held in place by layers of silver duct tape beneath the dented steel mantel, its milk glass top gone, exposing a tangle of burned out Lumiline bulbs and frayed cloth-covered wires underneath.

And then I saw it. The thing that finally brought the sting of tears.

An aluminum Christmas tree stood forlorn in the corner, still decorated, with long cobwebs stringing between it and the motionless old color wheel angled upward on the floor. A few presents wrapped in now vintage paper were fading and gathering layers of dust underneath, and I thought of Lillian, poor sweet lost Lillian, and her superstitions. I tried to wipe my eyes before Tally turned around. No such luck.

"What? What is it?"

"I was just . . . your mom was onto something. Bad luck to leave the tree up past New Year's."

Tally chewed her lower lip, the way Lillian had done when troubled. "I think I was ten or eleven when Dad insisted we get this tree. Mom hated it. She always wanted the smell of pine at Christmas, so Dad bought some kind of spray to make her happy."

"They stayed together?"

Tally nodded. "I was living back East, and I never really came home again, except for her memorial service."

"And now."

"Yeah," she said with a wistful sigh. "So this is why he insisted on flying up to visit me that one time. He didn't want me to know the truth."

I surveyed the open foyer where Benny Goodman's orchestra once played, the sweeping streamline stairs with their nickel handrail Fred Astaire had danced down a lifetime ago. It was forever after referred

101

to as the Fred Astaire-case. A pile of mail had collected under the slot, including untouched magazines that appeared to be ten years old. All three of the portholes in the front door were shattered, perhaps explaining the plywood bolted on the other side. Across the foyer was the small hallway to Milly's study, and, unable to stop myself, I headed over.

The light switch in the narrow corridor was dead, so I had to be careful as I walked in the semi-darkness, something crunching under my shoe as I recalled how starstruck I'd been by the conversation between Milly and Darryl Zanuck. It was impossible to determine the original color of the frazzled carpet; it was now stained and torn beyond repair. The room looked more like a storage unit, the billiard table piled high with more bulging boxes, the once gorgeous wood paneling scarred with nail holes and bleached by what sun had managed to seep through the half-closed wooden blinds drooping askew over the huge bay window. An old 16mm projector sat dusty in its still open cabinet, trained across the room toward a wrinkled sheet nailed to the wall over the torn and damaged pull-down screen. Spools of film, Milly's home movies most likely, were everywhere. As I took in the ruins all around me, I turned and spotted a 1970s console television, its screen completely shattered by something that had been angrily thrown. Drawing closer, I realized it was Milly's Oscar, lying amid the tangle of wires and broken glass.

The only thing that looked like it still got regular use was Milly's airplane desk. I flicked on a lamp.

A brown IBM Selectric dominated the space, a half-typed page still rolled around the platen. I scanned the last line Milly had typed:

"And so, I thank you for your kind indulgence. We're finally at the end now, at least I know I am, and I'd be happy to rest on my laurels . . . if I had any to speak of."

Next to the typewriter, an ashtray overflowed with cigarette butts, and a pair of reading glasses lay discarded atop an old cassette recorder surrounded by well over a hundred tapes hand-labeled with such titles as "Chapter One" and "The War in the Specific." I moved the ashtray to find at least 500 coffee-stained and cigarette-burned pages of a manuscript, covered with scribbled notes in ink, words scratched out and changed, some so illegible the author had then printed them in block letters a second time so he could decipher his own scrawl when he sobered up. Arrows and more gouging cross-outs marred the pages. The title read: *Milford Langen: A Hollywood Fairytale.* But an angry pen mark, so ferocious it had ripped through the paper, scribbled out "tale" so it actually read *A Hollywood Fairy.*

"What is it?" Tally asked from the doorway behind me as I quickly put the ashtray back to hide the title.

"Looks like your dad was writing a book. His memoirs."

"Fiction, most likely." She started to say something else, seemed to think better of it, then said it anyway: "You think it's worth anything?" Before I could answer, we heard a loud clattering overhead. We both tensed as something came running down the stairway accompanied by a jingling sound. Then a mangy terrier appeared, scrambling toward us and starting to bark.

"Holy shit," Tally said. "I didn't know Dad had a dog."

"Hey, hey, little guy," I said, kneeling down as the mutt scampered over, obviously agitated, but still allowing me to extend a hand and then scratch behind its ears. "How long have you been here?"

The dog wouldn't stop yapping and took several steps back toward the door and past a surprised Tally. It kept barking, loud, with unmistakable urgency, circling between me and the hallway.

"I think he wants us to follow him," I said, starting to do so.

"You first," was Tally's reply.

As soon as it realized we understood, the dog scurried off the way he'd come, and I trailed with Tally a few steps behind. He trotted up the curved stairway, circling back and glancing at us to make sure we were still there, all the while barking like crazy, until we made our way down an empty corridor toward what had once been a large guest suite in back of the house overlooking the pool. Lillian's preferred room for our long-ago trysts. The door was ajar, and the dog darted through. I held back for a second, glancing at Tally, then looked inside.

The room was dark save for a shaft of moonlight filtering through the dirty window, the one with the taped cardboard I had seen earlier. It was more orderly than the rest of the house, and I noticed the mirrored wall was now gone, replaced by plaster. A wheelchair was parked in the corner by the bathroom, and a rancid stench filled the air. The dog finally ceased its barking and leapt up onto the bed. I was so stunned even my hands were momentarily still.

An old woman was lying beneath a tangle of covers, the nightstand a sea of prescription bottles. At first, we were certain she was dead, but as I turned on a light, she stirred and blinked awake, groggy and weak. "Milly? Where on earth have you been?" she asked in a sedated Southern accent.

All Tally could manage was a whisper.

"Mother?"

TWELVE

On our last evening in Hollywood before Milly and I were to board a four-prop DC-6 for an overnight flight to New York and the start of our Europe trip, Lillian had insisted on a bon voyage party at the Mocambo. The joint was already past its prime, but the caged exotic birds still seemed to draw the likes of Clark Gable and Howard Hughes, and the night we were there, Milly, dapper in his impeccable white tuxedo, introduced me to Humphrey Bogart and Lauren Bacall. I nearly fainted. Did you ever see *Key Largo*? Now that's a picture. We had to step aside to allow Alfred Hitchcock and Mr. and Mrs. Jimmy Stewart to pass, while Milly said quick and cheerful hellos, and I gotta tell you, for this kid from Texas, it was aces.

I had smoothed things over with Milly after the backyard barbeque incident, telling him in sordid detail about the events of that afternoon. Milly's only response had been to hiss the word "reprobates." When I continued to apologize, saying how I would never doubt him again, he simply shrugged. "Don't keep pitching past the sell, Dex."

Lillian had reserved a table far from the tiny dance floor so she could hear herself think as she'd put it. She was to leave shortly after us for her stint in the Mojave with Joan Crawford on *Bring Them Back*, and she wasn't looking forward to the shoot. We followed the *maître d'* through the stylish throng, and out of nowhere Lillian grabbed my arm and gave a wicked laugh, feigning conversation so as to avoid eye contact with her nemesis Bette Davis who was two tables away sipping cocktails with her husband and costar from *All About Eve*—Gary somebody. No sooner were we seated than a crisp young waiter appeared with three perfect martinis. My dad was from Alabama, same state as Tallu, mind you, and if he had seen me sitting there in my blue serge and bowtie, sandwiched on the high-backed banquette between the woman who played Cora Wells in *Every Tomorrow* and the man who won an Oscar for producing it, well, shit, he'd have slurred out, "Ain't you stompin' in high cotton?" Screw him. I had embraced my new Hollywood life and was having a ball.

Appropriately enough, the swell little orchestra kicked off "Three to Get Ready," and a few dancers crowded onto the tiny floor. Everywhere I looked, there were movie stars, producers, directors, even a few writers (not that anybody would have known), and in truth, we had the best table in the joint, overlooking all that smart splendor.

"You're grinning like a jackass, as my mother would say," Lillian drawled, raising her drink in a toast, letting her native Southern accent glimpse through.

I lifted my martini to clink. "To jackasses."

Milly chuckled and tapped his glass with ours. "Three of them, to be precise." We all sipped in unison, and then the ritual of lighting the cigarettes followed.

"Dilly Dally! Who let you in?" asked a fellow in an impeccable suit and tie. I nearly swallowed my olive. It was Cary Grant. Sure, I should've been used to hobnobbing with the stars after six months, but *this* was cinema royalty.

"I bribed the *maître d'*," Milly grinned, putting his cigarette in the little ashtray and standing to shake Grant's hand. "And don't call me Dilly Dally."

Grant glanced my way with a hint of suspicion, then turned to Lilly. "Lillian, darling, you look positively radiant as always," he said, kissing her extended hand. She did. She was wearing a low-cut, off-the-shoulder gown that shimmered like black mother of pearl, her hair swept up to expose the nape of her perfect neck, which was encircled in a row of diamonds. The scent of gardenia was intoxicating.

"Oh Cary, you talk as if the cameras are always rolling. Allow me to introduce the next biggest star in all of Hollywood," Lillian smiled, gesturing toward me. Man, did I like the sound of that.

"Dexter Gaines, Mr. Grant," I said, shaking firmly with him.

"A pleasure," Grant said. "And please, call me Cary."

"Join us?" Milly asked, all too aware that Grant's presence at our table would turn everyone's heads.

"Can't just now. Betsy and I had a moment of insanity and ordered food." He winked and gestured toward a small table near the dance floor where his wife was taking her first sip of champagne. She smiled and waved our way; then we all exchanged a few more pleasantries before he headed off.

Milly picked up his cigarette. "For the record, I'm glad you convinced me to book a night flight."

"I know you well, Puppy. After *this* party, you'll be in no shape to travel for at *least* twenty-four hours," Lillian said with a laugh. "Now, which one of you fine beaux will dance with me?"

The thought of joining the crowd terrified me even after my exhausting lessons with Lillian, but Milly came to the rescue and, taking her hand, led her toward the floor. She glanced back over her naked shoulder, the flicker of sadness in her eyes telling me she was disappointed. As for me, I just sat there smoking, remembering to hold the cigarette the way she had taught me, taking in the Hollywood madness all around. I watched Milly and Lilly doing a cha-cha among the throng, like two old pros who effortlessly anticipated the other's next move. They were good together, as they'd emerge from the crowd, then get swallowed up again. After a moment, I realized my view of the dance floor was now blocked by the rotund stomach of a man standing over my table. I looked up and froze.

It was Henry Willson.

"We meet again," he said. "Clifton, wasn't it?"

"Yeah, um . . ."

"Don't fret. Oh, I forgot my manners. Allow me to introduce my client Guy Danvers," he said, indicating the handsome blond next to him. "He just finished his *second* picture. Nice featured role opposite Tab

Hunter and Linda Darnell."

Guy smiled and said hello, a bit self-conscious. Had Henry already pointed me out and told him about how I'd punched Rock Hudson in the face? There was no way to know. Whatever fun I'd been having was over.

"And you? Catch a break, yet?" Willson asked, obviously trying to bait me.

"I'm up for a role in *Titanic*," I said, measuring my words.

"Well, good for you!"

"And I'm Dexter Gaines now."

"Dexter Gaines?" Willson repeated, mulling it over. At length he pronounced, "That's good."

"Anyway, nice to see you again," I said, hoping they'd go away, but still pleased my new name passed muster.

"If you ever reconsider," Willson said, "call me. I still have your sandals." He gave a courtly half bow and added, "Mr. Gaines."

I responded with a tight smile and waited for them to leave. As they moved off to the next table, working the room, I saw Milly staring from across the room with concern in his eyes as if asking: *Are you okay?* I flashed my biggest smile to reassure him, then looked away, tapping the ash from my cigarette. After a moment I got up and headed toward the dance floor, eyeballing the tables until I spotted a four-top surrounded by gorgeous young women. Keenly aware Lilly and Milly were watching, I extended my hand to one of the girls and said, "Excuse me, may I have this dance?"

She looked up, curious. It was just my luck this fresh-faced beauty happened to be dancing up a storm on screens across the country to rave reviews, in Technicolor no less, in *Singin' in the Rain*. Cyd Charisse smiled, with just a hint of coy suspicion.

"I'm Dexter," I said, as if that would reassure her.

"Cyd," she said. "And I'd be *delighted*."

She grabbed my hand, and it certainly didn't help much when the bandleader spotted her and launched into a jazzy version of "Singin' in the Rain," ensuring all eyes in the room were on us. So I did the best I could to keep up with Cyd Charisse as we danced either a two-step or a foxtrot or something entirely new altogether. Even after my lessons preparing for the Europe trip, I really wasn't sure.

"Relax," she said with a reassuring laugh.

I tried, aware that Milly and Lilly were now headed back to the table. Cyd was fantastic, somehow managing to make me look good, and when the dance was over we drew enthusiastic applause from the celebrated crowd. After thanking Cyd, I kissed her hand, then squeezed through the crowd to join my mentors, flushed. Lilly teased me, saying perhaps I should sign with MGM rather than stay under Milly's tutelage. Milly scoffed, downed yet another cocktail, and snapped his fingers for more. A roving photographer stopped by our table, and the three of us scooched closer and posed while her flash eternalized the moment, my smile so big it almost hurt. Later, I noticed Tab Hunter dancing with Debbie Reynolds, and Lilly explained they'd been seen together quite a lot around town.

"She's his beard," Milly said, almost whispering the words so Lillian wouldn't hear. She just frowned and lit another cigarette. The three of us were soon toasted, and Lillian said she wanted to finish the party in the Urban Idyll. As we left, Milly, bolstered by the alcohol, drunk to the point I had to steady him, kept inviting everyone to the house. Just as Lillian explained she'd meant the three of us, not the entire industry, a man stopped to chat with her. It turned out he was Jack Warner, and he launched into a conversation about the upcoming shoot for *Bring Them Back*. Lillian lied to him through what looked like a real smile, saying how excited she was to be working with Joan Crawford again, when I realized what a brilliant actress she was *and* that Milly had disappeared— no doubt to avoid Mr. Warner. Lilly shot frantic looks my way, all the while smiling at her new boss but imploring me to go find her husband. I spotted Milly teetering as he handed some money to Xavier Cugat, who was now conducting the band.

"Dex, please go save him from himself," Lillian said.

"Excuse me, Mr. Warner," I said, then headed over as Milly turned to speak to Cary Grant again.

"C'mon, old man," I tossed it all off as a joke as I took Milly's elbow. "Let's get you home."

"Oh, all right," he said, doddering as I pulled him away. "Hell of a bon voyage."

"You bet."

By three-thirty in the morning, it seemed as if all of Hollywood had followed Milly, like their own pied piper, to the house on Windsor Boulevard. Xavier Cugat's orchestra was playing in the foyer, and Fred Astaire did an impromptu dance down the sweeping staircase. I spotted Debbie Reynolds and Tab Hunter, laughing from their chairs where they'd hidden in the dining room, sharing an amusing and animated conversation. I wondered what a beard was, even with the nagging thought it couldn't have been a compliment, not the way Milly had said it. Later, Darryl Zanuck pushed David Niven into the pool, fully clothed, and soon the water was undulating with everyone diving in without bothering to undress. Milly cannonballed into the deep end, no doubt ruining his white tuxedo. Their laughter and screaming rose above the thumping of the music even as the band now stood waist-deep in the churning water playing their instruments—the drummer and bassist choosing to remain on dry land. Still, their din was enough to drown out Lilly's orgasm in the upstairs guest room overlooking the debauchery.

She tried to catch her breath as I stared at our reflection in the enormous, unforgiving mirrored wall. Her gown was hiked up to her waist, her legs wrapped around me as I was still inside her.

"I love you, Dexter," she whispered.

"I love you, too," I replied automatically as she started to cry.

I'm pretty sure we both knew it wasn't true. Not yet anyway.

I was still a bit hung over, feeling queasy and exhausted, as the taxi drove us into the heart of Manhattan from the airport. Even a full day in bed hadn't been enough to recover from the scandalous decadence of Lillian's party, and when Milly and I had left for the airport late the previous afternoon, she had insisted we both down a Bromo before our final hugs goodbye. Though she tried her best to hide it, I could tell her heart was breaking. The flight had been an exercise in strained conversation with an equally hungover Milly, both of us feeling uncomfortable as we faced the reality of traveling together and the next few weeks of each other's company. The stewardess had been nice enough, and brought us some concoction that seemed to help. Guess she had a lot of experience with passengers suffering the aftermath of their bon voyage parties. I was pretty sure Milly was as relieved as I was when we finally retired to our respective sleeping berths, though I was far too excited to get any real shut-eye.

Despite my headache, driving into New York for the first time in my life on the morning of July 2, 1952, I was practically hanging out of the window, taking it in. All I knew of Manhattan were pictures I'd seen in magazines, the movies of course, and a color postcard a high school girlfriend had sent me before vanishing from my life forever. It had been nestled among my life's detritus in the suitcase stolen from The Buck's trunk—not the only time everything I owned would be taken from me as it turned out. But here I was, in the back of a taxi, sailing over some bridge and gawking at the most magnificent skyline in the world, seated next to an Oscar-winning producer who'd fallen sound asleep, immune to my excitement. I wanted to share the moment with him, but he looked so peaceful slouched against the window that all I could do was smile.

By the time the driver deposited us outside the Algonquin Hotel, I was already feeling better. I couldn't believe the masses of people everywhere, the sidewalks crawling with humanity, all walking with such purpose and determination. It was as if someone had taken the massive sprawl of Los Angeles and scooped it toward the clouds into the canyon of skyscrapers all around us. The hotel management knew Milly, and so we were checked in with no fuss even though it was barely ten o'clock in the morning. I enjoyed the way everyone fawned over us and was reading the card that came with the bottle of iced champagne waiting for me in my room: "I already miss you! Love, Lillian," when Milly knocked on the adjoining door and let himself in.

"Your accommodations okay?" he asked. I looked around, still unable to believe I was there.

"I'll manage," I said, grinning.

"Well, I'm going to spend the day in bed, and I suggest you do the same. We're meeting people at '21' at eight this evening. Wear the gray trousers and blue blazer. And no bowties. This is New York. See you at seven-thirty." And he was gone.

I swallowed my resentment over the way he'd dictated my wardrobe—I knew how to dress myself after all—then went to the brand-new Louis Vuitton steamer trunk already open near the doorway and rummaged until I found the items Milly had specified. Lillian had taken me on the wildest shopping spree of my life, and I now had a wardrobe to rival her husband's. I laid the pants out on the bed with the jacket, tucking a folded white shirt under the lapels, and set about choosing a tie from all the silk Lilly had insisted on buying for me. The window was open a crack, and the sounds of the city far below drew me over where I looked out on the unbridled glory of all of Manhattan. As usual, my hands were shaking, and I remembered the new match safe hanging on the chain around my neck. I fished it out and retrieved one of the six expertly rolled joints inside. I didn't want to waste any, knowing I still had days ahead on the boat, but I was in the mood to celebrate. Two nights before, as I was saying goodnight to Lilly after all the guests had left, she'd presented it to me. She told me she had badgered the prop department at 20th until they found a perfect duplicate of the one my grandmother had given me. She'd even rolled the reefers inside just the way I'd taught her, in her own maternal equivalent of packing a lunch for me.

Suitably buzzed, I considered going to bed as Milly had suggested, but the excitement of the city was too much, and I soon found myself joining the bobbing masses on the sidewalks, looking like a rube, I'm sure, as I walked around, unable to stop gazing upwards. I found my way to the Empire State Building and paid fifteen cents for a souvenir black and white Polaroid of me, again grinning like one of Lillian's jackasses, with what looked like the expanse of the whole world both behind and in front of me. Fueled by an unfamiliar elation, I'd taken in as much of the city as I could cram into a day, snacking on a hotdog from a street vendor, watching the toy sailboats in Central Park, and strolling beneath the marquees on Broadway advertising *The Male Animal*, *Pal Joey*, and *Of Thee I Sing* among a handful of forgotten others.

When a well-rested Milly knocked on the door at seven forty-five, I was buttoning my blue jacket. Showered, shaved, and scented, I had selected a bright red necktie to go with the white shirt. Milly was dashing as always, attired in a black blazer, white slacks, and a silvery blue tie. His lapel sported a rose he'd plucked from the flowers in his room. He scrutinized me, head to toe.

"What's wrong?"

"You sure about that tie?"

I gritted my teeth. "It doesn't clash."

"All right," he said with a shrug. "Let's get going. I'm afraid I overslept."

The minor rift behind us, we waited without speaking for the elevator to take us down to a cab, then we were off to the legendary '21.'

My two years with Milford and Lillian had been lovingly enshrined in a scrapbook Lilly gave me before everything went to hell in the late autumn of '53. It was a complete chronicle of our lives together, including photos Milly had taken of us clowning in the Urban Idyll, nightclub folders with black-and-whites of our trio with the cream of Hollywood, souvenir ticket stubs, matchbooks, programs, swizzle sticks, table numbers—you name it. I had shown her the shoebox full of mementoes, and while I was shooting my third and final film, *Hollywood P.I.*, she'd been assembling them as a gift for the last birthday I would spend with them. In January of '94, when I was locked out of the house Carol and I had shared, I was never allowed to set foot in it again, even to retrieve my personal belongings. As a result, that precious album had been lost to me.

Though I never looked back once I left, I did prize having those snapshots and souvenirs on the off chance some day would arrive when

I'd want to look at them again, or perhaps even offer up proof my story was true. Among those pictures was one of my favorites, a black-and-white five-by-seven in a fancy cardboard folder from the Bar Room at '21.' It showed me in my blue blazer and red tie, sandwiched between Milly and Noël Coward in a crowded booth, surrounded by Kitty Carlisle, Tennessee Williams, Margaret Truman, and the strangest, funniest little man I'd ever met, Truman Capote. He was the one who had raised a stink with the waiter that while all of us were puffing away, there was no ashtray on the table. The chagrined waiter brought another, everyone unaware the original had been stashed in my trouser pocket.

Coward was the first to join us and had taken to me immediately. "I'm relieved you wore that tie," he said, winking at Milly, who frowned.

"I advised against it," Milly said through pursed lips. "He looks like Uncle Sam in red, white, and blue."

"Nothing wrong with showing a little patriotism, dear boy," Coward said, then added, "Your tie is like an oasis in the desert. Or to be a bit more precise, a stuttering neon sign advertising cocktails for the parched."

"Thanks," was all I could manage, having no idea what he meant, but then I'm sure it was somehow related to his next move: he pressed his thigh against mine under the table. I shifted away so he got the hint.

"My apologies," he said with a prim smile as he folded his long fingers together. "These booths are rather cozy."

For the most part, Milford Langen was all work in Los Angeles, but there was something about being in New York that seemed to loosen him up, and I could tell he was having fun. Witty and wry, he charmed every one of those important people, me included. After the First Daughter settled in beside Tennessee, Capote at last arrived and the two literary giants had the most polite verbal sparring match I'd ever witnessed, both of them bleary-eyed with booze, and clearly with no love lost for the other.

"I'd join you," Capote said in his tiny, odd voice, "but with Tom here, there doesn't seem to be enough room."

"My lap's available," Noël Coward said with a yawn.

Margaret Truman scooted in, patting the seat next to her. "C'mon.

Squeeze in right here."

"Yes, and we'll be dancing cheek to cheek," Capote quipped, then joined us and soon the conversation at our table was off to the races. It must have been terribly sophisticated, because I couldn't follow half of what they were talking about, and each time Milly leaned over to explain, I waved him off, not wanting to call attention to my social deficiencies. I just laughed when they laughed, nodded in understanding when they spoke of the blacklist and that bastard Joe McCarthy.

"This H.U.A.C. thing is nothing but a witch hunt," someone said, to which Coward replied, "H.U.A.C.? How does one pronounce that? WHACK?"

I also couldn't keep pace with their drinking, and soon the room was spinning softly with laughter, traded barbs, and the music. Normally, such a situation would have been frustrating and humiliating for me, but that night, as Milly went out of his way to include me in the conversation, I was feeling like the luckiest guy on earth.

"You're sailing tomorrow?" Kitty asked, yanking me from my private thoughts.

"Yes, ma'am," I answered. "On the *United States*."

"A maiden voyage. What fun."

"What a delightful coincidence," the president's rather plain daughter added. "I'll be on the boat, as well. Representing the country and all that. Daddy couldn't make it, so he's sending me."

"Then save a dance for me," Milly said, lighting a cigarette with his usual flair.

I swear his words caused her to swoon; such was his effect on women.

"Goddamned waste of taxpayer money," Williams boomed out of the blue.

"What on earth?" Margaret Truman seemed genuinely offended.

"Read the papers. In another few years we'll all be crowded into those goddamned silver tubes and being rocketed across the pond in six hours. This boat's a little late to the party."

"That may be," Capote squeaked, "but a *real* lady is always *fashionably* late. It's the only way to be the belle of the ball."

"Really, Mr. Williams," Margaret Truman said, "It's quite exciting. Didn't you see Commodore Manning was just on the cover of *Time*?"

Williams harrumphed as Capote added with a twinkle, "And the ship made the cover of *The New Yorker*."

This brought a glare from Williams as he downed his bourbon and was just starting to say something when Kitty diffused the situation, confessing her preference for the ships of the French Line. Milly chimed in that his personal favorite was England's *Queen Mary*. As the three of us chatted, me pretending to understand the merits of various liners I'd never seen let alone heard of, I found Kitty Carlisle to be very genuine and warm. I was having such fun I really didn't want to leave when Milly abruptly rose and announced we had to get back to the hotel, but I thought better than to protest.

We said our goodnights, with Milly taking my elbow as he guided me toward the exit, leaning in to whisper, "Don't tell me that's an ashtray in your pocket?"

"Of course not," I answered, horrified, trying to walk so as to hide it in my baggy, tailored trousers.

As we stepped off the elevator and headed toward our rooms at the Algonquin, Milly asked, "So what do you think of New York?"

"It's the most amazing thing I've ever experienced," I said.

"Just wait'll you see Paris, kiddo." He lingered for a moment, tipsy and content, then with the slightest smile, he inserted his room key into the lock.

"Hey, Mill," I said, "what did Mr. Coward mean by all that stuff about my tie?"

"Like most true artists, Noël's half crazy or very insightful or both. So who knows? Good night," he said through a yawn, then went into his room and closed the door.

Sometime later, after I'd fallen asleep to the sounds of the city, I was awakened by his key in the doorway in the hall, then the unmistakable muffled curses of a man who's had too much to drink trying to change into his pajamas and go to bed. I held my wristwatch up to the sliver of night light that came through the dark curtains. It was 5:30 in the morning, and we were to set sail in just over six hours. I stared at the ceiling, too excited to go back to sleep, all the while wondering where Milly might have gone "horseback riding" in Manhattan until dawn.

THIRTEEN

The paramedics arrived at the house on Windsor within minutes of my having called. Unfortunately, they brought a van from Channel 4 news with them. Lillian had been delirious, incoherent and weak, recognizing neither me nor her own daughter. When she first turned to look at us, I was startled to see the left side of her face was sagging and misshapen, as if she'd had a stroke, and her lips were so dry they were cracked and bleeding. While there was still water left in the pitcher on the nightstand, it turned out she hadn't eaten since Milly had died four days prior. There was no trace of the ravishing creature I had known in my youth, save for her eyes, though they were clearly emptier than they'd ever been. Her hair, once always impeccably styled, was now oily and gray, clinging to the sides of her face and cascading down to her sagging chest that barely moved when she breathed. Tally and I both thought it best not to tell her the truth, even though she kept asking for her husband. I think we were both too shocked at having found her alive under what was left of Milly's roof.

I couldn't help wondering if the answers might be found in Milly's memoir and had stuffed the cassette recorder and a handful of the tapes into my overnight bag while the paramedics got Lillian onto a gurney. As they rolled her out of the house, she grabbed my hand. "Don't let them see me," she said with desperation. "Please don't let them see me." Unsure what to do, I pulled the sheet up over her head as we got her past the camera crew parked outside. We squinted as flashes exploded, and the next morning a photo of her shrouded body made the front page of the *Los Angeles Times* just beneath the headline: "Lillian Sinclair Dead Again?"

After the ambulance departed with sirens wailing, I found the dog's crusted bowls in the laundry room, just where Lillian had always kept them, and fed the anxious little fellow and changed his water, his puzzled look bringing pangs of guilt as we promised we'd be back, and then closed up the house. I made sure the dog door in the kitchen was unlocked, and the gate to the backyard fastened, then we headed for the hospital. By the time we had Lillian safely ensconced at Cedars Sinai, it was two in the morning. The story had broken that Hollywood legend Lillian Sinclair had been found alive in the squalid remains of her husband's home in Hancock Park, and Tally and I were surprised by the horde of piranhas waiting outside the hospital shouting questions. I sheltered her as we got into the rental car in the parking lot and sped away, unaware the next day Lilly would bump the O.J. story from the top slot on *Good Morning America*.

"This is . . . I don't understand," Tally said after a long silence.

"I know," was my only reply.

We found a cheap motel, the Hollywood Center on Sunset Boulevard, both of us having momentarily forgotten I was a newly minted millionaire, then said our exhausted goodnights and went into our respective rooms.

Once alone, I took a long, hot shower, my mind racing as I tried to wash off that extraordinary day. I was exhausted but knew there was no way I could sleep. Finding a T-shirt and shorts, I did fifty push-ups to get my blood flowing again, doing the exercises as I had my entire life, dipping just low enough that the now empty old match safe on the chain around my neck—one of the few things to survive my time in Hollywood—brushed the floor, then holding it there before rising up and starting over again. I liked the way my biceps burned. Even at sixty-three, I was still vain enough to take care of myself.

I unpacked the cassette recorder, unplugged one of the lamps to gain access to the only available outlet in the room, double-checked to make sure the sickly AC was on high, and then verifying the old machine was actually working, I popped in the first tape in the pile. As I pressed play, my finger was shaking, but not for the usual reason.

After a brief pause while the header tape cleared, I heard the sounds of a microphone rumbling over the faint background music of Milly's ever-present record player, bopping a slow and faint version of "Say It Isn't So." A deep exhale was followed by a racking cough; then ice cubes rattled in what was undoubtedly a glass of scotch, followed by the unmistakable click of a Zippo as it flared amid the sizzle of a cigarette lighting before the sharp metallic clunk of its being closed. Another long exhale, more ice cubes, and then the voice. Quiet. Hoarse. It almost didn't sound like Milly at all.

"Where was I . . .?" was all he said, his words slurred; then a chair squeaked, and some pages ruffled. "Right. God, why did I ever decide to do this? Somebody shoot me." His voice caught and he coughed before continuing: "I guess I have to talk about Michael Spencer . . . shit." Another pause as I remembered the name of the guy on all those check stubs. "As a producer at Twentieth, I was nothing but a glorified pimp. With casting and so forth, I was just another peddler in the flesh trade. And Michael Spencer was certainly flesh, all too ready to be pimped as it turned out. The arrangement with Lillian was straining, so when I met Michael at a casting session for *Brewing Storm*—ha! Never thought of that, what a perfect title—*Brewing Storm*." He mused for a moment, then went on, "Anyway, I invited him home for drinks. Lillian took a shine to him, and I excused myself, heading into my study to get good and properly drunk while I knew my wife was being pleasured by her newest young stud. At one point I'd even shut off the record player and listened, answered by the obscene moaning of the two of them, going at it right above my head." At this point he stopped talking because it sounded as if he had spilled his drink.

"Shit," he muttered, then the tape was nothing but static. I punched fast forward, only to get more hissing. Had any of this made it into the typed manuscript? I flipped the tape over and when I hit play, joined a story mid-sentence: ". . . was goddamned proud of my service to my

120

country, but I wondered if I'd be able to hide the truth about my days in the Navy. The studio guys seemed to have it all under control when the story broke in early '43 that I was coming home from the Pacific after being injured in hand-to-hand combat . . ." Here, he chuckled to himself. "Why does every goddamned thing in Hollywood have to be such a goddamned lie? I won an Academy Award, for Christ's sake." This part was especially slurred. "So fuck all of you!" There was the sound of something breaking amid the shattering of glass and electrical sparks, then a click as he shut off the machine. I wondered if it had been his Oscar, hurled in anger and bitterness at the television. It was becoming clear that if I hoped to learn anything about the years since I'd left Hollywood, I was probably going to have to read the manuscript rather than wade through the hours upon hours of ramblings of a drunk, resentful, and very broken man. My eyes were now bleary, my bones aching from exhaustion, and so I dropped onto the shabby little bed and fell asleep within seconds, soon to be dreaming of Carol, who quietly comforted me.

The next morning, I met Tally in a nearby coffee shop for a quick breakfast. She had already called the hospital and been told Lillian's condition was stable and they were feeding her intravenously. Tally was still reeling from the discovery that her mother was alive.

"It doesn't make any sense."

"Not a lot about your parents does, I'm afraid," I said, trying to be consoling. She glanced at her watch as she finished the last of her eggs.

"The doctor told me Mom keeps asking for Dad. And they suspect she's suffering from dementia."

"We should get over there," I said.

"First we have to go by the lawyer's office. He's expecting us."

"Oh," was all I could think to say.

We sat in the sleek lobby of the Century City law offices on the top floor of a glass and granite skyscraper just on the edge of what remained of Fox studios. Through its windows I could see the entire expanse of where the wondrous old 20th back lot had been, now nothing more than an ordered cluster of high-rises and shopping centers. I marveled at how much had changed. After a brief wait, we were ushered in to meet with Milly's attorney, a natty bald fellow named Jerry Mandelberg. As he walked us back to his office, he chatted about that morning's mind-blowing news of Lillian Sinclair's discovery.

"I have to hand it to Milly," he said. "He never once let on. I didn't understand why he suddenly canceled her life insurance shortly before she disappeared—against my advice, I might add—but now I'm thinking he didn't want any charges of fraud if the truth ever came out."

"Is there anything criminal in what they did?" Tally asked. "Assuming they did it together, I mean."

"Good question. Lillian's will left everything to Milly outright—except for the twenty-five grand she bequeathed to you, Tally. So I guess you could make the argument he did benefit from her death. Except everything was still community property and, hell, she didn't even *really* die. And anyway, he's not here to stand trial so . . ."

"What about Lillian? Could they charge her with anything?" I asked.

"Unlikely," Mandelberg said as we entered his corner office and he motioned for us to sit down in the leather chairs opposite his tidy desk. "From what I heard this morning, her mental state is diminished and she's not in the best of health, so . . ."

Tally nodded, but I could tell her mind was still spinning as wildly as mine. Mandelberg took out a thick pocket file and started leafing through the various official documents inside.

"So you're the famous Daniel Root," he said.

"That's me. But hardly famous."

"Around this office, you are. Good thing you showed up for the funeral. We were having a hell of a time finding you. We were just about to hire a private detective."

I shifted in my seat, uncomfortable. "There's been some kind of mistake, right? About the will, I mean."

"Not at all," he replied, then began to explain.

I'd be lying if I said I understood much of the legal and financial jargon he spouted as Tally and I sat across the desk from him. Only that I was to inherit everything Milly had at the time of his death, and there were no provisions for either Tally or her mother. It was further complicated by the fact Lillian wasn't dead, so an argument could be made she was still entitled to her half of the estate, but it had already been legally bequeathed to her husband, albeit under fraudulent circumstances. In truth, he said, Tally was the only person with a right to contest the will on that basis alone.

I watched Tally as she tried to comprehend before she said, "I'm not contesting it."

"Why not?" I asked, surprised.

"Because I'm not," she snapped.

Mandelberg shook his head. "Just as well. Both Lilly and Milly had provisions in their wills specifying if anyone *did* contest their terms, they were to be disinherited anyway. Interesting stuff," he said in summary. He seemed almost gleeful as he considered the ramifications of sorting everything out.

He droned on, speaking of estate taxes and probate court and letters testamentary. He explained he was the executor of the will, and his fees would have to be deducted, within reason, of course, and other things that didn't make a lot of sense to me. Milly had been "risk averse" and kept most of his funds in bonds and treasury bills with only a conservative amount in the stock market, so it shouldn't take longer than sixty to ninety days before I'd get the money and the deed to the house in Hancock Park. As Mandelberg talked, I could only wonder what Milly could possibly have been thinking in the twilight of his life. I had told Tally about the cassette tapes, and we were both anxious to see her mother and get back to the house, hoping to find some answers.

I was reeling and overwhelmed as the lawyer showed us out. Shaking our hands, he said, "Well, if it's any consolation, maybe the heart attack was a blessing."

"What do you mean?" Tally asked.

"Well, it certainly spared him from a more horrible death."

We both looked at him, having not a clue what he was talking about.

Mandelberg hesitated. "You didn't know?"

"Know what?" Tally was more insistent now.

"Oh, I'm so sorry to have to . . . I just assumed he would've told his own daughter." He exhaled, mustering as much compassion as he could before he finally said, "Milly had been diagnosed with AIDS."

FOURTEEN

Milford Langen was once again hung over and in a foul mood as we stood in the sea of passengers in the embarkation line, his demeanor very much in contrast with the festive chatter of the people all around us anticipating going aboard the brand spanking new liner, the SS *United States*. He didn't even bother to take out his cameras. I tried to amuse him with my unflattering passport picture, but he just waved me off, his face inscrutable behind the dark sunglasses he insisted on wearing even though we were inside. Milly was hard enough to read as it was, but his behavior that day made little sense. "C'mon, Mill, what's going on?"

"I don't like crowds," he said, grinding a cigarette out under his shoe even as he lit the next one. He'd been chain-smoking all morning. "I need a bit of dog's hair."

"We'll be aboard soon. I'm sure there's plenty of booze."

"Let's hope so."

All around us, rolling carts bulging with steamer trunks, suitcases, and provisions were being wheeled by stevedores in crisp coveralls. I figured Milly and I must have had a dozen bags packed with everything we'd need for our six-week location scout. The line was inching closer, but our view of the ship was obscured by the roof of the pier where we now stood. All we could see beyond the red, white, and blue gangways with UNITED STATES LINES emblazoned on their sides was a colossal wall of glimmering black steel dotted precisely with portholes. Other liners were in port, but none held the public's attention the way the

United States did. I had read in the morning *Herald Tribune* that when she'd arrived in New York after her sea trials, they'd had to turn away thousands who'd waited in line just to tour the new ship when she had been briefly opened to the hoi polloi at fifty cents a pop. All around us, people were chatting away in anticipation of the maiden voyage, and many were saying she was going to try and take something called the "Blue Riband" away from England's *Queen Mary*. To make conversation, I asked Milly about the Blue Riband, and he snapped at me, "It's the speed record for crossing the Atlantic. Don't you know *anything*?"

"Sorry I asked," was all I could manage in return, hurt and defensive. Still, I was determined not to let Milford Langen or the demons on his shoulders ruin my excitement, and wondered if his mood might be related to his wee-hours shenanigans. At last the line inched forward and we found ourselves inside the little embarkation office where we were checked in by a very courteous middle-aged officer who stamped our tickets, handed both of us a passenger list and a deck plan, then signaled for a porter to usher us toward the gangway. As we climbed to the first-class entrance, we could now hear the lively music of a society orchestra playing somewhere on deck, further enhancing the cheerful atmosphere. I looked out from beneath the gangway's canopy and was amazed by the sight towering overhead. The gargantuan hull was gleaming with fresh paint, a wall of black followed by the brilliant white of the superstructure, and, farther above, the twin rakishly tail-finned red, white, and blue smokestacks. She shimmered in the hot July sun, and I soon realized much of it was caused by reflections from her accents of bright, polished aluminum, like diamonds glittering on a beautiful woman. To hell with Milly's dark mood. I was going to Europe on the maiden voyage of the "the world's fastest and most modern superliner," if you believed all the hype.

We stepped into an elegant lobby on Main Deck, amidships, cool and crisp in its modern design, with patterned linoleum underfoot, and walls crisscrossed by decorative metal strips. To our left, opposite a row of elevators, two long black leather benches flanked either side of the grand staircase with railings that reminded me of the ones back in the house on Windsor. The new ship had a decidedly patriotic flair in its appointments, and I noted the cast bas-reliefs of eagles and flying birds adorning the landings as a fresh-faced and courteous bellboy ushered us up a flight of stairs toward Upper Deck, then rounded a corner to his left and started down the longest hallway I'd ever seen. The ship had an almost military efficiency to it, and later, as I read one of the brochures in our stateroom, I learned she had been built as a troop carrier disguised as a luxury passenger liner, but ever ready to be converted for active duty within days. I hoped she'd never be called for such service, even though I knew the Cold War was very real, and we were still in that mess in Korea. The only positive thing about my ever-quaking hands was they'd made me 4-F and kept me out of it.

We squeezed down the cramped hallway so swarming with people that bellboys toting elaborate bon voyage baskets had to hoist them over their heads to get through. As we finally neared our rooms, I noticed one of the doors was open, the raised numbers on a small plaque on the wall telling us we were to travel in U–87, 89, and 91—the "Duck Suite" to people in the know. For a moment, I thought the ship was sounding its throaty horn in anticipation of setting sail, but soon realized it was the familiar raucous blast of a woman's throaty laugh.

"Oh my god," I said to Milly, ignoring his scowl. "Tallu?"

It was, in fact—already waiting for us in the living room of our quarters with Truman Capote, Margaret Truman, and a crowd worse than the subway car I'd ventured on that morning while waiting for Milly to awaken from his coma.

"Oh dear god," Milly muttered, moving away. I noticed the bellboy loitering there, forgotten, so I jabbed my hand into my pocket and gave him a dollar from my money clip.

"Thank you, sir," he said with a sharp bow before backing out the door, off to the next tip from the unending stream of embarking passengers.

"Surprise!" Tallulah bellowed. "Can't have you going to Europe without a *proper* send-off, darlings!"

Never mind that two nights before I'd already had an incredible send-off with Lillian in the guest room overlooking the elite of Hollywood as they made fools of themselves in the pool far below. Now I was to be sent off across the Atlantic by the cream of New York society in my own private suite. Well, private except for Milly. This Dexter Gaines thing was pretty swell.

A breathless Tallulah came over and kissed our cheeks hello. "Dexter, darling, by *god* I could *devour* you," she said, laughing gaily before her eyes drooped and she deadpanned, "Milford, *you* look as if someone served you a castor oil martini."

"Hello, Tallu," Milly grumbled. "I wasn't expecting guests."

"Therein lies the *surprise*, darling," she drawled.

We squeezed our way through a narrow passage and I noticed the "trunk room" on my left, followed by a bathroom with a shower, and then into the sitting area, simply decorated in the most modern style I'd ever seen. Everything was bright, colorful, and clean in shades of dusty gray, beige and red, with three neat portholes and murals of ducks flying on the walls—thus the name of the suite, I gathered—and the room was festooned with cello-wrapped baskets and bouquets of flowers with happy little cards reading "Bon Voyage Mr. Langen & Mr. Gaines!" though I noticed at least one or two with "Mr. & Mrs. Langen." The crowd had spilled through the double doorway into one of the two spacious bedrooms on either side, and everyone was already drinking and eating canapés while a gray fog of cigarette smoke hung like low clouds overhead. A catchy tune was playing from a speaker in the ceiling, and I noted our rooms were not only air conditioned, but also had a small knob on the wall where you could adjust the volume of the piped-in music. Damn, they'd thought of everything.

Truman Capote shook my hand. "Well," he minced, "I'd trade places with you in a second. Or better yet I'd swap with Milly."

He chortled, and I went along, even though I didn't get the joke. Truman smiled with his tiny mouth and added, "I could stow away in a drawer, you know. I'd fit and promise not to be any bother." We all laughed. Margaret Truman, in her knitted blue dress with matching shoes, a pink hat and gloves, was grinning as if she'd just been elected prom queen as she moved toward the door, pausing to introduce us to a rather frumpy older woman who turned out to be the first lady of the whole country, nursing a bourbon while appearing anxious to get off the boat before it set sail. I grinned. High cotton, indeed.

Waving happily, Margaret shook our hands. "Don't forget you owe me a dance," she said to Milly. He just grimaced a smile. Whatever was going on with him, he soon put on his social mask, downed at least three drinks, and managed to get through the rest of what he later called a "surprise attack," before a bellboy lingered in the open doorway, tapping a little chime in his hand and announcing, "All ashore that's going ashore. All ashore that's going ashore."

A wave of hasty goodbyes followed, and the crowd filed out of our room, leaving discarded champagne glasses, half-eaten hors d'oeuvres, and overflowing ashtrays. Milly surveyed the carnage and announced, "I need to lie down. You can have the other room," he added, nodding to the one already trashed by our well-wishers, then went through the double doorway into the immaculate adjoining bedroom and closed and locked it. I shook my head, then smiled when I saw that my new steamer trunk and other suitcases were already lined against a wall. As I was starting to empty the ashtrays and tidy up, a horrified steward appeared.

"I'll take care of that, sir," he said, getting to work. "I'm Joseph, by the way. I'll be your cabin steward, so if there's anything you need, anything at all, please don't hesitate to press the red button on the wall sconce by the bed."

I smiled, relishing the idea of having the world at my fingertips. "I'm Dexter, and I don't mind helping."

"Please, sir, can't have the passengers cleaning up after themselves. You really should go up on deck for the sail away. And don't forget the safety drill at 3 p.m. sharp. Your life jackets are there on the bed. You're to put them on and report to boat station number seven, which is starboard on Prom Deck just outside the first-class ballroom."

"All right, thanks," I said, excited by the prospect. I grabbed my room key from the bureau, then, spying Milly's bag, retrieved his 16mm Bell & Howell camera. Sure that he'd thank me later, I headed out into the long hallway, hoping I could find my way up above in time. I wandered the long impeccable corridors, delighting in the fresh scent of the new ship mingling with cigarette and cigar smoke, brief hints of perfume and aftershave, and something I'd later find out was a wax used by the crew every single day to keep the superliner spick-and-span.

It wasn't hard to find my way up to the open decks. I merely allowed myself to get sucked into the horde of chattering passengers, many with champagne glasses and bottles in their hands, already celebrating the victorious crossing before it had even begun. I emerged into another exquisite lobby, and as I headed for the double doors leading outside, I was distracted by the gorgeous first-class ballroom, with red barrel-back chairs and a huge round black linoleum dance floor encircled by curved and illuminated glass panels etched with scenes of underwater life. In some ways, being aboard the *United States* was more exciting to me than all the parties in Hollywood combined. I'd never experienced anything like the buzz all around me. Shit. I was a kid from Tyler, Texas, and I was about to see the world in *style*.

Once out on deck, I realized I was on the enclosed promenade with its thick safety glass windows. Spotting a small stairway, I hurried over, lured by the sound of the society orchestra playing a jaunty version of "Anchors Aweigh," the music as appropriate as it was exhilarating.

Emerging on Sun Deck, I saw the place was swarming with passengers tossing streamers and drinking champagne, waving to their loved ones who had crowded onto the dock below to witness this historic occasion. Drawn by the music, I managed to squeeze into a spot along the jam-packed railing and scanned the throng of people on Pier 86, finally spotting Tallulah and Truman far below, but I couldn't catch their attention. Milly was going to regret missing this, so I wound the Bell & Howell, aimed, and pressed the button. It was already whirring, capturing the moment when a steward passed by, handing out more streamers. I tossed a few, watching the gay colors unfurl and trail in lazy spirals down toward the spectators, joining thousands of others in a glorious pastiche of utter, uncontained happiness. An attractive young woman in a crisp aqua-colored dress with a keen little matching hat joined me, and soon we were chatting the way strangers do when they find themselves in the most extraordinary of circumstances.

"Who's seeing you off?" she asked, smiling.

"Oh," I said, gesturing toward the teeming masses below, "everyone in Manhattan."

She laughed, and I grinned.

"Actually, my two friends down there haven't seen me yet."

"Who?" she asked, scanning the crowd.

"See the short guy in the white hat?"

"Where?"

"Third column over? With the woman smoking a cigarette."

She looked, and the strangest expression crossed her face. "You're friends with Tallulah Bankhead and Truman Capote?" she asked, the disbelief evident in her voice.

"Well, I know them."

She laughed. "You do not."

"Swear on my mother's life," I said. Never mind that meant very little to me. Finally, Tallulah caught sight of me, then nudged Truman who squinted upwards until he saw me, too. Capote waved his pocket kerchief while Tallu cupped her gloved hands over her mouth, filled them with air kisses, and blew them my way.

"Wow," my new friend said, impressed, "you were serious."

"I'm Dexter," I grinned, loving the ease with which name-dropping opened new doors for me.

She tried to introduce herself while waving to some people on the open balcony at the end of the pier, but we both jumped out of our skins when she was drowned out by the throaty, deafening roar of the ship's horn, signaling it was exactly twelve noon and time to go. In the ensuing silence, she laughed. "I'm Vera," she said. "My father's one of the vice presidents of the shipping line."

I shook her hand and smiled my most charming, "Pleasure to meet you." A ripple of excitement spread through the passengers like wildfire as a new sensation greeted us. It was a delicate vibration underfoot from the vessel's propellers beginning to turn while the dockworkers below freed the last of the heavy mooring lines. Colorful tugboats were already in place alongside the hull, gently nudging the ship from the dock, their whistles tooting to join in the celebration. The *United States* moved so smoothly that at first it looked as if the pier itself were backing away. Beside us, someone was collecting money for the first day's speed prize, and having no idea what I was doing, I picked a number and dropped five whole bucks into the box overflowing with cash. Vera grinned and did the same.

"Daddy would kill me." She winked.

"I'll protect you." I smiled and winked back.

"Mr. Gibbs!" Vera shouted, spotting someone. "Oh Mr. Gibbs!"

I turned to see a tall, skinny, grizzled and bespectacled man with a well-worn fedora perched incongruously atop his head, clashing with his fresh suit and tie. He gave Vera what looked like a forced, impatient smile.

"Mr. Gibbs, this is Dexter . . ."

"Gaines," I chimed in.

"Hello," Gibbs said, offering a perfunctory handshake before hurrying off, darting down the stairs just aft of us to lean over the very back railing and watch the progress of the ship as it was eased out of the quay and into the Hudson River. In his almost childlike delight, he looked for a moment as if he might flip and fall overboard.

"Don't mind him," Vera said. "He's understandably preoccupied."

"Who was that?" I asked, shouting over the enthusiastic din of the other passengers and waving streamers out of my face.

"Oh, that's W.F. Gibbs," she answered. "He designed the boat."

"Crazy," I said, my turn to be impressed, then helped Vera free herself from a wad of errant streamers now tangled in the tiny veil of her hat.

"Thank you," she said, laughing. "Well, I've lost my friends, but I'm sure I'll see you on the voyage."

"I'm not going anywhere." I grinned.

The liner was now slowing to a stop perpendicular to the pier, as the knife-like prow was nudged by tugboats to point us toward the open sea. I felt the deck beneath my feet rumbling as the propellers stopped before spinning again, changing direction, now pushing us forward and toward Europe as the well-wishers on the pier roared a cheer that sounded like a home run at the World Series. I stayed on deck until we passed the Statue of Liberty, shooting with Milly's camera, immortalizing on 16mm film the flotilla of boats of every kind riding alongside, crammed to the gills with more waving spectators. A ruckus of whistles filled the air, answered by the bellowing of the ship's horn that seemed so powerful it could change the rhythm of our hearts. I even spotted a newsreel crew documenting history in the making. Press photographers were snapping away, and a helicopter flew in low, thundering as it zipped overheard. A squadron of fireboats glided along with us, spraying huge plumes of water in salute, as I noted passengers crowding one another to have their pictures taken beside one of the neat white life rings emblazoned with "SS *United States*, New York," one woman rudely shooing children away so she could strike her own pose.

Once Lady Liberty was out of sight, and the boats began to vanish one by one like the passengers on deck, the ship headed toward the sun-dappled ocean, the city of Manhattan still radiant as it began to recede behind us. The most magnificent thing I'd ever seen. As we passed the Ambrose Lightship, signaling the beginning of our race for the Blue Riband, the *United States* almost leapt out of the water when the captain opened up her engines and set her out to sea. I glanced at the wristwatch Lillian had insisted on buying me for the trip. It was 2:36 p.m. and we were on our way.

Still, even in all that excitement, I couldn't shake the sense I was very much alone.

FIFTEEN

The celebration of the sail away lingered throughout the afternoon with continuous music, drinking, and boisterous laughter. I had explored most of the now crowded public rooms on Promenade Deck, shooting more film with Milly's 16mm and humming the bright melodies implanted in my head by the nonstop orchestra as the ship rumbled, faint and efficient below. Everywhere I turned revealed a new delight, from the first-class cinema aft of the red and black smoking room to the intimate bar off the main ballroom, so modern in its appointments, with walls smartly adorned with Navajo tribal sand paintings. I made a note I'd have to get Milly to come here for a drink.

Finally, growing bored and nagged by loneliness, I returned to our suite, where Joseph had now erased every sign of the bon voyage party, and the rooms were like new. My steamer trunk was open and stored in the closet with my other luggage, so I pulled out a drawer in the bedroom bureau and found everything had been unpacked, refolded, and put away—my suits, shirts, and pants now hanging in a precise row on hefty metal hangers in the closet. This was the life!

Milly's doors were still closed so I glanced at my watch, noting it was almost three. An authoritative recorded voice filled the hallways, announcing that all passengers were to put on their life vests and go to their muster stations for the mandatory safety drill. I picked up the two bright orange jackets from the bed, then knocked on the adjoining doors off the living room. Getting no response, I raised my fist to knock louder when Milly yanked it open and stared at me. He was just out of the shower, wrapped in a plush robe, and had a piece of blood-soaked tissue stuck to his jaw where he'd nicked himself shaving. He squinted at me through the smoke of a Chesterfield clamped in his mouth.

"Dexter!" he blurted, as if seeing me for the first time in years.

I held up the life vests. "We're supposed to put these on and head to our muster station."

"Of course, of course, can't have a leisurely afternoon at sea without being inconvenienced by the shipping line. I'm just getting dressed. The steward brought some food if you're hungry."

He stepped aside and gestured toward a fastidiously set table with silver plate covers and a just-opened bottle of scotch. Milly sure knew how to live.

"Thanks," I said, heading over. Whatever demons had been pestering him that morning now seemed to have vanished. I lifted one of the silver covers to find a plate of tiny sandwiches, and bit into a neat little BLT, the crusts of the bread sliced away, while Milly went into the trunk room where I could hear him rummaging around. A suitcase sat open on a rack near the bed, its contents natty and folded as if for a store window display. Beneath the handle were the gold initials MBL.

"The steward didn't unpack for you?" I asked, making conversation.

"Not yet. Honestly, I've been dead to the world for the past couple of hours. Nothing like the movement of a ship to rock you to sleep."

True, there was something soothing about the deck rising and falling ever so gently underfoot.

"So what's the 'B' stand for, anyway?" I asked as I took another bite.

"Excuse me?"

"Your monogram," I answered, trying not to sound like I was talking with my mouth full.

"What do you think?" he responded with a playful lilt in his voice.

"I don't know . . . Bart? Brian? Beauregard?"

Milly laughed as he emerged in a pale blue shirt, already tucked neatly into his gabardine trousers. He carried his shoes and went to the little suitcase to retrieve a pair of argyle socks, then plopped down on the foot of the bed and started to put them on. There was no denying the man had style.

"Bacchus?" I asked, noting the highball glass of gold-tinted ice cubes recently drained of scotch.

He laughed again, his mood having lightened. "No, dear boy, I'm afraid I was saddled with my dear mother's maiden name . . . Barnett."

"Milford Barnett Langen?"

"At your service," he said, tying his laces with a snap. He got up and joined me by the table, taking a bite of a sandwich and washing it down with more scotch.

"Maybe I'll start calling you Barney."

"At your own peril," he said, and I think he meant it. Still, it made me laugh. Milly returned to his suitcase, retrieved a screenplay, and tossed it to me.

"I brought you some reading material, for when you're sitting out on deck."

I looked at the title page.

"*The Trojan War*?"

"This draft is still a bit rough around the edges," he said, stamping out his cigarette in a little ashtray with the shipping line's spread-eagle logo on the bottom. I made a mental note to snag one before we disembarked in Le Havre. "I had to switch writers thanks to Joe McCarthy and his goons, so it still needs work, but be sure to keep an eye on the part of Achilles. I'm going to put you up for it."

"Achilles? He dies, doesn't he?"

"He's a hero, Dex, with one fatal vulnerability," Milly said, catching my eye. "What? You thought you'd get the role of Paris? The only way you'll be considered for that is if you get Gifford."

"When will we know?"

"Look at you," Milly said, smiling. "So ambitious. We're back in LA in six weeks. I'm sure they'll finalize casting for *Titanic* by then. Darryl loved your screen test, by the way. He's just nervous we might need more of a name."

"All right," I said, "I'll read it." Then, always feeling awkward in these situations where Milly was handing things to me: "And . . . thanks."

"Don't mention it. Now let's get this dreadful ordeal over with so we can go bribe the *maître d* and the deck steward."

"Bribe them?" I asked, helping him into his life jacket.

"To ensure we have the *best* accommodations for the crossing, of course," he replied, turning now to assist me with my vest, his worldliness impressing me. "You've got a whistle on yours. I'll stick close to you if we end up in the drink."

"I'm already in the drink. I've had a gallon of champagne since we got onboard. You should've been there for the sail away, Mill," I said. "It was *killer*."

"I apologize for my mood earlier," he said, opening the stateroom door and allowing me to pass. I was starting up the hallway when I realized he wasn't behind me. After a moment, he emerged with his Argus camera. "In case we want a few snapshots in these ridiculous get-ups."

As he locked the door and followed me, I said, "Step lively there, Barney."

"You better hope these jackets work, kiddo, because you keep that up, you're going for a swim," he said with a friendly chuckle.

I smiled at his newfound charm and felt as if I had just met the man with whom Lillian Sinclair had fallen so madly in love.

By the time we returned to our suite from dinner in the first-class dining room, my head was throbbing from even more champagne. First night out was semiformal as Milly had explained, so I obeyed without protest while he helped me choose my wardrobe for the evening—the new gray jacket with tiny silver flecks that Lillian had picked out at a high-end men's boutique on Wilshire in the Miracle Mile district, along with light blue trousers, and a steel-colored tie. Milly delighted in selecting everything from my pocket square to my socks and cuff links. As we prepared to leave for dinner, he plucked a rose from the arrangement of flowers in a tall vase on the bureau, snapping it off between his fingers and inserting it into the buttonhole on my lapel.

"Now you look like a proper gentleman," he said, beaming. "Let's go make some ladies' hearts flutter." Of course, I thought of Lillian, with a pang of guilt.

We dined at a table beneath the immense wall sculpture soaring up the entire two-story height of the swanky red and white room. At our table were my new shipboard friend Vera and her father, Major Clarence T. Donneville, vice president of operations for the United States Lines. Margaret Truman was there, too, with her charming friend Drucie Snyder whose father was Secretary of the Treasury, and a fascinating young woman who introduced herself as one of the artists who had helped adorn this magical ship. I had never seen Milly so relaxed, or so in command, as he regaled these East Coast people with semi-torrid tales of life in Hollywood, drawing gales of naughty laughter. The women were enraptured, batting their eyelashes as they hung on his every word. Sure, we had the president of the whole country's daughter at our table along with other VIPs, but Hollywood was an ace Milly loved to play. I relished being charming and sophisticated by association in my role as Milford Langen's dressed-to-the-nines traveling companion. He popped his cigarette case open, offered them around, and soon everyone was smoking as the conversation took more and more entertaining turns. I was in awe of Milly's social charms, and I blushed as he extolled how I was going to be the next Robert Wagner, eliciting squeals of delight from our female company.

The ship's orchestra was playing at the other end of the dining room, in a little balcony overlooking the sea of pristine white linen-covered tables with their elegant, embossed pattern of waves, all crowded with the most smartly dressed people I'd ever seen, and that includes the Mocambo, Ciro's, and the Grove, as well as all the other now second-rate Hollywood nightclubs combined. Our team of waiters made sure our glasses were always full, our ashtrays clean, and plate after plate continued to arrive with some of the best food in the world. I kept staring at the sculpture towering overhead, and when Drucie asked what I found so interesting, I said I wasn't sure, just that there was something deeply sensual about the abstract woman with her arms reaching skyward.

"You like it?" someone asked.

"I do," I replied. "Very much."

I didn't know it but I'd just hit a home run, as the young artist at our table turned out to be Gwen Lux, who had created the masterpiece. She laughed, explaining it was called "Expressions of Freedom," and saying my compliment made it worth all the aggravation, complaining about the difficulty of working in foam-glass because Mr. Gibbs had insisted everything, including the artwork, be not only lightweight, but fireproof as well. Major Donneville boasted that the construction of all the ship's components, from the carpeting to the navigation equipment, had challenged their builders and artisans in service of Gibbs' obsessive specifications.

Milly frowned. "Would it really have killed him to use a little bit of wood?" he asked of no one in particular. "The English ships are so much cozier."

The *United States* was moving with a purpose now, the deck underfoot rising and falling almost imperceptibly and causing the faintest tinkling of glassware. I knew I'd sleep well once I crawled into bed.

"Had a good day, have you?" Milly asked, as he rewound the film in his Argus camera, lingering in my bedroom doorway.

"Amazing," I answered, drunk and happy.

"Well, get some rest," he said. "Tomorrow we'll paint the boat red."

"All right." I grinned stupidly as I began to empty my pockets onto the bureau. My money clip, wristwatch, some change, and then the matchbooks and swizzle sticks I'd taken from the first class dining room, along with the menu and the little flags from the centerpiece.

"You're collecting souvenirs?" He seemed almost charmed by the notion.

"I just want to be able to prove this really happened," I said, my head swimming.

"Trust me, Dex, it's all impossibly real," he said, then stood with his hand on the doorknob, looking at me. The faintest glimmer of sadness crossed his face before he said a simple, "Good night."

After he'd gone into his room, I undressed, hanging my jacket and trousers and making sure my tie and pocket scarf wouldn't get wrinkled. My mouth was dry from all the champagne and scotch, further irritated by my having tried to keep pace with everyone's smoking, and I decided what I really wanted was a steaming shower before crawling between the unused sheets on the bed with its butterfly-patterned cover. I hopped on one foot as I took off my socks and underwear, then noticed the sensuous deep blue glow of the twin portholes. I was drawn to them and looked out at the rolling gentle ocean as it glided past, reflecting the sliver of moon hanging motionless on the horizon, almost as if we weren't really moving at all. Standing there naked in the cool, dark room, watching the water, I realized I hadn't had any pot for the entire day. I'd been too distracted. I held my hands up and smiled. They were hardly shaking now, barely so much as a quiver.

I took as hot a shower as I could stand, and as I rinsed the shampoo from my hair, I thought I caught a flash of someone moving outside the open bathroom door, followed by the soft click of a lock catching.

"Hello?" I called, wondering if the steward had wandered in, unaware I was there.

But the only answer was the relentless throbbing of the mighty ship's engines far below.

"Wake up, firecracker." It was Milly, jostling me.

"What?" I croaked, bleary-eyed and still half asleep.

"It's the Fourth of July, we're on a race into history, and we don't want to waste a minute of it." He was already dressed in casual slacks and short-sleeved shirt, impeccable as always, with a bright blue ascot and straw fedora, his 16mm camera hanging around his neck. He was sitting on the edge of my bed, looking down at me, grinning.

"Have we met?" I asked, sitting up, blinking awake.

Milly laughed. "It's the sea air. Now c'mon."

I looked at my wristwatch on the nightstand. "Uh, Mill? It's four-thirty in the morning."

"Six," he corrected. "Perhaps you forgot to set your watch an hour and a half ahead as the steward instructed? I heard a rumor if the ship keeps up her current speed, we'll have to set them ahead even more tonight. Imagine!"

"Oh, yeah," I grumbled, throwing back the covers and getting out of bed, waddling unsteadily toward the bathroom in nothing but my boxers as the floor rocked underfoot. Milly remained seated on the bed as he lit a cigarette, then toyed with his 16mm camera.

Once out on deck, he insisted we take a stroll before breakfast. The sun was still low in the sky, casting yellow light over everything, glistening off those magnificent red smokestacks while the sea hissed past us far below. Very few people were up this early, most likely sleeping off yesterday's celebration, so we had the entire deck pretty much to ourselves save for a young tipsy couple still giggling in their evening clothes, and a chipper steward already untying the deck chairs with their bright crimson webbing, lining them up with military precision in anticipation of a beautiful day. Milly insisted I pose with one of the life rings while he snapped away with his still and movie cameras, the entire expanse of the Atlantic clear to the horizon behind me.

"You're acting like a goddamned tourist," I teased.

"I *am* a goddamned tourist! Let's get some coffee."

"And breakfast," I added. "Please."

"Whatever your heart desires."

He put his arm around my shoulder and gave it a squeeze as we headed down to the dining room and the incredible day ahead.

Much of the trip remains only in vivid flashes of memory: a movie montage of endless meals, alcohol, cigarettes, and the ever-present babble about the day's record-breaking speed as we hurtled our way toward destiny.

On Saturday, our second full day out, Milly suggested we spend the afternoon in the ship's indoor pool down on C Deck. I wanted to see *The Man in the White Suit* with Alec Guinness first, so we sat in the dark watching the droll English comedy about a man who invents a white fabric impervious to wear and staining. It was hard to concentrate on the film with Milly's incessant whispered commentary, but we both enjoyed the picture nonetheless. Later, as I swam in the pool in my new black plaid trunks, braced by the cool salt water, I thought of our nights in the Urban Idyll, and missed Lilly terribly, while Milly sat at a white metal table nearby, watching. He thanked a steward for two waxed paper cups of champagne before signaling me to join him. I did, and we sipped the bubbly and watched the handful of other bathers splashing below. Then Milly chuckled, noticing something on the dark blue wall that rose behind the pool adorned with decorative nautical signal flags.

"What's funny?" I asked, downing the last of my champagne.

"Those signal flags," he mused, "do you know what they spell out?"

"Not a clue. Do you?" I asked, more than a little surprised.

"I was a signal man for the Navy during the war. They say 'Come On In the Water's Fine.'"

He had never spoken of his stint in the military, but I once read in a fan rag how he'd been injured while serving on a destroyer in the Pacific, cutting his career short and bringing him back to Hollywood before war's end, returning to his Svengali-like mentoring of Lillian's soon-to-be red-hot career.

"You were wounded, right? What was that like?"

He looked away, remembering. "Horrible. Ghastly, really. We'd docked at a small base on the tiniest island—I don't even recall the name—and that night, the Japanese caught us off guard with a surprise attack, not unlike Tallu's little bon voyage party." He chuckled sadly. "Only much, much worse."

He fell silent for a moment, and I didn't press until he continued, "I killed a Japanese soldier with my bare hands. His plane had been shot down by our anti-aircraft boys, and he'd parachuted out, landing on the beach. He came charging toward us, drawing a knife." Now he pointed to the scar in his abdomen I had noticed before. "Got me right here, the bastard, before I snapped his neck. I nearly bled to death, then got a particularly nasty infection so they had to send me home. Hail the conquering hero and all that." His mood turned somber as he added, "Not that my father saw it that way."

"Your father?" I asked, not knowing what else to say.

"Sergeant in the United States Army. He said I was a weakling for letting myself get injured in the first place. But god damn it, I *fought* for my country."

Sitting there beside the pool, staring into the bottom of his now empty cup, he exuded the air of a man still bitter over having his patriotic service cut short.

"C'mon, let's go spend some time on deck," I said, trying to lighten the mood.

"Excellent suggestion. I'm afraid this bubbly has gone flat."

Lounging on the open deck in the afternoon had become a favorite of our shipboard activities, second only to the sumptuous dinner parties and the endless miles of movies unspooling in the cinema. Relaxing while stewards tucked us into steamer rugs, bringing us hot bouillon in the morning, drinks after noon, and whatever else we happened to require in between.

I went up before Milly, stopping only to purchase a couple of five-by-seven black-and-whites taken at our first night dinner by the ship's photographer, while Milly insisted he needed a catnap in his room. So I sat beneath the canopy of blue sky, skimming most of *Trojan War*, looking for scenes that included Achilles, constantly distracted by the nonstop glorious sight of the ocean rippling past. It was a small but decent part, and I'd get to do some heroics like horseback riding and archery. The role also required I spend most of the two hours running time in nothing but a sort of loincloth, which meant I'd better stop gorging myself on the ship's endless tidal wave of food.

At last, Milly joined me, dropping onto the reserved deck chair next to mine overlooking the fantail and the endless white chop of the ship's wake, stretching all the way to the horizon because we were going so fast.

I swear it would've been a gas to water ski behind that boat. Milly wiped his nose with his handkerchief and complained the sea air was affecting his sinuses. Still, he remained upbeat, something I'd later refer to as Dr. Hollywood to his surlier Mr. Hyde. When I pointed out a line of description about my character and asked him what Achilles' quivering neck was all about, he burst into an uproarious laugh at my ignorance.

"The quiver around your neck is the thing that holds your arrows," he said, still chuckling. "And do me a favor, kiddo. I see you're making the classic actor's mistake. You're reading the script as 'bullshit bullshit my part.' Now go back to 'fade in' and read the whole goddamned thing. You love movies, so I'd like to get your thoughts for the next round of notes with the writer."

I couldn't believe Milford Barnett Langen was actually asking for my input on the project he considered most near and dear to his heart. I was both honored and touched. For the first time in my life, I felt my opinion mattered and I was somehow important. Milly, of course, seemed to have no idea how much this simple gesture really meant to me. After a lifetime of being told I was a "worthless shit" by my parents, to the point of having it beaten into me by my father's fists, I was almost moved to tears.

On the first full sea day, as passengers noisily celebrated the Fourth of July throughout the ship, I'd gone to the cinema to watch *Lovely to Look At* with Howard Keel and Kathryn Grayson, wondering if I'd ever get to be in a musical and how close the movie's back lot depiction of Paris would be to the real thing, when Milly appeared next to me. "Thought I'd find you here."

"Shhhh."

He lowered his voice. "I've booked some time in the ship's gymnasium. Can't be all play, you know." Lucky for me, the final credits had just started to roll. Milly glanced at the screen and sniffed. "A Metro Picture? Christ. C'mon."

Once in the gym on B Deck, Milly stripped to his white athletic shirt. I noted the dog tags and tiny key dangling just above the small tuft of hair in the middle of his chest and was still intrigued by what it might unlock. Instructing me to follow suit, which I did even though I wasn't wearing an undershirt, he then tossed me a heavy mesh mask and a foil.

"If you're going to be Achilles, you need to know how to handle a blade," he said.

"You fence?" I asked, surprised.

"I'll have you know I was a bit of a champion when I was in school."

"Then go easy on me."

"Don't worry."

He taught me the proper stance, putting a hand in the small of my naked back as he lifted my arms into the right position. "See, it's like floating . . ."

Turns out Milly was quite a good fencer, and even though he was teaching me, he was a tough taskmaster. With a blade in his hand, his face unreadable behind the screen of his protective hood, he barked orders as he critiqued and criticized my every move until I was getting frustrated.

"No, no, no," he snapped. "You lunge as you thrust if you hope to make a kill."

"Jesus, Mill," I said, exhausted, "I'm sorry. My damn hands are shaking again."

"You haven't been taking your 'medicine,' have you?"

"Not since we got on the boat," I answered.

"All right then, we'll call it a day and pick this up tomorrow. Run along and get yourself cleaned up for dinner. It's formal, so wear the white dinner jacket."

"Okay," I said, relieved this ordeal was over. Back in our suite, I cracked open the porthole and finally toked up, submerging myself into a relieving high before showering off the sweat still clinging to my flesh. While soaping up in the steaming water, I noticed a long raised welt on my left side where Milly had tagged me with his foil.

Our last day out was Sunday, and the weather was taking a gradual turn for the worse. Passengers were gossiping about how a gale or sudden fog might compromise our race for the Blue Riband. The sea was choppy with roiling swells as the wind whipped their crests into cloud-like spray that at times resembled vaporous sea horses racing alongside the SS *United States* in some mad frenzy. The ferocious squall then dispersed them, soaring up to whistle and moan through the steel rigging. The movement looked almost lazy, except for the way it was battering the ship, making her pitch and nearly throwing me into the empty bathtub as I tried to shave, a towel wrapped around my waist. Despite the liner's rolling, a near-giddy Milly appeared, bracing himself on either side of the bathroom door.

"Step it up. We should go out on deck and take some pictures."

"Are you crazy? There's a storm coming," I said, making sure I got the last little bit of stubble above my birthmark. I'd taken to covering it with makeup while on the crossing, which Milly hadn't noticed, and I wouldn't have dared let him catch me doing it.

"Then we'd best hurry. I'll grab the right wardrobe for you."

I frowned, doubting this plan, took another deep puff of the cigarette clenched between my teeth as I wiped my face with a washcloth to remove any remnants of shaving soap. Even over the rumbling of the ship, I could hear the metal hangers scraping sharply in the closet, then the drawers being yanked open one by one.

I came out into the stateroom where he had two outfits laid out on the bed like flat silhouettes of two men. One was more like Milly himself, patterned shirt and tailored trousers, the other, white dungarees and a striped sweater that looked almost like a sailor's. After a moment, with his chin in his fingers as he eeny-meany-miney-moed with his eyes between the two, he held a pair of my folded boxers over his shoulder with pointed nonchalance, never once looking at me. "And put these on," was all he'd said, still deciding about the rest of the outfit.

I hesitated. Milly shook the underwear with a hint of impatience, his eyes still darting between the two flat men on the bed. What the hell was going on? Finally, I took them from him and went into the bathroom. "Make up your mind," I shouted over the noise of the storm as I pulled on the shorts with my towel still in place, a trick I'd learned at the public pool back home. "I'm hungry."

"Done!" he called back. I wrapped the damp towel around my shoulders, covering my chest, as I returned to the room. He'd chosen the sailor outfit. "For the pictures," he said. "Lillian will love it!"

The mention of his wife, in that context, caused me to flinch.

"What?" he asked. "You know she will."

"All right, sure . . ." I said. "Okay."

I wanted to take the clothes into the bathroom to dress, but thought Milly might find it strange, which it might have been for all I knew. Frozen in indecision, I forced a smile. Finally, as if sensing my discomfort, Milly feigned remembering something. "I need to get the filters for the 16mm. Be right back."

He went into the adjoining room for maybe twenty seconds tops, but when he came back, I was already notching my belt. I even had my socks on.

Milly beamed. "Perfect!"

Milly was insane to have taken us out on deck. It was wet, and the morning's rising swells were just a preview of the full-blown gale speeding our way. As I understood it, the *United States* was doing about forty land miles per hour, creating a ferocious contest, the consequence to the human race being a ship bobbing like a toy in a bathtub, but hell-bent on defeating nature and winning the Blue Riband. Milly slipped on the wet deck and landed hard, nearly dropping his cameras. The small leather pouch of filters he'd gone to retrieve in our stateroom fell from his hand and bounced overboard before I could catch it.

I was holding onto the railing while Milly laughed and climbed to his feet. "Get *this* on a soundstage. This ain't a couple of grips rocking a platform while the effects guy throws a bucket of water on you!" He was turning around now in a slow circle, his arms outstretched like a mad man, his face soaked with spray and spittle. "This is reality, *right here!*" he screamed. His 16mm and still cameras were banging into each other on their straps around his neck, and I wondered briefly if they'd be damaged by the water.

"Uh . . . Mill," I said, "let's go inside. This is nuts."

"And miss this?" he shouted back at me as I clung to the railing by wrapping my elbows around it, causing my back to arch and my pelvis to extend toward him.

"That's it!" he cried. "That's the shot, right—"

I think he was going to say "right there," but just as he raised his camera to his eye, a ping-pong table caught by a violent updraft slammed into him, knocking him flat on his back as it sailed past, scattering errant deck chairs that had come loose from their moorings, then bouncing off the fantail and spinning end over end as it flipped and dinged the very aft railing before vanishing into the sea, no doubt to be sucked under and shredded by the churning propellers.

"Milly!" I screamed, rushing to him on the pitching deck. We got splashed again by another wave, and I wanted it to be the effects guy with a bucket, but as Milly had so vividly pointed out, this was real. I put a hand behind his neck, checking for signs of life, wondering if I'd have to carry him back inside, and whether or not I was even capable.

"Holy shit!" he said to my relief. "Did you see that?"

"Yeah, yeah, are you okay?"

He didn't move, lying there on the wet deck before raising himself up on his elbows as I knelt over him. Rivulets of water poured down his face, and the spray was now a heavy rain, drenching us both so that my striped sweater clung to me like brightly tattooed flesh.

"You were going to save my life, weren't you?" he asked, the most vulnerable I'd ever seen him.

"Well, yeah but—are you sure you're okay? That thing really beaned you."

"I'm fine, dear boy," he said with a fond smile. "Now let's get back inside before Lillian receives a very sad telegram. I must be out of my mind!"

"Let me help you up," I said, doing so.

"I've always depended on the kindness of strangers," Milly almost whispered. "Tennessee wrote that."

I laughed. "I know. Now c'mon before we get killed. Can you walk?" I asked, concerned.

"I'm doing so, aren't I?"

It wasn't Dr. Hollywood who joined me for lunch. The dining room was sparsely populated due to a wave of seasickness that had many passengers confined to their beds or kneeling with their heads in their toilets, begging God to let them die. Our plates were sliding around so the waiters made a fuss of misting the tablecloth and raising the concealed lip at its edges to keep the fine crockery and glassware from flying off.

"Did you use my movie camera?" he snapped so fiercely under his breath that I flinched.

"Well, yeah ... first day out, for the sail away. I thought you'd want to see it even though you were—"

"*Don't ever touch my cameras,*" he hissed, then collected himself as the waiters brought his poached salmon and a glass of white wine. He hadn't even ordered; they just somehow knew. He forced a tight, insincere smile as one of them snapped a fresh napkin into his lap, then leveled crazy eyes at me as soon as the servers were gone.

"Okay. I'm sorry, I just thought—"

"Don't," he said, ending the conversation.

Neither of us spoke another word through the main course, dessert and coffee. I was hurt and confused, wondering what had really set him off. But Milly wasn't forthcoming. At one point, the jovial ship's photographer stepped up to our table to frame yet another souvenir shot, but Milly waved him away, annoyed.

"There's another musical playing in the cinema," I said, uncomfortable and anxious to leave. "I'm gonna try and catch it."

Milly nodded, not even bothering to look me in the eye. I heard him asking the waiter for a scotch and milk on the rocks as I left him there.

I came in during the second reel of *She's Working Her Way Through*

College, another mindless musical, this one with Ronald Reagan and Virginia Mayo. I stayed all afternoon, watching the film twice, but to this day, I couldn't tell you a thing about it. Milly had ruined our short days of enchanted fun with a verbal smack that stung me far deeper than I knew it should, bringing with it the familiar slap of humiliation I'd known since childhood. Finally, I went down to our suite to change for dinner. The double doorway into Milly's bedroom was closed, and I certainly didn't dare to knock.

I showered and put on my formalwear and as I started out, I hesitated, then opened a porthole and smoked an entire joint.

Milly didn't show up for dinner, a gala affair where everyone wore festive paper hats. I made weak excuses for his absence to Gwen Lux, the only other dining companion hearty enough to brave the storm. We had a very forced, polite conversation throughout the five courses. Then I excused myself and went up to the enclosed promenade, walking forward through the smoking room now abuzz with passengers. I sat for a lonely hour sipping scotch in the Navajo Lounge while a gorgeous and intoxicated woman bought me drinks only to be insulted when I declined to visit her stateroom. Finally, I wandered into the brilliant red and gray sophistication of the first-class ballroom where the orchestra was kicking and passengers crammed the dance floor in anticipation of the ship's taking the speed record sometime before dawn. The crowd tossed red, white, and blue balloons overhead, tapping them when they got too near. I dodged one as I spotted Vera, Drucie, and Margaret clustered around a small table. They were chatting merrily, sipping their cocktails through tiny straws.

"Ladies," I said, channeling my best Cary Grant, "we missed you at dinner."

"We went to the private dining room," Drucie explained, gushing.

"Oo, the movie star." Margaret clamped her hands together in delight.

"Not yet," I said, popping open my cigarette case. "You mind?"

"Heavens, no."

"Please, go ahead."

"I'll have one."

After offering smokes all around and lighting them to bashful giggles before igniting my own, I put the case away in my breast pocket, for once in control and using every trick my mentors had taught me. Plucking an unopened bottle of champagne from the adjacent silver ice bucket, I tossed a clean napkin over the spout and proceeded to ease out the cork, just as Milly had instructed, then refilled the ladies' glasses. I was grateful the pre-dinner marijuana had steadied my hands.

"So," Margaret bubbled, "what's it like in Hollywood?"

"About like you'd guess," I said, flashing my best smile.

"I have a cousin who wants to be in pictures," Drucie said. "Any advice I can pass along?"

"Take Fountain," I said, smiling with my mouth open.

So were theirs as it turned out. Of course they wouldn't get the joke. In the ensuing awkwardness, I realized Milly was standing nearby, wearing an impeccable tailored tuxedo, a pink rose in his lapel, his face unreadable. My cheeks flushed as it dawned on me he had no doubt witnessed my attempts to ape his sophistication. When I looked at him and started to speak, he shifted his eyes away from me and grinned.

"Miss Truman, I believe I owe you a dance."

Margaret looked at her friends, excited. "Somebody take pictures!"

Vera and Drucie laughed gaily as Milly almost yanked the president's daughter onto the teeming floor. Just his luck, the band was ending their number to polite applause before a brief rustling of sheet music preceded the dramatic, cascading string introduction of a full-blown tango. Now bear in mind Lillian had schooled me in most ballroom dances, but the tango is a whole other ball of wax. As the melody vamped in, Milly seized upon it, snapping Margaret Truman's pelvis into his own to punctuate the sensual, staccato beat. She gave a nervous laugh through her shock as he twirled her by lifting her off the floor, then spun on his own heels so smoothly he might have been on a turntable. And the whole time, even as he twisted the Plain Jane around into a dip so deep her head seemed to kiss the floor, his eyes remained on me. I accepted his silent challenge, refusing to show any fear of whatever was really going on.

"C'mon," I said, snatching a startled Vera's hand from the table and leading her toward the floor, two couples over from Milly.

"Oh, I don't know if—" Vera didn't get a chance to finish her sentence. I'd already spun her around. It might have been a waltz move, but it worked, and she laughed uneasily. My eyes remained locked with Milly's.

"Step step back swirl aaaaand . . . dip," Lillian had said as we'd danced on the huge marble floor of the grand entryway to music from Milly's precious hi-fi. She'd laughed as she demonstrated how to spin and dip her, to snap our faces back into eye contact after each move. I missed her, but now called upon every trick she'd taught me in my foolish determination to prove I was Milford Langen's equal.

One hand on Vera's hip, the other clasping her wrist, I marched her backwards across the floor in perfect time to the flamboyant music, parting the sea of dancers who were stopping to watch in awe. A few even applauded as a sudden movement caught my eye. It was Milly, now giving Valentino a run for his money, flinging Margaret Truman out with a snap, then tugging her back toward him so she was coiled in his arms before he dipped her again, then miraculously slid her on her back through his legs. She giggled and cooed as he pulled her upright, repeating his pelvis snap move. He was so goddamned suave, so goddamned handsome, so goddamned sure of himself, that I refused to be outdone. I whirled Vera away from me before spinning her back and grabbing under her knee, yanking upward so her leg was now wrapped around my waist in a scandalously coital pose. She gasped in shock, as did many of the spectators. Milly and I continued our stare down throughout, and something in his eyes unnerved me and made my stomach flutter.

The number climaxed as we both dipped our partners low to the floor for the grand finale. I think Margaret Truman had fainted, as she swooned almost lifeless in Milly's arms. Vera was more polite but uncomfortable, hiding her mortification behind a forced smile. Milly and I just held each other's gaze, past the point neither was willing to break. Until, that is, I had to.

"Thank you, Vera," I said, kissing her hand as the orchestra notched it up with a rumba. I think she was all too happy to collect Margaret and lead her away, tossing pleasantries over their shoulders like confetti at a parade. The surprised onlookers began to retake the floor around us.

"Can I talk to you?" I said to Milly, now alone save for the jostling of happy dancers all around us, balloons still bouncing overhead, tapped from table to table. One landed atop his head before lazily rising as if yawning, off to find another port in the storm.

"Sure," he said with a shrug.

The roar of excited conversation, all about breaking the speed record unless the gale forced us to slow down, competed in volume with the thundering of the ship as it sliced through the relentless storm. Without a word, Milly led me out of the packed ballroom, past the jammed Navajo Lounge, and into a foyer where we descended two flights of steps to Main Deck, then proceeded down the port side corridor. Just as I was thinking he'd lost his way in the labyrinthine hallways but was too proud to admit it, he stepped into a waiting elevator. I didn't dare ask where we were going as he glowered at the control panel—seemingly annoyed that the operator was off duty—then jabbed the button for B Deck.

"Look, Milly . . ." I started, but he cut me off as we descended.

"Not yet."

The gymnasium was closed but unlocked, so after a quick glance around, Milly went inside. I followed him into the semidarkness as he shut the door behind us. The now deeper, steady rumbling of the powerful engines purred all around as the floor rolled beneath our feet.

"What's going on?" I asked, my voice echoing off the modern exercise equipment.

He looked at me, then went over to the fencing paraphernalia and picked up a foil, slicing it through the air with a loud hiss as he tested it. "Let's be gentlemen, shall we?" he asked, the first time he'd slurred his words. I then realized Milly was three sheets to the wind. It's a miracle he hadn't cracked the first daughter's skull on the dance floor.

"Forget it. Let's talk when you're sober," I said, starting to leave.

"You sound like my wife!" he roared. "Of course, why wouldn't you? You spend every minute of every day with her, don't you?"

"Milly . . ."

"And most of that time is spent *fucking* her, right?"

I froze, my heart now pulsing in my ears.

"At least you're showing me the decency of not denying it."

"Please, let's talk about it later," was all I could manage as I made another move for the door.

"Now!" he yelled as I grabbed the handle. The bell guard of the foil he threw at me cracked into my head so hard I saw a spray of stars before it clattered to the floor. Enraged, I turned to face him, standing there, his arm still outstretched, his breathing ragged.

"Be a man," he croaked in a whisper.

I lost it, scooping up the sword and lunging at him. He dodged backward, recovered his balance like a cat, then came at me, flailing madly, his foil whipping the air like an airplane propeller out of control. It was all I could do to fend him off so he wouldn't slice my face.

"You like fucking her, don't you?" he pressed, shouting over the clashing of our foils before stepping back to catch his breath.

"Milly, I'm sorry, I'm . . . I don't know what to say to you."

He screamed and lunged at me again, knocking the blade from my hand before whipping my arm so hard he sliced through the new tuxedo jacket and shirt. I cried out in pain, and after a moment, blood began to seep through. He staggered back, the bell guard of his foil clanging on the floor as it slipped from his grasp, both of us now dazed from our shocking skirmish.

"You'd better have the ship's doctor take a look at that," he said as he left me, more confused than ever.

I wandered through the throng of celebrating passengers, trying to stay up until I figured Milly would be passed out in bed, and ignoring the stares drawn by my bloody sleeve. We were set to break the speed record that night, but I didn't care. I couldn't think clearly, not with all the noise and laughter. Finally, around four-thirty in the morning, I made my way back to the dark and quiet Duck Suite. There was no sound from Milly's room, and I couldn't tell if he was inside.

The ship was moving at top speed as I started to undress, making it difficult to stand. I tossed my destroyed evening wear onto the back of a chair, my thoughts ping-ponging about things more important than winning the Blue Riband. My career was over before it had begun. Milly would ruin me. He'd brought me along on this trip to torment and humiliate his wife's lover. I examined the slash in my arm where he'd attacked me, grateful to see the bleeding had stopped despite the lingering, stinging pain.

I jumped as I heard him return to his cabin, then the sound of something crashing before he threw the double doors wide and stalked toward me through the wildly swaying living room. Only he didn't say anything, just stopped and stood there, hands on his hips, looking helpless. Tears shimmered under his eyes.

"God damn it," he said in a whisper.

To give him his privacy, I turned back to the mirror and resumed trying to remove my cuff links, but my fingers were shaking so badly I couldn't get hold of the clasp. After a frustrating moment, I gave up, shoving them down.

That's when Milly approached behind me.

"Let me," he said.

Startled by the unexpected tenderness in his voice, I was motionless for only a moment before I turned to him. He was close now, so close I could smell the scotch and cigarettes as he removed one cuff link, then the other, and I saw his hands were trembling, too. His upper lip bore traces of a white powder, and I now understood much of his erratic behavior since we'd left Los Angeles.

"I'm sorry, Milly," I said, nothing else to add.

"You should be," he answered, then ripped my tuxedo shirt open, the studs spraying the room like gunfire, one nicking the mirror over the bureau. I pulled away, but he grabbed me, tearing the fabric. He was stronger than I could have imagined, soon overpowering me as he pinned my arms tight to my sides. Thing is, I knew I could have kicked his ass if I'd wanted to, but I didn't.

By the time he had my cummerbund off and his hand down my pants, we were kissing like mad. I was surprised he was as good a kisser as his wife, but right then, my pot- and alcohol-soaked brain was blurring them into one and the same. He stripped me naked, then took me as I bent over the bed, and my cry was drowned by the rocking of the ship and the faint sounds of celebration on the decks up above where we could hear the rhythmic thundering of feet on the Promenade Deck in what I would later learn was a conga line dancing up to the bridge. In the distance, the orchestra had launched into the National Anthem as we made history that night. The ship was breaking the speed record, and Milly right along with it. He finished almost immediately, convulsing as he called out "Oh god, oh god," and then, in a coarse, almost inaudible whisper, "*Lillian!*"

A prayer of forgiveness.

He collapsed. The room was now still enough I could hear the music piped in through the little speaker in the ceiling, bouncing brightly as we both panted. He lay there on top of me, then without warning pushed away, pulling up his pants as he stumbled to the adjoining door, bracing himself on its frame as the floor rolled beneath us.

"That wasn't your first time, was it?" he asked, not bothering to turn around.

"No," I said, my face still in the pillow.

I was answered by the sound of his footsteps crossing the living room, then the metallic click of his door closing and the key turning decisively in the lock.

SIXTEEN

Lillian was asleep when we arrived at the hospital, and despite Tally's pleading, the nurse on duty could give no details of her condition, insisting we'd have to wait for the doctor to make her rounds. Distraught, Tally was chewing her lower lip as she repeatedly ran her fingers through her disheveled hair, unable to comprehend the onslaught of discoveries from the previous day.

"It's like seeing a ghost," she said.

I agreed.

Too restless to sit and wait, Tally decided to go and fetch us both a cup of coffee from the vending machine, leaving me alone in the sterile room with what was left of Lillian Sinclair. I pulled the uncomfortable chair up to her bedside and sat down, watching Lilly sleep, her dreams showing on her face as she furrowed her brow and smacked her lips as if trying to speak. She had been given a bath, and her hair was washed. The sagging, crepe-like flesh of her arm was covered in small bruises from where the nurse had tried to find a vein suitable for her IV. A monitor beeped in rhythm to her heartbeat, reassuring me she was, in fact, alive. The questions swirled through my head, about her well-publicized suicide, the note she'd left behind, and the devastation of her once exquisite face.

It was all wrong. Even the ravages of time, something I was all too familiar with as I considered my own reflection each morning, could not have been responsible for her damaged features. As for her supposed suicide, had she and Milly somehow faked the whole thing? And why?

As I watched her sleep, a soft tap came at the open door. Dr. Jameson introduced herself and asked me what relation I was to the patient.

"That's a loaded question," I said.

"Are you family?"

"No . . . just a friend, I guess. Her daughter's here. She went to get some coffee."

"Then I'll come back."

"No, please," I said, standing, "I'll go get her. We're both a little anxious to hear how she's doing."

The doctor sighed, checked Lillian's chart, then started to take her pulse as I stepped out into the hallway in time to see Tally approaching with cups of coffee. I motioned for her to hurry.

Jameson spoke in a hush as we sipped our coffees, listing a variety of Lillian's ailments. They were treating her bedsores, as well as feeding her through the IV, but still needed to do a thorough physical once Lillian regained consciousness.

"What about her face?" Tally asked. "Did she have a stroke?"

"It's possible, but we won't know until we see the test results."

"The prescription bottles we brought in with her . . . can you tell anything from them?" I asked.

"Not really. All of those were for someone named Milford Langen, so we're not even sure she was taking them."

I looked at Tally. Things were getting stranger by the minute.

Dr. Jameson continued, "They're medications for high blood pressure, depression, congestive heart failure . . ."

Lillian stirred in her troubled sleep, and her eyes fluttered open. "Milly?"

"No, Mrs. Sinclair," the doctor said, "I'm Dr. Jameson. You're in Cedars Sinai. We're going to help you get well."

Lillian's mouth tightened in disapproval. "Does Milly know where I am? I need to talk to him."

We all exchanged looks, then Tally took her mother's hand. Lillian blinked. "Who are you?"

"It's me. Tallulah."

It was the first time I'd heard her full name, unsure why it surprised me. It made perfect sense Tally had been named for her mother's best friend.

"Oh, Tallu. You've got some nerve showing up after all these years. And after what you did."

"What did I do?" Tally asked, puzzled.

"Your book. You never mentioned me once."

"What's she talking about?" Dr. Jameson asked.

"I don't . . ." Tally started, then shook her head in realization. "Mom, Tallulah Bankhead died years ago. I'm Tally. Your daughter."

Lillian searched her face, trying to comprehend, then raised a frail hand to touch her daughter's hair. "So you are," she said with the first hint of a smile. "Oh, my baby girl."

Tears sparkled in Tally's eyes. "Mom, can you tell us what's going on? Everybody thought you were dead . . ."

Lillian grew agitated. "I am," was all she said at first, then added, "You should talk to your father. He'll explain. Where is he?"

After a moment of silence, Dr. Jameson nodded to Tally. "You should tell her the truth."

"The truth?" Lillian asked, growing concerned.

"Mom . . ." Tally said as gently as she could, "Daddy died. He had a heart attack last Friday."

Lillian turned away from us, staring out the window. No one moved as we gave her the time she needed to let that sink in. There was a long silence before she whispered, "It wasn't supposed to turn out like this."

"What wasn't?"

Lilly didn't reply. After a moment, we realized she was crying. Dr. Jameson excused herself, leaving the three of us alone. Tally plucked a tissue from a box on the nightstand and offered it to her mother, but Lillian waved her away, instead covering her face with her skeletal fingers. I noticed her huge diamond wedding ring sparkling in the light reflected from the window. "Milly . . ." Her voice was muffled, her shoulders jerking as she started to sob. "You poor stupid bastard . . ." Tally sat down next to her, stroking her arm.

"I'm sorry," she said, her own tears spilling down her cheeks.

I looked away, feeling like an intruder.

"I want to go home," Lillian said.

"When you're better."

"Well, then, I guess I won't be going home at all," Lillian said, taking her hands away from her face as if trying to compose herself. It was then she seemed to notice me for the first time, a puzzled look forming on her distorted features. "Who are you?"

I cleared my throat, then looked at Tally. "I'm Dan . . ." I said, "I mean, Dexter."

Lillian's face was unreadable as she searched mine as if trying to place me. "Dexter . . .?" she asked, puzzled.

"Dexter Gaines."

Her eyes grew wide with some horrible recognition; then she turned away again. "No. No no no. I don't want you here. You can't see me. Not like this. Not like this." Her voice rose in agitation as she grabbed the railing on the bed and tried to pull herself up before collapsing back onto the pillow, distraught and hysterical. "Please go away. Please. Get out. *Get out!*"

I nodded, looking helplessly at Tally, then turned to hide the tears stinging my eyes as I made my way out into the hallway where I fell back against the wall, trying to compose myself. I looked up and down the corridor, taking in the hushed conversations of the nurses, the awful smell of the place, the sound of a man moaning in pain from the room across the hall, and behind me, Lillian's disturbed whimpers as her daughter tried to calm her. Eventually, Tally had to ring for a nurse to sedate her mother's manic outburst.

I couldn't stop the tears as I slid down the wall until I was sitting on the cold floor, burying my face into my sleeve as my shoulders heaved with sobs. But I wasn't crying for Lillian, and certainly not for Milly. It was for Carol, my dear sweet Carol, and the still raw memory of the last time I'd been ordered out of a hospital room.

At length, I became aware of Tally standing over me, her eyes glistening with compassion. She joined me on the linoleum and was

160

silent for a moment.

"What *really* happened?" she finally asked in a whisper. "With you and my parents, I mean."

I dug out my handkerchief and dabbed my eyes. "I'm not ready to talk about that, Tally. Not yet."

She gave an understanding nod as she eyed me for a long moment, then put a hand on my shoulder as I wept.

SEVENTEEN

Milly had planned for three days of sight-seeing in Paris before we were to fly to Barcelona, but as soon as the train arrived from Le Havre, I bolted and was swallowed up in the crowd. I'd managed to avoid him while the *United States* waited in the French harbor for several hours, having arrived so early the official welcoming ceremonies were not scheduled until the following day. I stayed in my dark stateroom, the doors locked and the little "Do Not Disturb" sign hanging from the knob in the passageway of the anchored ship, the curtains drawn and the covers over my head, fully paralyzed by the worst of my spells that had ever taken me siege.

I couldn't face him; in fact, I couldn't face anyone now that my darkest most despised secret had been exposed. The only solace I could find in the situation was Milly would never tell a soul what had happened, given how a man of his position had even more to lose by the truth being known. The unshakeable dreams haunting me in the darkness were of kissing him with too much passion to ever claim I'd been so drunk I couldn't have known what I was doing. Memories of fervent sex with Lillian would also invade my thoughts, churning in the mire of confusion.

Visions of my mother again boiled to the forefront, bringing with them the nausea of shame for that seminal moment when she'd caught me masturbating while spellbound by the near-nude muscle man on the cover of *Strength and Health* magazine before she had broken six of my fingers with her wheelchair, leaving my soul as damaged as the nerves

162

in my hands. And finally, a mischievous voice I'd heard so many times saying, "Hey Danny, let's go play in the woods," followed by the forbidden excitement of being naked with my cousin Bobby and exploring each other's bodies. In the darkness of my spells, I would continue to deny that the titillation of those episodes had outweighed the oppressive guilt, right up until Bobby's nineteenth birthday when he'd put the barrel of my uncle's shotgun in his mouth and pulled the trigger. I still felt remorse at the relief the news had brought me—our secret now being mine alone. As a kid, sitting in the flickering dimness of the Arcadia Theater, I already had a nagging sense I was somehow different from the other boys because of the way Johnny Weissmuller's Tarzan and Buster Crabbe's Flash Gordon excited me so. As I grew older, the sight of William Holden's bare torso in *Golden Boy* and, most recently, Marlon Brando's in *Streetcar*, had caused that same illicit thrill, one I tried to tamp down with vivid fantasies of Rita Hayworth and Veronica Lake. I had struggled all my life to shun those other feelings, but now they had donned flesh, and I had embraced them.

With only my nightmares for company in the dim stateroom, I'd lost all sense of time as the afternoon at anchor stretched into evening before I became aware of the static liner starting to move again when she was at last allowed to dock.

"Go away!" I shouted as Joseph the steward rapped on my door.

"Sir, we've begun disembarkation. I must get you packed!"

With no choice but to force myself out of bed, I somehow managed to let him in, then stumbled without a word into the bathroom. While I showered, I could hear him banging around, hastily packing my vast wardrobe. Milly was nowhere to be seen as I waited in the first-class observation lounge for the announcement that we could leave the ship. I was nursing a monstrous high and avoiding eye contact with people for fear they'd see through me and know the truth. So of course Margaret and Drucie came swooping over like excited birds. "There you are! We've been looking all over for you! We simply must have a picture with the next Robert Wagner before we go ashore!"

"Sorry," was all I could manage, "I'm not feeling well." I got up and moved off, ignoring their open-mouthed, twittering shock at my rudeness, going out on deck to watch while the *United States* was tied to her mooring lines at the dock amid a celebration to rival our New York departure. When we were finally allowed to disembark, I headed down the gangway, uncertain how I could ever face Milly again, and then managed to get through customs without incident before finding my way aboard the Paris-Le Havre train, my match safe undetected and holding my only salvation. I ducked into a restroom at the station and toked up before an attendant chased me out.

Once seated in the semi-private compartment, I shut my eyes, tensing when I heard the door open, then relaxed when I realized it was an overweight couple I'd seen traveling in cabin class on the crossing. I grunted in response to their chipper attempts at small talk until they mercifully gave up. Whatever panicked horror I was feeling, Milly must be experiencing the same, as we had both managed to remain invisible to the other throughout the day. With about sixty bucks American in my money clip, I was unsure of my next move. The only certainty was I had to somehow find a way back to the States on my own and vanish from Milly and Lilly's lives forever.

As the train hurtled toward Paris, a porter yanked open our compartment door, standing aside to allow Milford Langen to enter. While I was a disheveled mess, he was as natty as always in his impeccable traveling suit, his ever-present leather camera bags slung over his shoulder, and a fresh red rose in his lapel. He tipped the porter, exchanged pleasantries with the chubby Midwesterners, then tossed his fedora onto the overhead rack and plopped down opposite me, taking measured pains to tamp the tobacco in his cigarette against his silver monogrammed case before lighting it, most likely as a way of postponing the inevitable.

I stared out the window, never so much as glancing his way, even though I was well aware of his unavoidable reflection in the now black glass. My cheeks burned with mortification as I retreated as far back in my seat as possible, trying to maintain as much distance from him and the memories of the previous night as I could. At length, he spoke.

"I'm afraid I owe you an apology, dear boy," he said. I was horrified he thought he could have this conversation in the presence of the guileless couple seated with us.

"Not now."

"Well, I'd certainly feel better if you'd allow me to explain myself," he pressed.

I tore my eyes away from his reflection and met his gaze. He was grinning and unruffled as if nothing had happened. Was it possible he didn't remember? He'd been toasted on booze and cocaine, after all. I tried to silence him with my eyes, pleading for him to stop, but he shrugged.

"I merely got caught up in all the celebration," he said. "And you know how unpleasant I can be after mixing scotch and champagne. So my apologies if I acted in any way that might have embarrassed you or made you . . . *uncomfortable.*"

He smiled at me, and even though I realized he was sincere, it was all I could do to refrain from leaping across the compartment and strangling him. Instead, I got up, hovered above him for an uncertain moment, then left, finding my way through the rocking train to the bar car where I downed a half pint of bourbon before spotting an empty seat in one of the coaches where I tried to fall asleep for the duration of the trip.

I was awakened by a porter when the train arrived in Paris. Most of the other passengers were gone, and a new batch was already settling in. Without speaking, I hurried down the narrow aisle and out onto the platform. I had no idea where I was going or what I intended to do when I got there, but I almost ran through the station and out into the Paris night, leaving my array of expensive baggage behind.

I roamed the dark streets of the city with my hands dug deep into my pockets, my jacket collar upturned against the slightest night chill, smoking my last cigarette as I contemplated how I would get home. In my paralyzed state, I was unable to appreciate the still war-scarred beauty all around me. Even the enchanting sight of the twinkling Eiffel

Tower made no impression. Milly's unfazed apology bounced around my head where it clashed with his moans as he'd whispered his wife's name. Maybe he was fine with pretending nothing had happened, but I knew I wasn't that good an actor. What I really wanted to do was find a fleabag hotel and disappear into the darkness still threatening to consume me, but I knew I couldn't afford to spend what little cash I had. Finally, as my stomach rumbled to remind me I hadn't eaten all day, I found a small bistro, still open and crackling with nightlife even at this late hour. Once seated at a tiny sidewalk table, I studied the foreign menu card. It was, of course, all in French. I stared at the gibberish on the page, then became aware of something sniffing at my pants leg. I was surprised to see a little gray dog, looking to make a new friend.

"Hello," I said, reaching down to rub its neck. He jumped up with his paws on my lap and buried his snout in my crotch. I couldn't help but laugh as I squirmed to reposition him.

"Oh dear, I'm sorry, is he bothering you?"

I turned to see an attractive French girl, perhaps my age, sipping a glass of red wine and smoking a Gauloise, a dime store paperback open on the table in front of her next to a freshly cleaned dinner plate.

"Not at all," I said. "A friendly dog is always welcome. What's his name?"

"Sartre," she said. "I'm afraid he won't leave you alone now."

"I don't mind," I said, scratching Sartre behind his ears the way Puck loved. Sartre's eyes were glazed in ecstasy, his tongue panting long from the side of his mouth.

"Well, he's in heaven now. You've mesmerized him."

I smiled for the first time that day, then asked, rather sheepishly, "Would you mind helping me with the menu? About all I know is *oui*."

"Allow me," she said, all too happy to take the card, then translating in perfect English as she walked me through the café's offerings. At length, she ordered for me in French. Rare roast beef with horseradish, some vegetables, and a carafe of table wine. After the waiter had left, she offered me a cigarette, which I readily accepted, and soon she had brought her glass to my table while Sartre curled up and slept at my

166

feet. Normally, I would have avoided human contact in my current state, but there was something soothing about the way she spoke to me, befriending a stranger in her city. The comfort of the dog slumbering, its chin resting on my shoe, further eased my earlier distress. I glossed over the reality of my current plight as best I could, and when she told me her name was Daphne Ronget, I introduced myself by my real name. And why not? Despite my ludicrous attempts to become Clifton Garrow or even Dexter Gaines, I was now doomed to be Daniel Root for the rest of my life.

The food was excellent, and when the carafe was emptied, she ordered another. As she poured the last of the wine, we realized the place was closing and the waiters were clustered in the doorway, yawning and anxious for us to leave. I swooned when I stood up, knocking my chair over and rocking the table. She steadied me and laughed. "You Americans cannot, how do you say, 'hold your wine'?"

I laughed. "Sorry," I said, "I haven't eaten all day."

We strolled together now as Sartre strained at his leash, pausing to sniff every lamppost and leave a mark so other dogs would know he'd been there. She was an art student, and as we realized our evening must end, she said she wanted to paint me.

I laughed. "You're kidding."

"Not at all. I am intrigued by your face," she said. "And your eyes. I don't mean to be forward, but you have a sadness in them I'd like to try and capture."

I looked away, my smile fading.

"I'm sorry," she said. "I've overstepped."

"No, no," I stammered, "it's just . . . I have no place to stay and very little money."

"Then we will make a deal. You Americans are fond of such, no?"

"Okay," I said, grateful.

Daphne's tiny apartment was stacked with dozens of her paintings, mostly abstract but fascinating. The room was largely taken up by a giant easel and art supplies, with a hot plate and daybed shoved under the open double window overlooking a small fountain in the square below. We'd crept up four flights of ancient stairs so as not to awaken her landlady, and once inside she offered me more red wine and turned on the radio. Soon a woman's voice was singing softly in French, and I recognized the melody of "I Should Care."

"Your work is really good," I said, then added, "but I'm no expert."

"I hate experts," she laughed, then sipped her wine and curled her legs beneath her on the daybed. "And thank you for the compliment."

"I meant it," I said, studying a swirl of oil on one of her canvases that seemed to convey an angry sea, and reminded me of the events of the past twenty-four hours.

It wasn't long before we were naked in her bed and I was all over her, trying to absolve my sins with her flesh, her smell, the taste of her tongue. As we kissed, her hands moved down to position me, but I pulled away.

"I think I need just a minute," I said, gasping.

"You are tired?"

"A little." I resumed kissing down her throat to her flawless breasts, determined to silence Milly's cries still haunting me. My desperation was my downfall, and even though I at length managed to get inside of her, I was soon limp again. I collapsed, burying my face in her hair. The sobs shook my shoulders as Daphne held me, stroking the nape of my neck until we both fell asleep, Milly's voice as loud as ever in my dreams, "Oh god. Oh god. *Lillian!*"

Daphne was my savior during that dark night in Paris. She never spoke of my carnal shortcomings and didn't press for anything but the companionship of two strangers who've met by chance. As the sun rose, we finished the eggs she'd scrambled on her hot plate, washing them down with strong, bitter coffee. I thanked her for being so understanding.

"Your eyes, they are not so sad now," she said, touching my face. "But

I would still like to paint you."

"All right," I nodded, then sat for hours as she fussed and fretted over her work, refusing to show it to me until it was done. Her expression remained serious and focused as she dabbed at the canvas with her brush, then stepped back to scrutinize her progress before attacking with renewed fervor, her alert eyes returning to me in a way that made me feel appreciated. The same look I'd seen countless times in Milly's eyes—and Lillian's—but I jammed those demons back into the darkness. At length, as the shadows grew long and night began its inexorable approach, she announced she was done with an uncertain, "*Finis?*" My legs were stiff when I finally rose and walked around to join her.

The painting was in the same abstract style as her other work, but from its bold lines and colorful swaths of oil, my recognizable features emerged. I stared at myself, and at length another even more impressionistic image came into view—a second sexless face floating just behind my shoulder, its sensuous lips brushing against my ear. The experience was almost overpowering.

"The voices," she explained.

I didn't know what to say.

"It's too literal, isn't it?" she asked, misreading my reaction.

"No. Not at all. In fact, it's like I'm looking into my own soul," I whispered.

"It is shit," she laughed, nervous, then doused her half-finished cigarette with a hiss into the dregs of her red wine.

"No, no. It's . . ."

She took my face in her hands and kissed both cheeks. "Someday I will paint you again. In lighter colors. After you have made peace with yourself."

I stared at her, and tears stung my eyes. This woman had seen through me so clearly as to expose my essence on canvas, and I knew that pretense was futile.

"I'm sorry," she whispered, still holding my face.

I took her hands in mine, kissing her palms.

"Thank you," I said.

She smiled, then brushed my tears with her thumbs. She wiped them on the still wet canvas, just below the eyes.

"Now I will save a little part of you."

"I should go," I said, not wanting to.

"I know."

I turned and picked up my jacket, then lingered in the open doorway of her studio and stared at the now fading blocks of sunlight on her floor.

"Goodbye," I said, then knelt to scratch Sartre under his chin while he licked the inside of my wrist.

"*Trouves l'amour*," she replied, then translated, "Find love, *mon cher* Daniel. *Au revoir*. Until we meet again."

I could tell that despite his dour expression, Milly was relieved when I showed up at his room in the *Hotel l'Etoile*. I was incapable of admitting I felt the same upon seeing him again, however tinged with awkwardness it might have been. In the time I'd gone missing, he'd done everything short of hiring a private detective to find me. Still, when I told him I'd rather not talk about my whereabouts, he didn't press.

"Lillian was frightfully upset when I told her you'd vanished," he said while plucking ice cubes from a crystal bucket on the bar.

"You told her?"

"She called me transatlantic and wanted to say hello to you. I *had* to tell her. But only that you were upset about something and had taken off. She's very fond of you, Dex." He poured two shots of scotch and handed one to me.

I didn't say anything, just shook my head in silent confusion and guilt as we sipped, both of us avoiding eye contact.

"Mill . . . about what happened on the boat . . ."

"Let's not talk about that, shall we? There's no reason to. I think we both know how well we understand each other now. All too well, perhaps." He tried to chuckle before changing the subject. "Your luggage is all here, so you should get cleaned up. We still have all day tomorrow in Paris before our train to Barcelona."

"Okay," I said. I wanted to tell him about Daphne's portrait but decided it could wait. "How's Lillian's shoot going?" I asked instead, pouring myself another slug from the open bottle.

"She says she has some wicked Joan Crawford stories to share with us when we get home," he said, chuckling. Sure, we were both going through the motions, making idle conversation in a futile attempt to ignore the unspoken history now hanging thick between us. Still, there was no denying the prickly sensation as we tiptoed around the truth. After a while, I excused myself to take a much-needed shower, and Milly offered to order in a late supper so we could dine on the verandah overlooking the *Champs-Élysées*. I just nodded, then disappeared into the bathroom.

I stayed for a long time, pressing my face against the tiled wall and letting the hot water sluice over me like a baptism, washing away what traces of shame still lingered. I knew there was a chance Milly and I might never again succumb to our desires, but nevertheless found myself praying we would. There had been an urgent tenderness in the way he had touched me that last night on the ship, and it was an experience I now yearned to repeat. But even as I shaved and fussed with my hair, I couldn't look myself in the eye.

When I at last came out into the room, with nothing but a towel around my waist, I saw Milly standing in the open verandah doors, smoking a cigarette and watching as Paris sparkled below.

"Beautiful sight," he said, turning to me with a hint of melancholy in his eyes. My hands were quaking as he approached, then softly brushed the back of his fingers up and down my tingling stomach.

"We need never speak of it, Dexter," he whispered, a hushed tremble in his voice. "We *mustn't*."

"I understand," I said as he pulled me into a kiss. I gave in willingly, even as Daphne's painting reminded me of my own tortured darkness, and I felt a longing flutter throughout my body. We broke from each other's lips with nervous laughter. Then I began to unbutton his shirt, my shivering fingers savoring the warm firmness of his chest as I freed him from his clothes and let my towel slip to the floor.

It was the first time I'd ever made love.

EIGHTEEN

There was some brief confusion at the little hotel in Venice when Milly and I arrived with our panoply of suitcases and steamer trunks, fresh from four rainy but wondrous days in Barcelona. He had forgotten to wire a change in the reservation, and this being the peak tourism season, they only had a suite of rooms reserved for Mr. and Mrs. Milford Langen. With one bed. Milly feigned a fuss with the dapper Italian fellow behind the front desk, even as his eyes twinkled my way.

"We are happy to make up the sitting room for Mr. Gaines, with our apologies."

Milly sighed, tapping ash from his cigarette into the dish next to the bell, then turned to me. I could tell he was enjoying his little performance. "Would that be acceptable to Mr. Gaines?" he asked, a wink in his voice.

"I'll try and make do," I said, mimicking his weary, put-upon air.

"All right, then." Milly pivoted back to the man behind the desk. "I suppose it isn't your fault, after all."

"Very good, sir, *grazie*, sir," the fastidious Italian said, smiling his relief.

The bulk of the six weeks had been booked for pleasure as Milly and Lilly's second honeymoon to celebrate the eleven years of their marriage, and, as it turned out, pleasure was our paramount priority, too. Only a few days had been tacked on for the location scout in Greece for *Trojan War*, but before that we'd had Paris, Barcelona, and now Venice, one of Lillian's favorite cities. Mine, too, once I'd had a chance to experience it with Milly. Traveling with him was a daily revelation. He was fluent in French and Italian, and mostly in Spanish, and having a front-row seat as he charmed the locals in their own tongue, even making them laugh, was an exhilarating education. He knew which trains went where and the best restaurants, and his knowledge of most of the places we visited was more extensive and impressive than our tour guides'. I aspired to learn everything I could from him, now seeing him as the very model of a worldly, smart, and devilishly charming man. And it sure didn't hurt that I was seen as the same, even if only by association.

If Paris and Barcelona had been magical, then Venice was nothing short of supernatural, and Milly thrilled in pointing out various landmarks from our gondola as we drifted in the blazing sun, absorbing the sights and sounds of this enchanting city. Milly took endless photographs and home movies, delighting in devising various scenarios for me to pantomime while his 16mm consumed roll after roll of film. Quite by accident, I'd emerged from an archway in the Piazza San Marco in time to startle a massive flock of pigeons that burst into flight all around me. Under his direction, I spun round and round, my arms outstretched with the Bridge of Sighs behind me as Milly captured it all in a series of still photographs, an unexpected afternoon shower kissing my enraptured face with droplets. Later, he explained to me how the bridge got its name from the sounds made by guilty men on their way to prison. He caught my glimmer of concern and tried to reassure me, "Lillian need never know."

I nodded as he led me off to stroll the impossibly narrow, crowded streets. We found a table at an outdoor café and paused to fan ourselves with our hats as we ordered wine and smoked Italian cigarettes while watching the unending parade of sultry and fascinating people. Milly slipped on his reading glasses, produced a small moleskin notebook, and after uncapping his fountain pen, began to jot a few lines. God he was handsome.

"You keep a diary?" I asked, charmed.

"Not exactly. I like to write down impressions and ideas, that's all. You never know when inspiration might strike."

"Something inspire you today?"

"Any number of things," he said before slipping the journal back into his pocket and putting away his pen and spectacles. I smiled and sipped my prosecco, trying to hide my curiosity about whatever Milly had written down and wondering if he kept his little books hidden away in the locked desk drawer at home.

We sat in comfortable silence as we polished off the rest of the bubbling wine, then made our way back to our hotel to shower and change for dinner.

"Still plenty of time for a nap," Milly said as we neared the front entrance. "Nap" being the code word we'd adopted for unbridled sex.

We strolled through the cool marble lobby, greeting the hotel staff, maintaining the casual appearance of two gentlemen travelers before closing the door to our suite and ripping each other's clothes off. Milly sure was giving me a crash course in the ways of the world. I muffled my ecstasy as he came up for air, kissed me deeply before he pulled away, his bewitching eyes now an olive green in the dimming light as he searched my face and said, "I never knew it could be like this."

I grinned, fighting whatever guilt still haunted me. Emboldened by weed and bubbling Italian wine, I moved him from the chair to the bed and licked his dime-sized nipples, working down the fine trail of hair below his navel. "My god, Lilly's taught you well," he murmured.

"Please," I said, rising up, "that's not helping."

"Of course," he laughed, then wrestled me onto my stomach. When we were both sweaty and satisfied, he slid his tongue up my spine, and I could feel his little dog tags and key tingling along my flesh as he reached the nape of my neck, leaving his warm lips there for a long, long time. We lay sprawled in the tangle of dampened sheets, a stale breeze ruffling the sheers on the open window overlooking the lanterns along the canal. We listened to the faint voices of the serenading gondoliers, and ignored our dinner reservation, ordering room service instead and feeding each other through our giggles. And even while a hint of shame still lingered within me, I felt the embracing warmth of belonging for the first time in my life—the comfort of mutual adoration.

At length, Milly let his robe drop to the floor and stood there in the shaft of moonlight filtering through the window. He was devastatingly alluring, with a trim, lean body not quite as muscular as my own, but enough to get me going.

He pulled open a small drawer in his steamer trunk and produced an old typewriter ribbon tin, twisting it open to reveal the very white powder that had so bewildered me on the ship. He tapped some onto his shaving mirror, then proceeded to arrange it into neat little snowdrifts with a razor blade.

"Would you like some?" he asked.

I'd never tried cocaine before, though I'd been around it during my few short months in Hollywood. I was curious, but knowing full well how it could turn Milly's personality on a dime, I demurred. "I don't want to make Mary jealous," I said, holding up my half-smoked joint and smiling so as not to reveal a hint of judgment.

"Suit yourself," he said, pinching a nostril as he inhaled a line. He threw his head back, then filled his other nostril with the same before our eyes met and he smiled like a jungle animal ready to pounce. "Now come here," he growled. "I'm not done with you." I was all too willing to give in. For now, Milford B. Langen—Milly—had no distractions but me.

On our second day in Rome, after touring the ruins of the Coliseum and stopping to lunch on salad and veal near the Piazza Venezia, Milly announced he wanted to show me the sensual splendor of the Trevi Fountain. But as we neared the famous landmark, we were slowed by a crowd standing still, encircling the majestic, wet statuary as they watched something we couldn't yet see.

"Milly? What the hell?" A voice came from behind us.

We turned to see a small man headed over, waving his hat. "Are you spying on the competition?" he asked.

Milly seemed to freeze momentarily, just as shocked as the other gentleman, a forced smile on his face, as if he'd been caught in some impropriety.

"Billy?" was all that came out of his mouth.

"What are you doing in Rome?"

I had never seen Milly so awkward as he stammered, "I'm—on my way to Greece, of course. For a location scout."

"Ah," the man named Billy said, then looked at me.

Milly recovered his manners. "Sorry. Billy Wyler, have you met Dexter Gaines?"

"Not until now," Wyler said before we exchanged "how-do-you-dos."

"Dexter's up for a role in the picture," Milly explained, trying not to falter. "Method actor and all that. He insisted on coming along to immerse himself in the culture. Right, Dex?"

"Absolutely," I said with my most disarming smile.

Wyler seemed uninterested as he led us over to the film shoot that was keeping the crowd so riveted. He introduced us to Gregory Peck and a radiant, delicate creature whose name was Audrey Hepburn. They were on location filming a movie called *Roman Holiday*, which would be released to great acclaim the following year. Before long, Wyler insisted we join them for dinner that evening and a hasty plan was arranged. But for now, they had to get back to work, and Milly and I longed only to return to each other.

As we strolled toward our hotel, Milly shrugged with relief and said, "You see? You can go halfway around the world and you still can't get away from Hollywood."

"I've never seen you so nervous."

"Sorry. I was blindsided."

"I don't think he suspected anything," I said, trying to reassure him. "You were right about doing your best acting behind the camera."

In response, he tried to smile, but I could tell he was rattled.

Despite the unsettling chance meeting, Milly and I made love all night. It wasn't until two in the morning he realized we'd forgotten our dinner date. He laughed, then said he'd send a telegram to Wyler the next day making excuses. Besides, he continued, spending time with me was far more entertaining than dinner with Gregory Peck. I smiled and kissed him as he snuggled into me, his hand on my chest, then watched as his eyes grew heavy. He reminded me through a yawn to tousle the bed in the adjoining room before morning so as not to draw suspicion from the chambermaid, then fell asleep. I didn't move for the longest time, just relished his warm breath on my neck, the intoxicating scent of him, and the strange comfort that came from holding this fascinating, powerful man in my arms. As my eyes began to flutter closed, my breathing fell into sync with Milly's, and I realized for the first time in my life, I was as happy as all those rubes in the movies when they finally meet the right person and fall head over heels before "The End."

The next day, I sunned myself on the hotel verandah as a handsome Italian waiter brought my afternoon prosecco, lingering to practice his English, though more likely to enjoy the sight of my glistening torso. I was beginning to understand there were signals, the most subtle hints a man might dare project to let you know he was a kindred spirit. Milly had gone off souvenir shopping, and I'd spent the afternoon staring at the blank back of a picture postcard I'd bought at the Sistine Chapel. We'd stood there in the hushed crowd gaping up at the unspeakably divine ceiling, and then Milly had leaned in close to my ear and said, "Isn't it the most erotic thing you've ever seen?"

I nodded, my eyes still glued overhead, then confided without hesitation, "I've got a hard-on."

Milly stifled a scandalized laugh. "We're due back at the hotel then." A guard shushed us as we made our way out, blinking in the bright sunshine before exploding with laughter. To this day, I'm not sure what surprised me more: that I'd said such a thing out loud in such a sacred place, or that I honest-to-god hadn't cared.

The pen hovered over the back of the card, but my mind was as empty as the little space for a message. I had already stamped and addressed it to Lillian Sinclair, which was all I'd managed to write in the past hour. What could I possibly say to her? She was shooting, and Milly had said it's never a good idea to upset Lillian when she's working, not that I would have dared allude to anything remotely close to the real details of our holiday. So we'd cabled her a few times, glossing over the truth and always reassuring her we both missed her terribly.

I looked across the verandah and out into the square teeming with tourists before I spotted Milly, his white linen suit still impossibly crisp in the relentless heat like Alec Guinness's miracle fabric, as he side-stepped a beggar and approached, catching my eye and breaking into a grin. He held up a little shopping bag and headed toward me. I smiled, hastily scrawled *Rome is not quite as gay without you! Love, Dex,* then flipped the card over as Milly joined me, peeling off his jacket and helping himself to the last of my prosecco before sitting down in the adjacent chaise lounge and dabbing his forehead with his pocket kerchief.

"I've bought you something," he said with a grin, removing a small, wrapped gift from his bag. "Of course, I got our dear Lillian something a touch more expensive . . ."

I smiled, delighted. "What is it?"

"Good god, boy, why do people ask that when they receive a gift? Just open the damned thing," he said, teasing me.

I ripped into the paper and pried open the little box, moving the red tissue aside to reveal an elegant cigarette case. My mouth fell open as I picked it up, admiring its beauty as I held its heft on my palm.

"Solid gold," Milly said. "Only the best for you."

Without thinking, I leaned to kiss him in gratitude, but his eyes widened and he flinched.

"Sorry," I said, blushing, both of us looking around furtively to ensure no one had seen my hint of indiscretion.

"We must always remember ourselves," Milly said.

"I know."

"Now go on," he said, recovering. "Read the inscription."

I pinched the little clasp and the case popped open, revealing he'd already filled it with black, silver-tipped Turkish cigarettes. The inside lid glinted in the sun as I read the scrolled words: *To Dex. Fondly, Milly.*

"*Fondly?*" I asked, feigning outrage.

"It's code, dear boy; there isn't an adequate word in any language to describe how you make me feel."

179

I smiled at him. "Then I'm 'fond' of you, too," I said, before my smile turned melancholy. Up to that point, I'd been spinning in the whirlwind of unexpected happiness, and though I tried not to think too much about it, there was still something gnawing at my young and vulnerable heart.

"Mill . . . why were you so cruel to me? On the boat, I mean."

He looked away as he considered the question, a tinge of guilt now haunting his expression. "Because being so close to you—and alone with you—*terrified* me. Don't you see, Dex? I was trying to control myself and you were the object of my obsession, so I had no choice but to push you away." Here he paused before looking at me again. "Until I simply couldn't anymore."

His words meant more to me than I could acknowledge in the public setting of the hotel's verandah. So I just smiled and held out the still open gold case. "May I offer you a smoke?"

"Thank you."

His hand brushed mine as he took one, his now sea green eyes trained on me while lighting it, and I felt the familiar tingle of secret desire—now bolstered by the heady intoxication of what I believed could only be love. Something I'd never felt before.

Milly lit a cigarette for me and I signaled the handsome Italian boy for more prosecco. The lad opened a fresh bottle for us, pouring the sizzling liquid into clean glasses.

"*Grazie,*" I said.

"*Prego.*" He grinned, then bowed and stepped away.

"Careful, Dex," Milly said with a laugh. "That one's onto you."

"Yeah, well, I'm spoken for." I nestled back on my chaise lounge, dipping my sunglasses to eye Milly meaningfully, giving him a playful look I knew would drive him mad.

"So you are," he said. "Now, tonight we cannot be distracted. There's a restaurant I'm dying to take you to."

"Then let's finish our prosecco in our room." I grinned.

"Along with each other," he whispered. We resumed the guise of two gentlemen friends as we headed inside. For reasons I didn't entirely understand, I waited until Milly wasn't looking before dropping Lillian's postcard into the mail basket on the front desk, then joined my lover as we moseyed up the stairs, waiting until we were safely behind the closed door of our room before devouring each other once again. We were an hour late for our dinner reservation, but no one in the entire, lyrical city of Rome seemed to care.

Least of all me.

By the time our plane landed in Athens, my feelings for Milly were deeper than anything I'd ever experienced, even though I knew I could never speak of them. I understood him, too, and had figured out the best time to get him to talk to me—to really open up—was when he was delirious with contentment in my arms after one of our unending rounds of clandestine passion. He confessed how the moment he saw me, standing in his study in my frazzled waiter's attire on that now long-ago New Year's Eve, dog shit clinging to my shoe, he had known I was dangerous.

"Dangerous?" I asked as he lay with his face pressed against my bare chest, both of us sweating.

"You must know how hard it is to hide this . . . *thing* that overtakes us," he said. "I feared discovery over all else, which is why, I'm afraid, I was so unforgivably horrid."

"You let me spend a night in jail."

"I'm sorry."

"And you practically cut my arm off on the ship."

"Sorry for that, too," he said with a sheepish grimace. "Is there anything I can do to make it up to you?"

"Oh, I'll think of something," I teased, marveling at the distance we'd traveled since then. We lay there while I gathered my nerve before asking, as innocently as I could, "Who's Michael Spencer?"

"Michael? How on earth do you know about him?"

"I heard Deming and Blanche gossiping in the kitchen one afternoon," I lied.

"You mean they actually speak?"

"Only to each other."

Milly didn't move; instead he took a moment to kiss my nipple before he went on. "Michael was one of Lillian's lovers."

His candor surprised me. "One of?" I asked.

"Dear boy, Lillian is the most amazing creature, as you well know. And while I can take care of her in many ways, there are others in which I'm entirely deficient."

"She knows about you?"

Milly laughed. "Heavens no. But she's all too familiar with my war injuries which make me sometimes incapable of satisfying her."

"Sometimes."

"We do make love now and then, Dexter. She's my wife, after all."

"And you're okay with her affairs?" I asked.

"Let's just say I despise hypocrisy. I've told her I find it rather titillating, which I do, in fact. It's an arrangement that seems to work for us."

I fell silent, processing this new information, before I got up the nerve to ask what was really troubling me. "Did you pay him, too?"

Milly rose up and looked at me. "Why the sudden inquisition?"

"I think I have a right to know."

"All right, fair enough. Yes, we had a similar arrangement to yours and mine. A loan against his first movie role. The difference is, and it's a big one, Michael Spencer's acting made me look like Olivier in comparison, so the only return I saw on the investment was Lillian's contentment for a time. You, on the other hand, are destined to be a *star*."

"When did it end?" I pressed, thrilled by his words but pretending to ignore the compliment.

"Last year. Nice-looking boy, but nothing going on inside. Lillian soon tired of him and that was that."

"Did you and he . . .?"

"God no! Straight as an arrow, and as Lillian liked to say, 'dumber'n a bag a hammers.'"

I chuckled, well able to imagine those words drawling from her mouth.

"Of course, I fantasized about this happening with you, but I didn't dare pursue it. I knew it would be risking personal and professional disaster. But as time wore on, my lust got the best of me, I'm afraid. Because I realized the one thing I wanted—wanted most in the world, mind you—was to do with you what you were doing with my wife. And now, as for your affair with her . . ." He trailed off, this being the first time either of us had dared to bring it up since our insane fencing match on the boat.

"It'll stop," I promised. "The minute we get back to Hollywood."

Milly sat up, curling his legs beneath him as he drew a pillow over his lap. "But Dexter, it *can't.*"

I wasn't sure I'd heard him right. "Excuse me?"

"Dex, dear, dear, Dex. You and I can't disappear for six weeks on a European holiday only to have you shatter my wife's heart the instant we return."

"What are you saying?"

"I'm saying the only way to keep Lillian from ever knowing what she mustn't—*under any circumstances*—is for you to resume being her lover."

It took me a moment to find my voice again. "Milly . . . I'm not sure I *can.* Not after *this.*"

"There really isn't any choice."

"But . . . what about us?"

"We'll just have to manage somehow."

"*Manage?*" I said, getting up. "How's that going to work?"

He tossed the pillow aside and joined me, putting his hands on my biceps to steady me. "Look at me," he said, then waited until I did.

"You know how this could destroy us both. We have to be practical."

He was right, but I didn't want to admit it.

I touched his face and managed to whisper, "But I love you, Milly."

He darkened as he pulled away. "Then you'd better cut it out," he said, and went into the bathroom. I heard the shower start as I stood there motionless, dreading our return home now more than ever.

Greece was beautiful but left me anxious and unsettled as I tried to envision what life would be like once we got back to the day-to-day strain of image-obsessed Hollywood—an inconceivable future of only occasional and covert time with Milly. I understood his oft-expressed contempt for homosexuals now better than ever, given how I'd been guilty of the same strategy to ward off any hint of suspicion.

As we dressed for our first day in Athens, I finally brought it up. "So what are we now exactly? A couple of 'reprobate pansies'?"

Milly was wearing his reading glasses, slacks, and nothing else as he shaved at the mirror over the basin in our room. His eyes caught mine in the reflection as I zipped up my linen trousers.

"To some people, yes, I suppose we are," he replied. "Not that anyone ever has to know."

"So the whole rhubarb about me going to Henry Willson's barbeque . . . what was that all about?"

Milly ran his razor carefully over his Adam's apple before wiping the last remnants of shaving cream away with a towel. "You want the truth?"

"I'm asking."

"All right." He turned to me, leaning with his hands behind him on the edge of the sink. "I was threatened, Dexter. And jealous."

"What? That I might try to screw Rock Hudson?"

"Or the other way around."

"So you suspected . . . about me?"

"Not at first. I couldn't tell. And I sure as hell didn't want you to know how mad you'd driven me. So the easiest way to distance myself— and hopefully convince you not to go—was to make the whole thing sound criminal and perverse. Obviously you're no stranger to that tactic; otherwise you wouldn't have tried to break poor Rock's nose."

I approached him, confused and more than a little fragile. "You're right," I said, hooking my fingers through the belt loops of his pants then leaning close to kiss him. I liked the way his naked chest felt as it brushed against mine, and how he smelled of soap and cigarettes. "But I hate it."

"It's just the way of things, dear boy," he said, then cupped my jaw in his hand.

I wanted to tell him again how I felt, mostly in hopes he'd say the words to me, too. My youth and inexperience needed to know for certain that the secret he insisted we protect—at the cost of our own happiness— was deeply mutual. But it seemed foolish and cloying to request such a declaration outright.

"What is it?" he asked, so close it was intoxicating.

My grin was tinged with sadness. "Nothing. I was just thinking how good you look in your bookworms."

"Please, I loathe these damn things."

"You shouldn't. They make you look sexy."

"Sexy?" he asked, dubious.

"And powerful. And smart."

"Dear boy," he said, kissing me, "I *am* powerful and smart. Which is why you must *always* do as I say. And right now I say we eat. I'm famished."

I tried to smile as he moved away, wriggling into his shirt and signaling the conversation was over. As I was putting on my shoes, I thought about the difference between Henry Willson's party and what I was now experiencing with Milly. There had been no tenderness evident in the semi-darkness of Willson's spare bedroom that day. But here, watching Milly tie his ascot, unaware of my eyes on him, I wondered about his tacit rejection of any notion of romance once I'd spoken those forbidden words aloud to him, exposing my vulnerable, young, and very confused heart. Then again, Milford Langen was fond of his arrangements, after all; it was his own way of compartmentalizing and justifying.

Over breakfast at a café above the azure waters of Lake Vouliagmeni, he confessed to me there was to be no location scout. It had all been a ruse to get Lillian on a much-needed holiday. *Trojan War* would be a back lot picture all the way if he had any hope of seeing it produced.

"Then why didn't you cancel the trip when you had the chance?" I asked.

"Because, dear boy, I'm weak. I'd watched you floating in our pool enough by then. That's why I insisted Darryl loan Lillian to Warners."

I put my fork down. "You *arranged* that?"

"Of course. And I know she'll be brilliant in the picture. It's just the role she needs to platform her turn as Helen of Troy. I couldn't believe it when she herself suggested I bring you along."

"That's the most treacherous thing I've ever heard."

"Thank you." He grinned. "Everybody wins."

We spent the next three days sight-seeing or making love in our hotel overlooking the crumbling ruins of the Parthenon. Once, we found ourselves alone among its columns, and shared our first daylight kiss before recovering, mercifully unobserved. Milly laughed as we broke apart, and my heart fluttered when he said, "If only we could do this all the time." In one of the endless museums, Milly pointed out ancient decorations depicting love between men. "The Greeks and Romans were far more evolved than our so-called sophisticated society," he'd explained wistfully.

Two days before we were scheduled to leave, Milly came into our room, distressed, waving a Western Union envelope he'd picked up at the front desk.

"What is it?" I asked, pausing from laying my dinner wardrobe out on the bed. He just shook his head and handed it to me. The message was brutal in the clarity of its block letters: "LS fired from picture. Stop. You owe me. Stop." The telegram was signed by Jack Warner.

Milly sat down and rubbed his face. I went over and put my hands on his shoulder. "We have to go home" was all he said.

As we lay in bed together watching our final European sunrise, our bags already packed in anticipation of our premature return, I felt something wet on my forearm and realized Milford Langen was crying.

"I don't want to go back any more than you do," he said, holding his arms tightly, almost desperately, around me.

NINETEEN

Each leg of the trip home was excruciating, stopping to change planes or refuel in Rome, Zurich, and Paris before our transatlantic to New York, then more layovers in Chicago and Phoenix on our way to Los Angeles. Worse still, Milly groused the whole way about how cutting our trip short meant we had to fly "Air Tourist" rather than his preferred First Class. And all the while Jack Warner's cryptic "LS fired from picture" reverberated between us but remained unspoken. "No use speculating until we hear what happened," Milly had said, putting an end to the subject.

On the last stretch of our journey, still one more tortuous hour from Los Angeles, he sat staring out the small window at the dark clouds above and below, smoking pensively, one finger holding his place in his little pocket journal where he'd been scribbling. I was trying to steal a glance at whatever he had written when the attractive stewardess came over to freshen his second scotch, and Milly snapped the notebook closed and slipped it into his jacket pocket. I'll admit I was now tantalized by the notion his jotted "impressions" might include his real feelings about me, and itched to find out if I was right. For now, we were both exhausted, and the strident, steady droning of the plane's four engines was giving me a headache, so I turned my attention back to the draft of *The Trojan War* Milly had given me aboard the ship, determined to finish it. When I at last reached the end of the epic manuscript, I jotted down a thought I'd had while reading the climactic scene, then folded the upper corner of the last page the way I'd seen Milly do whenever he was preparing to give a writer notes.

Just as I closed the now dog-eared script on the little fold-down table in front of me, the plane shuddered from unexpected turbulence and Milly grabbed the arms of his seat, nearly dropping his cigarette onto his lap. "God, I hate flying," he muttered. The plane answered him by dipping beneath us, causing his highball glass to clatter on the table as he reached to steady it. The stewardess came by to make sure we were tightly buckled in, bracing herself on the seat backs, then returned to her own.

"You okay?" I asked.

"I will be once we land," he grimaced, then added, "safely." He glanced at the screenplay in front of me. "What have you done to my movie?"

"I just have a few thoughts," I said, feeling important. "Like you asked for."

"You've turned so many corners the script is fanning open," he observed, stubbing out his cigarette to mask his irritation before downing the last of his scotch. The plane heaved again, rocking side to side. It was more frightening than the rough seas we'd been through on the steamship given there was nothing below to keep us from dropping to the bottom.

"Well, let's hear your thoughts. I could use the distraction."

"Okay," I said, opening the cover and scanning the words I'd scrawled on the title page. "Overall, I think it's pretty swell."

"Swell?" His voice now had that trace of derision I hadn't heard for weeks.

"I mean it's really good."

"But?"

"Here's the thing. The love story? Aces. Paris kidnapping Helen and stealing her away, the whole doomed lover angle; the women are gonna eat it up. But unless you're gonna get George Cukor to direct—"

"What's that supposed to mean?"

"Right now, what you've got here is a woman's picture," I said.

"Oh, I see. And how would Dexter Gaines fix that?"

The plane dropped again, this time causing our stomachs to lurch into our ribcages. Someone two rows behind us let out an involuntary gasp. Milly set his jaw as he gripped the armrests.

"We can talk about it later," I said, closing the script again. "You're in a mood."

"Sorry, kiddo," he said, making the slightest effort to adjust his tone. "Finish your thought."

"I just think you need to take another pass and put some stuff in to get men into the theater. There aren't enough battle sequences."

"Featuring Achilles, you mean?"

"No," I said, truthfully. "Though that wouldn't hurt." I smiled at him, trying to keep things light. "It's called *Trojan War* not *Trojan Love Story*," I continued. "Needs more action to earn the title." Milly frowned as the plane tipped to the left, then back to the right, causing his drink to slide toward the edge of the table. I caught it barely in time. Milly took it from me and started anxiously munching an ice cube.

"You just need to find the right balance between the love story, which is already killer, and the reality of the war."

"What do you know about the reality of war? I don't see you in uniform going off to Korea. Dear old Dad could sure make a man out of *you*."

"I told you," I said, "I'm 4-F. Because of my hands. But I've seen enough war movies to know—"

"So your assessment of my script is based on your vast experience sitting on your ass in the dark?"

"Which is why you asked me to read the goddamned thing in the first place," I snapped. "Fine. Forget it. I thought you wanted to hear what I had to say."

"It's a script, Dexter. A mere list of suggestions for the director and actors. It's also a sales tool. I can't very well hand in pages upon pages of epic battle scenes. Why? Because Darryl would throw the damn thing right back at me. He'd only see dollar signs. You've obviously learned nothing from my tutelage and—"

He was cut off when the plane shuddered and rattled then dropped from under us as if we'd hit a pocket where there was no air to keep us aloft. As the plane fell, veering steeply to the left, Milly's glass and the screenplay slid onto the floor as I scrambled to grab the arms of my seat, watching in speechless terror as *The Trojan War* spun crazily down the center aisle, landing at the feet of the seated, ashen stewardess. The glass rolled with it, spilling the last of the ice cubes to skitter like thrown dice before it shattered against a bulkhead. Our stewardess closed her eyes as if praying for all of us who found ourselves at the mercy of the raging storm. Truth was, with my face still burning from Milly's dressing-down, I almost didn't care if we all died in a fiery crash.

Just as the plane started to level out, and the air seemed to calm, it lurched again, dipping to the right and plummeting anew, engines shrilling as the pilots scrambled to regain control of their aircraft. I knew it was bad when the stewardess let out a scream, then clamped both her hands over her mouth, her eyes popping and darting. By reflex, I grabbed Milly's arm in my panic, but he flinched and yanked himself free. Even faced with death, his most basic nature wouldn't allow him to risk exposure of his tortured secret.

"Keep your hands—*and your thoughts*—to yourself," he hissed. My cheeks flushed in anger and shame. It was merely a sample of the many burning rejections that were to follow—the first glimmering of Milly's desperate need to push his darkest truth away.

We remained strapped in our seats, teeth clenched, riding out the crazy violence of the flight, neither saying another word until, at last, the plane broke below the clouds, regained a more or less even keel, and we could see the vast sprawl of city lights beneath us, blurred by the pounding rain. Soon, our wonderful, torrid weeks in Europe would seem like nothing more than a dream.

The relentless rainfall continued unabated, dumping gallons as we made our way home. Milly had arranged for a studio car to collect us at the airport, and with the exception of a few instructions to the driver, we didn't speak for the entire ride. At one point I noted with a touch of sad fondness that Milly had dozed off, his troubled sleep reflected in the trickling wet window beside him. It was just past midnight when the car pulled into the splattering circular drive of the dark house on South Windsor, and I was surprised to see the Nash-Healey parked there as our driver held a drenched umbrella overhead in a weak attempt to cover us as we got out. Leaving us at the front door, he splashed unprotected to grab the small bags we'd taken on the plane. The larger trunks were due to arrive in a couple of days. We still weren't speaking to each other, and while Milly had some trouble finding his keys in the downpour, I noted a huge dent in the front fender of the sports car. Milly caught my concerned look and frowned when he saw the damage as well. At length, he unlocked the door and the chauffeur deposited our soaked suitcases in the dim foyer before Milly tipped him. No one had said a word.

I closed and locked the door, the click sounding hollow and reverberating through the silent house. When I turned, Milly was already peeling off his drenched jacket as he trudged up the stairs in the quiet, cavernous space, his wet shoes squeaking, the circular glass brick wall behind him alive with a steady rippled wash of wavering light and shadows as the rain cascaded down like Niagara Falls.

"Y'all're home," a weary Lillian said, appearing on the landing above. She looked as if she might have been ill. No makeup, her hair down and tousled, wearing nothing but one of the heavy cotton robes usually reserved only for the cabana. She wasn't the same woman we'd left behind all those weeks ago, nor would she ever be again. Before Milly could speak, the rain intensified, thundering on the roof overhead.

"We cut our trip short when I got Jack's telegram," Milly said, arriving at the top of the stairs and kissing her cheek.

"How was Europe?" she asked, glancing down at me.

"More importantly," Milly interrupted, "what happened on the set? And to the Nash?"

"Oh, Puppy," she said, tears welling in her eyes, "it's poor little Puck . . ."

"What's wrong?" I asked, concerned, looking up from the pattern of the marble floor.

She wiped away her tears as she shook her head, then motioned for both of us to follow. Worried, I trotted up the steps and Lillian led us down the corridor to her bedroom. Candles glowed softly, and a log in the fireplace still smoldered, providing the only flickers of light in the gardenia-scented room. Her usually pristine boudoir showed signs of a prolonged stay, and the gilt-framed floor-to-ceiling oil portrait of her in Civil War garb, a gift from the art director of *The Widows Wore Blue and Gray*, looked down upon us from between the two stately, curtained windows. As we entered the room, we could hear the raspy breathing of the little dog who had curled himself into a tight ball on a pillow on her bed. A full ashtray sat on the bedside table along with an empty bourbon bottle and a cloud of crumpled tissues, as if Lillian had been sitting vigil with her beloved dog. Trouble lay flat on his stomach near the fireplace, still as a statue, chin resting on his paws as his sad eyes drooped, one brow arching as he noted our arrival, but didn't move.

"Oh no," I whispered, and approached the bed. Lillian leaned against her husband and he put his arms around her.

"He's been like this for three days now," Lillian said, still crying. "Deming was having the car serviced so I had to drive to the vet myself and . . ."

The rest didn't require explanation. Despite my best efforts to teach her, Lillian was a terrible driver.

I sat down on the bed, careful so as not to disturb the dying dog, and no sooner had I reached to stroke the sweet spot behind his scrawny ears than his eyes flashed and his frazzled tail moved in a weak attempt to welcome me home. He could only manage to lick my hand once with his pale, dry tongue, and now I, too, felt the sting of sudden tears.

"Hey there, little fella," I said, my voice cracking. "Who's the best pooch in the whole wide world? Huh? You are, that's who. You know you are. Yes you do," I cooed as he tried to wag his tail again. Trouble whimpered from his motionless stance across the room, as if sensing what was to come. I looked at Milly, whose face remained unreadable as Lillian sobbed into his shirtfront. I stroked my hand up and down Puck's scrawny back, feeling the bumps of his fragile spine and ribs beneath my fingers. "It's okay," I said. "It's okay."

Puck drunkenly raised his head up, then struggled to stand on the pillow. The effort proved too much, and he collapsed again. "It's okay, it's okay," I kept repeating, trying to reassure myself along with him. His eyes seemed to glaze as they rolled back into his head, and his breathing became even more labored and shallow, sounding guttural and wet as if he had fluid in his tiny lungs as he started to fade. Trouble was whining now, a ghostly moan signaling the end was near as the rain drummed anew overhead.

"Lilly?" I whispered through the knot in my throat. "He's leaving us now."

Her face contorted into the saddest expression I'd ever seen. Milly walked her over to the edge of the bed as she looked at Puck with brimming eyes, then gently, so very gently, lifted his emaciated body and cradled him like an infant.

Puck licked an errant tear from Lillian's chin, and then with an almost imperceptible twitch, fell silent and still in her arms. My vision was blurred as I cried with her, but I still managed to see that even Milly's eyes were glistening in the silence now enshrouding us. The only sounds were the relentless battering of the rain, a short crackle from the dying fire, and at length Lillian's pitiful moans as she rocked her beloved Puck, then sought her husband's arms for comfort. He held her with genuine tenderness, never once looking at me.

The next morning, at Lillian's insistence, I drove with her to a pet cemetery in Calabasas, with Puck's body wrapped in his favorite blanket, resting atop his pillow. At the animal mortuary, we arranged for his burial, and while we waited, Lillian walked me through the green and soaked graveyard still dripping from the previous night's rain. The wet ground sucked at our shoes as we arrived at the small fenced-in plot she and Milly had purchased there years ago when her first dog had died. She bent to brush away some leaves and pine straw from two small granite markers inset in the ground.

Both of them bore the name Puck, with consecutive dates of birth and death that seemed to chronicle Lillian and Milly's eleven-year marriage. I noted with sadness there was still room for several more.

Lillian put her arm through mine as we stared down at the graves. "You took him from me, didn't you?"

I froze, unsure how to answer.

"What?" was all I managed.

"He never left my side until you came along," she said, further confusing me.

"He loved you very much, Lilly."

"Still, he held out to see you one last time before he died."

"Yes," I said, "but he did so in your arms."

TWENTY

As we let ourselves into the crumbling remains of the house on Windsor, Tally and I were loaded with grocery bags from our trip to the Ralph's at Third and La Brea. It was the first time we'd seen the shambles in daylight, and now that the low gray clouds of what Angelenos call "June Gloom" had burned off, the harsh surreal reality was laid bare by the California sunshine. We stepped into the sagging stacks of boxes and debris, grit scraping under our shoes, and I whistled and called out, "Here boy! C'mon!" Within seconds, the dog appeared running toward us, sliding comically when his paws hit the worn linoleum in the old kitchen, scrambling to brace his enthusiasm.

"How much you want to wager his name is Puck?" Tally asked.

"That's a sucker's bet," I replied as the dog leapt at my feet and I knelt down to say hello. I noticed his ID tag, then showed it to Tally for confirmation.

"I think I'll call him Puck the Eighth." I smiled.

Tally nodded. "Or the Twentieth for all we know."

I found his dish in the adjacent laundry room where I'd fed him the night before, then washed it out in the maid's sink before giving him some of the food I'd bought and changing his water. "You eat up, little guy. Then Uncle Dan's gonna give you a proper bath," I said, starting to unpack the groceries, setting aside the flea shampoo and comb I'd purchased with my nearly maxed-out credit card. Puck the Eighth gobbled his meal, then licked the empty bowl with such enthusiasm it slid across the floor. I chuckled while I watched him, then noticed Tally's strange expression.

"What's wrong?" I asked.

"Nothing. That was cute is all. How you were baby-talking just now. You're obviously a dog person."

"Yeah," I said, "but I've never really had one of my own. Carol was allergic, so . . ."

"Not even as a kid?"

"That's right," was all I could manage, then changed the subject. "Where should we start?"

Tally didn't press, just chewed her lower lip while she found the trash bags and cleaning supplies among our purchases. "Wherever you think."

"How about the room where we found your mother? In case they let her come home."

And so the two of us, acquaintances for just over twenty-four hours, set about the impossible task of making order out of Milly's mayhem. It proved to be an arduous undertaking, and one that would stretch well into the long months ahead. Tally had called some guy named Stefan who worked at her store in Haight-Ashbury, deputizing him to keep her vintage clothing business going while she tended to family matters. He was gushing so loudly I could hear his tinny voice buzzing through the other end of the ancient wall telephone, pressing her for details about Lillian Sinclair having been found alive. Tally told him she didn't have any answers, and that was only one of the reasons she wouldn't be able to return for a while. As for me, I had left nothing of importance behind. So little, in fact, it barely warranted a trip to San Jose to close out the furnished one-bedroom I'd been renting month-to-month since Carol died and I'd lost the house and a lifetime of memories.

The doctors had said Lillian should remain hospitalized for a few more days as they ran their battery of tests and billed the insurance company who refused to pay benefits for a woman who had died in 1982. It took some sorting out, hours on the telephone tethered to the wall, but because Lillian had no life insurance at the time of her infamous suicide, and because she'd never been removed from Milly's health policy with the Producers Guild, they were eventually forced to pay a portion of her medical expenses. The police, too, had come around the hospital to try to ascertain if any crime had been committed, but with Lillian still sedated after her outburst at me, they'd left with the same befuddlement as when they'd arrived.

While we laundered sheets and scrubbed the dirty walls of the old guest room, Puck the Eighth stayed close by my heels, even as I felt the gnaw of suspense in my stomach whenever I thought about sorting through Milly's memoirs and the hours of tape recordings in hopes of finding some answers. Tally and I chatted as we worked, speculating about what might have led to her parents' bizarre circumstances, and while I already knew some of the answers, I wasn't yet comfortable enough to share.

The sun was fading outside as she smoothed the covers on the freshened bed, and then suggested we take a needed break and walk the dog before his bath, so I managed to find a leash and the three of us set out on the wide sidewalks of Hancock Park. A new Lexus sports coupe pulled up in front of the house when we came out, and its power window whirred down as the driver, a fit man in his forties, leaned across the built-in car phone and a stack of what I could only guess were television scripts on the passenger seat. "Hi, I'm Rich," he said. "I live across the street. What's going on?"

"Oh, just trying to get this place back in order," I answered.

"Thank you *Jesus*," was the neighbor's reply. "Is it true he was holding Lillian Sinclair prisoner here all this time?"

"Is that what they're saying?" Tally asked.

"Some cop was interviewed on NPR just now," he said.

"We don't know yet," I said, doubting such a scenario could be true.

We introduced ourselves then, and it became clear Rich was a chatty gay man infatuated with the seamier side of Hollywood and all of its hoary legends. "It's a cool house," he said. "Too bad Old Man Langen let it go to hell."

Old Man Langen. How Milly would've hated that.

He wished us luck and then raised his tinted window with the touch of a button before the automatic gates across the street swung open and he disappeared. Tally and I walked in the approaching evening, the Hollywood sign hanging in a hot haze in the distance, while Puck the Eighth sniffed and peed.

"So," Tally ventured, trying to sound casual, "I'm guessing there's more to your story than you're letting on. I mean, my dad left you everything, but you said you only knew him for two years. And the way my mom spoke of you I can't help wondering if you two had a little thing going on."

I stopped walking, ostensibly to allow Puck a chance to nibble on some long stems of grass like a salad before his next feast.

"But I understand if you're not ready to talk about it."

I considered for a moment, then finally asked, "Think you can handle the truth?"

"I'd like to try," she said.

And so I started to tell her the whole sordid story, from the moment I'd arrived in Los Angeles forty-two years before to the life-altering six weeks in Europe. Sure I glossed over the more salacious details but managed to leave the gist of it intact. Tally reeled from the onslaught of tawdry tidbits as I recounted the period I'd lived with her parents, having sex with both of them, but stopped before telling her how the whole situation inevitably exploded.

"Both of them? At the same time?" she asked, trying to understand.

"'During the same time' would be more accurate," I said. "I told you it was a pretty horrible story."

"So my dad was . . . gay?" She tried to puzzle it through. "I mean, it certainly would explain his fondness for ascots, but still . . ."

"I doubt he would've used the word 'gay.' He refused to acknowledge his sexuality."

"Yeah and look where it got him." She now stood staring up at the decaying moderne mansion bathed in golden twilight as we arrived home from our long walk at what cinematographers like to call "golden hour."

"You know, Tally, back then the word 'gay' meant—I don't know—festive and carefree."

"Just like it will again someday. I know it," she said, and I smiled at the sentiment. Then her tone shifted. "Sounds like you were a pretty angry guy."

"Hell, I was just a stupid kid. I felt like the world owed me for every little injustice I'd ever suffered, and Hollywood seemed like the right place to cash in on the debt. Things didn't exactly work out like I'd expected."

"How did they turn out?"

I hesitated, feeling a little overwrought from vividly recalling a past I'd spent most of my life trying to forget. "You mind if I finish the story another time?"

"When you're ready. It's a bit much to take in anyway. I mean, considering."

Still, as we went around back and into the gloomy house once more, her nagging curiosity seemed to get the best of her. "So you're, what, bisexual?"

"That's direct," I said, chuckling.

"Well, since you're being so honest . . . are you?"

"Time was, I sure as hell wanted to be," I said with a sigh. "It was a different world back then, Tally. And what I *didn't* want was to be gay. So I dated women. Got pretty good at pretending with them, you know . . . sexually . . . not to get too indelicate."

"Pretty sure we crossed that line when you told me you slept with my mom and dad."

I smiled. "The truth is, I was half-crazy with denial. Took me a few years to figure it out, but to answer your question, these days I'm pretty much as gay as a party dress." She laughed, watching as I removed Puck's collar to ready him for his bath. "You have a partner?" she asked. "Now, I mean?"

My smile faded. "I did. He died at the end of last year."

"I'm so sorry."

"We were together for twenty-one years. Militant nonsmoker and he dies of lung cancer at the age of fifty-two. Go figure."

"That's horrible."

"Yeah," I said, "but that's life. And you know what? Carol was the best thing that ever happened to me. He was a drama teacher at Grant High in San Jose, and I took a part-time job building scenery for some show they were doing. One thing led to another and pretty soon I moved into his house with him. Best years of my life."

"This must be especially hard for you, then," she said with genuine understanding. "Dealing with this on top of that."

I nodded. "The worst part . . ." The catch in my voice surprised me. The conversation had been easy and casual up until then, but the sudden emotion I felt about Carol finally caught up with me.

"You don't have to talk about it," she said, putting a comforting hand on my shoulder.

"That's the thing." I wiped my tears and tried to collect myself. "I never get to. I'm sixty-three years old, Tally, and I've been in love exactly twice. First with your dad—at least I'd convinced myself it was love. Before then, I'd never felt wanted in my life, let alone desired."

"Sounds like the second time was a lot better."

"Yeah. It would've been perfect except for one problem." I then went on to tell her about Carol's family. How they'd never accepted that their son and brother was gay, and how they'd shown up at his bedside in time to watch him die, ordering me out of the room because I wasn't "really family."

"Carol had to die in the company of people who couldn't love him the way I did," I said. "It killed me, not being there to hold his hand while he moved on."

It felt good to talk about the injustices I'd suffered from the tyranny of Carol's family. When I told Tally about how they'd changed the locks on the house before I could retrieve my belongings, she was livid. She had more gay friends than straight back in San Francisco and was sympathetic to our plight in the face of so many injustices.

"Sure, it was Carol's house, but I paid what I could to help out with the mortgage. I wasn't freeloading," I said, defending my dignity. "They actually thought I was going to steal whatever I could get my hands on."

"People suck," she replied.

Puck endured his bath in the tub in the downstairs maid's quarters as night slowly overtook the old house. We turned on what lights were still working, and then Tally came out of the kitchen where she'd been cleaning.

"I have a surprise," she said.

"Not sure I can handle any more just now." I smiled.

She held up a bottle of decent red wine she'd purchased at Ralph's, already open and breathing. In her other hand, two vintage stemmed glasses dangled between her fingers and a plastic grocery sack hung from her elbow.

"Oh, you meant a good surprise."

"I also picked up some deli sandwiches. I hope you like roast beef."

"Love it," I said, feeling the welcome relief of honesty between us. We went out and sat down on the crumbling flagstone verandah steps overlooking the empty pool, and soon we were sipping wine and eating sandwiches in the pale glow from a distant streetlight, watching as Puck sniffed around the thick overgrowth of ivy, undoubtedly hunting for rats.

Tally recalled her childhood swimming lessons in that very pool with Esther Williams and told me how her father had drained it when she'd been in high school in the early '70s after her mother fell in while drunk and nearly drowned. It was difficult to imagine the Milly and Lilly I'd known so many years ago raising a little girl in that house, and from Tally's stories I gathered it wasn't the most conventional of childhoods. She had been mostly alone and without playmates until the age of six when she started school, but Lillian had tried to compensate with elaborate games of dress-up, reading aloud the books that delighted her daughter while acting out all the parts, and throwing festive if under-attended birthday parties. Her father would sometimes surprise her with the most astonishing presents, calling her "Daddy's little gift" and dancing with her to music from his hi-fi in the roomy old foyer, but those cherished memories were few as he usually remained distant and buried in his work while Lillian always doted. Tally said she adored them both but had grown skittish trying to predict her dad's moods. I laughed and told her I could relate.

Lillian had retired from the movies shortly after Tally's birth in

201

February 1955, and even though the offers continued to come in, she turned them down until they eventually dried up. "Let them remember me as I was," she'd said. "I have a precious little girl to take care of now."

According to Tally, the truth was her mother seemed to be losing her mind as the years began to take their unstoppable toll on her once perfect face, and she'd begun covering mirrors in the house and medicating with more and more alcohol. Once, for Teacher Appreciation Day in third grade, Lillian had presented Tally with an ornately wrapped gift for Tally's third-grade teacher, and Tally had been mortified when Mrs. Hartsell opened it to reveal a bottle of bourbon incongruous with the dainty packs of lace hankies and home-baked treats from the other children. For a while Lillian would only venture out at night, and usually in dark glasses and a headscarf. Late one evening a neighbor had called and asked Milly to please come and get his wife who was standing on their front lawn, apparently performing a scene from one of her movies while flinging her fur coat around. Another time she'd wandered into a store in Larchmont Village, approached the bald proprietor, lit a skinny brown cigarette, and announced, "It's never coming back, you know."

"What?" the proprietor had asked.

"Your hair."

Milly had been producing *Double Your Trouble* in 1971, one of his short-lived TV series for ABC, and while the show was on life support in the ratings, Milly used it as an excuse to spend longer and longer hours at nearby Paramount Studios where it was filmed—most likely as a way of avoiding his wife's increasingly bizarre behavior.

"When did he retire?" I asked, curious and feeling the warm buzz from the wine as I finished off my sandwich.

"He didn't," she said. "He got forced out. His taste was outdated, and after the whole disaster with *Trouble in Tinseltown*, he couldn't get arrested."

"Never heard of it," I said, wondering if all of Milly's TV series had the word *trouble* in their titles.

"It was this epic miniseries he was producing for Paramount and NBC. About the Hollywood Blacklist. He went so far over budget in just one week of shooting—insisting the period work be done just right—that the studio fired him and brought in Aaron Spelling to finish the project. From what I gather, Dad got drunk and marched into Barry Diller's office and peed in a potted plant."

"That's a career ender," I said, with no idea who Barry Diller was and trying to reconcile her stories with the impeccable, image-obsessed man I had so madly loved.

"My parents were insane," she said, pouring more wine, then toasting the cracked, overgrown pool. "I mean, obviously."

"Is that why you left?" I asked.

She looked away from me. "I was pretty rebellious. My folks were so self-absorbed I guess it rubbed off on me. By the time I was ready for college, Mom and I were fighting all the time—mostly because I was *me* and she was, well . . . completely *nuts*. I couldn't deal with either one of them anymore, so, yeah. Then I got my inheritance after Mom supposedly died and blew through it pretty fast. At least I had the good sense to start my own business."

A silence fell as we contemplated the ruins all around us; then Tally stood up and dusted the legs of her jeans. "Okay," she said, "I think I'm buzzed enough now. Let's start reading. C'mon."

I nodded and helped her gather the litter from our impromptu picnic; then we went inside to her father's study. She called the hospital and, after endless moments on hold, spoke with Dr. Jameson who informed her there was nothing new to report about Lillian Sinclair's condition. We were already on our second bottle of wine as we divvied up Milly's manuscript and started to read. Tally took the first half, and I took the last, and we read for hours, sometimes aloud, others simply summarizing to each other what we'd just skimmed. It was slow going as we tried to decipher the copious revisions Milly had scrawled on the pages, and we were disappointed when all that emerged was a fairly straightforward, rather dry chronicle of his career, with no apparent mention of me, and without a single whiff of scandal. He wrote one paragraph about Lillian's "suicide" in 1982, relating how each and every day since her death he felt she had never really left him.

"Yeah, 'cause he had her hidden away upstairs," Tally said wryly.

He wrote with eloquence of the two years he and Lillian had lived in Paris from December of 1953 through most of '55, and also repeated verbatim the same old tired lies about his heroic bare-hands slaughtering of a Japanese pilot on an unspecified island in the South Pacific, in denial to the very end.

"That's funny," Tally said. "I had to do a paper about World War II for history class in high school, but Dad refused to talk about his stint in the navy."

"Maybe because some of it wasn't true."

"How do you know?"

"I just do," I said, "but right now, I'm exhausted."

Whatever answers we were seeking clearly wouldn't be found in the chicken-scratched memoir, so I told Tally about the mountains of cassette tapes, showing her the ones that remained on his desk as I gathered them and tried to sort them into order. "We'll have to go through all of these, I'm afraid." I told her how the samplings I'd heard in the motel were drunken and far more brutal in their honesty. I noted how none of his rant about Michael Spencer had made it into the typed pages.

"Great," she said dryly, "something to look forward to."

As we went back to the kitchen, she asked, "Does it bother you?"

"What?"

"That he didn't mention you in the book."

"I never expected he would."

It was late when we locked up and headed back to our hotel, leaving the quiet old mansion with all of its still untold secrets. Driving over, we decided we'd attack the bedrooms the next morning, and hopefully get the place fit enough to live in soon. Once inside my squalid little room at the Hollywood Center Motel, I unwrapped Puck the Eighth from the jacket I'd used to sneak him in. He curled up next to me on the bed, but even his contented breathing couldn't lull me to sleep.

TWENTY-ONE

Lillian was in mourning during the hushed weeks following Puck's death, so mercifully there was no pressure to resume our affair. Lucky for me as I wasn't sure I would even be capable. She complained of an ongoing and chronic migraine and spent most of her time behind the closed door of her bedroom, drapes drawn tight and a sleeping mask over her eyes. She wasn't only grieving for the dog as it turned out. She had become upset after reading Tallulah's just-published memoir but refused to say why. Sometimes, I'd hear Blanche going up and down the stairs, bringing Lilly a bowl of soup or a pitcher of water.

Milly returned to the studio the day following our melancholy homecoming, and after reimbursing a portion of the production costs on *Bring Them Back* out of his own pocket, his spat with Jack Warner over Lillian's breakdown was settled. Lillian had tossed the whole thing off, saying the news of my disappearance in Paris coupled with Puck's failing health had simply been too much for her, and while she wasn't proud of the tantrums she'd thrown in front of Joan Crawford, Mervyn LeRoy, and the entire film crew, she was relieved to be freed from the picture.

As for me, I wandered like a sleepwalker back into my old schedule of acting class, getting high all alone in the Urban Idyll, drifting in the pool, and occasionally finding myself surprised when a memory trigger would be pulled and I'd expect to encounter Puck going about his daily doddering routine. I had spent my own fair share of time crying over the loss of my little friend. Trouble showed no interest in me and stood devoted watch over Lillian around the clock. Milly seemed withdrawn during that time, and his silence crushed my heart as I prayed for just one fleeting moment when we might lose ourselves in each other again. The Urban Idyll sat still and unused each night, as if we all three felt the permeating gloom that had settled over us.

Finally, with Halloween two weeks away, Lillian accepted a role in a thriller called *While a Clock Ticks*, so she was gone during the days, leaving me alone and lonely in the vast expanse of the empty mansion. I'd resumed my secretive searches through their belongings, mostly out of boredom rather than any desire to know more about these people. My curiosity about Milly's locked desk drawer still gnawed at me as I wondered if he'd written about us in his little moleskin notebooks, and was only temporarily mollified when I found, tucked beneath the lining paper under the socks in his wardrobe, an envelope containing his discharge papers from the navy. Dated April of '42, they revealed how Milly had left the service under dishonorable circumstances, not the heroic slaying of an enemy soldier as he oft repeated. More specifically, it had been a drunken fight with another sailor. When my eyes fell on the neatly typed carbon-copied words "homosexual conduct," I knew why the guy had stabbed him. I marveled that Milly hadn't burned those papers as I returned them to their envelope and hiding place under his fastidious rolls of expensive argyle.

I lingered in the stillness of his bedroom, taking in the burled wood paneling alive with slashes of sunlight through the half-open Venetian blinds. The big, comfortable-looking bed was slightly recessed into the wall, flanked by built-in shelves of illuminated milk glass. A massive painting signed *Francois* hung on the wall above it, depicting a French sailor surrounded by a group of cubist women in a Parisian bar done in muted dusty blues and golds. I longed to make love with Milly in this masculine room, and sleep in the comfort of his arms until morning, but knew he'd never risk it. For reasons I didn't entirely understand I avoided Lillian's opulent bedroom with its gargantuan movie prop portrait of her. Those oil-painted eyes had followed me around the first and only time I'd ever wandered in there alone.

A new mystery presented itself to me one day when I decided to watch a movie in the theater on the ground floor of the house's southern wing, directly under the guest bedroom that had been the scene of many unbridled afternoons with Lillian Sinclair. The theater held twelve comfortable leather chairs sloping down its raked and carpeted floor, and its walls were lined with olive curtains motorized at the far end so as to swish apart and reveal the silver screen at the touch of a button. Without speaking a word, Deming had shown me the spring-latched door hidden behind more draperies and leading into the narrow concealed booth, and then gruffly demonstrated how to operate the two projectors. I had let myself in that afternoon, and while I sorted through the alphabetized cans of film, I noticed a small hatch in the ceiling of the booth. Strangely enough, it had its own doorknob, but when I stepped onto a metal stool to open it, I discovered it, too, was locked.

I ended up sitting in the dark alone, crying through most of *Room for One More*, a sappy comedy about a middle-class couple played by Cary Grant and his real wife Betsy Drake who bring troubled orphans into their already full home. The picture's happy ending only left me feeling more abandoned.

Early one afternoon, I was sitting in my swim trunks on the bed in the cabana, idle and bored, sorting through the mementoes I'd collected since my arrival in Hollywood. I had a small record player of my own now and was listening to some of Milly's old jazz 78s, smoking dope and cigarettes, and drinking a post-lunch scotch. I was surprised by the soft tap at the open doorway, and even more so to see Milly standing there, still in the suit and fedora he'd worn that morning to the studio. My stomach fluttered.

"Dex?" he asked, his voice strained but polite.

"What are you doing home?"

"I came to see you," he said. I smiled, going to him, thrilled by his words. *At last.* As I moved to take him in my arms and kiss him, he pulled away, glancing toward the house.

"Don't be insane," he said. "I need to talk to you."

Stung, I turned away.

"Well, as you can see, I'm pretty busy," I said, realizing my words were slurred from the scotch. Milly came into the room and took off his hat, tossing it onto one of the matching chairs before plopping down into the other and lighting a cigarette.

"We need to talk business if you're sober enough."

"I'm fine," I said, lying back on the bed and propping myself up on one elbow, trying to adopt a sexy and alluring pose. But he wouldn't even look at me.

"I . . . actually have some bad news and some good news," he said evenly through an exhale of smoke that lazed in the dusty sunlight from the window.

"Great. Let's hear the bad," I sighed.

"Darryl's insisting on R.J. for Gifford. We knew this might happen. They're announcing it this afternoon."

"Yeah, well, I'm not surprised," I said, then decided to hell with it and poured myself another slug of scotch and downed it. "What's the good news?"

"I got you a bit in the movie," he said with forced enthusiasm, as if expecting me to be delighted.

"A bit?" The words came out with all the disappointment I could muster.

"It's a speaking part, in a little scene with Barbara Stanwyck," he said, trying a touch too hard to make it sound more important than it was. "Darryl thought your test was good, and he knows you're handsome enough to be a leading man, but he doesn't think you're ready yet, and he wants to go with a name and—"

"Oh stop pitching past the sell, Milly," I said, throwing his own words back at him, irritated.

"Okay. Anyway, I just wanted you to know." He rose to his feet, picking up his fedora by the sharp crease in the crown, then waved it slightly in his hand as he stood there, not yet leaving.

"You drove all the way home from the studio to tell me I got a bit part?"

He didn't reply, and I could see he was torn. This was my chance.

"I miss you, Milly," I said, getting up from the bed and approaching him. "It's been horrible since we got back."

"I know," he said, his voice low and strained. "It's been horrible for me, too."

"Maybe that's why you really came home?" I asked, drawing closer. "Knowing Lillian's at work, I mean."

"It's far more complicated than I ever imagined."

"Actually, it's pretty simple," I said, stepping out of my trunks. His eyes devoured me, even as I could tell he was trying to tear them away. Staying clear of the sight lines from the house, I shut the double French doors and pulled the cord to close the blinds. Within seconds, we were making up for lost time, our lips once more together as I pulled him onto the bed, tenderly exploring his now familiar body. His strong hands caressed me as I rode him, and I stopped myself just on the brink of shouting "Oh god oh god," biting my lip and shaking my head in ecstasy as he climaxed. The record had ended, and the only sound in the room was the rhythmic swishing of the phonograph needle bobbing idly in the trap grooves. I crumpled onto him, then maneuvered so he could finish me, but he pushed me aside and got out of bed, hastening back into his clothes.

"This shouldn't have happened."

"Of course it should've. God, Milly, you know we both want it. And nobody's gonna know. Now c'mon, you can't leave me like this." I rose up on my knees, exposed and throbbing.

"You're drunk," he said, "and I have to get back to the studio." He yanked the door open and walked out, leaving me unsatisfied and naked in my humiliated anger.

I went out and dove into the pool, still nude, and swam away my frustration, at length returning to the cabana to smoke an entire joint and polish off the bottle of scotch along with the last four silver-tipped Turkish cigarettes in the engraved gold case Milly had given me. I'd been rationing them for special occasions, but figured there might not be any more, so what the hell. As the afternoon crept toward evening, I heard Lillian talking to Trouble through the open kitchen windows, home from the day's shoot. I staggered into my tiny bathroom and showered, then shaved and brushed my teeth, spending extra time with the mouthwash before putting on my white dungarees and a tight tee shirt, then stomped barefoot across the warm grass toward the house. The kitchen was empty now, though something simmered on the stove. Heading for the foyer, I saw the ripple of black and chrome through the curved glass brick signaling Milly's limo was pulling into the driveway. Perfect timing, I thought, as I now sprinted up the stairs, two at a time.

Lillian was startled when I walked into her room.

"Dex? Are you all—?" I silenced her with a deep and hungry kiss, so filled with passionate desperation I could taste her lipstick as it smeared on my face. She resisted for only a moment before going limp in my arms as I lifted her up, kicked the door closed with a slam, and then threw her onto the bed, already unbuttoning her blouse and freeing her from her bra. "Yes, yes, please . . ." she said, breathless. I scooped her breasts into my mouth, fighting back the alluring vision of Milly's dime-sized nipples, licking their fleshy buttons the way I'd done to her husband. She heard Milly's voice in the foyer and tensed, but I didn't stop.

"Dex, it's too dangerous," she said, unaware I was now familiar with their arrangement.

"More than you know," I replied, raising her skirt and yanking her panties down.

"Then hurry," she said, gasping and overcome. I had her sprawled sideways across the bed and was kneeling on the floor beside her in an attempt to hide the fact that I was not aroused. Instead, I kissed down her body and held my breath while I finished her with my tongue, just the way I knew she liked. She smashed a pillow over her face and pinned it there as her body spasmed. "Oh god," she moaned, shuddering. When I pulled away, I saw lipstick now smudged on the pale softness of her inner thighs like blood.

I stood up, still fully dressed. "I better go."

She nodded, smiling as she tried to catch her breath. I walked out of her room, not bothering to be quiet about closing the door. Stepping out onto the landing overlooking the foyer, I locked eyes with Milly who was just starting up the stairs, a fresh scotch rocks tinkling in his hand. We approached each other, him coming up, me going down, and I didn't look away as we brushed past, making damn sure he saw the torrid display of his wife's lipstick on my mouth.

"She's a better lay than you are," I whispered as I passed him. I couldn't see his face, but I was sure it was ashen as he continued on his way upstairs. I heard him tap on Lillian's door, then her inaudible, muffled reply.

I returned to the cabana to relieve my pounding frustration, but only damnable thoughts of Milly would bring me any satisfaction.

The weekend passed with more somber tension strangling the house on Windsor. Lillian spent most of her time in the darkness of her bedroom, studying her lines and fearful of doing anything that might affect her appearance in front of the cameras. I had watched Tallulah's debut in *All Star Revue* alone Saturday night on the television in the kitchen, the laughter of the studio audience echoing through the silent house, and when I'd passed Milly's study, noticed a flickering gray light underneath the closed door. I could hear the 16mm projector whirring, and assumed he was screening rushes or home movies. When I tapped, stupidly hopeful, he didn't answer, so I skulked off to bed alone.

Monday morning brought two surprises, the first coming when the telephone rang in the cabana, its shrill clang pulling me from a troubled and erotic dream. I snatched the heavy handset from the cradle, pressed it to my face and croaked, "Hello?"

It was Milly's voice on the other end, instructing me to put on my gray flannel suit and meet him in the driveway at eight-fifteen sharp.

"What—?" I stammered, but he had already hung up.

I turned the alarm clock around, realizing I had forty-five minutes to get ready and to down whatever Blanche was serving for breakfast.

The next surprise came after I was dressed and finishing my second cup of coffee. The doorbell rang. A few seconds later, it rang again.

Annoyed, I wondered what had become of the servants, then made my way through the entry foyer and yanked open the door just as the bell rang with impatience yet again.

"Thank *god*, darling! I was about to break a *window*."

"Tallu!" I said, delighted to see her.

She was wearing a full-length fur and dark glasses, a pale blue chiffon scarf draped around her throat as she held a burning cigarette aloft, her huge leather purse dangling from her arm. "Well, don't look so surprised, honey-child. You *were* expecting me, weren't you?"

"I was? I mean, we were?"

"Perhaps Lillian wanted to surprise you. Would you be a *darling* and help me with my bags?"

I was still trying to process this turn of events as I saw the mountain of suitcases piled behind her. It looked as if she had come for a very long stay. While I brought them into the foyer and she admired how well I'd matured since last she'd seen me, Milly came downstairs dressed for work.

"Tallu?" he asked, bewildered.

"Why must *everyone* look at me as if I'd just shown up at my own *funeral*?"

Milly kissed her offered cheek. "Because we weren't expecting you."

"I don't understand," she said, tapping ash onto the floor, agitated. "I sent Lillian a telegram last week. Where is she?"

"She had a 6 a.m. call. And you know how distracted she gets when she's shooting," Milly explained. "She probably forgot to tell us. What are you doing here?"

"Making a goddamned movie, of course. I'm to play myself of all things in a little ditty for Metro called *Main Street to Broadway*. *Ghastly*, really, to have to *parody* oneself. I mean, *honestly*."

I knew what Milly was thinking. That Tallulah Bankhead was, by the fall of 1952, widely considered to be nothing *but* a parody of herself. Still, I adored her and was delighted she'd be staying at the house for the next few weeks of production. Milly rang for Deming and instructed him to take Miss Bankhead's luggage to one of the front guest rooms. We bid farewell to the flamboyant actress and got into the limo now waiting for us in the driveway.

As we headed toward Pico Boulevard, I turned to Milly. "What are you doing? Taking me somewhere so you can murder me?" I asked, Friday night's anger still boiling in my stomach.

"Quite the contrary. You have a meeting with the head of casting."

Milly's unpredictable swings were starting to make me dizzy.

"Oh," was all I could manage. While the limo crawled through morning traffic, Milly put on his reading glasses and turned his attention to making notes on the final draft of *Titanic*, folding the page corners with fussy precision as he did so. I thought about his airborne anger at me when I'd done the same, but knew better than to tease or bother him. The picture was due to commence principal photography in just a few days, and even though it wasn't a Milford Langen production, Zanuck had asked him to give the screenplay a final once-over. I could see the words on the pages shimmering in his spectacles and marveled at his keen intelligence and power. Whatever he was jotting down would surely make the movie so much better, and the writers, director, actors and everyone involved would benefit from Milly's behind-the-scenes contributions. Even the way he turned the pages, sometimes glancing at his wristwatch, told me his mind was crackling and alive as he planned the busy day ahead. I sat there mesmerized by him and realized I was willing to endure the unpredictable flashes of cruelty as I waited doggishly for even the tiniest morsel of affection from this intoxicating, infuriating man.

"Are you staring at me?" he asked, crossing out a line of dialogue and scribbling an alternative without so much as a glance my way.

"No, I was . . . just dozing off, actually. Sorry," I covered, finally tearing my eyes from him.

The head of casting turned out to be a stern woman named Mona Lucas whose office was piled with headshots and reels of film. Her male secretary cleared a sofa for me to sit down, asking if I'd like some coffee. "Sure," I replied, noticing in his expression a glimmer of the handsome Italian waiter who had admired me in Rome. I returned his smile with a playful bounce of my eyebrows. Milly had gone to his magnificent little office bungalow, giving me a perfunctory warning to make a good impression on the no-nonsense Miss Lucas.

Mona was finishing up a call as her secretary brought my coffee, serving it with the same knowing grin before exiting and closing the door. Mona at last hung up, put her hands flat on her desk, and looked at me.

"Okay. Dexter Gaines."

"That's me." I grinned.

"Age?"

"Almost twenty-two."

"Where are you from?"

"Texas, ma'am. Little town called Tyler."

"Where's your accent?"

"Left it back home, ma'am."

She grunted, asked a few more questions, then had me stand in the bright morning light from the window as she turned my face side to side.

"What's that on your lip?"

"A birthmark," I said, trying not to blush. "It covers up really easily."

"Good." She sorted through a stack of scripts that looked ready to collapse onto the floor, plucking one and flipping to a monologue. "Read this."

So I did, scanning the words and making sure my lips didn't move.

"Aloud," she barked.

"Sorry," I said, then cleared my throat. She went back to her desk and sat down, slipped on her big horn-rimmed glasses, then started jotting notes on a typed memorandum, not even looking at me.

"'Say, fellas,'" I started, "'why you carrying on this way?'"

"Deeper, from the diaphragm," she said, engrossed in her work.

I adjusted. "'Why you carrying on this way? We're all here for the same thing, right? We gotta kill us some Nazis and get back home to our girls. So come on . . .'" I continued to act as best I could, which was difficult because I had no context for my character's role or circumstances, and there sure as hell weren't any clues in the terrible dialogue. At length, just as I was settling in, she stopped me.

214

"Are you nervous?" she asked.

"Not really," I replied.

"Then why are your hands shaking?"

"Oh," I realized, "maybe I *am* a little nervous."

"Wait outside," she said. I started out. "And leave the script here, please."

"Right. Thanks." I put the script onto a pile by the door and, as I stepped into the waiting room, heard her voice buzz on the intercom as she told her secretary to get Milford Langen on the phone. With the door closed behind me, I sat down in the row of chairs against the wall opposite the desk where the finicky young man was already on hold, waiting for Milly to pick up. He smiled at me.

"Yes, I have Mona Lucas for Mr. Langen," he said crisply, then, after a moment, he covered the mouthpiece with his hand and gave me a conspiratorial look. "I can listen in if you like."

Before I could answer, he returned to the phone, "She'll be right with you, Mr. Langen." He cupped the handset between his shoulder and his ear and pressed the intercom button. "That's him," he said to his boss. He eavesdropped on their conversation for a moment, his smile fading before he hung up.

"What?" I asked.

"Oh, nothing," he said, "they're talking about something else." I couldn't tell if he was lying or not.

He returned to his typewriter where his fingers clacked across the keys. The intercom buzzed and he pushed a button.

"Yes, Miss Lucas?" he said.

Her voice crackled through the little wooden box. "Send Mr. Gaines to Building 58."

"Congratulations," he said with a smile.

"What's Building 58?" I asked.

"The portrait studio," he replied, then told me how to get there. I thanked him, my head swimming a little, and followed his directions once I got outside.

The 20th Century Fox lot was like a thriving ant colony, and for a moment I was briefly overwhelmed that I was actually there. I was walking through charming bungalows interspersed with giant sound stages, and in the distance I could see the sprawl of the massive back lot. Man, how I'd have loved to take a look around there. I passed the yawning open doors of Stage 14 and stood small and backlit as I watched a team of workers putting the final touches on a huge section of the *Titanic* set. I wondered if my bit would be shot there, then resumed my search.

When I arrived at the portrait studio, they were already expecting me, and two women fretted while they combed my hair and dabbed my face with makeup, paying particular attention to the "bittersweet chocolate" on my lip. A man in a billowy silk shirt and beret rolled a rack of clothes over for me to try on, and I did so behind a small trifold screen while he clucked and preened. The photographer was a gruff bull of a man, and he didn't waste any time putting me in various poses and outfits, adjusting his lighting, and barking orders to his assistants as he shot what felt like hundreds of pictures of me. First in black then white tie, open collar and sports jacket, an ascot I was sure made me look ridiculous, shirts of different colors and patterns, then just my undershirt, and finally several beefcake shots with no shirt at all.

"Okay. You're done." And off he went to his next assignment.

"Thanks," I said, then changed back into my own clothes before wandering out into the excitement of the workday at the movie studio. I saw Darryl Zanuck emerge from a long, low three-story building and get into the back of a limo before driving off with an air of authority, and I wondered if he'd remember me from that horrible New Year's Eve. I hoped not.

I finally made my way to Milly's bungalow and gave my name to his pert young secretary. She buzzed him on the intercom, and shortly his door yanked open and Milly ushered me into his sanctuary before closing it again. The room was bigger than his office at home, and equally masculine and important. Its walls were covered with framed posters from his movies, and the scent of tobacco and Milly's aftershave was both sensual and familiar.

"How'd it go?" he asked, grabbing his jacket from the back of his chair.

"No idea," I said. "They took a lot of pictures."

"That's a good sign. Now c'mon, I'm taking you to lunch in the commissary."

His mood had lightened since that morning, making me miss him all the more.

"Milly," I said, stopping him before he reached the door, "why're you doing this for me? Now, I mean."

"Because I promised I would," he said.

"C'mon," I pressed, "I'm grateful, believe me, but isn't there more to it than that?"

Milly sighed and half-smiled. When he spoke, his voice was low and honest. "I already told you I believe in your potential. I'm a producer through and through, and I know if you're handled right, you could make me, Darryl, the studio *and* yourself quite a bit of money. You can be a big star, Dex. What else do you want me to say?"

It was nice to hear, but not exactly the answer I had hoped for. "So it's just some kind of business deal? Is that why you're acting like Europe never happened?"

"Quite the contrary, dear boy. I'm acting very much as if Europe remains on my mind every minute. Which is precisely why I—*we*—must always be on our best behavior. We're in Hollywood now. And believe me, no one wishes that weren't true more than I do."

He looked at me, and I could tell he wanted the conversation to be over, but the hurt was already furrowed around my mouth and eyes.

"Look," he said, "I know I was horrible to you the other day in the cabana. And I'm genuinely sorry. But we have to be careful."

"I know, I know. But can't we figure out some way to get some time together? Something safe and discreet, I mean."

He put his hand on my shoulder and met my gaze. "Let me give it some thought. Now let's go. We need to show you off around the lot, get people jawing about you."

With that, he opened the door and ushered me out.

As we walked with purpose toward the commissary, Milly occasionally paused to answer the cheery and respectful chorus of "Good morning, Mr. Langen" from various underlings. I basked in his powerful aura, noting the approving and curious glances that came my way, once again relishing the stature afforded by being at his side and the focus of his attention, and was almost overwhelmed with relief when he finally said, "I really am sorry. About Friday."

"Me, too," I replied as he held the door of the Fox commissary open for me.

When I got home around three, I could hear Tallulah fussing with Blanche in the kitchen, instructing her on the right way to prepare her eggs. She had gone to sleep the minute she arrived, and had now emerged, coming out to the pool while sipping from a coffee cup (which I later learned was full of bourbon). While she waited for Deming to bring her breakfast, she watched me finish my regular afternoon swim. As I lounged on the pool coping, enjoying titillating her with all my firm, bronzed flesh, I complimented her debut as the hostess of NBC's *All Star Review*.

"You watched?" she asked, wriggling in her seat, immodestly flattered.

"Of course. Your sketch with Ethel Barrymore was a riot!" I gushed, meaning it. Tallulah had essentially played a more conceited version of her actress self, asking Barrymore for an honest critique of her performance in a play, only to be piqued by everything Barrymore had to offer. Sure, it was a rehash of the same bit she'd done on her radio show, but seeing this marvelous actress play the role with her expressive face brought a whole new dimension.

"Really? Did you think so? I thought I was perfectly *dreadful*."

"You were brilliant."

"I don't know, darling. My timing was off."

"Not at all! It was really funny, Tallu," I said, realizing we were reenacting a version of the skit for real.

"What did Lillian have to say?"

"Oh, I'm afraid she missed it," I said, measuring my words. "She had an early call the next morning."

"Really," Tallulah said flatly, her droopy eyes narrowing as she added, "She was filming on a *Sunday?*"

I realized my blunder and tried to cover. "Oh, uh, I think she'd gotten revisions for today's work and had to learn a whole bunch of new lines," I lied. I honestly didn't know why Lillian hadn't watched but wasn't about to start anything between the two friends. I was rescued when Deming arrived with Tallulah's eggs and toast. She put her cigarette down in the ashtray, took a few bites, then resumed smoking.

"Hard to believe you were on television night before last, and now here you are." I forced a laugh.

"It's utterly *exhausting*, honey-child."

I then went on to tell her how I'd devoured her memoirs and congratulated her on how well the book was selling.

"Devoured? Really, darling, they're just the white-washed *ramblings* of a *delusional* old broad. But thank you for the compliment. Now resume your backstroke so I can *enjoy* the scenery."

I flashed her a smile and dove back into the water.

Later that night, when Lillian and Milly were both home from the studio, Lillian made a valiant attempt at being gracious, apologizing for forgetting to inform us of Tallulah's visit, but I could tell from her demeanor something was up. Milly had his music playing in the backyard, and the Urban Idyll was once again alive with the twinkle of candles and the dusty, melancholy chalk of June Christy's voice, followed by the grits and honey growl of Billie Holiday, which brought a bittersweet smile to Tallu's face. While Milly and I swam a few lazy laps, Lillian and Tallulah sat on the swing, handing a reefer back and forth, passing it over the sleeping Trouble who was curled up between them, his chin resting in Lillian's lap.

"Well, now's as good a time as any," Milly said, climbing out of the water and toweling off. I tried to avert my eyes from his trim body, fearful of betraying our secret.

"For what?" Lillian asked.

"I have an announcement."

As was his habit, he milked the drama by lighting a cigarette and refilling his scotch glass, taking his time as he plucked an errant fleck of tobacco from his lower lip. After enduring all she could of this, Tallulah roared, "Oh *enough* of the stage wait, darling, what *is* it?"

"We're putting Dexter under contract."

I wasn't sure I'd heard him right. Tallulah clapped her hands and rasped her congratulations, and Lillian seemed genuinely excited for me as I stood waist-deep in the cool water, blinking like a fool. Just three days before, Milly had all but rejected me after we'd made love, and now . . .

"Well?" he said, grinning at me as I rose up out of the pool.

"I don't . . . are you serious?" was all I could manage.

"Of course I'm serious. You're already scheduled for your *Titanic* debut, and there are some other projects we have in development you'd be right for. It's two hundred dollars a week with various raises and options depending on how well you do, plus your per-picture salary, of course, so you're definitely on your way."

I was out of the pool now, and in my excitement caught us both off guard when I threw my arms around his naked torso and lifted him off his feet, spinning him around.

"Put me down!" he snapped, but I didn't let go.

"I love you, Milford Langen," I shouted. Lillian and Tallulah seemed to be oblivious, falling for my boyish horseplay and unaware of the truth lurking underneath. Finally, I released him.

He gasped and played along, joking. "Oh fine, Dexter Gaines. I love you, too."

It was the only time he'd ever say those words aloud to me.

"Awwwww," Lillian said, her eyes glazed from the weed.

"Champagne!" Tallulah barked.

Our euphoria was to be short-lived because Tallulah at last cornered Lillian. "All right, Lil. What's the matter? You haven't uttered *word one* about my book."

"Oh," Lillian said. "You know, Blanche picked up one of the last watermelons of the season today. I think I'll go and slice it up."

She rose from the swing and started for the house, Trouble leaping down and trotting close at her heels.

"What is it?" Tallulah pleaded, teetering as she got up to follow. The two women headed barefoot across the damp grass and Milly and I traded a look.

"Hold onto your hat," was all Milly said.

Lillian didn't stop as she went up the verandah steps and toward the kitchen, Tallu right behind. "You want to know why I haven't said a word about your goddamned book?"

"I *asked* you, didn't I?"

"Because you didn't say a goddamned word about *me!*" Lillian said, wounded. "I thought we were best friends!"

"*What?* Darling, I didn't write about you because you *specifically* told me *not* to!" Tallulah bellowed. Soon, the two women were locked in a ferocious argument. Milly and I stood there by the pool, watching as Tallulah shadowed Lillian all over the kitchen, gesticulating wildly while Lilly chopped into a huge watermelon, dicing it to pulp in her fury. Framed as they were by the brightly lit kitchen window, the whole thing looked like a puppet show, with both of them playing to the back of the house.

"You've not yet had the pleasure of witnessing one of these, have you?" Milly asked, leaning a little closer.

"Apparently not."

"Don't worry, it'll blow over soon enough and both of them will be sobbing 'I love you' into their mint juleps."

"Sorry about that, by the way," I said, meaning it. "Saying 'I love you' in front of them."

Milly delighted me with a smile. "I thought you played the scene perfectly."

"As did you."

Our eyes lingered for a long, sad moment as the argument boiled over from the kitchen. Tallulah was roaring and Lillian was weeping and Trouble was barking his fool head off at the two of them. At last Milly said, "I'm going to get dressed. Perhaps we'll screen a film later once the Battle of Gettysburg is over."

"Okay," I said, not wanting him to go. "I'd like that."

As he started across the lawn, I added, "Thank you, Milly."

He paused long enough to pivot on his heel and smile back at me. "Just don't screw it up." And he went inside.

"You're a *terribly* private person, Lillian, and *you* said you *didn't* want me writing about you!" Tallulah was still raging.

"You never even mentioned my name! You could have at least included me in your list of friends!"

"I'm *sorry*, darling!"

And so it went, until I noticed even the loyal Trouble had had enough. He was slinking out the open verandah doors, but when he saw me, scurried off and hid behind the bushes near the koi pond. I dressed and went into the house, careful to avoid the kitchen and the fight that continued unabated, their voices rising and falling with renewed rushes of indignation.

I started down the hallway toward the screening room when a new, more horrible sound now reverberated through the house. Trouble was yelping amid a violent roar of growls and the snapping of shrubs. Lillian and Tallulah arrived on the verandah at the same instant I did, and the three of us stood in open-mouthed, paralyzed horror as we watched a large coyote, fangs bared and dripping blood, circling the freshly wounded Trouble.

"Trouble!" Lillian shouted, starting to run over.

Tallulah grabbed her arm to hold her back. "Don't be a *fool*, Lillian! It'll kill you, too."

As Milly came racing out to join us, I sprinted back into the house to get Milly's gun, returning a few seconds later just as the coyote pounced on Trouble and clamped the little dog's throat in its angry teeth, flinging him side to side in an effort to break his neck, spraying blood onto the grass. Lillian was hysterical. "No, no, I can't go through this again!" Milly was throwing rocks at the beast, shouting at it, but the coyote was too hungry, crazy, or both to be dissuaded.

That's when I pulled the trigger of Milly's .22 and the blast shattered the October night, knocking the coyote sideways. They all turned, open-mouthed, to see me standing there, steadying the gun with both my trembling hands as I fired again, this time missing.

Wounded and covered in blood, the coyote released the struggling Trouble and hobbled away. I fired another shot as it leapt over the fence and vanished.

Milly ran to the blood-soaked dog, its whimpers pitiful and growing quiet. Lillian buried her face in Tallulah's shoulder, and her friend put her arms around her. No one said a word. I went across the lawn and joined Milly as he whispered, "Don't let Lillian see this."

I looked. The dog had been disemboweled, his stomach and intestines a gnarled and pulsing mass of blood and fur. His breathing was shallow, and we knew he was done for. Lillian collapsed to her knees behind us, and Tallulah sat down on the flagstone, never once releasing her friend. "There there," she cooed as Lillian sobbed, "don't look. Don't look."

"Dexter," Milly said in a low voice, "we need to put the poor thing out of his misery."

"You mean . . .?"

"You want me to do it?"

"I can't," I said, tears in my eyes. I handed him the gun.

"Take Lillian inside," Milly said.

I went over to her and gently pulled her to her feet as she sobbed. "I'm sorry, Lilly, I'm so so sorry," was all I could manage as we went into the house. Tallulah helped me get her up the stairs, and it wasn't until we were in the bedroom that we heard the single, fatal shot echoing from the back yard. Lillian rolled away from us on her bed, and I left her there with Tallulah caressing her back as I closed the door. The mournful wail of a siren announced the arrival of the police, undoubtedly in response to a call from a neighbor worried about all the gunshots.

When I rejoined Milly, he was saying goodnight to the two officers as he showed them out the back gate, the commotion having been reasonably explained. He came back and finished wrapping the dog in a towel from the cabana, his face unreadable.

"Dexter?" he asked. "How did you know where I keep my .22?"

I froze for a split second before replying, as calmly as I could. "I was getting stamps for Lillian," I lied. "And I must've pulled open the wrong drawer."

"I see," he said, heading off to put Trouble's body in the garage. "But I'd appreciate it if you wouldn't go through my things."

TWENTY-TWO

The autumn and winter of '52 proved to be my most magical time in Hollywood, winter being a relative term in the perpetual Southern California sunshine. It would also prove to be my most confusing. Tallulah had imbued the house with her infectious bawdiness, and Lillian had surprised us all when, ever the professional, she'd returned to work on *While a Clock Ticks* at 6 a.m. the morning following Trouble's tragic and violent death. The scene she'd filmed that day was one of her best, calling for her character to become distraught upon learning her daughter has been kidnapped in Amsterdam. When we screened the rough cut in the projection room, Tallulah had been devastated by Lillian's overwrought performance, and while we all knew she was drawing upon the events of the previous night to bring the tears and histrionics, no one dared mention Trouble's name.

On Halloween I arrived home from a hastily arranged lunch with Hedda Hopper as part of the studio's publicity push for their new "discovery." I was cradling a little bundle in my arms and found Lillian and Tallu chatting and making a mess of Blanche's kitchen as they fried something on the stove, their feud having been forgotten.

"I have a surprise for you," I said, playful, then delighted Lillian when I pulled back a corner of the blanket I was carrying to show her the half-terrier-half-god-knows-what puppy I'd picked up at the pound.

"Dexter!" she cried, "You've brought Puck back to me!" She scooped up the little ball of fur in her flour-covered hands and buried her face in his.

"Good *Lord*," Tallulah said, her eyes wide as she yanked her cigarette out of her mouth. "He's got balls bigger than *mine!*"

I stood there grinning as Lillian kissed my cheek in gratitude. "You're my hero," she said as the puppy licked her face. "How'd it go with that dragon Hedda Hopper?"

"No idea," I said. "She asked the usual questions and I told the usual lies, so . . . who knows if she'll even write about me. Something smells good."

"It's buttermilk fried chicken, honey-child," Tallulah said. "The way my granny used to make."

"And," Lillian said, pointing to the counter where caramel apples sat drying on waxed paper, "I made treats for later."

Milly came home in an uncharacteristically good mood as well, stopping to whisper in the foyer that he had a surprise of his own for me.

"What is it?" I asked, as pleased as I was impatient.

"Keep Saturday free," was all he replied with a wink before heading off to the liquor cabinet in his study. Although his erratic behavior toward me was dizzying, I was grateful for whatever morsel I could get, and was elated to see this latest thaw and the promise it held for the weekend.

The doorbell was ringing with a constant stream of trick-or-treaters, and the jack-o'-lanterns we'd all carved the night before while getting drunk and stoned in the Urban Idyll glowed on the front steps with the enticing smell of roasting pumpkin as flurries of dried leaves scratched across the circular drive. Milly was doing something in his study while Tallu, Lillian and I took turns delighting at the parade of costumes on the neighborhood kids, the new Puck barking nonstop in all the confusion. Tallu was wearing a pointed witch's hat with a campaign button for Adlai Stevenson on it and was particularly effective at terrorizing the children, offering the bowl of cello-wrapped candies and caramel apples and warning the little urchins of the horrific consequences if they didn't tell their parents to vote the Democratic ticket.

"I adore Halloween," Lillian said, picking up her new dog. "And I adore you, too. Yes, I do," she cooed as the dog panted and licked her face again. Lillian's eyes met mine in silent gratitude, as if she'd been talking to me. I smiled in return.

"All right, darlings," Tallulah bellowed in the cavernous foyer after the doorbell had at last stopped ringing, "we're going to a party."

"Not another fundraiser for Stevenson, I hope."

"No, honey-child," Tallulah rumbled, "it's a costume soiree."

"But we haven't any costumes," Lillian said.

"Oh yes we do," Tallulah replied, full of mischief. "Auntie Tallu made sure of that." She then showed us the trunk overflowing with pieces she'd borrowed from MGM's wardrobe department where she was filming *Main Street to Broadway*. Turns out the hat she had perched on her head was one of several worn by Margaret Hamilton in *The Wizard of Oz*.

"Milford Langen! Get out here!" Tallu roared.

"What now?" Milly asked, padding in from his study.

Soon, we were dressed and ready, piling into the back of the Cadillac as a put-upon Deming glowered at us. Tallu had thrown on a black robe to go with her witch's hat while Lillian had selected a rather tattered Bo Peep getup. Milly looked like a television test pattern in a Comanche Indian Chief headdress with his tailored jacket and slacks, and I felt pretty darn sporty in the white sailor suit and hat Gene Kelly had worn in *On the Town*. Sure the sleeves and pant legs were a little too short for me, but it was a costume after all, not a uniform.

Tallulah wouldn't tell us where we were going, but of all the nights I had spent in the already fading glamour of Hollywood, this one would be among the most electric. We made our way to the splendor of Beverly Hills, then meandered up a curving street called Warbler Way before stopping in front of a modest house festooned with Halloween decorations—Dean Martin's home. As the evening wore on, all of us drinking and smoking and laughing, Dean introduced Nat King Cole who smiled as he put his cigarette in the ashtray on the baby grand and started to play, a silk top hat perched rakishly on his head. Soon Dean was crooning, followed by Peggy Lee, as a tipsy Judy Garland joined in. They played well off each other, everything spontaneous and impromptu, as our laughter and applause echoed throughout the house, and no doubt the whole neighborhood. Judy's poignant rendition of her signature "Over the Rainbow" brought a momentary hush, beautiful and surreal as she sang while wearing cat ears and painted whiskers, but before she could finish, a human Tasmanian Devil burst into the room and spoiled the moment. It was Jerry Lewis, and while Garland looked miffed at having been upstaged, the crowd soon forgot her as we gasped for air at Martin and Lewis' antics. All eyes were on them as they clowned around, affording a furtive, private moment when Milly's gaze met mine and he smiled.

God, how I missed him.

Back at Windsor Boulevard, I helped Lillian clean up the little puddles Puck had left on the kitchen floor and promised to start training him the next day. Tallulah had passed out on the living room sofa, dead to the world, so Lillian pinched the still burning cigarette from between her friend's fingers, carefully extinguished it, then tucked Tallu in with a blanket and pillow and left her there. At length, Milly and Lilly went upstairs to their bedrooms, Lillian cradling the newest Puck in her arms. I heard their doors close and found myself again alone, my only company the coarse breathing of Tallulah Bankhead as she snored.

I went out to the cabana and was just drifting off to sleep when a shadow flitted across the window and I looked up to see Lillian framed in the open doorway to the patio, her pink chiffon negligée billowing in the gentle night breeze, her naked figure silhouetted in the glittering blue light from the pool. I was nervous as she lay down next to me, neither of us saying a word as she kissed me and reached into my boxers. I closed my eyes and gave in, conjuring visions of that first lustful night in Paris with Milly, and soon I was screwing Lillian for the first time since I'd returned from Europe. Just as her husband had insisted. My pent-up frustration from the awful Friday of Milly's rejection also helped me to perform well enough, and as Lilly straddled and rode me, her exquisite breasts bobbing, I saw Milly now standing in the doorway behind her. He was wearing pajama bottoms and an open smoking jacket exposing his tanned, lean chest. Thin wisps trailed from his cigarette as he watched for a moment, then turned and melted back into the shadows.

I felt cheated out of an opportunity to be with him, but still managed to join Lillian as she climaxed. Her breath was warm on my lips as she kissed me dreamily, whispering, "You really are my hero, Dexter Gaines," before bidding me goodnight and sneaking back to her own bedroom, leaving me alone in my confusion.

Saturday morning couldn't come fast enough, and Milly's surprise turned out to be exquisite. We'd bundled ourselves into the newly repaired Nash-Healey, and with Milly at the wheel, we drove through Los Angeles with the top down and the radio blasting along with the heater against the late autumn chill.

"Where are we going?"

"If I told you, it wouldn't be a surprise," was all he'd say.

At length we arrived at the Marina in Long Beach, and Milly greeted a dockworker as we moved down the narrow pier among every imaginable kind of sailing craft, at last arriving at a forty-two-foot Chris-Craft with the name *Jubilee* emblazoned in fresh paint on the bow.

"You bought a boat?" I asked, dumbfounded.

"No, I bought a *yacht*," he grinned. "Welcome aboard."

The *Jubilee* was a marvelous vessel, and Milly turned out to be an expert mariner as he guided us out of the slip while instructing me how to cast off the lines.

"You should have kept your little sailor's costume," he laughed. "You have no idea what that was doing to me!"

The sun was warm and the air cool as we anchored far offshore, the boat swaying in the rippling blue water. We put on the swim trunks Milly had stashed in the cabin and lay in the sun despite the chill as he opened a second bottle of champagne. After a while, I couldn't take it anymore, and we were soon naked and in each other's arms in the cabin below, the only sound the water lapping at the magnificent boat's new hull, and our own soft moans as we made up for lost time.

Later, as we padded around the little fantail, both still nude and not yet fully satisfied, he sliced up a fresh cantaloupe, a cigarette burning idly between his fingers, then fed me a piece, kissing the sweet juice from the birthmark on my lip.

"How was it?" he asked. "Halloween night, I mean. When you and Lillian . . ."

I blushed. "It was okay. Nothing like this."

"Were you able to perform?"

"Only while thinking about you," I confided.

"She must never know."

I nodded a bit sadly, then after a moment's silence: "Will it always have to be like this? In secret?"

He touched my cheek, then tousled my hair before taking my hand to lead me back to bed. "Of course it will, Dex. So let's make the most of these precious moments."

I had filmed my disastrous scene in *Titanic* in November, just a week before my twenty-second birthday. Milly had comforted me in my trailer after I'd showered Barbara Stanwyck in china and bouillon, sitting with me and holding my hands long enough to raise suspicion from anyone who might have clocked how long this powerful producer spent behind the closed door of a bit player's dressing room. I had been grateful knowing the risk he was taking, but it didn't seem to help much, especially when he broke the news to me that my scene had been cut from the picture. Lillian was supportive and kind after the day's shoot, cheering me with an anecdote about her first film role in a long-forgotten picture called *Better Dresses Fifth Floor* where she'd played Tough Cookie No. 3. She can still be glimpsed in the movie, but all of her dialogue was cut. Since that time, she had worked with a diction coach who helped rid her of her thick Southern twang. "We're all flawed in some way," she'd said. I tried to shrug off the whole episode, and we'd screwed again, this time back in the upstairs guest room while Milly was at work and Tallulah was shooting at MGM. I was finding it more and more difficult to satisfy her, as my heart was beginning to right itself with the dawning acceptance of my true nature.

Milly took me out on the *Jubilee* for my birthday, and I masked my disappointment that Tallu and Lillian had been invited as well. The weather turned out to be a bit rougher than any of us expected, and Lillian grew seasick while I cradled her head as she hung over the stern, retching again and again until she was dry-heaving and Milly had to turn the boat around and head back to land. Tallu fretted over her friend, insisting champagne with bitters was the best cure, but Lillian waved her off, weak and spent, at last regaining her land legs as we disembarked amid the warm hues of an autumn twilight.

The house was dark when we pulled into the driveway and piled out of the Cadillac, and I was feeling morose and lonely that Milly and I hadn't had a chance to be together on my birthday, but when he unlocked the front door and threw it open, the foyer was instantly ablaze with light and alive with people, all shouting "Surprise!" The piano had been wheeled in, and a small jazz orchestra fronted by Maynard Ferguson launched into a bopping version of some new catchy tune as I wore an astonished expression on my face, making the rounds and glad-handing with my new Hollywood friends. All the usuals were there, and Tab Hunter and I had a friendly exchange as he introduced me to a clean-cut and handsome young actor named Tony Perkins. There was much unspoken that passed between the three of us, just silent glimmers of secret camaraderie. Hedda Hopper had been very kind to me in her brief mention of our lunch in her column, calling me a promising new talent, "still a bit nervous from all the hubbub surrounding his rising star, the good-looking lad's hands were actually shaking from all the excitement." I'd taken to keeping them in my pockets as often as possible, giving me a casual and sexy affectation.

Later, after Marilyn Maxwell put on quite a show singing "Happy Birthday," Milly ushered as many of us as he could into the projection room. There were only seats for twelve, but the place was soon crammed to the rafters with people balanced on the arms of the chairs, sitting in the aisles, and standing around the small room's periphery. Milly assured those who couldn't squeeze in that there would be a repeat performance.

"Okay," Milly said, gesturing with his stemmed glass of champagne, "you all know we're here to honor my latest discovery, the inimitable Mr. Dexter Gaines." He paused for a round of applause and catcalls as I grinned stupidly, blushing from the attention. "I'd like to announce to you all, and to Dexter himself, that Mr. Ferguson and his fine musicians were hinting at a little something earlier with their introductory number. It's a brand-new tune called 'Shipshape,' written especially for our upcoming picture of the same name . . ." He paused to light a cigarette, his habit before one of his announcements, then continued, "Darryl and I—where are you Darryl?"

Zanuck waved his hand in feigned annoyance and bellowed, "Get on with it!"

The group laughed as Milly went on, "Darryl and I made it official yesterday. Dexter? You're slated to costar with Anne Francis in this terrific little romantic comedy."

The astonishment on my face brought more laughter, as Lillian gasped from her perch on the arm of my chair and squeezed my cheek. Tallu leaned in low from the other side and purred, "Well *glory hallelujah*, honey-child."

Through it all, Milly continued to beam with pride. "But before Dexter's star rises so fast that he'll leave all of us in its dust, let's take a look at his humble beginnings, shall we?"

I had no idea what he was up to, as I sat there drunk on champagne and happiness. Lillian squeezed my arm as Milly pushed the button and the curtains revealed the screen and the lights went dim, the projector flickering to life in its booth, lighting a shaft of smoky air over our heads and flashing a professionally made title on the screen: "Milford Langen is proud to introduce Mr. Dexter Gaines."

"That's Milly!" someone catcalled. "Always top billing!" This drew more chuckles from the audience. The title was superimposed over a cartoon comet and had obviously been created by the studio's graphic arts department to Milly's specifications. The first shot irised in, revealing

232

some of Milly's home movies. There I was, horsing around with Lillian in the Urban Idyll, the images dim and funny as some of Milly's jazz music played along. Then a quick shot of the two of us having one of our watermelon seed spitting contests brought more laughter. Another title appeared: "The whole world welcomes Hollywood's newest star," followed by shots of me posing with a life ring aboard the *United States*. I blushed deeper as some of the footage from our Europe trip unspooled: there I was doing my best Gene Kelly, dancing in the rain in Barcelona, then walking into a sea of flurrying pigeons in Venice, sunning myself on the hotel verandah in Rome, cavorting in and out of the columns of the Parthenon where Milly and I had stolen a furtive kiss. As the crowd laughed and applauded, I prayed I was the only one in the room who could feel the tenderness of the way the cameraman captured my antics.

A new title appeared on the screen, one that brought the first glimmer of rising dread: "A *Titanic* Comedy" it read, as the music faded into the background and we could hear the pop and static of the optical sound strip on the film as a crisp black-and-white image appeared on the screen. A clapper board snapped, then moved aside revealing Barbara Stanwyck reading her little book in her deck chair. My stomach curdled as I watched myself approach her, saying half my line before spilling the tray and its china cups all over her. The camera had continued to roll, and I watched the aftermath of the horrible memory playing out in front of the now roaring crowd, hollering and applauding all around me. I looked at Milly, whose profile showed he was smiling and laughing along with them, the light shimmering on his face as the outtake was repeated, this time in agonizing slow motion. Tallulah was gasping for breath next to me, laughing so hard I could smell her ashtray breath. Even Lillian was caught up in the hilarity as my cheeks burned and I wanted to bolt from the room, knowing I was trapped there by the crush of people and the paralysis of decorum.

Mercifully, the film ended, and I kept a smile plastered on my face as everyone congratulated me, complimenting Milly and patting him on the back. "Run it again!" someone shouted, but the crowd was already starting to disperse, off for refills of champagne and to dance to the music in the foyer. "Milly sure has a nose for talent," another voice said behind me. "Remember how steamed he was when Warner got to Doris Day first?" Even the encouragement of those words didn't soothe my wounded pride.

After the cake had been served, an elaborate thing made in the shape of the *Jubilee* as a sly wink from Milly, I wandered out to the empty and cold Urban Idyll and sat in Lillian's beloved swing while I watched three toy steamships rippling the otherwise mirror-like surface of the pool. They had been my birthday gift from Lillian and Tallulah, cunning motorized models of the *United States*, Milly's favorite *Queen Mary*, and Lillian's beloved *Ile de France*. The bebop and revelry wafted across the lawn and floated around me in the chilly November air as I smoked a joint and tried to recover from the exhilarating embarrassment of Milly's tribute.

It was as if the party never really ended, one gay gathering blurring into the next. Milly and I went sailing aboard the *Jubilee* when we could, and Lillian continued to come to me in the still of darkness, though with less and less frequency. She gave Blanche the day off for Thanksgiving and insisted on preparing the feast herself. It was honestly the first time in my life when I understood what the holiday was really all about. In December, we went to see Dorothy Dandridge perform at the Mocambo, and I added another fancy nightclub black-and-white of Lilly, Milly, and me to my growing collection. Christmas soon followed, bringing with it two enormous trees that Lillian and I decorated, and later an intimate holiday dinner party where I actually held my own discussing "the method" with none other than Montgomery Clift. Even Milly seemed impressed as he watched from across the table.

The next morning, the living room was overflowing with festive packages and we made short work of tearing into them. Lillian adored the bottle of gardenia perfume I'd bought for her in Paris, and Milly seemed especially touched by the leather satin-lined case I'd picked out for his reading glasses, paying a bit extra to have his monogram inscribed in gold. They gave me a pair of platinum cuff links in the shape of little movie cameras from both of them, and Tallu was delighted when she opened the silk scarf I'd been holding onto since I'd spotted it in a boutique in Venice.

At last, New Year's Eve made its lazy arrival heralding Tallulah's sad departure the following day along with the Christmas trees and signaling the close of my first full year in Hollywood. I found myself tuxedoed and laughing, shooting billiards and smoking a cigar in the crowded inner sanctum of Milly's study, surrounded by Darryl Zanuck and other important men. It seemed I'd found a place where I belonged—albeit a complicated one. I made a point of being gracious and kind to the fresh-faced and nervous young waiter who circulated among us, carefully balancing a tray of champagne.

TWENTY-THREE

The summer lingered and dwindled while an insatiable public remained captivated by the televised O.J. Simpson hearings, and Tally and I settled into as comfortable a routine as we could under the extraordinary circumstances binding us together. Mornings were spent at the Motion Picture Hospital in Woodland Hills where Lillian was now being tended to around the clock. She was not well enough to come home just yet if ever at all, so Tally and I would grab coffee and breakfast at the Astro Burger at Gower and Melrose before making the daily trek along Mulholland Drive, becoming fast and lasting friends, now forever connected by our mutual discovery of her parents' madness as we pieced together the fragmented and often obscured truth. I'd wait in Milly's gold 1976 Monte Carlo which we'd found filthy but still operational in the side garage, or stroll around the grounds of the so-called "Country House," Puck eagerly straining at his leash, while Tally sat with her mother who still refused to see me. Tally told me it was heartbreaking to watch her drift back and forth, bouncing from clarity to delusion during the course of their visits together. Lillian couldn't or wouldn't answer any questions about her staged suicide, and after a precursory investigation, the DA announced no charges would be filed. Milly had been characteristically meticulous in his planning in order to avoid any scandal, and now with his death they couldn't charge him with filing a false police report when he'd notified them of Lillian's disappearance in 1982. Of course, not even the truth could dissuade the handful of rabid entertainment reporters who refused to give up on the salacious tale, often shadowing us as we went about our daily routine.

I would fill my waiting time by popping Milly's endless stream of cassette-recorded rants into the stereo in the dash of the Monte Carlo, jotting notes on a dog-eared photocopy of his memoirs, trying to reconcile the truth with his fiction. Listening to the tapes had proven too painful for Tally, so I had taken on the enormous task myself. Milly slurred and cursed and broke things, drunk and bellowing at times, choking on his own sobs at others, to the point Tally's heart couldn't bear it anymore. Once, he'd left the recorder running after he'd dozed off, and I listened to twenty minutes of nothing but raspy breathing interspersed with the occasional troubled, indecipherable muttering. After Tally would return to the car with whatever precious little she might have gleaned from Lillian during that day's visit, we'd drive back to South Windsor and I'd update her about anything I'd learned from her deceased father's alcoholic diatribes—only maddening hints of the truth we were seeking.

Afternoons were spent immersed in the never-ending task of sorting through the detritus at the house. Tally was now ensconced in Tallulah's favorite suite in the north wing of the mansion, and I was more comfortable in the coziness of the newly cleaned maid's quarters, Blanche's former lair, a smallish space off the kitchen and laundry where I could be close to Puck the Eighth. Neither of us had dared or even wanted to stay in her parents' more capacious chambers, especially after the first week when we found Lillian's former bedroom had been sealed tight with a mass of overlapping strips of silver duct tape.

I'd peeled it off and opened the door to the dusty and stale air to find it exactly as I remembered from all those years ago, the cobweb-shrouded Civil War painting staring with dead eyes down from the wall, the drawn curtains now moth-eaten and sagging from rot, Lillian's still perfectly arranged cosmetics gathering dust under the silk-draped mirror, and her two massive closets lined with her impeccable wardrobe. As a vintage clothing dealer, Tally was torn as to what to keep and what to sell, given how her mother's closet contained some of the finest couture to ever come out of the golden era of Hollywood—with several one-of-a-kind gowns by Adrian and Edith Head. It was as if Milly had sealed it all up as a kind of shrine to the woman he remembered, not the one who lay weak and delirious in the rear guest room in the other wing of the house, her legendary face in ruins, secreted away as her aging body continued to betray her. Or, more likely, the hastily preserved memorial would have lent credence to his role as a grieving widower.

We had managed to spruce up the front of the house enough so it was no longer the festering eyesore it had been all those tragic years of Milly's decline, though it was still in desperate need of patching and painting. Tally was impressed by my handyman skills when I'd repaired the broken portholes in the front door, and we no longer had to trek through the heartrending back yard to gain entrance. Curious neighbors would drop by, including Rich the gay agent across the street, who told us there was renewed interest in Lillian's career, and several of her films were to be shown at the New Beverly Cinema over in the Fairfax District. Others came to ask about the latest progress, grateful someone was cleaning up the mess, though we were all annoyed when the Grave Line Tours hearse would pull up each day with gawking out-of-towners who'd pose and take pictures in front of the now infamous manse.

After sorting through the last of the screenplays, 35mm film reels, and countless boxes of dailies and rough cuts of every episode of every television series Milly had ever produced, Tally and I had been relieved when the truck pulled up and hauled it all away to the UCLA Film and Television Archive, where Milly's career highs and lows could be preserved for posterity. I was touched he had bothered to keep my note-covered and dog-eared copy of an early draft of his precious *Trojan War* and set it aside for myself.

Once they were gone, the downstairs of the house began to come together, and Tally and I would chat into the night while we patched the cracks and painted the walls, Puck the Eighth always nearby, shadowing me with his jingling tags. Even if I only moved across the room, he'd rouse himself and follow, then curl up again, dozing and content as we worked. We'd take breaks and listen to some of Milly's old records while we sat in the brush-cleared backyard, munching on ice-cold watermelon sliced just the way Lillian used to do. We slid comfortably into our unusual situation, waiting while the lawyers and other parasites settled Milly's estate, and living off our combined but dwindling savings.

For our sanity, we would sometimes make excuses to get out of that oppressive house for a while, like the afternoon we picked up sandwiches and had a picnic at the pet cemetery in Calabasas, our blanket spread on the ground by the neat little nest of tombstones, all bearing the name "Puck" and stretching a span right up to 1979, three years before Lillian's supposed suicide.

Tally mused, "It's like she was trying to make time stand still."

"What do you mean?"

"Well, Mom always made such a fuss about everybody's birthdays. Except her own, right? To this day, I don't know when hers is. Anyway, when I turned eight or nine—right after one of our dogs died—she gave me a puppy and I wanted to name it 'Eloise,' from those books, you know? I adored *Eloise in Paris* because that's where I was born. Anyway, normally Mom would give me pretty much anything I wanted, but not that time. She said we simply had to have a dog named Puck. It wasn't until I was older and she got battier that it started to make sense."

"How so?"

"Dogs live—what?—twelve, thirteen years or so, right? And she was so terrified of aging, every one that died meant that much time had passed for her. So by naming them all Puck . ."

"She stopped the clock?"

"Exactly."

We ate in silence for a moment, watching a small funeral procession in the distance, a family with kids following a pet casket toward a freshly dug grave. Tally shook her head.

"This place is a trip. I came here with Mom and Dad twice I think."

"I was here with your Mom when . . ." I paused to scan the little markers, then brushed off the one engraved 1938 to 1952. ". . . this one died. Before then, I never even knew such places existed."

"Only in Hollywood, right?"

I smiled. "No kidding."

Tally put her sandwich down and drew her knees up to her chin. "I truly adored her, you know. Even with all the nuttiness, she was still a pretty amazing mom."

"Sounds like she was crazy about you, too."

"Or just plain crazy."

"Well, she did give up her career so she could take care of you."

"Yeah."

Tally had grown thoughtful as we both watched the tiny coffin being lowered into the earth down the hill while the parents comforted their grieving children.

"What were your folks like?" Tally asked.

I considered my words before answering, "Raging alcoholics. Sick. Cruel. When my mother got tired of verbally abusing me, my father took over with his fists, so . . ."

"I'm sorry."

I shrugged. "Remember when you asked me if I had a dog as a kid? Well, I did once, for about three days. A stray I'd found. Next thing I knew, she'd vanished and my dad came home with blood spattered on his pant legs. He said she'd gotten loose and been hit by a truck, but I never believed him."

Tally didn't say anything, just gave me a sympathetic look.

"Anyway, once I left Texas and came to Hollywood, I never saw or heard from my parents again. Which was fine by me."

"Any siblings?"

"Nope. Only child like you." By now, I was eager to change the subject, so I asked, apropos of nothing, "What was your mom's last movie?"

Tally brightened. "Actually . . . Here's some Lillian Sinclair trivia for you. Everybody *thinks* it was *One Summer Midnight*, it's even in *Halliwell's Film Guide* that way. *But*, did you ever see that French film, *Une Voix de l'Ombre?*"

"Can't say as I have. What's it mean?"

"'A Voice from the Shadows,' or something like that. It's a thriller about a French diplomat who murders his American wife, only she keeps calling him up on the phone, from beyond the grave, right? But you never see her onscreen, you just hear this really creepy, unnerving voice. Came out in December of '55. *That* was Mom's last movie role."

"So she was the title character."

"Exactly. *But*, here's where the trivia gets even better. Originally, the character *was* supposed to appear—that's how the script was written, anyway—but by then Mom and Dad had been living in Paris for over a year and she was—as she'd put it—'obscenely pregnant' with me. The director was so enamored of having a genuine American movie star that he made the writer change the script so the famous Lillian Sinclair could be The Voice. Now *that* will win you bonus points next time you play *Trivial Pursuit*."

I laughed, then watched as Tally grew serious again while she fished out her battered and abraded Altoids tin. "You mind? All this talk . . . I need to dull the edges."

"Go right ahead," I said. "You're not driving."

"When did you give it up? Pot, I mean?"

"Same time I quit cigarettes. Carol didn't approve of either, and he was more important to me. By then my hands were immune to it, so I haven't really missed it."

She nodded as she took a drag, and when she stubbed it out on the inside of the open top, the little wire hinges broke.

"Well damn," she said as she tried to put the lid back on. I watched her with a growing fondness, this funny, somewhat scattered young woman, then reached to unsnap the ball chain around my neck and pressed my match safe into her hand.

"What's this?" she asked, examining it, puzzled.

"It's an exact duplicate of the one my grandmother gave me. The police confiscated the original when your dad had me arrested for possession the night I met your folks. Lillian found this one for me, and since I don't need it anymore, it's my gift to you."

"That's so sweet," she said, and I could tell she was moved. "Thank you, Danny."

"It's the closest thing to a family heirloom I've ever had. Take good care of it."

"I promise." She put the charred joint into the little cylinder, and I snapped it around her neck. "Mom wasn't kidding. You're all right." After a moment, she sat cross-legged and plucked at some blades of grass.

"I felt so *guilty* when she died. All that unfinished business. And now here she is alive again, but with her health and all, I don't know if I'll get a second chance."

"Looks to me like you're off to a good start."

"Did you know anybody named Harry?" I asked one afternoon while we were both on our hands and knees, polishing the marble entry floor.

Tally sat back on her haunches and wiped sweat from her forehead, carefully moving a tuft of errant hair back into her vintage headband. "Harry who?"

"I don't know. Your dad was talking about somebody named Harry on the tape I listened to this morning. Sounded like he might have been a doctor."

"Oh," Tally said, remembering, "Doctor Harry. Well, that's what we called him. His last name was B-A-L-Z."

"Harry Balz," I repeated, then realizing what I'd said, gave her a look. She laughed at her little joke.

"Balfour," she admitted. "But that was Mom's nickname for him. Doctor Harry Balz."

I couldn't help but chuckle.

"What'd Dad say about Dr. Harry?" she asked, sipping from a plastic water bottle.

"I think he might have helped cover up Lillian's suicide."

Intrigued, Tally got up and brushed off her knees, went into the living room and dialed 411 on the antique rotary phone, then asked for the number for Dr. Harry Balfour in Beverly Hills.

"You're just going to call him up and *ask*?"

"Unless you've got a better idea," she replied, jotting down the phone number.

I went over and leaned in the archway, trying to wipe the oily floor polish off my hands with an old dinner napkin, watching as Tally's finger zipped the numbers around.

"Yes, hello. This is Tallulah Langen. May I speak with Doctor Balfour?" She listened for a moment, then went on, "It's about my mother, Lillian Sinclair. Will you tell him it's urgent?"

She cupped a hand over the mouthpiece.

"Hold music," she said. Then, hearing a voice on the other end, "Yes, Doctor Balfour . . . oh, you remember me? Uh-huh. Well, I just wonder what you might know about my mom's supposed suicide. Uh-huh. Is that right?"

Here I noticed her tone shift. "Well, then let me tell you something. If I find out you had anything to do with it—and I have really good reason to believe you did—then you can bet your life I'm going to sue you for inflicting mental distress on me for the past twelve years. *I thought my mother was dead because of you*, and if you helped my parents commit fraud, so help me I'm going to take your house, your medical license, your reputation, and everything else you've ever cared about."

I looked at her with alarm, but she gave me a playful glance to assure me she was bluffing. *Damn.* When it came to acting, the apple stayed close to the tree.

"Oh I've got proof," she went on. "And the only way you can avoid a lawsuit that I promise will ruin your whole family is to tell me the goddamned truth."

She listened again, then grinned. "I'm at the house and—hello?"

She put down the phone and stood there with her hand still on the receiver. "Bastard hung up on me."

"That was scary," I said, "and more than a little impressive."

"Let's see if it worked." Tally exhaled sharply, then to distract herself: "Hey, there's some of that pasta left from last night, maybe I'll bake it into a casserole."

"Sounds delicious," I replied. "I got stuff to make a salad."

"White or red wine?" she asked.

"Whatever's open."

I finished up in the foyer, and while the floor was still dingy and in need of professional restoration, at least it now gave off a faint glow in the afternoon sun outside the curved glass brick wall, recently stripped of its invading ivy. The carpet on the stairs, indeed throughout the entire house, would have to be replaced, but we didn't have the funds for that kind of expense. Not yet anyway.

Tally was puttering around the now orderly kitchen as I passed in the rear entry foyer, pulling on a threadbare but cherished baseball cap embroidered with "Grant Thespians" and little comedy and tragedy masks over the bill, a gift from Carol when I finished the set for their high school production of *Ten Little Indians*. "I'm gonna start on the cabana," I said with a hint of dread in my voice.

"Why don't you take a break? You work too hard," Tally said, spinning the knob on the old 1950s stove to preheat the oven.

"Keeps me sane," I replied, then went outside into the dwindling afternoon sun and surveyed the ruins of the Urban Idyll. We had hired some laborers in the parking lot at Home Depot the week before, and they'd spent all day clearing the overgrowth of greedy ivy and weeds, exposing the stark decay of the old patio and walkways along with the skeleton of a large raccoon. In the far corner of the yard, we found two handmade tombstones marking the final resting place of still more Pucks, as if Lilly and Milly had opted to inter the dogs at home rather than risk any hint of suspicion by burying them publicly in Calabasas. The faintest outline of the koi pond peeked through the now denuded dry dirt, and I remembered the night I'd shot the coyote as it attacked poor Trouble.

I stood looking at the dilapidated, boarded-up cabana, gnawed by curiosity, waiting to find more pieces to the puzzle. I took the heavy bundle of keys out of my pocket. We'd discovered them hanging on a nail in a cabinet in the laundry room one day, finally providing unfettered access to every locked door in the place. I was just sorting through them when Tally blustered out onto the verandah.

"He's here!" she said, drying her hands on a dish towel. "Dr. Harry!"

"You're kidding."

"Said he drove right over after I called."

244

"Can't say as I'm surprised after your little Oscar-worthy turn on the phone."

The cabana would have to wait. I headed back inside, and soon Tally and I were greeting the gaunt, nervously guarded doctor in the tidy but tattered living room, the aroma of roasting garlic and pasta filling the old house. Neither of us had been able to face removing the decrepit Christmas tree, and Balfour glanced at it curiously as he sat down. We could tell he'd been rattled by Tally's phone call.

"Yes, I knew Lillian was still alive," he told us as Tally poured him a cup of coffee. Suspicious of her hospitality, he gingerly scooped sugar into it and stirred, his teaspoon dinging as he sighed, preparing himself to tell the truth. "I was vacationing in New Zealand when Milly died, but I wasn't surprised to get your call."

"Look, we just want to know the truth, that's all," Tally's tone was oddly reassuring.

"Why'd they do it?" I asked.

Balfour hesitated, considering his words. "You were an actor once, weren't you?"

"A very long time ago," I answered, surprised by the question. "Briefly."

"Then you understand the vagaries of Hollywood and the emotional toll it can sometimes take on a person," he said.

"All too well," I replied. Tally gave me a sympathetic look.

And so he at last opened up and told us what we'd been dying to know. He had been their family physician since the early 1970s, as his father had been before him.

"That's right," Tally chimed in. "Your dad was my pediatrician."

Dr. Balfour nodded, then continued. Lillian was terrified of aging, and in her lucid moments, knew she was behaving irrationally with her late-night furloughs in the neighborhood and her ever-growing fear of her own reflection in the mirror. With their daughter out of their now empty house, Milly had insisted the best thing for Lillian would be to make a comeback in television, and set about looking for a project for her under the terms of his overall deal at Paramount. Milly soon found it when a young writer came in and pitched a sitcom about a busybody in a fading Los Angeles neighborhood who takes her dog out for walks so she can spy on the neighbors. Milly had suggested they name the dog Trouble, and the show would be called *Walking Trouble*. The busybody had just moved back into her mother's home, and the writer said he envisioned the character of the mom as a sort of a grand dame, half-crazy Tallulah Bankhead type, with a dash of Norma Desmond and Margo Channing. He suggested Ann Bancroft for the part, but Milly had a better idea.

The role would be perfect for Lillian's return—who better to mimic the legendary actress than the woman who had been her best friend? She'd be a supporting character and wouldn't even have to work many hours per episode, and though she resisted at first, Lillian had been intrigued by the idea of playing the zany matriarch as a tribute to the actress she considered her sister. Tallulah's death in 1968 had been an especially difficult time for Lillian.

I thought sadly of dear Tallu. Hers was the only career I'd followed after I fled Hollywood, making a point to catch her old films whenever they were shown on television and delighting in her appearances on talk shows and as a mystery guest on *What's My Line?* My heart ached for that incomparable creature when Carol and I rented *Die! Die! My Darling!* In the twilight of her extraordinary career, Tallu's deranged portrayal of Stefanie Powers' dead fiancé's mother made me wonder if perhaps Lillian had had the right idea when she'd retired in her prime. I had read with an amused sadness that Tallu's last, rasping words had been, "Codeine! Bourbon!"

Dr. Balfour went on, "Lillian loved the pilot script, so she finally agreed." He paused to take another sip of his now lukewarm coffee before putting the cup back into the saucer and sliding it away on the end table. He stared at it, fidgeting, then continued.

"Lillian insisted she'd need to have some work done before stepping in front of a camera again. She was approaching sixty at the time, and aging gracefully if you ask me, still incredibly beautiful. But Lillian couldn't see herself objectively."

Tally nodded, and I noticed tears in her eyes before she dabbed them away.

"Plastic surgery?" I asked.

Balfour nodded. "I referred her to a doctor in Beverly Hills, a man of very good reputation . . ." He trailed off before continuing. "The first surgery was a disaster. And the one to repair it even worse."

"So it wasn't a stroke?" Tally asked, hushed.

"No. Lillian insisted on far more work than she needed, and it became a series of botched procedures from which there was no recovery. Milly was beside himself, having already boasted of her comeback, and obviously devastated by what had happened to his wife. After all, what does an actress have once she's lost her face?"

"But why the suicide thing?"

The memories haunting Dr. Balfour now seemed to make it difficult for him to finish his story, but at length he did. "Photographers were hounding her every time she came and went from the cosmetic surgeon, always wearing a hat with a dark, almost opaque veil to hide her destroyed face. She was already emotionally fragile and became terrified of someone getting a shot and publishing it in one of those awful magazines or flashing it across the nightly news. I was with them, right here in this room as a matter of fact, the night she became so hysterical, shouting over and over how she wanted to die until I finally had to sedate her."

He was staring at the threadbare carpet now, and I looked around the room, imagining Lillian's pitiful wails echoing through the home that was soon to become her prison.

"Milly," Dr. Balfour continued, trying to cover the crack in his voice, "was beside himself with worry she might try something drastic, and he broke down and sobbed like a baby to the point I could barely understand what he was saying."

"What *was* he saying?" Tally asked, no longer fighting back her tears. They cascaded down her full cheeks so she blotted them with her wrists.

Balfour exhaled and shrugged. "He said it was all his fault. Everything. Sobbing like you wouldn't believe. Saying over and over that he should just kill himself. He was the one who had destroyed his wife.

Saying again and again he was to blame." The doctor shook his head as if to dispel the memory. He went on to tell us Milly had convinced Lillian he couldn't live without her, and she had insisted she could never be seen in public again, so they settled on a plan.

While Milly was at a holiday party surrounded by hundreds of witnesses who knew him well, Lillian would take the *Jubilee* out to a rendezvous point off Catalina. A small rented boat was to meet her there and take her to a secluded spot where they'd hidden one of the cars that afternoon.

The *Jubilee* would be found the next day, as luck would have it, by the harbormaster who recognized it immediately and called Milly with the news. There was no sign of Lillian save the note authenticated to be in her own writing, reading simply, "I'm done." With the ruse perfectly executed, Lillian Sinclair would then live out the rest of her years hidden away in the house. Dr. Balfour dropped by from time to time, and whatever ailments she needed treating, he'd diagnose Milly and write the prescriptions in his name. Lillian's life insurance wouldn't pay in case of suicide, so Milly felt safe from any accusations of fraud. If anyone came to question him, Lillian would hide in the little attic above the projection booth. Balfour recalled sitting with the two of them and watching the news of her suicide, and she'd insisted Milly have her memorial service and funeral videotaped so she could see who turned out.

"I don't know why I went along," Balfour at length concluded. "Except I've never in my life seen two people in such despair. Your parents loved each other very much, Tally," he added, no doubt thinking he was comforting a grieving daughter.

"In their own way," I said in a hush, starting to believe it was true.

The sun was now setting, and Tally turned on a lamp as we all sat in contemplative silence before I asked, "Who was in the other boat?"

Balfour looked at me. "It was their driver. The Chinese fellow."

"Deming?" I asked, surprised.

Balfour nodded. "Took their secret to his grave."

After a moment, he added, almost timidly, "Please understand. I was only trying to help two very broken, desperate people. Your mother even told me she thought you'd be better off believing she was dead."

Tally softened. "Look, I'm sorry. It's just you were so hesitant when I first called you—understandably so, I mean—and that's why I threatened to sue. But now that you've told us the truth ..."

Balfour seemed relieved as he was leaving, and he told Tally her parents had both expected Milly to outlive Lillian, who had already been diagnosed with congestive heart failure, which might explain why he'd made no provisions for her in his revised will.

"When this gets out, in the news I mean," Tally said, worried, "you know it will kill her."

I nodded, then closed the door after the doctor said his goodnights. I made it as far as the bottom of the stairs before I sat down, exhausted, and Tally joined me, gently leaning her head against my shoulder as darkness overtook her parents' faded Xanadu. At length, she smiled tightly and went off into the kitchen to finish making dinner, but I didn't move until she called me, telling me it was ready.

The next morning, we stopped at Astro Burger where the girl already had our orders waiting for us, then ate in the car as we snaked our way along Mulholland on our daily trek to see what remained of Lillian Sinclair.

"You gonna tell her we know the truth?" I asked.

"Not yet," Tally replied.

I nodded as she got out of the car and went inside, then popped in the next cassette, listening while Milly droned on, the tape finally running out as he repeated, apropos of nothing he'd been saying, drunk and self-loathing, "It was all my fault."

One afternoon, while I was spackling some nail holes in the kitchen walls, the phone rang. After Tally spoke with the caller on the other end, she hung up, her hand still on the receiver.

"Was that the hospital?" I asked, worried.

She shook her head. "Dad's lawyer. He wants us to come by his office this afternoon."

"What's up?"

"They've settled the estate," she said, then walked out of the room.

As we drove to the offices in Century City, I tried to make conversation by pointing out various landmarks where the Fox back lot used to be, but Tally didn't seem very interested. At last, we sat across the desk from Jerry Mandelberg as he explained how the title to the house would be transferred to me, then I signed an endless mountain of documents, the lawyer flipping the pages and holding them open for me until my signature and initials no longer looked like my own. A courteous and quiet woman notarized everything. It appeared Milly's finances had been in far better order than the rest of his life, and with no criminal charges and no contests, everything had been settled in short order. At last, the lawyer produced a final document, explaining how once I signed it, Milly's entire fortune would be mine. After estate and other taxes and administrative fees, the unimaginable sum of three-point-three million dollars.

I exhaled sharply.

"And how would I go about giving it all to someone else?" I asked.

"Well, first you'd have to pass a mental competency test," he quipped, but grew serious when I glared at him. "We can handle that for you, minus gift taxes, of course. Who's the lucky beneficiary?"

"Tallulah Langen."

"What?" She blinked.

"I'm giving it all to you," I said.

"Are you crazy?" she asked, then put up such a fuss. She didn't want her father's money, and it was obvious he didn't want her to have it, so no, she wouldn't take it, though the tempted look in her eyes betrayed her words.

"Then we'll split it," I said. "And I'm not going to argue about it."

"I told you—"

"I said I'm not going to argue about it!"

She fell silent and we waited while Mandelberg drew up the paperwork. Once Tally and I were signed, sealed, and notarized, we shook the lawyer's hand as he gave us the cards of various business managers and financial planners. I told him I'd call to make an appointment to draft my own will—something I'd never needed before.

He waited for the elevator with us, and I finally asked the question gnawing at me since my return to Los Angeles. A small thing, but one that had come to matter to me, nonetheless. "I assume you handled the funeral arrangements personally?"

"That's right. Exactly as Milly specified, down to the last persnickety detail. I can show you the provisions in his will if you'd like," he said, sounding a touch defensive.

I shook my head. "I was just wondering about his reading glasses. Did he ask to be buried in them?"

Both Tally and Mandelberg gave me a look. I knew it was a strange question, but I still wanted to know.

"He did. I thought it an odd request at the time. Why?" the attorney asked.

"No reason," I answered, my curiosity mollified. The truth is, I wanted—or *needed*—to believe it was because I'd once told him he looked sexy in them, and my youthful affection had still mattered to him after all these years.

Tally was numb the whole drive home, both of us newly rich, and we agreed we would split the cost of restoring South Windsor before we put it on the market, a little business venture together. We envisioned top dollar, upwards of eight or nine hundred thousand, the house having bona fide Hollywood history.

"You're a really good man, Daniel Root," she said, dabbing still more tears.

"Nah," I said, chuckling, "maybe I am just crazy."

The following week, after our daily morning visits to Woodland Hills, we interviewed money managers and soon hired a reputable guy in a little office downtown, entrusting him with our new wealth, then set about finding a contractor to finish the house and grounds. The work was to take at least three months and wouldn't be cheap, but for the first time in our lives, neither of us had to worry about money. Lillian remained our chief concern, especially when Tally reported her mother seemed to be fading and had no appetite.

Tally and I had already returned some semblance of order to the rooms inside the mansion, tossing what we didn't want or giving it to charity. I managed to organize all of Milly's cassette-recorded memoirs and the mountains of his rusting cans of home movies before sending them out to be transferred to video. An army of laborers and craftsmen had invaded, and Puck the Eighth was being spoiled by scraps from their lunches as the mansion gradually came back to life.

I then turned to cataloging Milly's extensive collection of jazz 78s, LPs, cassette tapes, and compact discs, sampling as many of them as I could. It was the lyrics to Dean Martin's recording of "Money Burns a Hole in My Pocket" that not only made me laugh in light of my new financial circumstances, but also gave me an idea. I telephoned Jerry Mandelberg and hired him on the spot to represent me in a lawsuit. Once I explained the circumstances he was delighted by the prospect, and said he'd get on it right away.

If my ploy worked, it would go a long way toward silencing the most voracious of my personal demons.

"Who was that?" Tally asked as she came home through the front door carrying a shopping bag.

"Mandelberg," I replied, getting up. "Not important. Your turn. What's in the bag?"

"You'll find out. You busy tonight?"

"I'll check with my secretary."

"Well, have her—or him—clear your schedule and be ready to leave at six-thirty, okay? And wear a jacket."

"I might even shave," I said as she winked and then, humming to herself, sashayed out of the room.

That evening, after I showered and dressed, I sat watching the slashes of sunlight turn from yellow to amber in the foyer when Tally at last appeared at the top of the stairs. She was wearing another of her vintage dresses, this one a Lucy Ricardo-inspired orange number with a Peter Pan collar and cuffed elbow-length sleeves.

"Wow," I said, as she paused halfway down the grand staircase to curtsy. "This is my only jacket I'm afraid. Same one I wore to your dad's funeral. Hope it'll pass muster."

"You look very handsome," she said, joining me. She had a clutch purse from the same fabric as her dress in one hand, and the shopping bag I'd noticed earlier in the other.

"So what's the occasion?" I asked, intrigued by her festive mood.

"Oh, just celebrating your kindness. Let's—"

The tap of a car horn in the front drive interrupted her.

"Perfect timing. That's our cab. Trust me, neither of us is going to want to drive home tonight. Shall we?" She grinned with mischief and offered me her elbow.

Twenty minutes later we were being seated in a half-round high-backed white leather banquette in an otherwise empty restaurant on North Vermont called The Dresden. While Tally asked our gray-haired waitress for two Blood and Sands, the joint's signature cocktail, and an order of calamari fritti with marinara to share, I took in the posh elegance of the place with its brick-colored walls, dark mahogany floor-to-ceiling parallel posts encircling some of the booths, and the frosted and etched glass panels separating the dining room from the adjacent bar where a handful of lifers hunched over their beers. The room had a dated elegance to it, and for a moment, as Dinah Washington's piped-in voice crooned from overhead, an odd sense of déjà vu made me feel as if we were surrounded by ghosts from my own time in Hollywood.

I waved my hand at the ambience. "I take it we're somewhere special?"

"My folks used to bring me here when I was little. I remember wearing crinoline slips under my dress, and little white gloves. Deming always drove us because Mom hated to drive and Dad usually couldn't by the time we had finished dinner. He especially loved this place."

I took it all in. "Well, it does look like the inside of a super swanky yacht, so I can see why he might."

"Anyway," Tally said, "I thought this might be a suitable place to lift a glass and celebrate."

As if on cue, the waitress arrived with our Blood and Sands. She asked if we were ready to order, but Tally said we needed a few minutes, so she bowed and gave us our privacy.

As Tally slipped her fingers around the stem of her glass, I noticed how the flattering glow of candlelight danced across her features. With her vintage dress and her hair pulled tight into a stylish updo, her face conjured memories of her legendary mother. She raised her glass, and I did the same.

"Shall we drink to Milly and Lilly?" I asked.

"Maybe later, sure," Tally said, her voice becoming serious and fond. "But first, I'd like to drink a toast to you, Dan. For your generosity. And on behalf of the Langen family, as the sole surviving member, I'd like to extend to you our deepest and most sincere apologies."

"None necessary," I said, clinking my glass with her. "But appreciated all the same."

"Good." She smiled and we both took a sip of our sweet, crimson cocktails. Tally next lifted the shopping bag from the banquette and put it on my lap.

"Now then. A little 'thank you' present," she said, handing it to me. I gave her a puzzled look, so she added, "Just open it."

Curious, I reached in and removed something heavy wrapped in tissue as she watched me with a smile both excited and satisfied. I put the parcel on the table and peeled back the paper to reveal a large coffee table book: *The Art of Daphne Ronget*.

I stared at it for a moment before asking, dumbfounded, "Where did you . . .?"

"At a used bookstore on Third. It's out of print, you know, and I had a helluva time finding a copy so I asked them to special order it."

"Is it . . .?" I trailed off, caressing the glossy dust jacket, unable to finish my question.

"Page ninety-three."

I gingerly flipped through and let the book fall open. There, above the simple caption "Daniel, 1952," was the portrait Daphne had painted of me. The one that had exposed my soul and helped steady my heart.

"I was going to buy you the original, but last time it sold at auction it went for just over two million, so .. ."

Only I wasn't really listening, moved as I was by both the sight of my youthful, tortured face and by Tally's generosity.

"I'm sorry," she said. "I didn't mean to make you cry."

I smiled and wiped my eyes. "Doesn't take a lot these days. And these are happy tears for a change," I said, then squeezed her hand and added a hushed, "Thank you, Tally."

"You're welcome, Danny."

The day before workers were scheduled to start on the pool and cabana, I realized it was the only place I hadn't cleaned out, so while Tally went to Ralph's to buy groceries, I took the bundle of keys into the September afternoon and finally unlocked the door, bracing myself for the memories that might be stirred once I went inside. The door creaked in protest as I opened it, and when I fumbled for the switch, a bare bulb hanging from a cord in the ceiling sputtered to life in the swirls of dust visible through what little sun permeated the plywood-covered windows. The dim light revealed boxes upon boxes of empty scotch bottles, as if Milly had been too embarrassed or too drunk to put them out with the recycling.

As I shook my head and started to cart them out onto the decayed patio, my excavation revealed a little nook in the very back where my bed had once been adjacent to the small but efficient bathroom. A tattered and stained vinyl recliner sat facing a small television with a VCR on top. A carpet of dog-eared gay porn magazines littered the floor around the chair and the built-in bookcases, and as I gathered them, I shook my head and marveled at Milly's self-loathing—a hatred so intense it had clung to him for a lifetime, only expressed in the privacy of this dirty, secret lair. I wanted to clean it all up before Tally got home, so I started tossing them into a trash bag, then turned my attention to the VHS tapes piled around the television, their cover art advertising more of the same. I pitched them in with the magazines, then found one last empty cassette case. The VCR fired to life when I pushed the power button and hit eject, and the tape that clattered out stopped my heart.

On its spine was scrawled a single word:

"Dex."

My hands trembling, I pushed it back into the recorder and turned on the television. After some nervous fiddling with the controls, a picture appeared. It was the reel he'd made for my birthday all those years ago, and I was soon mesmerized by the overwhelming melancholy of seeing my youth played out on the screen as I laughed and clowned for Milly's camera. I sat down in the battered recliner and watched my disastrous turn with Barbara Stanwyck and was surprised to see this version of the film contained more footage.

There I was, all of twenty-one or twenty-two, swimming lazily in the Urban Idyll while Milly's camera roamed over me, luxuriating in every muscle of a body I hadn't possessed in years. There was a lingering, aching fondness to the color footage as he'd followed me while I rose from the water, smiling at him, the truth so evident from the love in my eyes it's a wonder no one ever figured out what was really going on between us—that remote world having been so sophisticated and yet quaintly naïve. At length, the film ran out, the screen went white, and I realized I was crying.

For all this time, while I lived in silent desperation and heartbreak over what had happened with Milly, that seminal formative period in my life from which I'd eventually escaped with Carol's help, Milly had been returning to the past again and again in the privacy of his tortured sanctuary. He had never been capable of saying the words to me when we were together, but his love was as deep as it was tragic, and the only way he could beg for my forgiveness was to leave me his fortune in hopes I would take care of his wife and daughter. Despite everything, he had *entrusted* me.

I sat there weeping for what felt like hours, tears for the loss of so many years and the tragedy that had come from Milly's self-hatred. Still, my love for him, however childish it might have been at the time, had eventually given me the strength to accept my own truth and find happiness with Carol. I realized I'd been lucky to have met Milford

Langen, lucky to have been freed by him, and now lucky to have returned. My shoulders were heaving when I felt a touch and looked up to see Tally. She, too, was crying.

"What's the matter?" she asked.

"You first," I said, wiping my face on my sleeve.

"The hospital just called. They say Mom should be moved to hospice. She . . . doesn't have much time left."

I hugged her as she cried on my shoulder.

"She keeps saying she wants to come home," Tally said, her voice choked and muffled on my shirtsleeve.

"Then let's grant her last wish," I said. "God knows we can afford it."

Tally nodded, still holding onto me. At length, we composed ourselves and started back toward the house to make the arrangements. I put an arm around her shoulder as we climbed the sweeping stairs of the verandah in the encroaching gloom of dusk.

"Maybe you should tell me the rest of the story before she gets here," she said.

And so I did.

TWENTY-FOUR

Production on *Shipshape* started in early January of 1953, and while I wasn't yet attracting the kind of buzz Milly wanted, he did manage to cajole the publicity department into landing me on the cover of *Photoplay* with the caption "Milford Langen's Newest Discovery: Rising Star Dexter Gaines." The accompanying article was all fluff and included a few quotes from my interview with Hedda Hopper. One of the photos they used alongside the text was a small black-and-white "candid" staged on an unused living room set on the Fox lot. In it, I'm sitting cross-legged on the floor, in dungarees and a tight white T-shirt with rolled-up sleeves to show off my physique, sorting through a stack of records next to a console hi-fi, a burning cigarette perfectly posed between my fingers. The photographer, wardrobe people, and editors at *Photoplay* had all somehow missed the hole in the bottom of my sock that nevertheless made the photo both sexy and adorable. The little caption underneath had my name misspelled: "Rising star Dexter Ganes relaxes to jazz when he isn't working."

I had to laugh when I read it because at the time the magazine came out, the only thing I'd done was my excised turn in *Titanic,* so if *Photoplay* were to be believed I must have been listening to a lot of jazz. Still, legions of my nonexistent fans would never know the difference, so I was making the rounds of interviews with Louella Parsons and Sheila Graham, telling them how I had been surprised when packages of new socks began showing up addressed to "Dexter Ganes c/o Fox Studios," all from teenage girls who'd seen my picture in the magazine. It was fun being a cover boy, however briefly, and I was enjoying what little attention my fledgling career was garnering and glad to be away from those lonely days on South Windsor.

Anne Francis was gracious to me when our first day of production rolled around. Although we were more or less the same age, she had already appeared in several films and television shows, and she willingly gave me discreet suggestions about acting in front of a camera, never in a way that would tip off the crew I was still more or less a movie virgin. I found her charming and likeable, and nick-named her "the Old Pro" which made her laugh. She set me at ease as the shoot wore on.

Shipshape was an ensemble comedy with a large cast and several overlapping plotlines, featuring Rosalind Russell, Celeste Holm, Edward Everett Horton, Leo G. Carroll, Mary Wickes, Anne Francis, and, of course, "introducing Dexter Gaines." Not exactly the "costar" billing Milly had announced at my birthday party, but a decent part with some real screen time. The film was set entirely—no surprise here—on another transatlantic voyage aboard a fictional ocean liner. I wondered if I'd ever get to do a movie set on dry land. In his legendary knack for saving a nickel, Zanuck had ordered the art department to pull the sets from *Titanic* out of storage and rework them into a more contemporary ship for this low budget black-and-white comedy. I was somewhat apprehensive when I found myself back on Stage 14 for much of the production, praying the film wouldn't sink at the box office.

In our story, Anne played the haughty debutante daughter of a wealthy East Coast financier who takes a dare from her college friends and trades her first-class ticket with a girl traveling tourist. My character was a handsome male gold-digger who starts off romancing the girl pretending to be the "rich" Anne in first class; then, after some shipboard hijinks, he abandons his "marry into money" scheme when he meets and falls for the "poor" girl traveling in tourist. They share a big movie kiss, and only then does he discover she's the real Anne who's loaded. With a happy ending to tie up all the plotlines with a neat little bow before the final fade-out, the film played better on the page, as Milly was fond of saying.

During production, all of the scenes from the various plots were scheduled to shoot on whatever set was already lit for the day, so I usually worked only a few hours before saying hello in passing to the other actors, then spent the rest of my time wandering around the enormous Fox back lot that sprawled all the way from the sound stages on Pico to Santa Monica Boulevard. Sometimes, Anne would join me for a stroll through the fake buildings, nibbling on takeout from the commissary as we drifted from Paris in the fourteenth century to the Old West simply by rounding a corner. I even recognized some of the sets from the hundreds of films that had enthralled me growing up and pointed them out to her. Anne was the only person I ever allowed to tease me about the permanent spot of brown on my lip, mostly because she called it a "beauty mark" just like her own. In fact, she made me so comfortable I even confided my wildest dream had been to one day appear in a movie with the most magnificent logo in cinema history—20th Century Fox— the sight of which had always assured me I was about to see something *really* good. She smiled with kindness and said, "Well, this *is* the town where dreams come true, right?"

"They're supposed to, anyway."

I was nearly suicidal the night Milly brought home the first rushes and screened them in the projection room, smoking and making notes for the director and editor while Lillian wandered in and remarked how handsome I was on the big screen. My acting was wooden and arch, the lightweight banter sounding forced and ridiculous coming out of my mouth. Lillian tried to reassure me, and Milly told me to be patient, it was just the first day, and the alchemy of editing had only begun. Over the course of the month-and-a-half shoot, Lillian would become my personal acting coach, rehearsing my upcoming scenes nightly, helping to shape my performance, while Milly paid obsessive attention to even the most minuscule aspects of the production. He insisted on approving every costume, hairstyle, set decoration, and prop, all while running the show with tight reins and impeccable taste. If anything displeased him, he'd fire off one of his infamous memos (having learned well from his own mentor, Darryl Zanuck). It was fascinating to watch him work, and

I was to ultimately benefit from his masterful touch and keen eye for detail all the while hiding my devotion to him as best I could.

During the second week of production, Milly came home with another reel of film. I assumed it was that day's rushes and said I'd forgo the torture of watching myself flub lines, but Milly insisted. The footage turned out to be a rough cut of the first two scenes I'd shot, already assembled by the film's editor under Milly's meticulous supervision. Their collaboration deserved an Oscar, because working together they had managed to make my leaden performance seem lighter and much more charming.

She had even cut around my ever jittering hands, except in the scene where I lit a cigarette for Anne like Paul Henreid did for Bette Davis in *Now Voyager*, putting two to my lips, touching the flame to them, then handing one to her. Unlike that now classic moment in cinema history, *my* tremulous fingers dropped Anne's freshly lit Camel into the multiple folds of tulle in her Orry-Kelly gown, which promptly burst into flame. Panicked, I doused it with the prop cocktail I'd just been served and the only damage done was to her dress and my confidence. Thing is, it wasn't in the script, so her shocked reaction was spontaneous and real, the camera lingering on both our stunned faces in a comic reprise of my ill-fated turn with Barbara Stanwyck. It had been so funny they decided to keep the bit, and the writer even adjusted the dialogue for us right there on the set to accommodate my gaffe—with something about my character being nervous around this gorgeous young woman. Lillian found it hilarious and told me I had a knack for comedy as I watched her smiling in the flickering light from the projector. My screwup stayed in the picture, but I had very mixed feelings about it when I heard the laughter at the test screening.

"You see?" Milly said, flashing a grin as the last of the film ran out, flooding the room with a sudden, stuttering brightness. "Real magic only exists in the movies."

I was exhausted during most of the shoot, even with my light schedule. Pretending to be someone I wasn't both on and off the silver screen was draining. Milly and I would take the *Jubilee* out for afternoons of furtive lovemaking whenever he could get away on the weekends; then I'd drag home and find Lillian waiting for me in the cabana, or luring me to the upstairs guest room. Somehow, I managed to function with both of them in the blur of that year, and it wasn't until later I realized the only thing keeping me going was a very mixed-up and damaged love. Not just for Milly—for whom I constantly, foolishly pined—but for Lillian as well. In a way, I suppose sex with her was my own demented means of being close to Milly, especially during those interminable lapses between our stolen hours aboard the *Jubilee*. And, as he'd said, he wanted my affair with his wife to continue, so I complied with a blind and aching stupidity.

Besides, as I was to come to understand, I was trapped by my own inability to break her heart, even as I grew to resent her more and more. She was always seated next to Milly at lavish dinner parties, always on his arm at premieres and screenings. With their alliterative names, *Milly* and *Lilly*, they projected the photogenic aura of two people destined to be great together—just as Milford Langen must surely have envisioned when he created Lillian Sinclair from the raw clay of Edna Mae Loudermilk. Of course, I had a festering and crazy notion that in a far more perfect world, the person at Milly's side should have been Dexter Gaines. But it could never be, as he made damn sure to keep up our charade of being two friends who enjoyed doing manly things like boating together. It was especially difficult to hide our shenanigans from Deming and the nearly invisible Blanche, but if they were onto anything, they liked their paychecks well enough to keep their mouths shut. The only consolation for my third-fiddle status came when I helped Lillian plan a soiree for Milly's thirty-fourth birthday, a really swanky white-tie-and-tails sit-down dinner for 260 people at the house. I convinced her to fire An-*ton*-ia the caterer just as I had vowed to do my first night in Hollywood and actually felt I had accomplished something.

Some evenings, when Milford and Lillian were out at yet another Hollywood premiere or function where my presence couldn't be explained away, I'd taken to going out on my own. A favorite destination was the Formosa on Santa Monica Boulevard, where I was always sure to encounter established stars I'd met at parties on South Windsor, and then use them to impress whatever young up-and-comers I happened to be drinking with at the time.

One night, shortly after I'd settled in at the bar and ordered my usual scotch neat, a young fellow asked if the next stool was taken. I turned to look at him. He was handsome in a bookish sort of way with tousled hair and round clear acrylic spectacles. I knew by then I was a sucker for a man in glasses. He had a writing tablet tucked under his arm and his tie was already loosened. "It's all yours," I said as he smiled and joined me. When he took off his tweed jacket, I could see he was built like a wrestler. Maybe a couple of years my senior, he was pleasant enough, and told me he'd t arrived from Madison, Wisconsin, to pursue a career writing for the pictures.

"Alden Metford," he said, extending his hand.

"Dexter Gaines," I replied as I shook it firmly, summoning all of the masculinity I could. My own name still sounded false to me, but I did have a movie opening soon, so I knew I had to get used to it.

"I know," he said. "I saw you on the cover of *Photoplay*."

We shared a laugh together then, both drawn in by each other's friendly smiles, and Alden seemed fascinated as I began to tell him how I'd arrived in Hollywood with nothing but a similar dream and had just wrapped my first picture for 20th. In fact, he was so impressed, he bought the next round of drinks, and the two of us proceeded to get pretty toasted together. When the conversation turned personal, as they invariably do in such circumstances, I confided I was in a relationship with someone who was married but took special care to omit any references to gender. Turns out, a similarly unspecific situation had led to his hightailing it out of Wisconsin, so we became fast friends. Careful not to betray the truth of my domestic situation, I was nagged by the idea that my life might be easier without Milly and Lillian and the prison of secrecy—but such thoughts were always quashed by my unshakeable feelings for Milford Langen. Still, I did get a tingle when, at one point in the conversation, Alden put his hand on my arm and gave it a squeeze. So casual.

"Who is she?" he asked, unable to conceal his curiosity.

I hesitated, having no prepared answer other than the unutterable truth. Alden smiled at my silence.

"Somebody famous?" he pressed, as if hungry for gossip.

"I . . . really can't say," was my answer, and not a good one. I honestly wasn't sure if I'd been talking about Lillian or her husband.

He nodded and smiled again as I changed the subject, asking what kind of pictures he wanted to write.

"Oh, you know, action-adventure, romantic comedies, Westerns . . ."

We then talked endlessly about our favorite movies and music, and he was impressed by my extensive knowledge of jazz—even though I was only naming the artists I knew from Milly's collection. At length, after the two of us were hoarse from cigarettes, laughter, and booze, he grabbed a cocktail napkin and scrawled something down.

"Here's my number," he said, sliding it across the bar to me. "Give me a bell sometime."

I couldn't help but like the idea, even though I was fully aware of the potential consequences.

The first test screening of *Shipshape* was held in Westwood Village, and afterwards Milly sorted through the scribbled comment cards ranging from "stinks up the joint" to "very funny" and "Dexter Gaines is dreamy." Apparently, it didn't matter if I could act or not, so long as teenage girls would shell out half a buck to see my full lips on the screen. One woman had especially liked my scene by the ship's pool where Anne shoves me in so violently I lose my trunks before she snatches them out of the water and exits in a huff, leaving me stranded in my waist-deep nakedness. The woman had written gushing words about how I could be the next Tarzan. When I pointed it out to Milly, he glanced around to make sure no one was listening then chuckled. "How do you know it's a woman?"

I blushed.

Through it all, Lillian was once again on loan, this time to Universal, shooting some melodrama with Douglas Sirk called *Tomorrow Will Bring Heaven*, and truth be told, she seemed to be doing well. Milly, on the other hand, continued to battle with both Zanuck and his revolving door of writers, trying to get *The Trojan War* down to a manageable running time and budget. Production was ready to start one minute, then pushed back several weeks the next. Through it all, Milly never gave up on his masterpiece, even while being forced to spend much of his time on the lesser, frothier projects he'd been assigned. When Darryl Zanuck closed the deal for the patent to the CinemaScope process and announced that all of the studio's pictures would be produced in the new colossal format, Milly again held up his precious *Trojan War* as a perfect candidate.

Shipshape at last premiered at the Orpheus Theater downtown, and there I was, walking the red carpet behind Milly with Lillian's arm draped through his, watching them charm reporters and pose while flashbulbs exploded all around.

Milly and Lilly. The fabulous and famous couple with the assonant names.

I was escorted by a young starlet whose name and personality were entirely forgettable and struggled to make conversation throughout the evening. Milly had encouraged me to date her afterwards, saying it would be good for my image and even better for our secret, but I decided to save my acting for the cameras.

I was nervous when the lights came down and the plush velvet curtains glided apart, my dream coming true as searchlights swept the majestic 20th Century Fox logo, the signature fanfare thundering and trumpeting the premiere of another Milford Langen production. Even if I wasn't fond of my new name, I was in awe when the words "and introducing Dexter Gaines" blazed across the screen accompanied by the cornball music that bubbled and bounced. Lilly applauded and the crowd followed suit, more out of respect for her than me. They laughed in all the right places, and my confidence grew as the film continued. I looked away only during the scene where I'd set Anne ablaze and the audience howled. Afterwards, I accepted a shower of compliments, posed for a few pictures, and even signed a handful of autographs, all while tasting a future I now thought possible. At one point, I caught Milly's eyes and was thrilled by their silent gleam of pride and affection.

The film opened to a polite reception and did modestly well at the box office. I was already shooting my second picture for the studio while *Shipshape* debuted on screens across the country. I wondered if my parents would sober up long enough to catch it at the Arcadia.

Probably not.

Milly made damn sure to have the woman who'd cut *Shipshape* edit my next film, another romantic comedy called *Gravy Train*, and this time I found myself bound for Chicago on the 20th Century Limited, playing second banana to Tony Curtis as two soldiers home on leave trying to outmaneuver each other for the attentions of Cyd Charisse, who played an exotic jewel thief posing as a showgirl. It seemed my movie self was always destined to be going somewhere exciting, while my real life was becoming mired in the immobility of deceit and duplicity. When Cyd and I realized we were both Texans, we became friends almost immediately, further bonding over our unfortunate real names. She won the contest by confiding hers was Tula Ellice Finklea. She was even gracious enough to act like she remembered our long-ago dance at the Mocambo. I also liked working with Tony, and in fact had to hide the crush I developed on him, but as Milly would bring home the rough assemblies of our scenes, I noticed I was getting less and less screen time, much of the dialogue I'd worked on with Lillian having been excised. Milly privately admonished me that if I needed to pretend I was flirting with Tony in my scenes with Cyd, then I should, because Zanuck had made a crack about me batting my lashes at the wrong costar.

"Cut it the hell out," Milly warned. "I can only do so much to protect you."

"And more importantly *yourself*," I shot back.

The incident threw me off, and while the picture went on to do pretty well at the box office when it came out later that year, my sidekick role was so butchered I was barely mentioned in a single review, and my promised costar billing after Tony and Cyd was bumped down a notch to "featuring." When we screened the finished film, I slid lower and lower in my seat, terrified that others might see me as I was beginning to see myself—a creature becoming more and more difficult to hide. If

Darryl F. Zanuck had seen through me, how long before the Heddas and Louellas and other chittering gossips would expose the dirty truth, and drag Milford Langen down with me into the quicksand of scandal? And it angered me as well, knowing the judgment of others held far more power and importance than my own happiness.

My salvation came in the form of the impressive paychecks I got for both pictures—well above and beyond my contract salary—and I began to repay the advance Milly had been giving me since my arrival in Hollywood. That money was important to me, too, because it allowed me to return often to the Formosa to surround myself with the insouciant freedom of my peers.

Driving home one afternoon from the studio, I stopped in for happy hour and was both delighted and thrown by a voice in my ear: "You never called me."

I turned on the bar stool to see Alden Metford, giving me a look of feigned hurt. "Alden, hey," I said, indicating the next stool, "let me buy you a drink and tell you why."

He grinned and joined me, and I explained how busy I'd been.

"I know," he said, smiling. "I saw *Shipshape*."

"You did?" I asked, flattered. "What'd you think?"

His face betrayed the truth. "Not really my kind of picture. But you were terrific. That scene where you set Anne Francis on fire . . ." He trailed off, chuckling. I made a point of putting my hands flat on the bar to hide their trembling.

"Yeah," I said. "That wasn't in the script."

"It was an ad lib?" he asked, surprised.

Sure, why not? "Anne didn't even know it was coming. Her reaction is a hundred percent real."

"And here I thought you actors *always* stuck to what's on the page," he said and I laughed at his sarcasm. He sipped his scotch for a moment, as if steeling himself, then said, "And the scene where she leaves you naked in the pool? *That* was something else."

Here he chuckled at the memory, and I wondered exactly what he meant but didn't dare ask for clarification. After a moment of silence, he said, "Hey, some friends of mine are throwing a little bash later. You in?"

"Sure," I said.

He glanced at his wristwatch. "It doesn't start for a while yet. We could grab some dinner first if you want." He was still smiling at me.

"I do," I said, really liking this guy and grateful for some uncomplicated company my own age.

We took our cocktails to a vacant booth, and as we smoked and scanned the menu, I asked, "So how's the writing going?"

He tapped the writing tablet beside him. "Slow but sure. I'm working on a thriller."

"What's it about? Or can't you talk about it?"

"I trust you." He smiled, and I tried to quell the stirring I felt. Then he launched into the pitch, putting his elbows on the table and using his hands for emphasis. "It's about this Nazi officer who escapes during the American occupation of Berlin. He goes underground and manages to get to present-day New York . . . on a war bride ship or something—I haven't quite figured that part out, yet—and his English is perfect, not a trace of an accent—so he passes himself off as an American in polite society, but he's secretly trying to find other Nazis to band together and overthrow the government."

"Wow, sounds ambitious," I said, chewing on the steak that had just arrived.

"Yeah, the first draft's almost finished. I really like the theme of people leading double lives but pretending everything's normal, you know what I'm saying?"

I nodded, deciding not to admit I knew *exactly* what he was saying even as I started to choke on my steak. Alarmed by my coughing, Alden made a move to pat me on the back, but I waved him away as I managed to swallow.

"Sorry," I said, embarrassed. "I'm fine. Please, finish your story."

He shrugged and went on, "That's pretty much it. Anyway, all I need now is to get it to somebody." I thought for a moment about how easy it would be for me to help him, and how he'd probably end up in my bed as a result, but decided to keep my cards close to the vest. After a while, he asked about the process of shooting *Shipshape*. I enjoyed being the "old pro" as I told him and he listened attentively, allowing me the spotlight. After I'd babbled on for about twenty minutes, he finally asked, "Who's Milly?"

"Oh," I said, realizing the familiarity with which I'd been referring to my "boss" on the picture, "Milford Langen. Everybody calls him 'Milly.'"

"Oh, right. Of course. Have you met his wife?"

"Sure," I said. "I'm renting the cabana behind their house."

"No kidding," he answered, intrigued. I thought it best to steer the conversation toward something less treacherous, and soon we had finished dinner and were walking outside toward the curb where the Nash was parked. Alden had taken the streetcar, so I was happy to volunteer to drive the two of us to his friend's shindig. The night traffic drifted by on Santa Monica Boulevard as I fished my keys out of my pocket.

"Dex?" Alden said, stopping with his hand on the door handle and eyeing me over the roof. He seemed sheepish and uncomfortable. "I sort of left something out."

"What?" I asked, unlocking the car.

"This party. It's . . ." He trailed off, shifting his weight as he looked away, then lowered his voice and said, "Well, there aren't going to be any girls there. If you catch my drift."

I froze. This was now moving much faster than I was comfortable with, and entirely in the wrong direction. To risk being seen at such a gathering could put my burgeoning career in real jeopardy, and I could only imagine what Milly might think if he ever found out—especially after his infamous reaction to Henry Willson's backyard barbeque. To step outside my tortured relationship with my benefactors could derail my entire trajectory.

"Oh," I said.

"I mean I sorta gathered you and I were on the same wavelength, so . . ."

I'd be lying if I said I wasn't tempted in that moment. But I also knew I couldn't allow myself to think with anything other than my brain.

"Then, um, sorry but I'm gonna have to pass."

With that, I got into the car and drove off, leaving him standing there on the sidewalk. When I glanced into the rearview mirror, my heart ached as I saw Alden snap his head downward as he cursed, then spun around as he hurled the writing tablet against the side of a building, no doubt feeling like a fool in the wake of my rejection. I considered slamming on the brakes and returning to apologize and explain the whole sordid situation. Instead, I tore my eyes away from his ever-receding reflection, then whipped the Nash onto La Brea and headed back to my own deceitful prison.

Earlier that year, when February faded through to March, a film Milly produced was up for an Academy Award for best black-and-white cinematography. It was like a wish come true when Lillian suggested I accompany Milly to the Oscars in her place because she'd come down with the flu. I knew it was crazy, but I couldn't help thinking it would be a little ember of Europe all over again, with me at last in the coveted role of Milford Langen's "companion," however briefly. But Milly balked at the idea, surprising me with his candor when he told Lillian he was concerned how it might appear, two gentlemen walking the red carpet together. I gave him a pleading look, and by the time it was all sorted out, I learned the true meaning of "beard" when we got into the Cadillac in our tuxedos and were greeted by two starlets from central casting, gushing and giddy at having been selected from the stack of photographs Milly had requested and babbling on about the "nifty" fold-down seats they'd commandeered in the back of the limo while fretting about what the light rain might do to their expensive hairdos.

I endured the evening at the Pantages Theatre with the two birds between us like an uncrossable barrier, and my beard chattered away in a voice that sounded like fingers squeaking on a balloon. At least it was easy to tune her out given how I was fascinated by seeing Bob Hope both at the microphone center stage and projected live on a big movie screen hanging overhead. *What would they think of next?* I also marveled at the choreography of the huge NBC television cameras broadcasting the whole shebang for the first time ever, and wondered if Lillian might catch a glimpse of us while watching at home. I was pleased to see *The Greatest Show on Earth* take home the best picture Oscar for no other reason than I'd watched it aboard the maiden voyage of the *United States* all those months ago, and also because it signaled the evening was almost over. Later, when I escorted my beard to her apartment door, she tried to jump me, but I declined, promised to call her, but of course never did.

A week or so later, I padded from the cabana into the kitchen and found Lillian, wrapped in her peignoir, sitting in the breakfast nook, smoking and staring in a melancholy daze at the lifeless television.

"What's wrong?"

She roused herself, but hardly moved.

"I just heard the most dreadful thing," she said, dropping the remainder of a Chesterfield into her now cold coffee. I sat down opposite her, concerned.

"What's happened?"

"I never wished her ill, Dexter," she said, her voice distant and rattled. "I resented her, true, but that's not the same thing."

"Lil? Who are you talking about?"

"Poor Vivien. Poor, poor Vivien."

I had never seen her like this. "Vivien Leigh?"

Lillian nodded. "She's had a complete nervous breakdown."

I vaguely recalled reading that Leigh was shooting *Elephant Walk* with Peter Finch in Ceylon, and there had been some trouble on the set.

Lillian continued, "The director decided to move the shoot here, and as their plane was taking off, she started banging on the windows, hysterical, shrieking to be let out." She trailed off into silence, closing her eyes as if to shut out the horrible image. I put a comforting hand on hers.

"That's terrible," I said. "But why are you so bothered by it?"

"Don't you see, Dexter?" she replied, meeting my gaze for the first time, looking frail and afraid as she whispered, "Sometimes I know exactly how she must feel."

One afternoon when I'd wrapped early, having finished all my work on *Gravy Train,* I sat in the cool spring of the Urban Idyll, embracing the rare gift of the boredom that had once so troubled me. I still didn't know what my next contract picture was to be, and Milly seemed to be growing more and more distant whenever I tried to strategize my career with him. He assured me my role as Achilles was safe, and the studio was trying to find just the right script for me in the interim. I was delighted to see him through the kitchen window, getting ice cubes out of the Frigidaire before coming outside.

"You're home early," I said with a smile, hoping I might lure him into the privacy of the cabana. "And you're in luck, Blanche and Deming won't be back for another forty-five minutes . . ."

"Dexter," he said, his tone foreboding as he sipped his scotch and lit a cigarette as if stalling for time.

"What now?" I asked.

"It's just . . ." he said looking out over the pool, "we have to stop seeing each other. For good."

I barely made a sound. "What?"

"Darryl called me into his office and gave me a very uncomfortable talking to. There's been some gossip at the studio."

"About us? That's impossible!"

"Not after you making goo-goo eyes at Tony Curtis and then accompanying me to the Oscars. And everyone's jawing about how you're still living in our pool house even though your career is taking off."

"People talk, Milly, you know that—"

"Somebody mailed pictures to my office," he said, cutting me off. "Of you and me aboard the *Jubilee.* Nothing terribly incriminating, but suspicious to say the least. It's a blackmail threat, obviously, and—"

"Then we should leak my affair with Lillian! God, Milly, whatever it takes."

He shook his head. "We both know we can't do that to her. None of this is her fault, after all."

I felt a rush of uncomfortable adrenaline bringing tears to my eyes.

"But I *love* you, Milly. And you can't deny you feel the same way."

"I have to deny it, Dexter. We both do. There's a witch hunt going on. And they're not just looking to round up the Commies. If you or I were exposed, it would—"

"I don't care about that. All I care about is you. And *us*."

"Stop it, Dexter," he said firmly. "We knew this might happen. And I can't risk—*I won't risk*—any whiff of scandal. It's over. It *has* to be."

He got up then, threw his cigarette onto the lawn, then followed it with the now drained ice cubes in his glass as he walked away from me and toward the house, pausing only once to look back and say, "You'll have to move out immediately, of course," then went inside.

I stared at the lazy wisp of smoke rising from the grass in the chilly afternoon.

At length, I staggered to my feet and into the cabana, closing the blinds before crawling into my unmade bed, pulling the coverlet over my eyes and spiraling downward into a dark and impenetrable spell. I don't know how long I was there before I heard Lillian's excited voice as she barged in.

Oh god. Not her. Not now.

"Hey sleepyhead, wake up. I have the most marvelous news."

"I'm not feeling very well," was all I could manage from my cocoon. Fueling my unhealthy state, she pulled the covers back and pressed her hand to my forehead.

"You're not running a fever," she said.

"I have a migraine," I snapped. "And you're not my mother."

"All right," she said, stung with disappointment. "I'll save my news for another time. Feel better."

Mercifully, she left. My mind was racing as my heart seemed to wither in my chest, the nightmares returning to swirl around me as I sought the forgiving relief of sleep. When I didn't show up for dinner, Lillian brought me a tray of soup and some dry toast. I tried to tell her I wasn't hungry, but she wouldn't take no for an answer, especially when she saw my pillow was soaked with tears and snot.

"What's really bothering you, Dex?" she asked. "I know you well enough now to suspect you're hiding something."

I fought the surge of panic and tried to steady my hand as I raised a spoonful of soup to my mouth, feigning hunger to avoid answering her question.

"It's us, isn't it?" she pressed. "I've been exhausted commuting back and forth to Universal every day. I promise we'll steal some time together this weekend." Then she touched my chin and forced me to look at her. "Okay?"

I nodded, playing along, anything to get her out of there so I could return to my demons.

"We'll have more opportunity in the weeks ahead," she went on, misunderstanding the whole sordid situation. "I was going to tell you I've been given the lead in Milly's next picture, *Three Minutes to Curtain*. I play a movie star nervous about my Broadway stage debut, and you won't believe who's going to be my costar."

"Tallu?"

"How'd you know?"

"Lucky guess."

"Imagine," she said, "the two of us finally getting to work together."

"That's great, Lilly," was all I could manage, silently imploring her to leave.

"All right then," she said, rising. "You rest up and feel better. You'll need your strength for this weekend."

She left me, and I stayed in bed until late the next afternoon. The house was empty and the doors locked, signaling Deming and Blanche were both out, so I let myself in and found my luggage from the Europe trip in the closet hidden under the curved wall of the main staircase. I tortured myself by lingering in the doorway to Milly's study while I momentarily considered breaking into the locked drawer to satisfy the ridiculous notion I had that its contents might reveal irrefutable proof of Milly's love for me—scrawled in his own hand in those little journals— then came to my senses and went back outside. I packed hastily, and even though I knew it wasn't mine for the taking, I put what few things I had into the Nash-Healey and drove away, directionless and adrift again. I hadn't even left a note and relished the idea of their panic upon returning home and finding me gone. That would sure as shit show them. My thoughts of vengeance brought the tiniest comfort, knowing at least they would care that I'd left—unlike dear old Mom and Dad back home.

As it turned out, I didn't get too far before I spotted a "for rent" sign outside a poured concrete art deco apartment tower on Sycamore just above Third Street. Mrs. Carnahan, a plump former New Yorker with a cockatoo perched on her shoulder, showed me a furnished studio on the second floor in back, with a Murphy bed and its own private doorway to a small terrace spanning the width of the building. Sure, it overlooked a dingy alleyway and wasn't exactly the Urban Idyll, but in my state of mind, I didn't give a damn. It had purple-and-black tile in the bathroom and a kitchen that looked like something you'd find on a train. The rooms were airy and light enough so I signed the lease and lugged my suitcases up, venturing out only once for bread, peanut butter, scotch, and cigarettes. When I returned, I locked the door, then closed the blinds before crawling onto the bare mattress of the fold-down bed, curling into a fetal position as I cried myself to sleep, sheltered in the darkness from the panicked drama that would play out both on Windsor Boulevard and at 20th Century Fox when they realized up-and-comer Dexter Gaines had vanished.

I awoke a week later in a malodorous holding cell not unlike the one where I'd spent New Year's Eve the night I'd arrived in Los Angeles. The day before, while drunk and high, I'd ventured out of the *El Palazar* apartments in search of food, when a crazy notion overtook me to keep driving and flee Milly and Lilly and all of Hollywood for good. I didn't even know what part of town I was racing through when I heard the wail of a siren, signaling me to pull over. I was arrested by the motorcycle cop and booked on charges of auto theft. It seems Milly had reported the Nash-Healey stolen when I hadn't returned after three days, and, as he would later explain to me, it was the only way he had of tracking me down. He arrived at the police station in Glendale to clear up the misunderstanding and get the charges dropped, and we'd been swarmed by a phalanx of photographers waiting for us outside, snapping pictures and shouting questions as Deming spirited us away in the Cadillac.

"What the hell is wrong with you?" Milly was almost spitting at me. "Lillian is beside herself."

"And you obviously don't care."

"Stop it, Dexter. Be a man, for god's sake."

"Oh, that's rich, coming from you."

He silenced me with a quick jerk of his head toward Deming's eyes in the rearview mirror, stealing glances toward us.

"Darryl's livid at your little escapade," Milly went on, barely able to calm the fury in his voice. "He had appearances scheduled for you to promote *Gravy Train*, and I looked like a jackass with no clue where you were."

"Oh, I get it," I said. "It's all about *you* looking like a jackass."

"We'll finish this at home," he said, his tone suggesting it was the end of the conversation, but I wasn't having any of it.

"Yeah, well whose home is that? I got my own place now. Just like you told me to. And frankly, I don't care if I never set foot in your house again. Or see either one of you for that matter."

"Stop it. Do you have any idea what you've done to Lillian? She's fragile enough without convincing herself you'd been abducted and murdered."

"Right, we know how much you're concerned about your precious wife."

"Dex, listen to me—"

"Fuck you," I said, just as Deming stopped for a red light at Los Feliz Boulevard and Riverside, right by the giant art deco Mulholland Fountain, its jets sending loud plumes of spray into the warm spring air. I threw the door open and bolted.

"Get back in the goddamned car!" Milly yelled after me.

Ignoring him, I hurried through the intersection as cars whizzed past, some laying on their horns. Then Milly was behind me, snatching at my elbow. I shrugged him off and kept going. When I reached the other side of the fountain, I could feel its showering mist as Milly grabbed my arm and yanked me around to face him. "You're acting like a heartbroken schoolgirl," he said.

"Maybe because I am. You might be able to turn this thing on and off like a goddamned light switch, but I *can't*," I was yelling.

"Keep your voice down."

"It's all about your precious image, isn't it? It's all about Milford Langen being the big-dicked producer with the gorgeous wife and house, everybody kowtowing to you. And that's more important to you than being honest with yourself. Or me. Because I've got news for you, Milly, *you're just like me*. Only you're something worse. Worse than even Henry Willson, you know that? You destroy and hurt the people who love you because you can't face the truth!"

"Shut up, Dexter, shut your goddamned—!"

"You're *pathetic*, Milly," I shouted over him. "You act like you hate homosexuals to protect yourself; only turns out it isn't an act after all, is it? Because *you're* a homosexual and you obviously really do hate yourself *so* much—!"

My head snapped back as he punched me in the mouth, knocking me so hard I lost my balance and fell, cracking my skull on the concrete encircling the fountain. I staggered to my feet, dazed, feeling the pulsing sting from my split lip and tasting the metallic tang of blood. Before I could turn around, he shoved me in the middle of my back, pushing me headfirst into the ice-cold water. I rose up, stupefied and coughing, then collapsed, sitting on the little wall and burying my face in my hands.

"Leave me alone," I said, starting to cry, broken and helpless.

"Pull yourself together," he snapped. "You signed a contract, Dexter. You have binding legal obligations to both me and the studio and if you can't—"

I cut him off by standing, facing him, and screaming at the top of my lungs, my eyes wild and furious as all my impotent rage exploded in a violent, insane roar. Soon my throat was raw and I was coughing on my own blood. Milly stood frozen, and I could see the alarm in his face before he spoke in a sedate voice that betrayed how deeply my outburst had rattled him, "Just get back in the car."

I wanted to run from him and keep going, to disappear for good, but I knew I had no choice. I was trapped, already so enmeshed in his web of deceit and self-hatred I couldn't have gotten out if I'd wanted to. I still clung like an idiot to my dream of stardom, even as I watched it decay into an inexorable nightmare. At length, still weeping, I did as I was told and Milly ushered me into the back of the limo. From my scrambled and desperate thoughts emerged the image of Vivien Leigh pounding madly on the window of an airplane, beseeching her demons to set her free.

Neither of us said another word until we got to the house on Windsor, and I found myself apologizing to a wildly relieved Lillian while Milly simply went into his study and locked the door, no doubt drowning himself in booze and loud music. Lilly and I had both noticed how he seemed to be drinking more and more lately, and while she attributed it to the stress of producing *Trojan War*, I knew better.

Lillian tended to my wounds while I explained I had gotten into a fight with some hooligan in the cell. Fortunately, my shirt was dry enough I didn't have to invent a story to cover that as well, though by now lying was as second nature to me as it was to Milly—one of the many ways he'd infected me with his own self-loathing. The only difference was I had grown weary of the merciless deception.

"It's my fault, isn't it?" she asked, seeming vulnerable as she dabbed my aching lip with a damp washcloth.

"No, no," I said, desperate to avoid further conversation.

She turned to rinse the cloth, then froze in place, and I could tell she was crying.

"You vanished so suddenly—without explanation—I couldn't help but think you'd grown tired of me."

I was silent, my mind racing as I felt the trap closing ever tighter. Milly had said I mustn't break her heart, after all. When I didn't answer, she asked, "I'm right, aren't I?"

"No," I lied yet again, "it's nothing like that."

She smiled through her tears, then kissed me when I promised to return to her bed.

TWENTY-FIVE

Milly went back to work, and I went back to screwing Lillian. My passion was fueled by my unspoken fury at Milly's rejection, and in my muddled state of mind I had managed to convince myself that sex with Lillian was the best way to exact whatever emotional revenge I could. The studio had spun the whole car theft episode into a wacky comedy of misunderstandings, even going so far as to have me pose for a fake mug shot with a look of open-mouthed surprise. Milly then made a huge and very public fuss of giving me the Nash-Healey as a gift so he'd never need to have me arrested again. He didn't bother to tell me until sometime later he'd also shelled out two thousand smackers for some negatives taken by an opportunistic photographer who'd captured a whole series of compromising shots of the two of us cavorting aboard the *Jubilee* and of our overwrought brawl by the Mulholland Fountain. The studio system was alive and well, cunningly washing its stars' dirty laundry before delivering it freshly pressed and scented to the gossipmongers.

Somehow, I managed to return to work, making guest appearances on local radio shows to promote *Gravy Train*, all the while drifting as if in a daze. I'd recite the now well-rehearsed lie about why I'd disappeared for a week, explaining how I'd moved out and into my own apartment, and before I could have a phone installed, I'd come down with a very bad flu. This evolved into a piece in Louella Parsons' column about the poor, valiant young Dexter Gaines, and how I'd been to death's door and back, making me sound like some tragic hero. After that, I started receiving

280

flowers and get well cards from teenage girls who'd seen my *Photoplay* story and had loved me in *Shipshape*. The morass of lies grew deeper and deeper, and I'd vent my frustration with loud and fervent sex with Lillian, fighting away the wretched images of Milly when he'd ravished me the way I was now doing his wife. In short, it was exhausting.

I kept my place at the *El Palazar* apartments, and only came by the house on Windsor for my trysts with Lillian or a handful of mandatory parties as that untenable year wore on. One night, as I was dressing to leave the upstairs guest room with its taunting mirrored wall, careful to avoid catching a glimpse of my reflected delusions and shame, Lillian expressed her disappointment that Tallu had backed out of *Three Minutes to Curtain* because she'd accepted a nightclub gig at the Sands Hotel in Las Vegas, of all things. Tallu was to be replaced by Thelma Ritter, whom Lillian adored, but she had so wanted a chance to work with her best friend. To cheer her up, I suggested we steal away and see Tallulah's nightclub act, and she delighted in the idea of a weekend together away from the house. *And Milly*, I thought, but kept my mouth shut.

Milly seemed to invent excuses to see me, always speaking with a strain that betrayed his inner struggle to resist what we both knew he fervently desired. Deciding I had to move on, I tore through every drawer in my apartment until I found what I was looking for: the crumpled cocktail napkin with Alden Metford's phone number scrawled in pencil.

The muted sound of typing stopped when I knocked on the door to his drab studio apartment in a ramshackle building on Franklin. After a moment, it opened a crack and Alden looked at me curiously. No wonder, considering I hadn't made a lot of sense on the phone.

"May I come in?" I asked.

"What do you want?"

"To talk. Explain even. Look, when you told me that your friend's party was gonna be—"

Alden's eyes widened as he caught sight of a neighbor approaching down the hallway. He cut me off. "Come inside."

I stepped into the shabby room, noting his ancient Royal typewriter and endless reams of neatly typed pages. The space was cozy and masculine. He closed the door as I shoved my shaking hands deep into my pockets, feeling like my skin was on fire.

I swallowed, nervous. "Got anything to drink?"

"I'm all out. What is it?"

"Okay, look. We *are* on the same wavelength. It's just, at the time, I couldn't risk letting anybody know."

I was astonished by the frankness of his next words:

"Are you telling me you're a homosexual?"

I tried to smile, unable to read his look.

"I'm telling you," I said, "that it's okay."

I leaned in to kiss him and was shocked when he shoved me away, then wiped his mouth with the back of his hand. "What the *hell* are you doing?"

I blinked at him, trying to comprehend.

"Get out of here," he said.

"What?" I asked, surprised. "Look, Alden, it's okay. I know I was rude before, but I gotta be discreet. It's just, things have changed for me now and . . ." I approached him, unaware that I was, in that moment, a pleading and desperate creature, putting my hands up to touch his face.

"Whoa whoa whoa," he said, "you got the wrong idea."

"How? You invited me to that party. I was the one who said no . . ."

"There was no party. I was just gonna pretend like I couldn't find the place while you drove around."

I looked at him, then croaked a baffled, "I don't understand."

"Look, I just figured you were probably queer from the way you were making girly eyes at me, and since I knew you had connections with Milford Langen, I thought if I strung you along you might slip him my screenplay."

My cheeks burned in humiliation, and I turned away from him to hide the tears now blurring my vision. All I could manage was "You're an asshole" before I hurried out of there, feeling like the most ridiculous man alive.

Jesus, this whole fucking town was full of nothing but whores.

My luck improved when I made an awkward pass at another student from Dante's class one night while we were rehearsing a scene in my apartment, and after we shared a joint, found him all too willing to join me in my bed. Scott Presscott was a good-looking blond, freshly home from the war in Korea, who had moved to LA to chase the same dream I had. Still, the sex wasn't the same as with Milly, lacking the comfort and tenderness that comes from caring. After he dressed to leave and we were saying goodnight, I was stunned to find Milly in the hallway outside my door when I opened it, just standing there with his hands in his pockets, making no move to knock, a cigarette dangling from his lips, as if he'd been caught in a moment of paralyzed indecision, his nose pink and his eyes red from booze. I wondered how long he'd been there, and whether or not Scott and I had made any telltale noises. His eyes flashed as Scott shook my hand and said we should rehearse again sometime soon. Milly watched, then dropped his cigarette onto the tile floor and ground it out with his shoe—next to three identical extinguished butts, indicating he had, in fact, been standing there a long time. I didn't bother to introduce them, but as Scott walked down the hall, Milly couldn't help but cover, saying loud enough for him to hear, "We need to talk about your next picture." The slur of his words betrayed his now constant drunkenness.

"What next picture?" I asked, closing the door after he followed me inside. The dial on the radio glowed a pale amber as Nat King Cole crooned "Lost April." I didn't shut it off or even bother to fold up the still-tousled Murphy bed, instead folded my arms and stared at him, waiting. Milly eyed me, then turned away as he realized I was wearing nothing but my boxers.

"Who's your friend?" he asked, feigning interest in the label of the scotch bottle on the counter in the breakfast nook before pouring himself a shot.

"Help yourself," I said dryly, watching him take a sip. He stared at me over the rim of the glass, his eyes demanding I answer his question.

"He's just some guy in my acting class," I said.

"Some guy you're sleeping with?"

"I'd hardly call it sleeping, and it's really none of your business. You're the one who said it was over. Scott and I have a great thing going," I went on, turning the knife with my lies. "You know, I thought you were hung, but Scott. Criminy!" The truth was Scott's equipment had been wholly disappointing, but if Milly wanted to torture and toy with me, I was all too eager to parry his every thrust.

"Dexter," he said, eyes closing to shut me out, the pain aching in his voice, "please. Put some clothes on so we can talk."

"About *what*, Milly? What the hell are you doing here?" I asked, not bothering to mask my impatience.

"Apparently," he said slowly, still without looking at me, "making a grievous mistake. Good night."

He started for the door, but I snatched his elbow, tight, and wouldn't let go. I was still buzzing from the marijuana and the lackluster sex with Scott.

"Get your hands off me," he said, his tongue thick as he failed to shrug me away. I spun him around to face me, pinning him.

"That's not what you want and we both know it," I hissed, my lips close to his as I grabbed his crotch through his trousers. Just as I suspected, he was already stirring, even as he struggled to free himself.

"No," he said, but it was barely a whisper.

"Stop lying to me, Milly. And to yourself." I wasn't sure what had taken over me, but the power and control brought a wild rush of adrenaline. I yanked his hat off and flung it across the room, then tugged my boxers down and kicked them away as I put my hands on Milly's shoulders and forced him to his knees in front of me.

"Stop it, please . . ." It was only a hoarse, pathetic whisper, and I realized he was crying.

"You *do* want it, don't you?" I teased, waving my crotch near his face, my voice husky and cruel.

He struggled against me, trying to stand, but he was no match for me.

"Tell me the truth!"

"Yes," he murmured, "god damn it, *yes*." As he leaned in, I shoved him away and he fell flat on his back, his knees twisted behind him. He lay there for a moment, dazed, blinking in drunken confusion as I stepped into my boxers, then found my athletic shirt still on the bed where Scott had left it.

"Well, you can't have it. Now get out of here," I said with a smirk. "When you come to your senses, let me know."

He made an effort to rise from his awkward position, but I didn't offer to help him. Instead, I turned to pour myself another drink. That's when he seized me from behind, pinning my arms with his own as he hoisted me, writhing, and threw me face down onto the bed. He clutched at my clothes, pulling so hard I heard the fabric rending as he tore them away, all the while fumbling with his belt.

"Now who wants it?" he rasped, positioning himself to take me.

"Wait," I said, the sudden softness in my voice catching him off guard, "not like this. Milly . . ."

I rolled over onto my back so I could look up at him. Our eyes met as he loomed over me and I began to unbutton his shirt. Milly gave in, and we kissed fervently as he rasped "yes oh yes" before taking me.

The thing is, by then, we were both crying. I ran my hands all over his body, so grateful he'd come to me, and for the feel of his skin, the scent he exuded, and the way he looked at me as waves of pleasure rippled over and over throughout my body. Gordon MacRae's mournful version of "Blame It on My Youth" now wafted from the radio, providing a bittersweet underscore.

When Milly finished, we lay sated in each other's arms, listening to the music. And though I still had tears in my eyes, I was smiling. I kissed the top of his head.

"I'm sorry, Dexter," he said.

"Me, too," I replied. "But everything's okay now."

He lay there for an indecisive moment, then disentangled himself and got out of bed.

"No," he whispered as he dressed, "everything isn't okay. Far from it."

"But Milly, you—"

"It can't happen again," he said, distraught. "No matter how much you or I or *we* want it. That was—it *has* to be—the last time. Goodbye."

I was too shocked to speak, tears welling fresh in my eyes. Before I could recover, he was gone. I wanted to run after him, plead with him, make him understand. Instead, I picked up his empty scotch glass and hurled it against the door, making damn sure he'd hear its explosion before he reached the stairway in the hall.

By the time May came around, my phone had stopped ringing and there were no scripts arriving on my doorstep. I dialed my agent, a no-nonsense woman named Sylvia Henley at William Morris, and asked her what was going on. She said she'd have to call Fox and get back to me.

"Who're you gonna talk to?" I asked.

"Milford Langen, of course," she said. "He's been your greatest champion."

"Don't bother," I muttered, then hung up. After a half-second, I snatched the receiver again and dialed Scott's number, letting it ring thirty times before I disconnected. Mind racing, I grabbed my keys and drove to the studio on Pico. The guard waved me through, and I was enraged to find a battered Studebaker parked in my space. I pulled behind to block it, got out, and headed off toward the back lot. Lillian was shooting exteriors for *Three Minutes to Curtain* on New York Street, the set dressers having transformed it into a semblance of the real thing with cabs and working traffic lights. As I approached, the second assistant director stopped me while they finished a shot.

I watched at a distance while Lillian, in character as the terrified and flustered movie star, filmed a take of the scene where she arrives at the theater for her first opening night. My heart fluttered with hope and annoyance when I saw Milly sitting in a canvas chair watching over the director's shoulder. Fortunately, his back was to me. Lillian's scene was with Thelma Ritter and a cute young guy I didn't recognize playing the writer who had convinced the movie star to be in his show. My stomach boiled. There's no reason I couldn't have played that part. I'd read the script with Lillian one night but hadn't dared suggest myself for the role. Still, I resented it like hell.

The scene was long and full of banter, and after an eternity, the director at last yelled "Cut!" and the freeze-frame of grips, gaffers and other workers came to life as they all scurried to prepare for the next take. Lillian made a beeline for the shade of the fake theater marquee, complaining she needed a hat with a wider brim to keep the sun out of her eyes. This sent the wardrobe girls and the director of photography into a scrambling tizzy. I shook my head, knowing the only reason she wanted a bigger hat was because she'd become more and more terrified of anything that might damage her skin and begin to expose her age. I waited while Milly went to her and they chatted briefly before he started right toward me.

Damn.

Milly caught my eye, forced a half-smile and nodded as he passed, "Hello, Dexter," before continuing on his way.

I didn't bother to reply, and instead made my way over to Lillian under the marquee. She seemed delighted and surprised to see me, and while the crew was relighting to accommodate her new chapeau, she led me through the double doorway and behind the façade of the theater. We stood in the cool dimness among the exposed beams and electrical cables hidden by the illusion.

"Could you please ask your husband what's going on with my nonexistent career?"

She looked at me, surprised. "Why don't you ask him yourself? You just missed him."

"I tried, but he's not exactly the chattiest Joe these days," I said, wanting to add "about my career among other things," but of course left that out. Even if my affair with her husband was over, he was still dangling the carrot of stardom in front of me.

"Are you two having a quarrel?" Lillian asked.

"I don't know. I just thought you might be able to help."

"I'll try," she said, ever supportive. "Dexter, as long as you're here . . ." She trailed off, a troubled look on her face.

"That doesn't sound good," I said.

"I'm sorry, but I think I shouldn't go with you to Las Vegas on Saturday."

"Why not?" I asked, surprised. "Tallu will be devastated."

"It's just . . ." She stopped, realizing she was chewing her lower lip and mussing her makeup, then continued, "Milly said we shouldn't be seen traveling together. He's worried about any damaging rumors that might get started."

"Of course he is. Great. Fine. Perfect," I said, irritated. It wasn't directed at her, but she was the nearest person at that moment. "Suit yourself. I'll go without you."

"Dex," she called as I walked back into the sunlit counterfeit New York street, aware of the unapologetic phoniness of everything in Hollywood. But I didn't bother to stop and turn around, though as I passed Milly's office bungalow, I did consider going in and confronting him. When I returned to the Nash, a pudgy and irate delivery guy was gesticulating to a security guard, enraged that I had blocked him in.

"It's my car," I said, approaching.

"You got some nerve, fella," the porky guy said, picking the wrong time to cross me.

"Me? You can go to hell. That's *my* goddamned parking space."

I got into the little convertible, drove back to the *El Palazar*, and rang Scott's number every ten minutes until at last he picked up, sounding out of breath as if he'd dashed to catch the phone, probably hoping it was his agent. By that time, I was pretty toasted on pot and scotch, but invited him to go with me to see Tallulah's nightclub act anyway.

"Tallulah who?" he asked.

I rolled my eyes. "Tallulah Bankhead."

I waited, but there was no response, so I tried to mask my irritation as I said, "You remember *The Big Show* on NBC?"

"Oh yeah," he said to my relief. "She's that old campy broad, right? If you want to, sure."

I let his casual insult slip past, then arranged to pick him up on Saturday. As soon as I hung up, I cursed myself for making the call, but was now stuck with its consequences.

The drive to Vegas was interminable, with patches of slow traffic and only the radio to give us anything to talk about. Scott was a sweet guy, but as Lillian would've said had she ever met him, "duller'n an ol' butter knife." Once we checked into our two-bedroom suite, I ditched him while he took a shower and went down to the casino where I proceeded to lose a hundred dollars while getting drunk. We had dinner in our room, and afterwards he wanted to fool around, but I made excuses, apologizing with all the feigned sincerity I could muster. I had been out of my mind to invite him along; in fact, I had been out of my mind for the past few weeks, but it wasn't his fault, and now I'd have to make do.

It seemed like hours as we waited for eleven o'clock to arrive, wandering the endless slot machines and game tables while struggling to chitchat, and at last it was time to file into the nightclub for Tallulah's show. As we settled in and ordered drinks, the orchestra took their positions. Then their conductor, Ray Sinatra—Frank's second cousin—entered to polite applause and gave a crisp bow before sitting down at the piano. Finally, after the requisite dramatic musical introduction, Tallulah herself burst onto the stage, sparkling and radiant in the spotlight as the crowd roared. I was enamored of her and found everything that came out of her mouth hysterically funny, though Scott didn't seem to get the joke. I glanced at him to share a laugh after a particularly good zinger and saw he was scanning the table card advertising various exotic cocktails, apparently bored. I knew as soon as we got back to Los Angeles, I was getting a new scene partner.

At one point during a dramatic and moving performance of a monologue about a woman waiting for a phone call from her lover, spellbinding all of us with its reminder of her enormous talent, I was certain she caught my eye and was thrown for one fleeting instant, though she recovered for an electrifying finish. The audience ate it up, awarding her enthusiastic applause as she now segued back into more bawdy comedy, then surprised us with a very poignant version of "Don't

Tell Him What Happened to Me," singing as soulfully as that inimitable contralto of hers would allow.

Sure, she was no Dinah Shore, but listening to her interpretation of the song I realized that Dinah Shore had never brought me to tears. Scott gave me a strange look as I wiped my eyes with a cocktail napkin, but I didn't care. I had come here to get as far away from Milly as possible, and yet he had followed me, still piercing my soul as Tallulah sang the final heartrending lyrics, then lowered her head, bringing down the house while I struggled to collect myself.

Tallu took her bows and winked and blew a kiss at me, and I now noticed a large portion of the audience appeared to be kindred spirits, all nattily dressed men and a fair sprinkling of women whistling and applauding their devotion to her. It seemed there were, in fact, a lot of other people out there like me.

We rose to leave, and a waiter appeared, handing me a hastily scrawled note on a cocktail napkin. I was delighted to see it was from Tallulah, inviting me backstage to her dressing room.

"Sounds good," Scott said with a bored shrug.

"Actually . . ." My mind raced, looking for a good lie, then opting to go with some version of the truth. "Look, Scott, Tallu doesn't know about me, so . . ."

"Oh," he said, only mildly disappointed. "I'll just see you back upstairs."

"Great. Thanks."

I was relieved as I watched him go, then went off to find Tallulah's dressing room.

As usual, Tallu made a very theatrical display of welcoming me, no doubt still high on the success of her performance. She eyed me head to toe and said I got more and more *scrumptious* every time she saw me as she smothered my face with kisses. She introduced me to some friends I no longer recall, then announced she was famished and simply had to eat or she'd die before her next show at one-thirty in the morning.

Fans and other well-wishers continued to interrupt our quick meal in the restaurant, dropping by our cozy table in an endless stream to ask for autographs or a picture. Tallulah was gracious, always enjoying the spotlight both on and off the stage. A couple of teenage girls even recognized me and nearly fainted as I signed their autograph books, though I felt like a fraud. During the brief respites between these little onslaughts, Tallulah expressed great disappointment that Lillian and Milly hadn't come to see her.

"You know how Lillian is when she's working."

"Yes, darling, and how *Milford* is in general," she said, downing another drink and calling for more as she chain-smoked and howled. At length, she invited me to watch her next show from backstage, and I accepted without hesitation.

Standing in the wings while Tallulah bewitched another full house made me feel like a part of her delicious magic, and I realized regardless of her flamboyant and wicked reputation, she was, at heart, the consummate professional and a brilliantly gifted actress and entertainer. I'd forgotten all about poor Scott when the audience at last let Tallulah go, and while the applause continued to rage, she came into the wings between bows and invited me for a nightcap in her room.

"Tallu? Are you trying to seduce me?" I joked.

She roared a throaty laugh, then said, "Darling, to paraphrase our ol' friend Tom, I'd *best* keep my hands *off* the children. Besides, you certainly aren't aroused by an ancient hag like *me*."

Before I could reply, she whirled and took to the stage again, bowing deeply to the unabated roar of her adoring fans, all on their feet now as they begged her for more. She was glittering and beguiling in the spotlight and the flush of her own triumph as she gave them a demure curtsy, fanning her gown out with her hands. After her second encore number, when she turned and came backstage again, she wobbled, feigning comic exhaustion. "That's that. Now come with me, it's a little soiree in my room, *not* a seduction. How deliciously *naughty* you are!" She looped her arm through mine, her gown a susurration as we walked, and soon I found myself toasted on pot and booze, lounging in Tallulah Bankhead's suite at the Sands Hotel with only a handful of her inner circle and assorted hangers-on while Tallulah sat on the bed with her friend Marlene Dietrich having a very bawdy conversation. Marlene was also performing in Vegas, as it turned out, and the two were seeing as much of each other as they could.

I had heard them performing skits and songs together on *The Big Show*, but being there in the room with these two legends made a profound impression on me. I was drifting and musing, deep within my own thoughts, wondering what Milly was doing that night in his big, cold mansion, when Tallulah's words brought me back to the scene playing out before me, spoken through a lascivious laugh: "Well how should *I* know if Monty Clift likes cock?" she roared. "He's never shown the slightest interest in *mine!*" The room exploded with laughter as Tallulah exhaled a plume of smoke and extended her now empty bourbon glass. It was immediately refilled.

I didn't know at the time that it was a version of a joke she'd use so often it would end up in her friend Truman Capote's final, unfinished book. But in the haze of the moment, I realized I'd missed a pretty important segue in their conversation, as they were now having an open discussion about what I had thought to be the most forbidden subject in the world.

"It's true," Marlene purred in her distinctive accent. "The best lover is one who knows how all the equipment works."

"Precisely, darling," Tallulah said. "Or in my case *doesn't*. At least not as well as it used to."

More laughter, then Marlene continued, "Let's be honest, men are always telling us exactly how they want us to pleasure them." Here, she dipped her voice to a masculine growl and said, "Oh baby oh baby, more tongue, that's it." Then, in her own voice, "It would save womankind a great deal of trouble if they'd all just take care of each other!"

"*Imagine*, darling," Tallulah said, throwing her head back and spraying the room with the infectious machine-gun fire of her staccato cackle. In the ensuing pause, her eyes fell on me and her wicked smile evaporated. "Dexter? What on earth's the matter? Don't tell me we've offended the boy from Texas."

"No, no," I stammered, realizing I had no explanation ready other than the truth, and I wasn't going to open up about that.

Marlene smiled. "We're sorry. I know some men have trouble with the subject of homosexuality."

"And the lousy lays have trouble with *heterosexuality* as well!" Tallulah bellowed, and everyone laughed, reinvigorating the conversation and mercifully taking the spotlight off of me. I poured myself another drink, sitting on the floor near the bed as the party loitered well into dawn when it at last began to disperse.

"Just a moment, Dexter, darling," Tallulah said, taking my arm. "I want to talk to you."

Once we were alone, she eyed me shrewdly. Her words were genuine and kind. "I'm truly sorry if we offended you. Marlene and I simply *adore* being scandalous."

I faltered, drunk and buzzed. "It's just . . . I've never heard people talk about, you know, *that* the same way they'd jaw about a ball game."

She put her cool palm to my cheek. "Did we hit perhaps a touch too close to home?"

My face burned as I tore my eyes from hers.

"Oh, honey-child," she said, every trace of outrageous affectation gone, leaving just a wise fifty-year-old Southern woman who'd seen more than her fair share of the world. "It happens to the *best* of us. Well, some of us are *omni*-sexual, but others . . ."

And so I sat and talked with her, telling what I could without bringing Milly and Lilly into it. I told her I'd been seeing someone, but he'd ended it, and I was hurt and bitter.

"I always *did* wonder about dear ol' Milford," she said absently, stubbing out a cigarette.

"What? Wait. I never said anything about Milly!"

"You didn't have to, darling. Lillian and I are *best* friends, you know, and *best* friends have a tendency to tell each other *everything*. So *naturally* I already knew what a *lucky* lady she's been these past two years. The rest of your story was merely fill-in-the-blanks."

I was both alarmed and horrified by my indiscretion, but Tallulah took my hands in hers, looked me in the eye and promised, "Don't worry, darling. I won't breathe a *word* to anyone." And as far as I could tell, she never did.

"I shouldn't have told you," I said.

"Don't be ridiculous. Carrying something that big around all by yourself, *heavens*, darling, it's a wonder you haven't suffered a *debilitating* rupture."

I laughed a little, then she grew serious and pinched my chin between her thumb and forefinger, forcing my eyes to meet hers.

"It's a *fucked-up* world, Dexter, full of *fucked-up* people," she said. "And the only thing you *truly* have is yourself to get you through. *Trust me*, honey-child. I *know* whereof I speak."

I was grateful for her supportive words and touched by the respect she'd shown me, feeling for the first time what I can only describe as a dawning maturity, unaware as I was it would be the last time I'd ever see her.

When I got back to our suite, still dazed but lightened by the extraordinary candor of my conversation with Tallu, it was already morning and Scott was surly while he gathered his things. He'd spent the night alone in our rooms and was anxious to leave. The drive back to Los Angeles was even quieter than the previous day's as I thought about my conversation with Tallulah and how I'd told her the truth and she'd still embraced me. If only the rest of the world and especially all of Hollywood could feel the same.

I apologized to Scott as I dropped him off at his apartment. He smiled sadly and shrugged it off as no big deal, but I could tell I had hurt him. With nothing further to say, I drove off and left him there.

I never saw Scott again. Until, that is, many years later when I was pretty sure I recognized him in a grainy 8mm gay porno loop unspooling in a very dark and underground little theater in San Francisco, his film career apparently having lasted well beyond mine.

In the months that followed, lazing through the infuriatingly hot

Hollywood summer, I was still drawing my studio salary, which I was sure must have been an oversight on the part of Fox's accounting department because the film offers had dried up like the chaparral on the Hollywood Hills. I wasn't working and spent interminable hours in the oppressive heat of the *El Palazar* with an oscillating fan roaring inside the open icebox. Sylvia continued to represent me, but sometimes it would be days before she'd return my calls, and always with the same bad news. Even parasites give up on their host once there's no more blood.

I'd rediscovered my old friend Mary Jane and spent much of those forgotten days drifting in the fog of her enchantment, feeling sorry for myself and seeking the only comfort I could with Lillian. Milly was ignoring me now, as if we had never taken that life-altering voyage together. When the despair of my fraught loneliness became too much for me, I'd seek out the comfort of men when I could, but it was dangerous and unsatisfying, as my heart wanted romance, and nothing could ever compare to the extraordinary feelings I'd had with Milly. Love and lust were confused with all of the foolish passion of my wasting youth, and I had convinced myself Milly felt the same—he *had* to. Only I knew he was all too willing to deny himself, to allow propriety to forever overrule passion.

It wasn't Milly who got me my third and final film; it was Lillian, who'd used her star power at 20th to insist I be given the role of a cub reporter looking to expose the seamier side of scandal rags like *Hollywood Confidential*. It was a movie that screamed of Darryl F. Zanuck's frustration over dealing with the emerging so-called journalism of an increasingly salacious press. It wasn't Milly's picture, and Lillian had prevailed with the young producer who was clearly afraid of crossing his star. I'd been grateful to her, but if you've ever seen *Hollywood P.I.*, you'll know it wasn't much of a part. Only six of the eight scenes I shot survived the final cut, and by that time, my credit was buried down the list of other players in a block of titles at the beginning of the picture beneath the demoralizing word "with."

Still, I was working again, and got to play the one and only scene of my short-lived career with Lillian Sinclair, which meant a lot to me, regardless of the fact it consisted of a mere three lines of dialog, one of them only one word. Her role in *P.I.* was more or less a cameo, essentially playing her movie star self, as she was also shooting another film called *One Summer Midnight*, a Southern Gothic murder mystery. The pace was grueling, and I sometimes had to remind her to hide her natural accent as we rehearsed her scenes for both films each night before shooting. My sole consolation was that according to the script, my character always had his hands in his pockets. Then again, I had to wonder if Lillian had tipped off the writer. The best thing to come from the experience was the additional salary, which allowed me to write my final check to Milford Langen, squaring my "loan against impending stardom" for good.

While I was circling the drain of depression, Lillian was planning an intimate dinner party for my twenty-third birthday after the picture wrapped and November at last rolled around, trumpeting the beginning of my second holiday season in Hollywood.

The night before the shindig, Lilly showed up at the *El Palazar* and surprised me with the scrapbook she'd put together of my time in Hollywood thus far. I was touched by her gesture, and sex with her was now my only fulfillment, no matter how void of real passion or feeling or lust. I knew Lillian sensed my withdrawal, but she seemed unwilling to let go of whatever dream life she had playing out in her head. She hadn't wanted to give me the scrapbook in front of others, as it was too personal, and might betray the truth of our now two-year-old affair. I smiled sadly, thinking of how Milly had at least taken a risk when he showed those home movies to the whole town on my last birthday. Lilly insisted we flip through the book together, page by page, and I was dying inside as she pointed out the pictures of her husband and me in New York, aboard the ship, in Europe . . .

Sweet, tragic Europe.

When that torture ended, she closed the book and excitedly told me they'd invited Anne Francis, Tab and Debbie, and the Tony Curtises, said they'd try to make it. for the soiree the next night in my honor. I feigned enthusiasm and thanked her, even as I dreaded the thought of sitting across their delicately set dining table and play-acting with Milly.

Only the pathetic hope he might have a change of heart got a nod of agreement out of me.

My birthday dawned chilly and clear, another deceptive day of bright and dappled California sunshine. I treated myself to breakfast at a diner on La Brea where the girl knew me and brought my eggs without my having to order. As I finished my coffee and smoked a cigarette, I noticed the couple who'd just vacated the adjacent table had left yesterday's *Daily Variety* on the banquette next to me. I hadn't read the trades for days because I frankly didn't care about all the fabulous people who weren't me, but a creased photo of Lillian above the fold intrigued me, as did its headline:

"IS THIS THE FACE THAT LAUNCHED A THOUSAND SHIPS?"

I quickly snatched it up and spread it out on the table. My heart stopped:

"Langen's *Trojan War* a Go at Fox."

My pulse racing, I skimmed the article. Lillian hadn't bothered to mention this news to me when I'd seen her just the night before. Was it possible she herself didn't yet know? The Technicolor CinemaScope picture was to start filming in January, with a script by "newcomer scribe Alden Metford."

I blinked in shock. Could it be some wild coincidence, or was something more insidious at work here? How did Alden get a script to Milly? And so quickly? Unless . . .

The theory taking shape in my mind was overwhelming. I knew Alden was capable of playing me to advance his career—he'd made that abundantly clear—but was it possible he'd been following me to boot? Worse, had he been lurking with a camera while shadowing me around town? And once I'd confirmed the truth to him in his dingy little apartment where I'd made such a fool of myself, had he played his cards with Milly and blackmailed his way into his first writing assignment? That's how cynical I'd become after barely two years in Hollywood.

The remainder of the article revealed the more likely explanation for Lilly's silence: she couldn't bear to break the news to me. She had inked to play Helen of Troy, of course, opposite Charlton Heston as Paris and in the role of Achilles—*Tony fucking Perkins?*

My heart was racing now, throbbing in my temples. The remainder of the article was a bunch of hot air from Milly about this being his passion project, so I paid my check before tucking the *Variety* under my arm and getting behind the wheel of the Nash-Healey, now fueled by fury and humiliation as I raced to Hancock Park to confront Milly once and for all. When I careened around the corner at Third and Windsor, the stoic palm trees no longer special, I slowed as I neared the house, just glimpsing Milly in his riding clothes as he got behind the wheel of the Cadillac limo, Deming nowhere to be seen. I zipped behind a milk delivery truck half a block away and was relieved when Milly came out of the driveway and drove south in the opposite direction, having opted to take the tree-shrouded expanse of Sixth Street as he headed east.

I followed at a respectful distance, and realized I was playing out one of my scenes from *Hollywood P.I.* where I'd tailed an actress involved in some scandal. Of course, following a car in real life is a lot more difficult than in the movies, but I managed by running a couple of red lights. And Milly's weaving as he drove, apparently drunk at eight-thirty in the morning, certainly helped—as did the light Saturday morning traffic. The black Cadillac headed up Wilton all the way to Franklin, then made a left onto Western and slid around the right angle turn where it becomes Los Feliz Boulevard. He sailed past the pocket of lush mansions set well off the street, and I was alarmed when I saw an empty scotch bottle hurl out the window and shatter on the curb. Milly drove all the way down to Riverside before turning left at the very fountain where he'd punched me in the mouth.

Making sure to keep other cars between us, I followed as he sailed past the riding stables, snaking his way through the park until he took another left and started winding up a narrow ribbon of hilly road surrounded by nothing but trees. He slowed and parked near two or three other cars already sitting idle and empty along the otherwise deserted, wooded stretch. I stopped before rounding the curve completely, and even though Milly looked back when he emerged from the limo, he didn't see me. Instead, he staggered toward some shrubs and disappeared. Within seconds, I had parked the Nash and gotten out, noticing the barely discernible footpath he'd taken. I followed, my eardrums pulsing like bongos.

Milly had vanished. The woods were dense here, with low-hanging branches and shrubs I had to brush aside to continue along the path. I moved deliberately, allowing the slight breeze rustling the foliage to mask the sounds of my progress. At last, I arrived at the perimeter of a small, lush glen, with moss-covered boulders and low-hanging branches. A tree limb bowed lazily in front of my face, and through its swaying leaves I caught a glimpse of the back of Milly's tan riding jacket.

I froze, not daring to move. It looked as if he had stopped at a huge pine tree to relieve himself, but as I watched through the flashes of dappling leaves, I saw two hands appear on the seat of his unhitched trousers. Immobilized by the shock of Milly's infidelity, I watched while a young, pudgy and unattractive man serviced him, the only sound the rustling of the breeze, the occasional lonely bird, and then the whispered cry, "*Lillian!*" There was no hint of eroticism in the moment; instead it was pitiful and fraught with despair.

I exploded through the branches and stormed toward him just as he was hitching up his trousers.

"What the *hell* are you doing?" I yelled.

Milly whirled to see me and the stubby guy took off, scrambling into the bushes, terror in his eyes.

"Get out of here!" Milly snapped, keeping his voice down.

"This is what you're driven to every Saturday?" I couldn't believe it. In my shock, I'd forgotten all about *The Trojan War* and Tony Perkins and Alden Metford. My eyes were wet with the bitter sting of an even deeper, more palpable betrayal. My voice crackled as I went on, "It doesn't have to be like this, Milly. You don't have to keep shoving me away and disgracing yourself or, or . . . *us!*"

"There is no 'us,' you stupid fool," he said, starting to brush past me, but so drunk he tripped on a stump and fell flat on his face. He tried to get up, groaning, but only managed to turn over, splayed on his elbows as he avoided my gaze.

"Get out of here," he repeated.

"No," I choked the words out, crying now, aching for what I knew should be. I knelt beside him and continued, "We could be together, Milly. I know you love me. I know you're crazy with—"

"I don't love you! That's impossible!"

His words hurt, but I pressed on, frantic and desperate to convince him. "Cary Grant and Randolph Scott didn't care what other people thought! Neither does Rock Hudson! For *god's sake, Milly*—"

"I'm not a *faggot!*"

"But you are, Milly. My god, *we both are . . .*"

"I love Lillian," he said, then started to cry, his voice an almost inaudible, pathetic whisper. "I love Lillian."

I don't know how I found my way out of there. I ran, hysterical and sobbing, furious to discover Milly's depraved perfidy, my mind racing madly about what other secrets might yet be revealed. The motor of the Nash roared to life and its tires left smoking skid marks as I made a violent U-turn, racing away as fast as I could, leaving him to the coyotes.

By the time I burst through the front door of the mansion, I was driven by nothing but blind rage. Lillian looked up from where she was toweling off the Steuben glassware for that night's party in my honor, her smile upon seeing me fading to a look of terrible concern. Puck sensed something was wrong, too, and scurried off to hide in the kitchen.

"Dexter?"

I grabbed her, wild with confusion and betrayal, and I could tell it frightened her.

"I'm sorry," I gasped, struggling to compose myself. "I have to, I need to, I—"

"Come upstairs," she said in as soothing a voice as she could muster. "What's happened? What's wrong?"

We climbed the steps in the stillness of the vast foyer, and she led me into the guest room and closed the door. I pulled her into a kiss, fraught and forlorn, unsure why I had come to her. Within moments, I was inside her, crying madly as I thrust again and again and again until at last my body shuddered and she gasped, both of us sweating atop the expensive bedspread. If Lillian was the only thing he loved, then I was determined to take her from him. I collapsed on top of her now, my shoulders heaving as I sobbed, distraught with grief and heartbreak.

"Dexter, poor, poor, Dexter," she said, stroking my hair. I heard the cavernous echoing boom of the front door slamming and knew her husband had somehow managed to get himself home, no doubt pursuing me.

"Hurry," she said, "he mustn't know you're here."

"He already does," I cried. "Stop pretending he doesn't!"

Her expression was unreadable, but her tears told me everything. That's when the door burst open and Milly stood there, enraged, waving his .22 in his hand.

"Milly!" Lillian cried. "No!"

He staggered, his clothes still disheveled with dirt and twigs, looking more impotent and ridiculous than dangerous.

"Get away from my wife," he slurred, trying to steady the gun. He didn't know I had an advantage over him. I knew for certain he was incapable of murdering me. The scandal and resulting trial would be a swirl of tawdry and salacious secrets that would irrevocably destroy his precious reputation. As Lillian screamed, I lunged at him, wresting the gun from his hand and shoving him so hard against the wall his skull dented the plaster.

That's when my eyes fell on the dog tags and key dangling in his open shirtfront. What could be so sacred to this man that he didn't dare risk hiding the key anywhere other than on his own flesh? It must have been proof of his love for me. The love he so denied with such cold vehemence. Determined to confront him once and for all, I clutched at the chain as he struggled, shouting "no" over and over and trying to fend me off. I managed to tighten my fist around the tags and pulled so hard the chain dug into the skin of his neck as it broke, cutting deep and drawing a gush of blood that stained his white shirt.

"Dexter, stop it! Stop it!" Lillian pleaded, grabbing at me, but I shrugged her off as Milly slid down the wall, injured and broken, crying pitifully.

I bolted from the room, Lillian tending to Milly, but I didn't care what they were saying as I sprinted down the foyer steps and into Milly's study. My hands were trembling more wildly than ever before or since as the key clattered against the metal lock until I was finally able to insert it and turn, then yank open the lower left drawer. It was heavy and stubborn, but at last its contents were revealed—not the little moleskin notebooks professing his love for me as I'd imagined; instead it appeared to be crammed full of manila file folders.

The topmost held a series of Milly's paycheck stubs from the studio, with itemized bonuses and deductions, all of them bearing the neatly typed notation "$200 per week deducted for D.G.'s salary as arranged."

It was as if all sound in the house fell away, leaving me alone to face the stark reality that my whole life in Hollywood had been a sham with Milford Langen pulling the strings. It was as humiliating as it was enraging, and then, newly fueled by both, I hurled the file across the room so that the hundreds of papers documenting my fraudulent career fluttered around me like the flock of birds in the Piazza San Marco. I was out of my mind, tearing into the first of several manila envelopes, the horror dawning raw and ferocious as I flipped through picture after picture of me screwing Lillian in the upstairs bedroom. Pornographic and disgusting, the photographs, perfectly framed from the foot of the bed, cheapened and destroyed whatever it was I'd thought we'd had so long ago.

The next envelope was marked "Michael," and bore more of the same, this with Lillian being serviced by a man who could only be Michael Spencer. The next envelope had "Reed" scrawled on it, the next "Alan," until they were gone and I saw what had made the drawer so heavy. Stacks of 16mm film cans, all with scraps of tape on them bearing names to match the envelopes, undoubtedly home movies of the same wretched scenes as the photographs.

I was reeling, overcome and crying, as I gathered up a handful of pictures, mingling the images of my own torrid history with Lillian among the others who'd been so desperately used, and staggered out of the study. Milly was lurching down the stairs toward me then, his shirtfront soaked in crimson, Lillian following, begging him through ragged sobs to tell her what had happened. I came up the stairs, saw the terror in Milly's eyes when he realized I was holding the truth in one hand, the loaded .22 in the other. He seemed to collapse when I kept moving, shoving past as I threw the photographs so they swirled around him. Lillian's eyes grew wide with a ghastly confusion as she at last saw what they were, but I didn't stop.

"Dexter? Milly?" was all Lillian managed as I crossed the landing and headed straight for the south wing and the guest room with its bed still tousled from my final passion with Lillian. Specks of Milly's blood trailed beneath the dent in the plaster where he'd fallen. Driven by a force so unspeakable I was helpless in its spell, I picked up a nightstand, causing the lamp to clatter and fall, sparking as the cord was ripped from the outlet. I raised the table over my head, then hurled it across the room as hard as I could into that goddamned mirrored wall at the foot of the bed. The glass shattered, shards exploding in a violent shimmer as it dropped like a sparkling sequined curtain in a magician's act, exposing a tiny beamed and unfinished attic with a hatch in the floor below a retractable ladder. The little door had its own knob, and I knew it led to the projection booth below. In the now revealed space, two tripods held a 16mm and a still camera, trained into the room. The horror of realization spread like a wildfire as I ran my fingers through my hair, feeling the hot sweat on my scalp, my tears continuing unabated. A dirty sheet was draped over something in the farthest corner of the secret room, and I whisked it away amid a flurry of dust and scattering spiders.

My battered old cardboard suitcase.

The one that had been lifted from my Buick what seemed a lifetime ago.

My mind raced as I struggled to comprehend this undeniable proof of Milford Langen's demented desperation, so powerful it had driven him to take the first step in an elaborate ploy to ensnare me forever in his own treacherous nightmare.

Trembling, gasping for breath, I staggered backwards as Lillian appeared in the doorway, her shoes crunching on the carpet of glass shards as she sobbed and took in the destruction all around, unable to grasp the secret now revealed. A paralyzing wrath overtook me then, and I stumbled down the staircase for the last time, dazed and enraged by the depth of the depraved ruse that had stolen my life for the past two years and made me no better than a whore myself.

I still held the gun, quaking, as I came upon Milly who was groveling in his own insanity, trying to gather the lurid photographs from the marble floor. I raised the .22 and pointed it at him as he looked up, his eyes fervent with misery, staring into the trembling void of the pistol's barrel.

"How do you know Alden Metford?" I screamed at him.

Milly blinked stupidly, his mouth hanging open.

I cocked the gun. "*How*?!"

He lifted his arms to shield his face, cowering. "It's *your* fault. *Yours*! He threatened to sell the story. He was going to expose me . . ."

"So you hired him to shut him up?"

"Yes," he croaked, "he said you told him *everything*—"

"That's a lie!"

"And he was the one who took the pictures. Of us aboard the *Jubilee*. And the fight that day at the fountain."

"Pictures? Of you and Dexter?" It was Lillian's small voice from the top of the stairs, where she stood clutching the railing as if on the verge of collapse. I scooped up a few of the pornographic images now littering the floor and shook them at her.

"Pictures just like these," was all I said. Her shocked expression distracted me long enough for Milly to lunge, and as we wrestled for the gun, it discharged and Lillian screamed. I threw Milly off of me and he lay sprawled on the marble floor as I again pointed the .22 between his eyes. Lillian was sobbing now as she staggered down the stairs.

Milly looked at me, begging in a whisper, "Go ahead. You've already destroyed me. So please . . . just pull the trigger."

I screamed with impotent rage, knowing full well I couldn't, then hurled the pistol across the room where it nicked the edge of the dining room table before skittering across its surface, sending the Steuben flying, the sound of shattering stemware reverberating throughout the house, mingled with Milly's wails and my now labored breathing. I leapt at him, grabbing him by the throat and tightening my grasp.

"*You* did this! *You* did *all* of this!" I yelled as Lillian now came racing down the stairs, begging for me to stop. She clawed at me, crazed and catlike, trying to pull me off of her husband. With one hand, I pushed her away and she stumbled and fell against the curved wall under the stairs and lay there, splayed like a broken toy. Milly's eyes met mine as I strangled him, my hand already bleeding from Lillian's fingernails. She was pleading with me, gasping, "I don't understand I don't understand" over and over again as she crawled toward us. I saw in her eyes a reflection of what I had become. What Milly's self-loathing had done to us all.

Overcome with horror, I released Milly with a shove and stood, looking away as my delirious mania gave way to shame and revulsion, moaning again and again "oh no oh no." He grabbed his bruised and bloody throat, gasping, "Get out. Please, get out."

I looked at Lillian now, her face streaked with rivulets of mascara as our eyes met and she nodded; then I turned to flee the room, to free myself of their madness. As I yanked open the heavy front door, I was aware of Lillian scrambling across the imported marble to her husband, both of them sobbing as he whimpered, "It's the only way I could love you. It's the only way. The only way . . ."

Crying and hysterical, I stopped at the apartment just long enough to grab my few possessions before racing out of Los Angeles and the lives of Milford Langen and Lillian Sinclair forever.

Or so I believed at the time.

TWENTY-SIX

Milly and Lilly's youthful, joyous faces flickered through the dust and scratches of their home movies as they stood holding hands and swearing eternal devotion, their words to each other lost in the radiant black-and-white glow of the silent film. Milly, all of twenty-two, had worn his Navy uniform and Lillian a white gown that evoked images of Juliet, another tragically doomed lover. The incomparable life they had shared in the ensuing years had been immortalized through the eye of Milly's camera, little monochrome vignettes that chronicled the sprawling decades of their complicated togetherness. There they were at a party when Milly had returned home from the service, then celebrating endless Christmases, moving into the house on South Windsor, now joined by their adorable daughter Tally while Lillian doted and fussed over the child, always accompanied by their unbroken chain of dogs named Puck. When one reel ended, Tally would get up and go to the little television and VCR we had moved into Lillian's old bedroom, the place where she had said she wanted to spend the dwindling moments of her life. Her daughter would insert the next cassette and press *play*, then return to her station on her mother's bed, holding the dying woman's hand as Lillian drifted in and out of sleep and delirium, between lunacy and lucidity. The hushed hospice workers regulated her medication and tended to her failing body as she sometimes stared with smiles and tears at the condensed passage of time playing out on the screen.

I stood in the corridor outside the open door, leaning against the wall, hidden from Lillian's sight, or pulling a chair up to the doorway's edge to sit and watch, ever respectful of her wishes not to see me. Puck the Eighth seemed torn and confused as to where he should be, sometimes curled on the bed at Lillian's feet, others on the floor next to mine in the corridor, while the films brought to life the memories of an astonishing romance: Milly clowning around on the rare occasion he'd allow someone else to run his precious camera, waving and smiling on a long-ago sunny day aboard the *Jubilee*, then Lillian, who as time wore on and the films became more vivid and in color, seemed to shy from the camera's unforgiving eye, shooing Milly away. Briefly, an aged and decrepit Tallulah scowled at the lens, still smoking in spite of the oxygen tank that was by then her ball and chain, on what must have been her last visit to Hollywood before her death.

I had been careful to exclude any of the miles of footage of me out of respect for Lillian, not wanting to upset her. Still, I yearned to talk to her one last time. I also omitted the videotape Tally and I found of Lillian's "memorial service" in 1982, though the two of us marveled at what we called the "cavalcade of costars" who'd turned out to eulogize the woman they believed to be dead. When fleeting footage appeared of a dinner party in their dining room, with Milly and Lilly as I remembered them best, entertaining Tab Hunter and Debbie Reynolds, and Anne Francis, and a sequence of Tony Curtis and Janet Leigh arriving with a bouquet of flowers and a bottle of wine, I noticed Milly had been wearing an ascot that seemed higher around his throat than was his usual impeccable style.

As I watched, noting the haunted, forced smiles of the host and hostess, I realized this could only have been taken the night of my violent exit from their lives, his scarf hiding the still fresh gash in his neck. Incredible, I marveled, how they must have insisted to each other that the show go on, even allowing the madness of preserving the event on film. A splice jerked the images away, replacing them with shots of Milly and Lilly on the deck of the *Ile de France*, the same vacant expressions on their faces as they waved amid the streamers evoking my own sail away all those years before. Here, the camera caught a closeup of Milly, and I got a glimpse of a bandage on his throat where the chain had cut his flesh when I'd exposed the last of his secrets. In the wake of my leaving, they had booked an impromptu European holiday together, no doubt to get away from the house on Windsor and all its memories. It had been snowing as they posed with half-hearted and forced smiles by the ship's railing, and they both looked cold in their hats, gloves, and overcoats as streamers swirled among a sprinkling of lazy snowflakes. A fleeting shot of Lillian revealed the still fresh shock in her eyes.

From Milly's recorded rants and the untruths of his typed manuscript, I learned their official story had been that Milly's doctor had diagnosed him with exhaustion in November of '53 and had encouraged the two of them to take a long respite from the pressures of the studio. Their planned holiday stretched into two full years abroad, resulting in the birth of their daughter while they were living in Paris in 1955—Milly's proof to the world that he was, in fact, capable of anything. I realized with sadness the house must have been dark for the holidays during those years, for the first time since they'd lived there.

I had leaked to one of the determined reporters that Lillian was to be taken to Cedars Sinai, outsmarting them so she could arrive at the house on South Windsor undetected in her ambulance. She'd been unconscious on the gurney at the time and hadn't stirred until the medics made her comfortable in bed with an IV drip to feed her and relieve the ever-present pain. Tally and I had scrambled in the days before her homecoming to bring her bedroom back to its former glory, with new drapes to match the originals, fresh paint, and numerous vases of her beloved gardenias delivered regularly at my precise instructions. The workers continued their quiet restoration of the remainder of the house and grounds, careful never to disturb its dying occupant.

Lillian surprised us all with her tenacity, clinging to life far longer than the doctors and hospice workers had predicted, but then, there had never been anything ordinary about her. When I'd venture out, I always had the overwhelming sense of stepping through time upon my return to the now restored mansion, the gardeners at last finishing up the landscaping. Tally told me her mother had been delighted when we'd had the old speaker system replaced, filling the rooms with Milly's ancient jazz. The music seemed to soothe Lillian as her body continued its slow betrayal of her soul. Once, I'd been listening to the last of Milly's recorded memoirs and had inadvertently piped his rasping voice throughout the house. Tally said this had agitated her mother, and for a while Lillian insisted Milly was still alive and had been vexed he wouldn't come in to see her, perhaps confusing her own staged suicide as an explanation for her husband's absence. Her room was kept dim, the curtains drawn and candles flickering to provide the only light Lillian would allow, the mirror over her dressing table sheathed in silk, as if she were the art director of her own deathbed scene.

Tally remained as stoic as she could during that time, only breaking down in tears when we'd get together each evening on the verandah for a glass of wine after Lillian had slipped off to sleep. We'd talk about the progress on the landscaping, or how much we thought we might get for the place once we were ready to sell. Sometimes, she'd tell me about her incoherent conversations with her dying mother, but if she'd rather not, I never pressed.

As the music lilted through the house, I'd at last finished listening to the tapes Milly had left behind, piecing together some semblance of a bizarre but undeniable truth. It seemed one of Milly's greatest regrets had been his aborted *Trojan War*, as he spoke with bitterness about how Zanuck had pulled the plug once and for all. The ultimate blow had come when Warner Brothers released *Helen of Troy* in 1956, with Rossana Podestà in the title role. Darryl Zanuck had abandoned his exalted position at 20th by then, and Milly had turned to the burgeoning medium of television, no doubt keeping his demons at bay by expending all his energy producing fluffy comedies and escapist fare at the expense of his relationship with his daughter.

Lillian had stayed with Milly despite my having exposed his psychotic deceit, growing more and more mired in their mutual dependency and diminished sanity until they had become inseparable. From his ramblings and the home movies emerged the tragic and doomed love story of two people so tangled in the darkness of denying their secrets that the risk of discovery had bound them in an inevitable life together. He spoke of his love for Lillian, which I now believed was genuine, but as the truth was sorted from the fiction, it became clear he needed to love her more than he hated himself. I found no clues to illuminate the psychology of his self-loathing, other than the few veiled references to his strict Catholic upbringing and his need to please his military father, who must surely have known the once shameful truth behind Milly's discharge from the Navy. I remembered the genuine dignity Milly had exuded while speaking of his service to his country, and how he'd worn his Navy seaman's tags for the rest of his life as a token of his bitter patriotism. He spoke in a hush, his voice cracking, of how his mother's death had devastated him when he was eleven years old to the point that he vowed to live his life in a way that would have made the dead woman proud, especially if she might be watching from Heaven.

The only theory I could devise to explain his voyeuristic obsession was his desperate need for the vicarious thrill of watching other men enjoy pleasing his wife the way he himself could not, and to experience their passion with the almost magical ability of movies to spin reality from make-believe. He had mentioned me only one time in his recorded ramblings, not by name, of course, and just to say that once he'd fallen in love with one of his surrogates, and it had "nearly destroyed the life and reputation" he had built. I now understood with an aching sadness Lillian's long-ago heartache when she'd been omitted from the memoirs of her cherished friend. Even then, after so many years, hearing the words "fallen in love" brought an unexpected comfort, as if that sole confession somehow justified everything that had happened between us.

Lillian must have felt some complicity in all of this, and had remained at his side, even as it drove her ever deeper into the paralysis of her own insanity. On the final tape, after a long silence, Milly had almost whispered his last recorded words before shutting off the machine forever: *"Oh, the things that might have been."*

I wondered if he meant a life with me, or one with Lillian unfettered by his detested homosexuality. I realized with an inescapable sadness that while Lillian hadn't killed herself, it was her husband who had committed a slow and excruciating suicide, with alcohol, cigarettes, and furtive, dangerous sex with faceless strangers.

One morning, the electricians told me they needed access to the little attic over the projection booth. I hadn't dared open it since my return to Windsor Boulevard but knew I should go first in case there was anything unseemly that might be revealed. When I finally got the door open and climbed the ladder, a flashlight my only illumination, I was moved to tears by what I saw. There, stashed away in the secret silence of the little room, were the photographs Milly had taken during my days with them. Not the pornographic images which seemed to have disappeared, rather the shots of me twirling near the Bridge of Sighs, neatly matted and framed and hung in a series on the wall where the two-way mirror had once been, my eyes closed and my young face basking in sunlight and happiness. Another frame held a picture of Milly and me, posing in our ridiculous life jackets from that long ago voyage. The three model steamships given to me by Lilly and Tallu sat dusty but neatly displayed on a makeshift shelf, and I realized the hidden room was Milly's shrine to what we had together. My old suitcase was still there, untouched, along with a few burnt candles, and I took small comfort knowing Milly had retreated here sometimes to remember what he would never allow to be. At last, the aching, tragic confirmation—far more valuable than the inheritance he'd left me—showing he *had* loved me deeply and throughout his lifetime, and while it shouldn't have mattered anymore, my tears betrayed the fact it did.

Oh, the things that might have been . . .

The sound of the doorbell chiming throughout the house pulled me from my reverie, and I climbed down the little ladder and made my way to the bottom of the grand staircase where Tally was already signing for a delivery of several large parcels, all of them addressed to me. The UPS guy helped bring them into the foyer, and once he was gone, I tore into the first of them with a rush of delight, rummaging through the clothes, books, and bric-a-brac inside.

"What on earth?" Tally asked as I moved on to the next one.

"My stuff from Carol's house," I replied, unable to hide the glee in my voice.

"Okay, how did *this* happen?"

"You get most of the credit, young lady. I hired Jerry Mandelberg to threaten a lawsuit if they didn't return all of my belongings. Like your little performance with Dr. Balfour. And it worked equally well."

I found the thing I most wanted in the bottom of the third box. An object I had kept tucked away in the back of a closet for most of my life: the precious scrapbook Lillian Sinclair had made for my twenty-third birthday, its now brittle and faded souvenirs and snapshots preserving my life with those two astonishing people. I sat down at the foot of the stairs, trembling, put the book on my lap, and opened the cover. Intrigued, Tally joined me and we pored over its pages, with me filling in whatever lingering gaps remained in my story. When my eyes fell upon the picture of me posing with Lillian Sinclair and Tallulah Bankhead at the beginning of my Hollywood journey those many years ago, a rush came over me.

"The last time I looked at this was a few months after I met Carol. I needed to prove it was all true."

"He didn't believe you?"

"I meant to myself," I said, my voice cracking. Tally gave me a warm smile, and we spent the remains of that lyrical afternoon sifting through my newly salvaged treasures.

It seemed, for now, I was finally getting my life back.

As October dissolved to November, with the memories of holidays past now lurking on the horizon, Lillian grew weaker, and after a hushed conversation, Tally emerged, crying as she whispered to me, "She's asking for you."

I nodded and swallowed, then stepped into the gardenia-scented candlelit shadows of Lillian's sanctuary, a fire glowing beneath the ornate mantel, flickering its light over Puck the Eighth who lay still, his chin on his paws, mirroring Trouble's final vigil when Puck's namesake had died in Lillian's arms. The old portrait stared down at me from the wall, but

Lillian's face was turned away, even as she sensed my presence and feebly patted the bed next to her. I went over and eased down onto the bed so as not to cause her any pain. She spoke to me only in profile, still hiding the shame of her destroyed face.

"Dexter . . ." she said as I strained to hear.

"I'm here, Lilly."

"Happy . . . birthday . . ."

It was still a week away, but I was surprised she could have possibly remembered. "Thank you," I replied in a whisper.

"Lillian . . . I'm sorry, I'm . . . for everything . . ." I trailed off, devoid of words to express what I was feeling.

"You . . . mustn't be," she said as a hint of relief washed across her ravaged features. "You have to know . . . none of it . . . was your fault."

I nodded, grateful for this final release.

The melancholy music from Milly's records wafted in the distance, echoing through the freshly restored, wondrous old house, first a sad June Christy song that at length gave way to a mournful jazz piano solo of Noël Coward's "Mad About the Boy."

"We . . . loved you . . ." she managed through coarse intakes of breath.

"I loved you, too," I said, realizing there was now an undeniable sincerity to the words. "Both of you."

A pale smile curled her lips, and she was silent for a long time, her eyes half closed and her breathing coming in shorter and shorter rasps. I watched as she turned her hand over in an offer for me to take it, so I did. She somehow managed to put her other hand on mine, and I was moved by the twinkling of her diamond wedding ring. I thought of Carol, and how I hadn't been allowed to be with him in his final moments as he'd slipped away, surrounded by his family, but unspeakably alone.

And then, almost as if drawing strength from the faint music, she pulled me closer and began to speak, labored and difficult. From the warm whispered words brushing my ear, the last of their secrets—perhaps the biggest one of all—at length emerged before she stopped mid-sentence, noticing something behind me.

"Look . . . who's here," she said, her eyes opening wide.

313

I turned to look over my shoulder toward the open doorway to the hall, but it was empty save for a circular patch of moonlight glowing through the huge round window at the end of the corridor—looking for all the world like an empty spotlight.

"Oh look," she said, the weakest glimmer of delight in her voice as her eyes sparkled with tears, "he's brought his little movie camera."

Then her hands went soft and still as they held mine, and Lillian Sinclair made her final exit. This time for real. I sat there crying as a kind hospice worker touched my shoulder, saying simply, "You stay as long as you like. We'll make all the calls."

I nodded without speaking and sat with Lillian for a few more moments before at last mustering the strength to stand, gently pulling away from the dead woman's still warm fingers. Crossing the room, dazed, I lingered in the doorway while the smoldering log in the fireplace collapsed amid a hiss and crackle of tiny sparks that swirled up the chimney as if in slow motion. Puck rose to his feet, whimpering as he shook himself and joined me.

I trudged in a daze down the old staircase in a house now shrouded in the hush of death, Puck following at my heels. We went through the elegant foyer, then down the corridor to the rear entry where the French doors were once again open to the splendor of an autumn night. We found Tally sitting on the back verandah steps, knees pulled up to her chin, toying with the old match safe around her neck as she stared into the freshly filled, glimmering pool of the restored Urban Idyll. The lights glowed softly inside the cabana, conjuring fleeting phantoms of happiness and despair. The music continued from the house as Tally turned to look at me, my expression telling her everything she needed to know.

I sat down next to her, and Puck the Eighth rested his chin on my thigh. Tally exhaled, both of us weary but somehow relieved.

"She's gone?" she asked, and I nodded.

We sat for a moment in the finality of it all—a silent wake for Lillian, Milly, and all that had come to light in the few short months Tally and I had known each other. At length, she asked, "Was she able to talk to you?"

"Yeah . . ."

"Did she make any sense?"

"She told me . . ." I faltered, overcome.

"What?" She looked at me, her tear-filled eyes searching mine.

"Tally, she told me your father's still alive."

She frowned as she exhaled and shook her head. "In denial to the very end."

"Thing is," I said, "she was telling the truth."

"But I don't . . ." Tally said, unable to complete her thought.

It took me a moment to compose my voice before I said, with great difficulty, "You were born in August 1954, Tally. Not February of '55. Your parents faked your birth certificate. That's why they stayed so long in Europe. To cover up the scandal."

Our eyes met as the astonishing reality settled over us, then my daughter slowly laced her fingers through mine, both of us smiling as we wept.

"So, I guess I can stop dreading my fortieth birthday," she said in a hush, trying to make light of this overwhelming revelation. "Since it's already passed, I mean."

I nodded, watching her process the many implications.

"No wonder my horoscope never makes any sense," she said, her voice now quivering between laughter and tears.

She leaned against me then, resting her head on her father's shoulder as Puck at length dozed off, his chin warm and motionless on my leg. We stayed that way, the three of us, for what seemed like a pleasant and promising eternity, watching as the twinkling lights of the Urban Idyll began their slow, almost imperceptible fade to black.

And at last, my hands were perfectly still.

ACKNOWLEDGMENTS

In writing a work of fiction set in a world as familiar as Hollywood's Golden Age, it would be impossible to achieve any semblance of verisimilitude without the inclusion of real movie stars, directors, writers, and other well-known personalities weaving in and out of the narrative. I have endeavored to use as little creative license as possible in a respectful attempt to portray these legends with the accuracy and dignity they deserve.

The following sources were enormously helpful in that regard: Tab Hunter's (with Eddie Muller) heartfelt and candid autobiography, *Tab Hunter Confidential: The Making of a Movie Star*, in which he writes openly about closeted gay life in Hollywood in the early 1950s; Robert J. Wagner's (with Scott Eyman) honest and touching *Pieces of My Heart: A Life*; Tony Curtis's (with Peter Golenbock) wildly entertaining and salacious *American Prince: A Memoir*; director Jean Negulsco's insightful musings in *Things I Did and Things I Think I Did: A Hollywood Memoir*, which brings Darryl F. Zanuck to life as a man rather than a mogul, and vividly recalls life in Hollywood both in front of and behind the cameras; Leonard Mosley's equally indispensable *Zanuck: The Rise and Fall of Hollywood's Last Tycoon*; Robert Hofler's invaluable *The Man Who Invented Rock Hudson: The Pretty Boys and Dirty Deals of Henry Willson*; Lawrence J. Quirk & William Schoell's detailed and delicious *Joan Crawford: The Essential Biography*; Sam Kashner and Jennifer MacNair's tantalizing *The Bad and the Beautiful: Hollywood in the Fifties*; James Robert Parish's wonderfully tawdry *The Hollywood Book of Scandals: The*

Shocking, Often Disgraceful Deeds and Affairs of More Than 100 American Movie and TV Idols; all the incomparable writers who contributed to *Vanity Fair's Tales of Hollywood: Rebels, Reds, and Graduates and the Wild Stories Behind the Making of 13 Iconic Films* (edited by Graydon Carter); Thomas Schatz's remarkably thorough *The Genius of the System: Hollywood Filmmaking in the Studio Era*; Alexander Walker's heartbreaking *Vivien: The Life of Vivien Leigh*; every delicious word Sam Staggs has written about behind-the-scenes Tinseltown first in *All About "All About Eve": The Complete Behind-the-Scenes Story of the Bitchiest Film Ever Made*, then in *Close-up on Sunset Boulevard: Billy Wilder, Norma Desmond, and the Dark Hollywood Dream*, and, of course, *When Blanche Met Brando: The Scandalous Story of "A Streetcar Named Desire"*; and, finally, the inimitable Tallulah Bankhead's simply titled memoir *Tallulah: My Autobiography*, which gave a mere peek into the reality of her life later so brilliantly laid bare in Joel Lobenthal's *Tallulah! The Life and Times of a Leading Lady* and Lee Israel's *Miss Tallulah Bankhead*.

Without these fine writers and their devotion to their respective subjects my humble story would not have been possible. Also of invaluable assistance were the cheerful and helpful researchers at the UCLA Film & Television Archive, the USC Cinematic Arts Library, and, of course, the Academy of Motion Picture Arts and Sciences Margaret Herrick Library. Deepest gratitude also goes to my priceless and precise editor, Alice Peck, my fellow ship geek Dan Grossman with his encyclopedic knowledge of vintage aircraft and timetables, author Georgia Kolias for introducing me to the wonderful team at Amble Press, and all of my friends and colleagues and a few strangers who were kind enough to read early drafts and weigh in with their praise, critiques, and encouragement. A very special tip of the fedora is reserved for author and friend Patricia V. Davis, whose love for my characters is solely responsible for raising them from the dead and breathing new life into my moribund novel. Words are inadequate to express my gratitude to her.

Last but not least, a toast to the perpetual magic unspooling around the clock on Turner Classic Movies, providing daily inspiration and wonder.

ABOUT THE AUTHOR

Mark B. Perry is an Emmy and Golden Globe Award-winning writer and producer whose credits include *The Wonder Years* (1988), *Picket Fences*, *Law & Order*, *Party of Five*, *Brothers & Sisters*, *Ghost Whisperer*, and *Revenge*. He's also been nominated for both The Humanitas Prize and a WGA Award. His 'Two Doors Down' episode of Netflix's *Dolly Parton's Heartstrings* won a GLAAD Media Award in 2020. Born and raised in Atlanta, Georgia, Mark moved to Los Angeles in 1986 to pursue a career in film and television.

AMBLE
PRESS

Amble Press, an imprint of Bywater Books, publishes fiction and narrative nonfiction by LGBTQ writers, with a primary, though not exclusive, focus on LGBTQ writers of color. For more information on our titles, authors, and mission, please visit our website.

https://amblepressbooks.com

www.ingramcontent.com/pod-product-compliance
Lightning Source LLC
Chambersburg PA
CBHW050522110726
47899CB00005B/1551